For Carol,
Thank you for friendship and inspiration throughout the years,

Audrey:
A Book of Love

A Novel

Beate Sigriddaughter

With love,
Beate

This is a work of fiction. Names, characters, places, and incidents either are the product of the author's imagination or are used fictitiously, and any resemblance to actual persons, living or dead, business establishments, events, or locales is entirely coincidental.

ELJ Publications, LLC ~ New York
ELJ Editions Series

Library of Congress Control Number: 2015942019
ISBN 13: 978-1-942004-15-8

Praise for Audrey: A Book of Love

Beate Sigriddaughter's writing is fearless and lovely all at once. Her new novel, *AUDREY: A BOOK OF* LOVE, examines our most precious, (and often all too fleeting), emotion in an honest, lyrical, and forthright way. Sigriddaughter's language is musical, her characters spring from the page fully formed. We want to know them. We want to embrace and protect them in their vulnerability and honesty. This book reinforces my belief that poets do indeed write the best prose. Here is a new fictive work with a voice that refuses to be silenced. Everyone should purchase and savor this novel. It's truly one of those rare books other writers of any stamp will appreciate and save to read again and again.

—Joani Reese, Editor, *MadHat Lit* and author of three books, including the new collection *Night Chorus*

What is love? Beate Sigriddaughter explores this timeless question with a confident, wise, and poetic hand in her intimate story of Andrea, a young woman riven by her simultaneous passion for two lovers of opposite genders—and a steadfast commitment to her own personal power and freedom. Compelled to trust in love's profound truths, follow her hungry heart, and embrace life fully, Andrea must navigate strong, perilous rapids—both figuratively and literally. Sigriddaughter's perfect-pitch recounting of Andrea's sensual journey of self-discovery will resonate with anyone who has ever ignored the prescriptions of society in order to care for another deeply, soulfully, and without reservation.

—Richard Mahler, author of *Stillness: Daily Gifts of Solitude* and *The Jaguar's Shadow: Searching for a Mythic Cat*, among other books

Audrey: A Book of Love is an important look at intricate facets of love as it surprises, delights, challenges, sometimes defeats, and always honors our lives.

—Alex Marcoux, award winning novelist and New Thought author

Audrey: A Book of Love is a story of tender and long-suffering love confused with rage and powerlessness, youth and healing, loss of craft, broken promises to oneself, and endless misunderstandings. It's also a compelling and masterfully written tale of the equally destructive powers of jealousy and alcohol, and the restorative power of love and forgiveness, especially for oneself.

—Susan Clay, Librarian, University of Georgia, Athens, GA

Audrey is a bold and compelling novel. Sigriddaughter gives us insight into the world of a woman who loves both a man and a woman, while she strives to be true to herself and her art.

—Elise Stuart, Poet Laureate, Silver City, New Mexico

SPRING

She came with a painted dragon and cinnamon hearts for Valentine's. Her name was Audrey and I am hard pressed to remember what anyone else brought to the party.

Thirty friends crowded the red wall-to-wall carpet of our one-bedroom apartment. The festive anticipation of starting a new decade, the 1980s, still hung in the air. Kay, my roommate, and I moved in artist circles, more to Kay's credit than mine, as I already showed early symptoms of being a recluse.

Despite the crush, even those of us who wore long skirts managed to maneuver without knocking over the candles that burned in cereal bowls on the floor. The magic of candle flames, long skirts, seven guitars complete with accomplished players, laughter, murmurs, and cheap wine, made even me give up a good portion of my customary February gloom.

Several men courted me all at once. Even Toby, nobly invited after I had recently conceded him the glory of rejecting me, seemed confused. Was there something to me after all? He sat with me at length instead of treating me with his special brand of benevolent disdain. I recited a few poems, sang with the singers, and kept bringing my eyes back to Audrey's painting of a mystical green dragon.

Did Audrey watch me stare at her dragon, which hung over a collection of rejection slips Kay and I used as world-defying wall decoration? I couldn't tell. But just in case, I did my best to look intrigued, intelligent.

A misty blue planet floated on a background of swirling black paint. From this planet the dragon burst forth into the universe, crossed the entire canvas, and tried to transcend the canvas's borders into our space. Its left paw, or claw, or whatever it is that dragons have, reached out in a tentative gesture—groping to fly out with those enormous wings, despite being mythical, despite being trapped there on canvas. Later Audrey told me the dragon's name: Serena.

Midnight came and Audrey began leaving. This took a long time. We lifted Serena from the wall. I touched the dragon's nose briefly when the painting stood upright against Kay's desk, ready to be shipped home again.

Where was home? And who was Audrey, come to stand behind me, telling me that I had lovely energy?

I never took compliments lightly. This was no exception. To hide both thrill and embarrassment, I launched into a long speech about the dragon, its gentle, timid, fawn-like nose, the forceful amber eyes, which, Audrey explained, were modeled on the eyes of a nun she once knew.

"I'm so glad you like Serena," she said. "Some people are afraid of her."

Afraid? I tested the feeling. No. I told Audrey the painting gave me a sense of woman spirit emerging.

Audrey smiled.

For the first time I looked deeply into her own fascinating eyes. They were the color of nothing definite, and had the depth of everything all at once, gray, blue, brown, green, blended with the spice of joy and sorrow, and just a hint of attractive danger. The candles, some of them flickering toward extinction, didn't do anything to help with definitions.

"Good thing I never killed a dragon," I said.

"You were tempted?" she asked.

"Well, sure. I used to have to play by myself, so I took turns being princess, prince, and dragon. Mostly I ended up being the prince and waiting for the dragon. Good thing I couldn't be both at once because then, out of sheer ignorance, I might have actually slain the dragon. After all, that was the traditional thing to do."

On her belt Audrey wore a dragon buckle. A blue porcelain dragon hung on a satin ribbon from her neck. Another dragon rode on a silver ring on her left hand.

I boldly asked if she would loan me the painting of Serena for a while. Regretfully she said that she had to varnish it in the next day or two, so the answer was no.

The least I could do then was to carry Serena out to Audrey's green Volkswagen beetle. Sparks flew between us that could only be born at all by looking up and discussing the moon. Howling a little. Moaning the joy of something ineffable into the sky and into sleepless neighbors' ears.

Audrey felt so safe to me—a woman. So I need not, could not, fall in love, since, after all, I was a woman, too. Also, she had to be at least ten years older than I was. Twenty-three years, in fact, as I learned later on. Most of all she felt safe because I recognized a familiar sadness filter through the joy gloss of her impossible eyes.

I watched her drive off, took a deep breath, and returned to the tap dance of congenial indifference in the apartment. When Kay talked of Audrey at one point, I earmarked for future recall the mosaic pieces of a once-upon-a-time solitary writer working in a cottage and one day burning her whole manuscript with total satisfaction. An art teacher nowadays.

"By the way, I'm having dinner with Audrey next week," I bragged. My enthusiasm was undaunted by the less than reverent reception of this, to me, overwhelming news.

§

The next week, however, came and went without dinner. Almost literally so, as was often the case in our household. I'd open the refrigerator door when I came home from my day job, slap mayonnaise on a slice of bread, and devour it on the way to my room. Extreme appetite would send me back for more of the same. I didn't like to spend a lot of time on the necessities of corporeal sustenance. As to Audrey and not having dinner with her, I don't remember what transpired.

Often Kay didn't come home at night but spent the evening with one of her two lovers at his place. On nights when she did come home directly from her job, she would take a nap, and I raided our bread and mayonnaise supply on tiptoe. Thence to my room where I would arrive with every intention of working, as distinguished from doing the day job that paid my bills. Work equaled writing.

Kay kept better contact with the outside world, including Audrey. Kay had lots of gossip about Audrey, of which she divulged or kept to herself according to her unpredictable judgment. I, on the other hand, had the mystification, the wonder, and the admiration that comes of not knowing a person at all, but getting to taste all the legends already.

§

Audrey was Kay's art teacher. One night Kay stormed into my section of the apartment, ignoring the bed sheets that were hanging down in token of my wanting to be undisturbed.

"Best thing that's ever happened to me," she shouted.

"Do tell," I said, taking my hands off the typewriter keyboard.

"Audrey invited me to paint with her in her home studio some Saturdays. It's such an honor. She only invited one other student. I am so excited. She's such an inspiration."

Aside from being an honor, it was also a godsend for Kay, because normally Kay's studio was the wide world at large, consisting of streets and parks, provided that it was warm enough outside and not raining. Her artist's bane was our cheap basement apartment that offered shelter, privacy, atmosphere, everything a budding artist could possibly desire, except light.

I couldn't share the heady sense of being chosen, but I had to agree with the inspiration element. By now I knew Audrey was fifty-two. Amazing, and comforting to my twenty-nine going on old age, to see her energy and creativity blazing into middle age. She intrigued me. I didn't yet know her, but I felt I had it in me to be a worthy friend to this magnetic woman. Eventually.

For the time being, however, I didn't so much as pick up the telephone to do anything about my anticipations. It was a busy time. Audrey's absence in it became presence.

§

One evening I opened the door, threw down my handbag on the red carpet, and checked the mail on the table. Nothing for me. A travel magazine for Kay. Some stale corn chips in a rattan basket. I ate one to reassure my stomach that I would attend to its needs shortly.

On the dresser—strictly Kay's territory—was an envelope, ripped open, sender's name visible on the back flap: "Audrey" in turquoise calligraphy. I turned over the envelope. It was addressed to Kay. I refused to accept that it did not concern me. I eased out the small folded sheet with the beautiful handwriting, and, with the frailest remnant scrap of ethics, I ignored all of the brief note's contents, but canned down to the last phrase above the signature: "Love to beautiful Andrea. I'd love it if you'd bring her along to our Saturday studio session."

I stared. I felt joy. Warmth. I had it in writing. She had thought of me, considered me beautiful. Sent love. Invited me.

Or, rather, Kay had it in writing. But she would have to relinquish it to me sooner or later.

I danced to my room singing "Audrey" and "Andrea." From the first Audrey always pronounced my name correctly, with the accent on the second syllable, and without demanding, "say that again?" Though in my teens I had briefly allowed slacker variants like "Andy," I was meanwhile convinced that I had the right to insist on having my name pronounced the way it was meant to be, an honor which I was perfectly willing to accord anyone else.

"Love to beautiful Andrea" had great rhythm, I thought. What's more, no one had ever invented that particular rhythm before. Or had I simply not read enough mail not addressed to me?

Kay had already left for the evening. I didn't see her again until the following night, by which time Audrey's letter had been multiply rearranged the exact way I had originally found it: carelessly thrown on the dresser, back flap of the envelope in sight, with the left upper corner just touching Kay's grandmother's yellowing lace doily.

Hungrily I trailed Kay through the apartment, ready to pounce on any opportunity that would present itself to bend the conversation to the subject of Audrey. I talked about art, talent, and, in growing desperation, even studio space, until Kay was finally obliged to begin a sentence with "Audrey, for example . . . ."

"Have you heard from Audrey?" I interrupted.

"Yes. I had a note from her yesterday."

And? And? I looked at Kay expectantly.

"She reminded me of our studio session on Saturday."

"Did she say anything about our party?" I tried again.

"No. I'm sure she liked it."

Oh, please, Kay, don't let me down, I pleaded silently. Give me her invitation.

"So how is she doing these days?" I continued grasping, then decided to put myself more firmly into the picture: "I haven't heard from her at all."

"She doesn't say," Kay said. "It was just a very short note."

I know, Kay. I know. One page of five by seven paper with large calligraphy. Please tell me what she said about me.

"You know who's coming to town this weekend?" Kay asked suddenly.

I shook my head in despair.

"James," she said triumphantly. "You know, he's the guy who lives up in Woodstock. He wants to film a documentary on shopping-bag people. You've met him. When he was here last fall? At the festival in the park? Tall guy with blond hair. Talks about spirituality a lot. Remember him?"

Dejectedly I nodded my recollection of James.

"He'll be staying close by. One of his friends lives just a block up on Wisconsin. Most of the time he'll probably. . . ." Kay interrupted her enthusiasm for James. "Andrea, is something wrong?"

"No, no," I said. "Just tired, I suppose."

"You look pale all of a sudden."

"I guess I'm ready for a nap."

All I had to do was ask if Audrey had said anything about me. But how could I ask that? I wanted the answer as a gift that would validate my stolen knowledge. Why wouldn't Kay absolve me from being a thief?

I stalked off to my room, sulking privately, to take my nap. Unobtrusively, I took a glass from the kitchen which I filled with wine from my stash in my closet three times before falling asleep with the phrase "love to beautiful Andrea" pleasantly expanding in my mind, then fading into the easy phase of no consciousness, not even dreams.

§

Audrey and I made star-crossed telephone calls. I would resolutely pick up the phone, for example, and replace it with relief when I heard a busy signal at her end. My own line was even less accessible, Kay being popular.

It was almost time for our second art party that year when Audrey and I finally managed to set a dinner date. She was to pick me up at the apartment at a quarter to eight. This gave me time to hurry home from my own secretarial playpen at the computer firm, where I kept ordinary nine to five hours, and to take a quick sleeping draught and refresh myself with a nap. I set my alarm for half past seven to wake up in plenty of time to get ready for Audrey's arrival. She was supposed to knock at the side door of the apartment which opened into an alley. Lulled in anticipation I fell asleep.

When the rattle of the alarm clock finally got to me, I sat up electrified. It was eight o'clock.

Never mind, I tried to console myself. I'm too groggy to go anywhere anyway. Maybe she hadn't been able to make it herself. I hadn't heard a knock. Still, I jumped from my bed, sped to the bathroom, splashed water in my face, combed my hair, grabbed coat and scarf, and dashed out of the apartment, up to the lobby, heading for the glass doors with my crushed hopes.

I saw her kneel on the red carpet in the entry way. She was writing something on the upholstered round bench in the center of the lobby.

"Hi!" I exclaimed, startled by her sudden presence in my path while my body was still poised to lunge past her for the street. "I'm sorry. I overslept. I came home and took a nap. And now I overslept."

She looked at me with amazing crystal lights in her eyes. Then, somehow, she cut off that look, as though deliberately replacing it with something simpler.

"I was just writing you a note," she said.

"This is awful. I simply didn't hear, slept right through the alarm. For half an hour! Didn't you knock?"

"I knocked at the door," she said.

"You should have knocked louder."

"I thought of knocking on your window," she said. "But then I thought you were probably asleep and so I didn't want to disturb you."

"You should have! I most particularly wanted to be disturbed!"

She shrugged her shoulders, laughed. "Anyway, here we are. Where shall we go?"

I was filled with a surging sense of well-being, though picking places to go was not my forte, since I rarely went out. The place I suggested turned out to be an awful choice, noisy and crowded. It was one of their "All-You-Can-Eat" nights. Neither of us was prepared to vie with the din. We looked at each other and left.

"Next choice?" Audrey asked.

I deferred to her presumably vaster experience.

"You commit yourself into my hands?" Her eyes glittered.

I did.

By the time we reached her car, the March night wind had awakened me completely.

"I swagger, don't I?" she asked just before she opened the passenger door of her car.

"Yes. Will you teach me?" I replied.

She sat behind her steering wheel, meditating for a moment about the best way to get from here to wherever, which fascinated me, for I was one of the few stubborn non-drivers left in twentieth century America. Officially I was following the example of Einstein who had claimed that driving was too complicated for the Herr Professor. In reality I was merely enslaved by my fear of aggressive drivers, undersized city streets, and lack of parking spaces.

While Audrey picked a shortcut across a succession of parkways, I confessed my fascination. She tried to make it sound like a small thing, explaining that she had been a cab driver in one of her lives.

Except for a few men at the bar, we were the only customers at Mama Ayesha's, which earned us a quiet booth. I wanted to know more about the various lives she had mentioned. But she refused to enlarge on them, even though I prompted her by telling her I already knew that she had, in one of them, been a writer. All she conceded was that there must have been approximately seven lives in all.

"All in this body?" I asked.

That, according to Audrey, depended on how one defined "this body." Since she was being enigmatic, I bragged about approximately three and a half lives of my own, wondering immediately whether, if challenged, I would be able to substantiate such a grandiose claim.

Audrey told me she was in the process of conceiving another dragon, a golden one this time. She drew a sketch of her intentions on a napkin. In exchange I told her a few hazy ideas about my latest writing project, which was to be a piece dissecting religion, and then, if possible, putting it back together again. Since this was to be my first large-scale single work, I was shy of touching it, much less completing it. I told Audrey grandly that I had my last major work of art planned already, also. The reason I thought it would be my last work was that I felt I would have to experience most of it first. I rambled on and on.

"I'm talking too much," I finally said.

She shook her head, ready to defend me against self-censure.

I laughed. "It's not so much self-criticism as it is a wonder to me, Audrey. I don't think I've ever before in my life talked too much!"

"Oh." She slid the plate with bread and baba ghanoush dip, of which we had both eaten virtually nothing thus far, closer to me.

Like a trapeze artist climbing down after a performance, I came back down to earth, hungry, and ready for more mundane curiosity before we had to go home.

"So, you're a real inspiration, you know, supporting yourself with your art," I said. "Maybe one day I'll be able to do that too."

"I only teach part time," she said as she dipped her pita bread. "I do other stuff to make ends meet."

"Like the rest of us." I sighed, nodded. "What do you do?"

She shrugged her shoulders. I pegged her for being involved in some kind of crafts business. When she finally gave me a metaphor for her job, the crafts image fit perfectly.

"You know the particles that dance around in the sunlight in the morning?" She held up her palms, then closed her hands. "Let's say I gather sun dust."

"And what do you do with it?" I pictured her, climbing up into a hill at dawn with a basket under her arm. She wouldn't even have to stoop to gather herbs or twigs. She would simply stand there and pluck sun dust from the air with her bare hands.

"I share it. Sometimes I transform it," she said.

I, too, came up with a metaphor for my secretary's desk in the computer company. I told her that I helped guard information. "Mind you, I don't personally stand watch. I merely see to it that the guardian dragon has all the necessary breathing fire in perfect condition."

"You work for a dragon?" She clapped her hands.

"But of course," I said.

§

Two days later Kay and I gave our second party. The theme was adolescent art. We asked everyone to bring what they had created ten, fifteen years ago. Some of our friends balked. Audrey had the most cogent reservation of all: did it have to be work from ten or fifteen years ago, or from adolescence? If you were in your fifties, the distinction mattered.

By the afternoon of the party, Kay and I flitted around the apartment, dusting recessed corners, looking for missing poems, running into each other's rooms, shouting, "Listen to this!" The most disturbing discovery I made during that preparatory afternoon was that, given ten years of so-called maturing, I hadn't come all that far. I was still picking my way among images of unrequited love and pits of despair.

I put my hair in curlers for the first time in several years and donned black tights and the one miniskirt I still owned. I'd found it buried in some luggage I had dragged from place to place. Folded up in its generous pockets, I carried with me a few of my old poems, and some of my old scars.

Toby had decided to deal me a final coup de grace the day before. Our relationship had already ended and now he came to visit for the express purpose of telling me so once again with all the noble clichés that he had in him. At every syrupy phrase I wanted to scream, 'So, get out! Must you come here to tell me all this when it's so obvious?' But he had to accommodate his need for a histrionic farewell, hardening his clichés into knives, investigating the wounds they dealt, judging their depth, then offering the band-aids of his choice.

"You're not beautiful," he said. "But you are so good. You really haven't lost anything by losing me."

Only time, some money, and some respect for myself. Besides, my not being beautiful was a matter of opinion.

Solemnly he laid his hand on my head: "We'll be so much better off without each other in the long run."

It rose like a growl from the pit of my stomach, my counter cliché fleshed out by disgust: "If you go now, Toby, you may indeed go far!"

This did the trick. At the door he looked back. Apparently it wasn't the effect he had intended. Should we have wept together, kneeling on the floor, perhaps? What novels had he been reading lately that seduced him to his tear-thirsty performance?

What shamed me the most was that I recognized major pieces of myself in his soggy flirtation with melancholy. The true suffering I felt, while growling at the vanishing Toby on his way out of my life, was the gnawing suspicion that I, noble thinker and striver for the sublime, got exactly what I deserved: a cloying entrapment in a love affair into which I had voluntarily entered on the strength of the other commonplaces that amused me. It had been love at first sight. Artist met artist. Since there had been sex, we had to have been in love. From all of which followed that, if this was a breakup, then I was obliged to experience the glory of pain instead of prosaic relief. Here was a real situation no more wholesome than many of the adolescent poems that were, because of our party, neatly typed up in my miniskirt pockets.

I drank a lot of wine that night, crossed my black-stockinged legs defiantly, and smiled copiously to cover up for anger and confusion, wearing charm like precious jewels, ruby, anger, and moonstone.

As soon as I sat down on the carpet or stood still anywhere, I found myself the center of a circle of men whom I instantly despised for directing all of their comments, unsolicited, to me. Was I some queen bee to them, capable of justifying or destroying their unnecessary verbal droning? I felt unbearably alone.

By the wall, near the door to my room, Audrey sat with Kay, having a one on one conversation of which I was envious. Pretty soon I forbade myself to look their way again, lest my envy should show or grow. When I did look again, I saw them hug. I could hardly bear it.

Compared with our Valentine's party, this second fête was a flop. The only young man who could play a guitar strummed along nicely until someone said, "play louder." Suddenly he protested that he couldn't play at all.

Instead of viable musicians, we had, through friends of friends, attracted a small cluster of magicians who competed with card tricks and tied sausage balloons into poodles. Someone kept pestering me about giving him my phone number, which was absurd, because he already had Kay's, which was mine too. Meanwhile, the currently active magician asked for an assistant who had to be female. All of us qualified muttered and avoided eye contact, except for Audrey who jumped up from the floor.

"I'll do it," she said.

She made a perfect magician's apprentice, standing, legs apart, pelvis tipped forward, black pants, white shirt, and underneath the dark vest the familiar silver dragon belt catching the light of the candles.

Her short brown permed hair flew out in a semicircle at chin level as she moved her head in staccato motions to end each soft sweeping gesture of her arms. Her eyes looked soft gray tonight, as though hidden lights poured out from behind them. I couldn't afterwards remember the magician himself, except that he stood behind Audrey, taller, wider, and infinitely paler, like an amorphous background shadow. We did all, in the end, applaud their performance, so that something or other must have worked out as far as his tricks were concerned.

Audrey took a bow, then sat down against a wall quietly, sinking back into herself, as though to give the shape of the magician's assistant a chance to linger, independently, in the air.

Later she recited, from memory, a poem she had written when she was nine. It was about a lamb lying down in soft grass, warmed by the sun. Then she recited one about distant love, with the worshipful lover subjecting herself humbly and in total devotion.

"You too?" I asked, turning to face her fully. Audrey shrugged her shoulders and frowned, as though asking what exactly I meant. But her eyes glittered with laughter.

"Why did you ask me that?" she said later.

"I don't know," I said. "I guess I just wanted to say something. Your poem struck a familiar chord. Was it written with someone specific in mind?"

"No." Audrey shook her head in several quick jerks. "No, I just wrote it. Felt like that. Grand feeling, you know."

Yes, I was familiar with grand feelings.

I went to bed long before the party was over. There were two people left, Audrey included, to whom I thought I owed a personal and friendly good night, but some hostile silence took over instead. All I wanted to do was slip away, withdraw to my bed, and reject the rest of the night.

§

I had taken Monday and Tuesday off in order to do some writing I felt ready for. Only to find I wasn't ready at all. Instead, I found myself reading, drinking wine, and sleeping a lot, unwilling to tackle anything more demanding. Least of all myself.

By Tuesday Kay hadn't talked to me for two days. She came to my room, woke me up and offered me food, which I didn't want. I tried to be as friendly as possible to keep a lid on the concerned look in her eyes. Since it was easier to avoid Kay than myself, I simply told her that I felt miserable and hinted at the desirability of being left alone.

"Look, Audrey sent you these flowers," she said.

Listlessly I looked at the white chrysanthemums in Kay's hands. Three long-stemmed flowers, like cranes with fluffed head feathers, coming at me through my fog wall.

"Where do you want me to put them?" Kay said unhappily. Her unhappiness offended me. Didn't a person have a right to suffer in peace?

"I'll put them here on the floor by your bed," Kay said when I didn't answer.

"Yes, please," I said. "Thanks."

She stood in the middle of the room for a time, then decided to leave. "Do you want me to turn off the light again?" she asked.

"Yes, please."

After she left, I guilt-tripped myself into a less miserable public appearance. I went to the kitchen and started making noises. When Kay showed up in the kitchen door, I offered to make us coffee. I thanked her for bringing in the flowers.

"They've been on the dining room table since yesterday," she said.

I caught her eyes for a moment. She quickly looked away.

Next day I wrote Audrey a note during lunch hour, apologizing for not thanking her for the flowers earlier, calling them "guardian flowers." I reported that I had been depressed on account of men trouble, which sounded more plausible and sophisticated than merely being depressed on account of my inability to write and drinking too much to avoid the depression while involuntarily increasing it.

§

Audrey called to thank me for the note and we made another

dinner date for the following week. I asked her to be sure to give my love to her dragon.

"Oh, Serena will be so excited," Audrey said. "She's been impatient for news of you. She's been terribly unruly. She wanted to make such an impression on you. I had to tell her to cool it."

"Well, you can tell your dragon that I'm perfectly in love with her. She's very beautiful. And tell her also that I've never been in love with a dragon before."

"Beats being in love with people, doesn't it?" Audrey asked crisply.

"It sure does," I said.

§

Everybody was solicitous regarding my allegedly wounded heart these days, though what was truly wounded was my ego, of course. My best friend Sharon and her fiancé Benny invited me to dinner. They had also invited his best friend, an unattached young man passing through town. Sharon and I quipped about the fact that this was tantamount to matchmaking, and wasn't it an indignity that we had to go to such lengths on my behalf?

They picked me up and I sat beside Joel in the back seat of their car. It was dark, and I could only make out his features vaguely, especially since it wasn't appropriate to look too often or too directly.

On first impression, Joel didn't strike me anything near as beautiful as advertised. Nevertheless, I did my best to dazzle. We had dinner uncomfortably, both being aware of the fact that we were deliberately being set up for one another. We exchanged essential information. He worked as a river guide for a rafting tour company out west. When he talked about his river, he lost some of his reserve and became more attractive, his black eyes gleaming with love for the river and for nature and long days of silence in it. We politely regretted that he would only be in town another ten days, for otherwise we might have gotten to know each other.

I liked Joel's face. Weathered brown skin, thick long black hair. His black eyes were full of warm lights that danced. His teeth seemed too large and too white. I particularly liked his tall, lean, angular body with its deliberate, sinuous, unselfconscious animal movements. There was a certain animal shyness in his face as well—not fear, simply caution.

I began feeling romantic, just in case. No matter how free I was in other respects, I still subscribed to my old personal conviction: if there was going to be sex, then I had better be in love.

Joel seemed polite, gentle, and very attentive. The final straw for me was when he groped for words to compliment me. I let him grope for a while, unwilling to help, but wanting very much to hear. As soon as he started to speak, he stuttered, apologizing for the triteness of his words. I was enchanted. Here was a man who spurned clichés. The soft spot I already had for him expanded and grew softer.

My romantic feelings about Joel developed just in the nick of time, for two days later we found ourselves in bed together. It started innocently enough, the two of us sitting on the carpet of our friends' living room, drawing closer, accidentally touching while I reached for a cigarette.

I couldn't remember a time when making love had been such a delicious prospect, unclouded by fears, duties, or other restrictive complications. I felt no responsibility toward him. He would be gone in a matter of days, too far away to make any permanent relationship viable. With so little time, it made sense to skip all preliminaries. It wasn't possible, or necessary, to find out who he was.

Privately I already schemed that I would see him once or twice a year, which would leave the remainder of my life uncluttered for my writing, and free also of the bothersome fear that my work would prevent me entirely from leading a life of pleasure. Who, in this day and age, respected a woman who, no matter how productive, didn't have a lover and some experience of the world to her credit?

The more it became apparent to me that I was well on my way to using Joel for selfish purposes, the gentler I became toward him, hoping to give something in return for my self-centered taking. I didn't want him to lose out. And through such complicated reasoning I conceived an amazing tenderness for him. I wasn't going to belong to him or satisfy any of his needs if they in any way went against my agenda. But I was going to be so kind that he would hardly notice anything was missing.

For the remaining days he was in town, I took a vacation from writing and from any other social life, determined to do nothing but enjoy him with an abandon I had never before experienced. I accepted no other dates, though the requests suddenly poured in with unprecedented quantity. Or had I simply never noticed? It gave me an imperious chance to inform all unwanted suitors that I was having a fling and was therefore busy.

"End of winter episode?" one of them asked.

"No, more like early spring," I said.

§

I also canceled all of my prior engagements, except the one dinner date with Audrey. I bragged to her about Joel.

"I met the perfect young man. He'll be gone in a week."

"That's sad," she said.

"No," I explained. "That's what makes him perfect."

We went to a Japanese restaurant. I had no idea what to order, so I relegated that chore to Audrey's vaster experience. She ordered gently, keeping raw fish to a manageable minimum. Meanwhile I studied the menu and made a mental inventory of the cash in my pocket. Good, I was solvent enough for this.

"And, by the way, do let me pay for dinner tonight," she said.

I muttered protestations of independence.

"That's all very well," she said. "But what's really relevant is this: I'm not exactly rich, but I have a hell of a lot more money than you do."

A Japanese girl in a blue robe took our orders, brought sake and the first round of raw fish, which was unobtrusive, because it was generously seasoned with ginger. I still had Audrey's "hell of a lot more money than you" on my mind and finally brought the conversation back to her mystery work.

"So I take it, you still won't reveal to me the true nature of what you do besides teaching?" I asked.

She studied her chopsticks with great concentration.

"It can't be that bad," I said, softly enough to accommodate the delicate atmosphere of the Japanese restaurant. "I, for one, work as a humble secretary to earn my living, and am often duly ashamed of it. Except that it's not really too bad. And," I added into her continuing silence, "now that you know what a lowly person you are dealing with, you better tell me your own vile secrets."

Audrey was still unwilling. "If I tell how I make most of my living, you'll never talk to me again."

I told her I didn't think so.

She took a deep breath, making my expectations rise, then deflated her chest again. "Promise you'll talk to me still, no matter what?" she asked in a small voice.

I swore by all that was sacred to me. "I won't even look at you while you make your confession." I selected a print with a genteel Japanese lady holding cherry blossoms on the opposite wall to focus my eyes on.

"Well, here you go. And remember what you promised."

Audrey spoke with menace in her voice. "I make most of my living as a psychic healer. Mind you, a more or less reputable one. No neon lights and crystal balls and tarot cards. Though I do own tarot cards, but I never use them. I basically use my hands and my intuition. So there. "

"Hm," I said, concentrating on the white skin of the Japanese lady, the stark outline of her painted face, a violently red mouth above the soft tribute of almost amorphous flowers. What was Audrey's problem? Being a psychic sounded more glamorous to me than shameful.

"See? Already you're not talking to me," she said. "It turns people off. It frightens them. Nobody wants to talk to me again. Unless it's by appointment."

I took my eyes off the Japanese lady and smiled, probably stupidly, and informed Audrey that I was neither frightened of dragons nor of psychics.

"Then why are you silent?" she demanded. "Afraid I'll read your thoughts?"

"What do you mean?" I said. "I'm talking. And if you were to read my thoughts, and if that frightened me, then I'd be up and gone, wouldn't I?"

"Promise you won't do that?"

The stark loneliness in her eyes touched me. That, if anything, was what truly scared me. I considered myself somewhat of an expert in loneliness. My own. Even that of others. But it had never before touched me so deeply in another human being as it did just then, looking into Audrey's pleading eyes.

Audrey had already told me, proudly, that she had never been married, and, though she had lived with lovers, that she preferred, in the end, to live by herself. It seemed to her she couldn't compromise with others. In the end, it never seemed worth the sacrifice of self. I wanted to embrace her with the part of me that was lonely also and felt a bond between us. I wanted to wrap my arms around her like a blanket of comfort. Instead, I self-consciously played with my chop sticks and said cheerful and irrelevant things.

I had to get home early, too early for my taste now. I wanted to stay with Audrey and talk. But a friend was coming over to take photographs of me for my new book of poems which was due for publication late spring. Joel was also planning to come over.

"When will I see you again?" Audrey asked.

"When do you want to see me again?"

"Oh, not too early." She looked past me. "I don't want you to get tired of me too quickly."

I looked at her from the corner of my eye.

"And not too late either." She laughed.

"Hm," I said. "That's difficult."

"How about next week?" she said jubilantly.

"How about Thursday next week?" I said. Joel was leaving on Wednesday.

On the street, a block away from her car, Audrey took a strand of my hair in her hand and said, "You're lovely, Andrea. You truly are lovely."

I touched her shoulder, not knowing what else to do. "By the way, what color are your eyes?" I asked. "They seem to change all the time."

"You noticed!" Audrey exclaimed. "Hardly anybody ever does."

How brave she was in her loneliness. As perhaps all of us are who know about being alone. We laughed all the way back to my apartment. Once, at an intersection, Audrey's car stalled and knocked us back in our seats.

"Weeeeeee," she sang. Then she explained, "This was a sake stop. I distinctly feel the sake taking over. Do you still trust me to deliver you home?"

"Of course," I said. "I had as much sake as you, if not more.

That makes my trust equal to your driving ability."

§

My photographer friend failed to show up that night, but Joel came as planned. I tried to be my usual intriguing self and failed. Joel was confused. I was helpless. I tried to tell him about Audrey, but quickly gave up. To me, what had transpired between me and Audrey that night had been like a recognition of something that I couldn't yet put into words. I wanted to keep it to myself, unshared and untouched.

I managed to send Joel away without actually having to tell him to go. Then I paced back and forth on the red carpet of my room, not, as usual, thinking and phrasing my thoughts to myself, but instead as though waiting for something to come through to me.

I could feel it come slowly, painfully almost, but bringing its own consolation in its wake. It came, not like a monster, but like a deep peaceful sadness. I went to my desk, mechanically opened my notebook, and wrote down the cry in me.

"Audrey, I cannot take away your loneliness."

Seven words in my notebook. Yet it seemed as though I had performed a strenuous task that required all my energy. I sat down on my bed, trembling.

§

Joel was pure joy. I surrendered to the playful essence of his being. We were inseparable for the remaining week he was in town. We went for walks, we went to cafés, we renamed every statue we saw, we went to a concert, we went to dinner. We went on and on and on.

At night we went to bed. I was immersed in him and felt revitalized and giddily avoided all troublesome intellectual matters. I was on vacation from myself, a holiday of undiluted joy. I knew I would soon be back to my usual self. I chose to distance myself for a week and I soared.

I even ignored Audrey during that week.

She called one night, just as Joel and I were about to storm out of the apartment into some new adventure. Since Kay didn't lunge for the phone, I answered, breathlessly and mock-forbiddingly: "City morgue."

Audrey's laughter rang through my ears larger than any reality. She sounded uncanny. In the process of confusion I managed to unplug the phone for a moment and tried with feverish hands to reconnect it. Miraculously she was still at the other end of the line when I succeeded. Even after I had relegated the telephone to Kay's much calmer ears, mine were still ringing with her unearthly laughter.

Probably there had been nothing uncanny about her laughter at all. What made it ring in my ears so strangely was my own response. There was awe, almost fear. I wanted to speak to her so desperately. But not with a lover hovering behind me, listening in on words that couldn't be private enough for my taste. I was beginning to be afraid of the almost toxic way in which Audrey affected me. I wanted to flee.

Once, when I was out at the store to buy dinner fixings, Audrey called while Joel was alone at the apartment.

"What did she say?" I felt uneasy.

"Just that she called. No message. She would probably like to be called back."

But I escaped. I did not call back. I wanted to. And at the same time I did not want the joy I danced with Joel troubled by the dark essence within myself that I would have to recognize again if I so much as talked to Audrey. I wanted to be free of her, and yet, in some part of myself I already knew that I wasn't, that I could only momentarily escape from that part of myself which responded to her so strongly by further immersing myself in the light-heartedness of Joel's companionship.

§

Joel traveled seventeen miles across town in the evenings to come to me. In the mornings he left at four o'clock to return his father's borrowed car in time for his father to take it to work. I got up with him, fixed coffee, kissed him goodbye and then went back to sleep for another two hours.

I loved the soaring sensation of being with Joel, floating across the fence posts of the universe. By the time he left, I'd already made arrangements to visit him in May. He promised to take me on a raft trip. I yearned to see what made his eyes come alive, the love for his job and his river. A refund from the IRS was earmarked to pay for my extravagance.

The only uneasy moment I had with Joel was on March 28. He announced that one of the rides he had counted on for part of his way back had fallen through and he therefore considered, since everything was so wonderful between us, staying on another week or two.

I didn't protest. I was prepared to welcome him. But I did not want him to stay. That, to me, wasn't part of our romance. In order to fulfill my needs, it was imperative that he leave as scheduled on April 1st. I had reserved for him exactly so many days of my vacation from myself, no more. I knew if he stayed I would be resentful and, as a consequence, cruel. I wasn't tired yet of Joel. But I needed him to leave before any tiredness had the slightest chance of setting in. I didn't like my calculating thoughts and was determined to keep them to myself. However, they were there, undeniable, and mine.

Joel spared me the necessity of having to strike a balance between what I wanted and what he might want by leaving on schedule after all. He gave me back the gift of undiluted joy of having, but not having to keep.

The night before he left I came out of the bathroom after brushing my teeth and found him on my bed, naked, lying on his stomach, unselfconscious of his beauty. His dark skin, his long, slender body, stretched like a cat's before me. His long black hair spilled out against the white of the pillow. He was beautiful. Completely still, mine for the moment, without demands. He had the rare gift of offering himself without struggle, without pride, without self-serving. I had never experienced a man like him before.

He was able to stay all night, not needing to return his father's car for once, and he walked me to the bus stop the following morning. The bus came. I moved toward it, turned and waved. Joel said something about April Fools. There was sadness in his eyes, but not despair.

"See you at the end of May," I said.

I elbowed my way to a place by the window and waved again. The bus pulled away. That was that.

§

I returned to the solitary business of writing. Scheming. Plotting. I felt no sadness. I felt as though I had been given a gift.

Next I started catching up with the social obligations I had neglected for nearly two weeks, beginning with Audrey whom I called to remind her of the dinner I was scheduled to cook for her that evening, a Thursday. Like an exuberant child, having just discovered something important, I planned to give her all the enchantment I had recently received from Joel.

She came and I carried her on my wings. I gave her what joy I had in me, translated into words and gestures. It translated well. I was, that day and for many days to come, so much in charge of freedom, light, and joy that even what was merely in my vicinity blossomed. The spring trees in the business district around Dupont Circle—trees I had passed for months without so much as noticing—puffed out into extravagant white and pink flowers.

No one questioned the price of the magic I was spreading. We all drank the elixir of exuberance I had concocted without bothering about ingredients or recipes. Like a good chef, I was determined to keep my recipe a secret. It wasn't necessary to see anything except the light on the face of whoever was drinking from my cup of enthusiasm. It wasn't necessary for anyone to know the steps of the dance I performed, so long as the dance was good and full of life.

§

Audrey and Kay came up with the idea of painting me at one of their Saturday painting sessions. I was flattered. I promised to visit them during their next painting session to see their works in progress, still lives at the moment. So, on the first Saturday in April, I set out with my notebooks in my shoulder bag and a crumpled and often examined piece of paper with instructions as to how to get to Audrey's house in my coat pocket.

I approached the house with a feeling of awe and anticipation. She had promised that some dragon, probably Serena, would sit on top of the roof, tooting with joy when she saw me coming so that I wouldn't miss the place. But, just in case, I also scanned the house numbers before I turned toward the red brick building and stood still at her door, marveling at the commotion in my chest, before knocking my first feeble knock. This went unheard and unheeded. I knocked louder and still got no response. Finally I tried the door, which opened to chiming bells.

"Anybody there?" I asked into the smell of turpentine layered with incense.

Audrey floated through the two large dark rooms that opened out before me, dressed in jeans and a splattered, gray shirt, a wet brush in one hand, a sweeping gesture of welcome in the other.

She exhaled. "So here you are!"

I looked around for green Serena first of all, and there she stood, on a cabinet in the second room, drifting down toward her yearned-for universe.

Both rooms were cluttered with paintings, plants, statues, knick-knacks, antiques. The walls were a bold dark blue, like an invitation into the comfort of darkness. I was stunned not only by the beauty of the place, but also by its wealth of playful detail. Chimes, oriental carpets, gold basins, white statues. A silver dragon dangled from the ceiling drop that separated dining area from living room.

Still, it wasn't cluttered. Everything had breathing space. Darkness and space. Briefly I forgot to breathe.

§

Awe yielded to a poodle that came tumbling toward me, past Audrey who remained fixed in her posture of greeting. A Lhasa followed, waddling at a slower rate of excitement, as though dragging under the weight of its long hair. I swallowed in one single gulp my longstanding tradition of despising small dogs, specifically poodles. But in the process of swallowing and bending down to pet the animals, which were now jumping up the length of my legs, I felt irrepressible laughter rise up in me. So Audrey's place was not only sacred but also delightfully mundane. Meanwhile an ancient orange tabby cat dragged itself into our direction to inspect, with diffidence, what everybody seemed to find of so much interest. Almost at once it turned away again, having satisfied itself that it was nothing more exciting than merely another human being come to visit.

With an entourage of two dogs we made our procession through the living room, dining room, kitchen, and a tiny hallway to the studio where we found Kay, proudly focused on pale oranges, on and off canvas, while giving me a casual "hello."

I asked for a basket for the grapes I had brought, feeding some to Kay's mouth directly because she couldn't, just then, let go of the brush in one of her hands and the turpentine rag in the other. I sat down on the floor. With the two easels in the room, there was no room for another chair.

I had intended to write, but found I could only manage to watch, fascinated, very still, as though in a dream state. From time to time, one of them would address a comment or question to me. I had to make an effort to pull myself out of the magic where I had been floating.

Soon Audrey decided that she was through with painting for the day. Kay said she would take a break as well. I could have sat there for a long time still, dreaming myself further into the atmosphere. But at their change of rhythm, I too rose, ready to leave, or do anything else that might be suggested. I just wanted to be.

Kay talked of possibly resuming her painting again in a little while and withdrew to one of the rocking chairs in the living room. Audrey still bustled in the studio, cleaning brushes, skipping to the kitchen for water, coming back, looking at me, then again at the rag and brush in her hands.

With her back to me she said,"I have a small gift for you. Do you mind?"

What kind of a question was that? And how to answer, except with huge eyes and raised eyebrows that went unnoticed because her back was turned.

"Do you want to see it?" Her voice squeaked. She finally turned around. "You may not like it, and if you don't, you'll have to promise you'll let me know and won't take it." Her hands painted nervous patterns in the air. "I just walked through this little store with a friend, looking, you know. And there it was. It made me think of you, and I wanted to give it to you. Well, can I give it to you now?"

"Sure," I said, amused, but also protective of her peace of mind and determined to like the gift, no matter what it was.

She danced off into the room adjoining the studio and reemerged with a small brown paper bag, once more reciting conditions for the increasingly unlikely chance that I would dislike her gift. By the time I held the package in my hand, I was nearly as apprehensive as she. Tension surged between us as we went through the ritual of "well, open it, open it," and hesitation, and further prodding.

I closed my eyes as I folded away the paper and reopened them on a silver chain with a pale green carved scarab in a delicate silver setting.

"If you don't like it . . . ." Her voice trailed off.

"It's beautiful."

Her hands fluttered, her voice fluttered. She reached for the necklace and apparently wanted to relieve me of it again. I closed my own hand around the pendant and took a step back, telling her that she could only take it out of my hand again if she promised to put it around my neck.

"Come, I'll show you the house," she said as I inspected my new necklace in the large mirror in her studio. The scarab looked unfamiliar, but perfect and permanent.

She led me through the house with its circular layout where the living room joined the dining room and the kitchen beyond it on the right-hand side. On the left, opposite the kitchen, was the large studio, followed by the bedroom and a small bathroom. Another cat, with beautiful black and white markings, came to inspect me.

"That's Missy. She's very shy of people," Audrey said, just as the cat proceeded to rub herself against my legs in answer to my human rendition of meows.

I laughed.

Audrey shrugged. "Guess not with you."

Past the hallway, between living room, entrance door, and bathroom, was a closed door. I was curious, but didn't ask about it. This was Audrey's tour. With all the other doors in the house open, one could walk a complete circle, omitting just that one closed door off to the side.

On our second round through the open rooms, we inspected the paintings on the wall. Most of them were not Audrey's work, but there was one in the living room which, after my beloved green dragon, I liked especially, and it turned out to be Audrey's. It was a portrait of an old woman with careworn lines and pale colors of age, gentleness, and peace in her face. I also particularly liked Audrey's crayon self-portrait that stood propped up against the window in the studio.

Audrey told me the story of the old woman's portrait in the living room. Audrey had gone wandering along a beach when she saw an old, solid-looking house, which she suddenly felt she simply had to paint. She decided to knock at the door to ask permission to paint the house. The woman in the portrait opened the door. "I came to ask permission to paint your house," Audrey had told her breathlessly, "but now, I believe, I am asking permission to paint you." Besides the woman and her husband, there was also a young son whom Audrey described as so beautiful that she immediately wanted to go there and live with him.

"Did you?" I asked.

"Did I what?"

"Go and live with the young man?"

"No, of course not," Audrey protested.

"Why not?" I asked.

"Well, he was much younger. And one doesn't just go and live with someone merely because one wants to. I just sort of loved the way he looked and moved. I have some slides of him. Do you want to see them?"

I didn't really, but it was something to do, so I said yes. We lay down in the open doorway between studio and bedroom and used the one bare wall of the hallway as a projection screen. Audrey had slides of the beach, the house, the woman, her husband, and then of the tall blond son, a minor giant.

"Isn't he beautiful?" Audrey urged.

"Wish I could have seen him in person," I said.

In fact, I wasn't impressed at all. He looked bland to me. He always leaned against some truck or fence or door, squeezing himself against it, or alternatively out of the picture in one direction or another. I asked to see more slides, and Audrey began putting them into the projector indiscriminately, landscapes, seascapes, a harmony of birds against wire poles.

Kay wandered in on our slide show, restless after looking at drawings in one of Audrey's books in the living room rocking chair.

"Ready to paint some more?" I asked.

No, she'd also given up for the day. Besides, she had to go soon to meet one of her boyfriends.

"What are you doing tonight?" I asked Audrey boldly. "Rather, are you doing anything? More rather, do you have any plans?"

"Nothing. No. No. In that order," Audrey replied. "Do you want to do something? Together?"

There was the exhibit on Alexander the Great in the East Wing of the Smithsonian. I had wanted to see it for months and it was now in its final few weeks. We decided to go and see that.

We walked across the Mall toward the East Wing building, breathless with being together. It felt bewitching to have Audrey by my side. It made me feel important. As did the prickly wind of spring and the gleam of white buildings in the moonlight and lamplight around us.

We talked just for the sake of talking, for the sake of having sound between us, for the sake of doing justice to the fact that we were together rather than on lone pursuits, which, as we both knew by now, was the habitual way with which both of us navigated in the world. We had no subject, no theme, merely a loose string of casual thoughts we showed to each other, like merchants in the market place displaying their wares, smiling, putting things into curious and attractive lights. Suddenly, as we stood waiting for a traffic light to change, Audrey turned to face me with a puzzled look in her eyes, then shook her head lightly.

"There's something about you I don't understand," she said.

"What's that?"

"I don't even know how to explain it."

"Try?" I said.

"It has to do with innocence."

"I'm not particularly innocent," I said with the requisite modesty, while privately feeling flattered.

"I know that," she said. "Still, it's there. There's a childlike quality about you. I don't mean childish. It's spontaneous. Playful. Searching, and, yes, innocent. It makes me feel very comfortable around you, Andrea. And then again, sometimes it unsettles me."

I thought I knew what she meant. I looked younger than my twenty-nine years, incipient laugh lines crinkling the skin at the eyes and all. Apart from that, I had a knack for having people respond to me with tacit offers of protection. There were advantages to that. The child was like a shield around me that kept me out of the way of the brutality of which most human beings are capable. It had disadvantages as well. Often I felt pushed around and ordered into poses of compliance against which the adult in me rebelled.

"Now I've offended you." Audrey placed her hand on my arm

and stepped around in front of me, blocking our progress across the mall. "I didn't mean to say you were childish. I was merely talking about your aura of innocence."

"I think I know what it is," I said. "I've done a lot of things, I've been a lot of places, and I've been through twenty-nine years of this. But when I look back, it almost seems to me as though nothing has ever touched me to the core. If there is such a thing as a human core. I've merely moved through things, you see. And when I was through, they closed behind me and didn't become part of me, just as I didn't become part of them. It seems as though every experience I've ever had really happened to someone else, not me."

Audrey gave me a quizzical look. "I guess that makes sense." She stepped to my side again and we resumed our walk.

I gave her an evening of childlike enthusiasm, and she reciprocated. We pulled each other through rooms full of medallions, with the young and always handsome face of Alexander, and rooms full of gods and golden trinkets.

I found the golden ears of wheat I had particularly wanted to see, kept separated from the jewelries and statues on a small pedestal, encased in glass, and playing their mild golden glimmer against the background of midnight blue velvet. I stood in front of them, trying to let the sense of awe and ancientness pervade me and merge with the longing within me. They were disappointing and exhilarating at the same time. You couldn't wear them. Couldn't follow them down some trail of ancient human memories. You couldn't even pray to them. They simply existed, and I was drawn to them, again and again, while Audrey inspected reconstructed tombs and enormous golden earrings made in the shape of chariots.

Audrey wanted to show me something in the main building of the National Gallery. We arrived just before closing and rushed past urgent admonitions by a guard that we only had a minute. Audrey showed me the satin shimmer of women's white dresses, and the reflections of windows in the eyes of one of Dürer's portraits. She infected me with her excitement.

"It's impossible to making oil paint glitter, you see," she said. "But he did it anyway."

She wanted to achieve that effect in her new golden dragon. It would be difficult, but she would learn to do it. Her new dragon would fly through both the warmth of gold and the coolness of the gold's shimmer. She would fly through the flat of the canvas as easily as through the depth of the universe. She would fly through impossibilities made possible.

"It's like the concept of transformational grammar," Audrey told me on the subway escalator on our way home.

On top of the escalator, I didn't know what transformational grammar was, and by the time we reached the bottom, I had a fair working knowledge. Surface structures of communication versus the underlying images and associations, which the communicators filled in from common mental constructs as well as from personally unique ones. I also grasped the miracle, in view of all these complications, of people understanding each other at all.

Most impressively to me, I suddenly knew about the artist's dream to translate her impossibly personal and unshared vision with others through the careful balancing act of supplying sufficient recognizable structure to keep her audience comfortable, while simultaneously supplying enough gaps in the structure to force the audience to look again and again, driven by the slight unease of not understanding the how, the why, or the what. These gaps, much more than the structure, it seemed, were what determined the quality of any given work of art. The gaps were what attracted attention.

When we got in the train, Audrey had a headache. Sympathy with her pain brought me down to earth again and kept me there. At every station the breaks screeched. I finally pressed my two hands over Audrey's ears when the noise came on again. I couldn't take away the pain, but I was able to transcend its presence with the sweet shared knowledge that I was touching her deliberately and without any semblance of accident.

I knew how much I loved her then, how much I would always love her. Touching her was strong with meaning and helpless with futility. Earth-gesture in the face of heaven.

§

Parting that night was difficult. Back at Audrey's house we ate the afternoon's remaining grapes. A neighbor came over to visit. The subject of travel came up. Audrey mentioned she still had to make reservations for a trip to New Mexico for Memorial Day weekend. Suddenly she asked if I would come along.

"New Mexico?" I asked. "Just for the weekend? Why not Paris?"

"No, it'll have to be New Mexico," she said, then mentioned that she could easily manage to pay my way.

The neighbor watched with interest.

"I'm going away on vacation around Memorial Day myself," I said. Audrey looked disappointed. The neighbor looked relieved.

"How long will you be gone?" Audrey asked.

"Oh, just ten days," I said.

"Ten days!" Audrey regretted again later on in the car as she drove me home. "You'll be gone for ten days."

I laughed. "You'll be gone for part of the time yourself. And we don't even see each other all that often."

"But if you're gone for ten days, I won't even be able to call you if I choose to," Audrey said sulkily, underlining the word "choose" with her voice.

At the glass door to the apartment building I turned around nine times, and nine times Audrey still sat in her green Volkswagen, waving to me as I turned. I only refrained from turning around a tenth time by admonishing myself that there had to be a limit and that I had to get inside somehow before the night was over.

I found a letter from Joel waiting for me on the living room table. It was the first of his letters, postmarked in Texas. A week ago, when I had sent off my first batch of affectionate letters to him, I would have expected to tear open communications from him with impatience. Instead I was capable of fixing myself a leisurely cup of tea first.

His letter was full of joy and zest and gratitude for having known me. He made it sound as though he were turning somersaults in Texas on account of me. It brought back all the exuberance of our time together.

I opened my notebook. I wrote down the date. I wrote a dedication of the rest of my life and my writing: "For Joel and Audrey." It was the purest feeling of love I ever felt in my life. I was in love with both of them, and deeply proud of my love. I felt so deserving, so dizzy with life's grandeur.

§

Audrey and I met nearly every day the following week. My solitary hours of writing became endangered. I took that risk gladly.

Besides, old specters currently haunted my typewriter. Toby had reappeared with the humble request to use my typewriter for a few nights in order to type up applications for graduate school. With habitual nobility, I granted his request, provided he used the typewriter at my place, rather than, as he had envisioned, abducting it for several days. It was my moral security blanket which could, under no circumstances, leave my abode.

Kay, Audrey and I dined scrumptiously on fish at the dining room table one night while Toby spooned vanilla yogurt, standing, when I couldn't bear it any longer and asked him to sit down and share our meal with us. Soon Kay's boyfriend joined us too, and we engaged in the posturing of wit one puts on display when men are present. Suddenly I felt angry because nothing of interest was being said at all anymore. My soup was praised, my fish was praised, and Toby, indelicately, suggested that I would make a good wife, would I marry him?

"Or me?" Audrey joined the banter.

It didn't look as though Toby was going to revert to his work on the typewriter, now that his conviviality had been aroused. So I went to my room, uneasy about abandoning guests, but confident that Kay would entertain them more competently than I could ever hope to, especially while feeling moody. Leafing through an old book of myths, I began to feel more at ease. After a while Audrey came in.

"Where are you?" she said.

"On the carpet. As you can see," I said.

"Are you angry with me?" she asked.

"Not that I know of."

"Then why did you leave?"

"There was nothing interesting I could contribute to the conversation."

Suddenly she seemed old, wise, motherly, bending over me, sympathizing with my graceless sulking. "I think I understand," she said. "Sometimes witty people simply have to be tolerated. And sometimes it's better to leave."

"I can hardly tolerate my own wit anymore."

I continued sulking. She sat next to me on the carpet and looked at my book with me. It was one of my oldest personal possessions, a collection of medieval romances. I had lived many of the tales myself. I had been Tristan, Isolde, and King Mark. I had been Erek and Enide, Merlin, Morgan le Fay, and Lancelot. I turned the pages to show Audrey my favorite illustration.

"It's someone like you," I said.

The drawing showed the successful Perceval, still very young, kneeling in front of the Holy Grail, his arms flung wide in an exuberant gesture of joy. The legend underneath the drawing read: "Mine is God."

I showed Audrey another Perceval illustration also, the young fool setting out into the world on a sad-looking nag, dressed in the rags of a patchwork coat—all the scraps his mother was able to find in her desire to keep him from attaining any knightly respect in the world, so that he would come home to her unharmed. Audrey looked up from the book, then back at the illustration, then into my eyes again. The grail itself couldn't have received a more enchanted look.

"I love you, Audrey," I said quietly. "I hope I'll know what to do with it."

"With what?" she asked in a whisper.

"With my love for you," I said with all the calmness and rapture of fearlessness in spite of fear. My eyes locked with hers.

The moment fled. Kay came through the room to go to the bathroom. My bed sheet curtains were not in place. Audrey and I sat, almost touching, on the red carpet, neither of us looking up to acknowledge Kay, but both of us excruciatingly aware of her presence and probable judgment.

"Like that," I said. "I hope I'll know what to do with it."

Audrey laid her hand on my hair for a moment. "I will never go very far away from you," she said.

Images crowded in on me. I saw myself back in time at some French castle with other girls from school. My best friend Susanna already asleep, I stole away from her to sit with others who were still awake, three or four to a bed, our voices intimate and quiet in the circle of flashlights and sips of May wine. Suddenly, as we too lay down to sleep, the curious question from the tall and beautiful Mira:

"You and Susanna, are you lesbians?" "I don't think so, no," I said, bewildered, then yawned and stretched my body into sleep, my arms against hers. Next morning, the first moment I had to myself in the bustling of girls and breakfast and workshops, I raced to the dictionary, trying to find out what lesbian meant, and finding nothing except the cold and clinically unsettling "homosexual." I didn't know what that meant either. But it was mildly reassuring, since, as far as I knew, I was hardly sexual at all.

After Audrey and Toby left and Kay and her boyfriend were asleep next door, I paced the worn red carpet again under the violent colors of a Matisse print hanging by the bed. I let myself feel all of the beauty of my knowledge rise in me, though the tormenting voices of the past, their insistence on twenty-nine years of forbidding, still circled me with all their crowding pressure.

"I only LOVE her!" I defended myself. And the voices drowned right before me, lost their power over me that night. I felt as though I had a shield of warmth and peace around me.

§

"Where is she?" was Audrey typical exuberant cry for me at the door. This always startled Kay enough to keep her from recognizing her potential role as chaperone before it was too late and Audrey was already in my room, filling the air with the patchouli of her presence.

One night she sat beside my bed, straddling the chair she had turned out from my desk. I sat on the bed, cross-legged, leaning back slightly as she leaned toward me. And we, who usually had to speak so quickly that Kay once remarked we spoke to each other in a shortcut language that no normal human could keep up with, had run out of words to say to one another. We merely looked into each other's eyes and shared the silence, her gray diamond eyes holding still, her cherub hair surrounding her small face.

Gradually the sparks between us changed and suddenly I found myself locked into a quiver of trance.

As I let my eyes drift with the strong current that drew me toward her, Audrey's face began to blur. It took on softness. The colors changed. Red became pale, dark became light, outline became formlessness. Then the vision took on shape and definition once again, though it remained in flux and change.

It was as though I saw her age before me in a matter of seconds. Her skin became gray. Deep lines formed, settled in. Her hair turned gray and thin, and in her tiny smiling mouth her small and slightly pointed teeth separated, trace by trace, and became smaller still, as they would in the mouth of a skull. The vision threatened to become one of death. I saw challenge in Audrey's laughing eyes. Would I be able to bear seeing what she looked like in old age or in death?

I kept my own knowledge. You are beautiful, my silence answered hers as she kept changing further into age. I saw her wash away into the drift of time, and I grew afraid. Still, I stayed locked to her eyes, bound to this trance, but growing sad within myself, making my eyes ask her, are you sure I can bear this, my love? Are you sure you're not showing me too much? And all the while the other silence in me chanted, you are beautiful to me, and there is nothing you can do to change that.

At last her face became old and fragile beyond bearing. Her teeth looked small and separate and stained with brown, her lips fell away, as though in a grin.

My mind battled itself, not her. It challenged: "Stay, she has things to show you even here." But it said also: "Break this spell. What if she does show you death? What if you can't bear it?"

I felt dread inside me, and growing regret, moaning that my courage wasn't stronger. After sending her my voiceless greeting once again, that she was beautiful no matter what, I broke eye contact and turned my head aside.

I felt her hand on my arm.

"What's the matter?" she asked.

I couldn't yet look at her again. Or answer her.

"Andrea." She spoke softly. "You look so sad."

Finally I forced myself to look at her. Her face looked normal, if anything even younger than usual. I was glad. She held her head tilted to the left, and her eyes feigned such amazing innocence that I couldn't help but laugh.

"What just happened between us . . . ," I started, serious again. "Did this . . . did you . . . ? You did something to me on purpose to make me feel this, didn't you?"

She didn't answer right away.

"Did you?" I prodded.

"Yes, I suppose I did," she said. "I'm sorry. I shouldn't have done this, should I? I shouldn't tamper with your mind like that. I shouldn't do something like this unless you asked me to."

Audrey sounded confused now. But also sweetly satisfied.

"It's all right, Audrey," I said. "It's just, you might warn me before you do something like this."

"No, no, I shouldn't do this at all," she said.

Oh, yes, you should, I thought, knowing that I would follow wherever she was prepared to lead me, priestess of God only knew what.

§

April unfolded. Trees in the busiest streets of the city kept bursting into bloom right before my eyes. It happened to me, too. I broke into colorful intensity, then stood helpless in some rain or storm, all blossom colors dashed to the ground, lying on the asphalt, wet, torn to fragments underneath healing branches that didn't seem to run out of fresh color. Everything changed every moment. I felt

April over April, inundating me and touching me as though it were the end of winter forever.

There were letters from Audrey, and once a poem in which she promised me freedom in a careful construct of rhymed pentameter.

She removed a blue dragon painted on white porcelain from her neck and gave it to me as a charm. I wrapped the blue cord around my hand at night and slept with the cool porcelain against my cheek. It still carried her scent of patchouli mixed with musk. It made me think of her fine brown angel hair, the silken shirts beneath her velvet vests.

Joel sent me flowers, a basket of daisies and red carnations, and I loved their presence too.

§

Her only client of the day successfully dispatched, Audrey danced around the dining room table at my apartment one Saturday afternoon. She and Kay had stopped painting together on Saturday afternoons.

"I would like to make love to you, but it's probably too early," she said.

"Yes, it is probably too early." My teeth felt complicated, my eyes focused on bread crumbs on the table.

I felt heavy and clumsy with the weight of terror, while the joy underneath welled up like a fountain. Recklessly we went to her house anyway—to listen to music, and to talk, perhaps. We lingered in her kitchen over tea and jumping animals when she informed me that, as far as she was concerned, she was going to make love to me after all, and would I let her? Of course I would let her. Never mind how early it was.

She danced around me all the way to her bedroom, with its blue mystical painting hanging over the bed, a golden road narrowing upward into a vision of blue and gold geometry. I wasn't sure whether I was dancing or merely witness to a dizzying merry-go-round within me.

Audrey closed the bedroom doors to banish the animals, for whom I instantly felt sorry, knowing that they otherwise always had complete run of the house. To the melancholy meow of disappointed cats, I quickly undressed, and even more quickly hid underneath protective sheets and comforter. Audrey went through the process more slowly and with patient finesse, showing me her body, though I had cheated her for the time being of mine. She unbuckled her red bra and flung it cavalierly on the floor. She was beautiful, her body stepping out of all cover and mask, her tiny child-sized shoulders, her firm mid-moon crescent breasts, large nipples, a slender long waist, wide hips and buttocks, wide thighs.

I asked her from somewhere within my dizziness how she could be so beautiful. Audrey told me she had worked as an artist's model in one of the lives of her endless past.

"I didn't have the money for a real robe," she said. "Instead I had this long shiny yellow piece of cloth I'd wrap around me. So there I was. In front of everyone. Nervous as all hell. There wasn't anything I could do except eventually drop my piece of cloth. I didn't dare look up at first, though I could hear the whole class draw in breath. Finally I did look, of course, and they'd all stopped whatever they were doing. The teacher said, 'No doubt the perfect female figure.' And then, pretty soon they were all working again."

No doubt the perfect female figure. How I wished I could have seen her enjoy that moment. I could see her youth now, all the way through the traces of aging that her body managed to render irrelevant. I could see the art teacher's pose of studied sanity. Looking up from his own easel to see why it was suddenly so quiet in the room. Taking in the sight. Then turning back to his easel with his cool comment of artistic indifference. Either having seen it all before. Or else incapable of admitting that he hadn't.

Audrey inched toward the bed and looked at me imploringly. "This has to be done, you know," she said apologetically, then pulled away the comforter and sheets.

I lay still in a last moment of delicious terror before she flung herself across my body into our first naked embrace. Every shred of terror melted into the music of her touch.

"Hello, perfect female figure," I said.

"Oh, not anymore," she said.

"But yes, still," I said or thought, impossible to remember which.

I stayed with her that night, my arm around her narrow shoulders, her head against my own much wider shoulder. I fell asleep with flowers on my mind.

§

How easy love was at her house. But out in the world, the rains of April shook our blossoms mercilessly.

Kay came into the kitchen once, singing, as Audrey had her arm around my shoulders. I quietly withdrew, went to my room, lay down on my bed, my face to the wall. It wasn't long before Audrey followed me and sat down at my desk. I could feel her eyes on me, but didn't look up.

"It is difficult, yes?" she said.

I was confused and angry at my fear and at my shame. Yes, it was difficult. There would be so many versions of "I didn't think you were that kind" to face. And so many ways of saying, "I love her, that's all."

The whole world would assume that something was wrong because I didn't take my love to the arms of some man. This wasn't new to Audrey. She had been in this before with other women. But it was new to me.

She had her own grief. I looked up when I heard her move. I saw her stand up from the chair. I saw her look at me, her eyes clouded with pain and with pity.

"In another life I was the right gender," she said.

I wanted to protest. I wanted to tell her that everything was right, that I had enough courage, given time, to face up to everyone. I was sad to have caused her sadness, but I was, for the time being, too weak to undo it. I was angry, too, despite all my love, that she couldn't be stronger just then herself, to help me over this first hurdle. All of me wanted to cry out, help me, don't pull away into your own grief for now. Just for now, help me, be with me, Audrey.

She stood still in the middle of the room, as though undecided. Then she turned to leave, her hand reaching for the door.

"Don't go, Audrey," I said. "Don't go like this. Give me time. I will conquer this fear. Be here. To give me courage."

She stopped. I saw indecision in her eyes. Don't run, I begged her silently. Not until we have settled this between us. Only then can we settle anything about this with the rest of the world.

She stayed and the strength of my loving her returned to take my fear away, to turn it into hope and happiness that would defy the world's mixed messages. Love your neighbor as yourself. But don't you dare love another woman. Love your neighbor, and know your neighbor can only be a man, if you were born a woman. Man to love God, and woman to love God in man. Rain of April. Merciful Aphrodite, Artemis, Athena, help us now.

§

It became unbearable to live around Kay. She always talked to me about her lovers. Now she only got silence from me. I'd come home from my job and rush to my room to avoid her. Audrey's sad words in my mind: "In another life I was the right gender."

I went to the kitchen half a dozen times one night when I should have been working, to fix myself cups of coffee that I didn't need. Finally I met Kay there, stirring noodles in a pot.

"I'm fixing spaghetti. Want some?" she asked. Her voice sounded cold.

"Can I help?" I started picking up dishes around her, feeding them to the dishwasher.

"You are my friend," I said, far from boldly. "Tell me what you think."

She had her back to me, a black vest with a shiny yellow embroidered flower design. Her slender arms moved, cutting tomatoes, peeling garlic, shaking salt. Like a priestess administering, silently, some ritual. Long wisps of light-brown hair escaped from the pins on the back of her head. A slight shrug of her shoulders. She didn't speak.

"I'm so much in love with Audrey. I thought it would be easier. I'd simply not care what anybody thought. The hell with the world. But it turns out it isn't that easy. I do care a whole lot what some people think. You, for example."

I said this to the bright yellow flowers on her vest. I remembered standing in my room a few weeks ago, the chrysanthemums that Audrey had brought still fresh and beautiful, saying to Kay excitedly, "I love Audrey. I really do." Kay, with brightness in her eyes, replying: "Does Audrey know that?" Feeling that Audrey should be told. "Oh, sure she does," I had said. But we were talking about a different love then.

Now Audrey and I had taken the strings into our own hands, knitting together something unforeseen. Perhaps an element of regret was also involved. And perhaps even an element of fear. If you suddenly love a woman, Andrea, then what does that mean about your friendship with other women?

Having our respective men in our lives, and talking about them, had been easy, predictable, cathartic. Suddenly everything was changed.

The water in the pot boiled over. I lunged for the pot with the nearest kitchen towel and removed it from the gas flame.

"Audrey loves you very much, too," Kay said.

"It's strange and new to me." My eyes held tears I didn't want to cry. "I've always liked and loved women as friends. I remember, though, being unsettled, even hurt in the past, when somebody would so much as suggest anything else. A professor once, drunk, confided to a friend, 'Andrea? She's a switch-hitter. Wouldn't surprise me at all, I can tell you that.' The comment traveled back to me. I felt the urge to kill. My friendships with women were sacred to me. I could never conceive of myself as a lesbian. Admired Sappho, of course. But lesbian love was not for me. Twenty-nine years worth of brainwash cling. The fear of being labeled. Perverse. I love her, and I don't feel perverse."

Kay listened to my soliloquy without interrupting. Not so much as a "hm" at breathing pauses.

We were still standing in the kitchen, though we hadn't done any chores for a while now. Just standing and talking. While the noodles on the plate slowly got cold and the butter that had melted on them began to congeal again.

"Andrea," Kay said, gently and with admiration, "You are an artist. Of course you would love a woman. Of course you would love one of your own."

I felt as though Kay were inviting me into the circle of my friends again, being the harbinger of acceptance.

§

Unremarkable weather followed, memorable only for its ordinary human happiness.

Audrey called one Saturday, pleadingly: "Andrea, can I come home now?"

"But Audrey, I thought you were going to come here! I'll even put mushrooms in your eggs for lunch, so that you won't be too bored!"

"That's what I mean, Andrea. Can I come home?"

"Oh, of course. Come on home now, Audrey."

She stopped at the door, the diamonds in her eyes sparking love. "I had lunch with my friend Karen the other day. I told her about you, Andrea. When I told her your name, she put up her hands in mock despair, 'Of course her name would be Andrea!'"

I could understand that too, the grudging despair over our beauty, even in name. Audrey. Andrea. World, we challenge you to come up with better than that.

Karen had apparently also cautioned Audrey. "Don't make yourself too available. You don't want to be taken for granted, you don't want to kill the suspense of romance."

We laughed about that, too. Why would we need suspense?

I wore Audrey's porcelain dragon day and night, falling asleep to its cool polish under my cheek, more romance in that than in any artificial taxing of our self-discipline by not seeing each other. When I was with Audrey, I often took a strand of her hair to smell it and compare it with the scent that lingered in the porcelain. Audrey's hair was brown, very fine, brittle with the frizziness of the perm. Angel hair.

§

I made attempts to cling to self-discipline regarding the rest of my life. Evenings and weekends were the only times I had for my writing. Evenings and weekends were also the only times I had for

Audrey.

The first thing that fell by the wayside was reading books already written by others. Next came weekend writing. Audrey had a lot of work to finish on a house she had bought in Maryland, which she was now getting ready for renting out and which needed a lot of repair. I went along to write while she was taking care of her property; I ended up helping her as much as I could.

She said a lot of the repair was necessary because of deliberate sabotage and betrayal. I was puzzled. Why did the magic field of energy she had around her not protect her?

The energies around her did baffle me. Talking on the phone she would describe to me the clothes I wore that day. She said she sent me love and energy and promptly my nerves started spinning.

Beyond any undercurrent of negativity, though, the reality was simply that the house in Maryland needed a lot of repair. Audrey accomplished much of this work on Fridays when she didn't have classes or clients. Some of the work, however, did spill over into our weekends.

We compromised. I'd bring my work along. There was, after all, a chair in the damaged house, and, if the weather permitted, the large garden. It was, of course, impossible to plug in my electric typewriter in the garden, however well the latter was equipped with green and flowers and tranquility. So I went along to the house with merely notebooks and pens in my bag.

Audrey went about her business in a yellow cutoff sweatshirt. I tried to go about mine.

I found myself unable to concentrate under these transitory circumstances. So I wrote letters, some of them way overdue, or quaint disjointed observations into my notebook. Nothing of substance. It was frustrating. One time I fell asleep like a cat in the sunlit garden, then woke up to a suspicious neighborhood pincher barking at my limp body from across the fence, shushed by its human owner, not remaining shushed, reminding me once more of my many unused talents lying there asleep in broad daylight, hours stolen from myself. I sat up, bearing the officious dog no grudge, opening my notebook again, failing to fill it with substance once more, watching Audrey come up the garden steps, hands splattered with white paint, even her hair speckled, ready to take a rest, a talk with me, a cigarette or two.

After a time I asked: "Do you want me to help you with anything?"

Seeing that I wasn't terribly productive on my own account, it was only natural to chip in with her monumental task. But underneath I felt with equal force a silent apprehension that begged her, please, Audrey, say no. Say you don't want my help. Say that we had agreed that I could simply come along to be here and to write.

"Oh, if you want to help," Audrey said, laughing.

No, Audrey, no, I pleaded silently. What will become of my discipline, such as it is, if I don't stick to it? What was becoming of it already anyway, when I couldn't think of anything but her, and the sweet, sad peace I felt in being? Simply being. With her.

I borrowed one of her work shirts and plastered a hole in the wall, polished wood, or washed doors. I felt both happy and torn apart.

During the week, too, I tried to cling to discipline. Some time ago Kay and I had made a pact. Three nights of the week were taboo for anything except our work. It didn't mean we couldn't work on other nights as well, should the spirit move us and life's busy agenda allow it. Unfortunately our grand scheme of solid work never got off to a solid start. There was a lot of life out there, tempting us into all directions all the time. Nevertheless, we kept the myth of our working nights alive.

I mentioned this work night pact to Audrey once. When she asked which were the week nights that were taboo, I hedged. First of all, to my private regret, I discovered that I had been extremely flexible with them. I had not kept much to any schedule at all. Secondly—and this I told her—revealing my secret was risky. Toby, for instance, had sorely tested the boundaries of my work nights. He had managed to create such a mesh of complications that mysteriously all the nights when I was scheduled to work became the only nights on which he would call me up with irresistible longing to see me. The nights on which I was free, according to my own scheme, were nights that turned equally mysteriously into nights when he could not conceivably make the effort. Life over art—a noble concept. But what do you do when life decides to engage with art in a competition for precedence and power?

Audrey listened to this exposition of my trials as a would-be disciplined person with amused compassion. She promised to respect my discipline. So, after the long preamble, I felt confident to tell her my working nights, both of us knowing, with small sighs, that those would now be nights off limit to us.

Pathos of human discipline. On my next working night, a Wednesday, Audrey got sick. She'd been dragging with symptoms of a minor cold for a while, but now, when she called, which she usually did from school once or twice during that day, she sounded horrible. She was on her last ounce of energy, and all she could think of was the moment of salvation when she could go home to lie down.

I thought with dread of her bare refrigerator shelves.

"I'll come over and bring you something to eat and sing you a lullaby," I said.

"It's not terribly convenient, is it?" she said. "This is your working night."

"But you're sick, Audrey. That changes everything."

I paused to listen to myself. It was true, it did change everything. I only felt compassion for her illness now. As a child I had become an expert on illness, its loneliness, its dream of being taken care of in the hours that drifted away between fever and a fuzzy, aching head. No focus. Just the yearning for tenderness.

"You'll let me use your typewriter, I'm sure," I said. "So that's settled. What would you like to eat?"

"Oh, anything you bring will be fine," Audrey gave in with lurking enthusiasm.

"That's not the point," I said. "Don't you know that being ill gives you great privilege to get dormant desires fulfilled?"

"No, I didn't know that," she said. "I thought you were supposed to be as inconspicuous as possible, and you were to humbly accept whatever solace was on offer."

"I can see you don't have the fine art of being ill mastered at all, Audrey. You lie still, perhaps. But at the same time you make extravagant wishes. Then you submit to having your wishes granted. You even submit to having fairy tales read to you out loud. You suffer through all that with divided feelings, because, after all, you are tired and would just as soon sleep, but you also know your duty toward compassionate souls around you."

"You'd read me a fairy tale?" Audrey rejoiced with a hoarse voice.

"Of course," I said. "But the important thing is, you must decide what you would like to eat for supper. Since you probably don't feel like eating anything at all, it had probably better be something terribly appealing to senses other than your appetite."

"Then perhaps you could bring me some fish," she said with hesitation in her voice. I didn't believe her.

"Is that really what you want?" I asked sternly.

"No," she confessed. "I'd really like shrimp, but. . . ."

"That settles it." I cut her off.

I went to the bank during my lunch hour, since I didn't have enough cash on me for shrimp, and after work I set out to gather all the shrimp I could find. As luck would have it, I had to visit three stores before I found any at all. I also picked up grape juice, and honey, lemon, and milk, to be covered for all eventualities.

I loved her so much. I was tired from work and I walked through the streets, from store to store, with my tiredness trailing behind me like a triumph on a leash, something I didn't have to pay attention to if I so chose. I even managed to stop at the apartment to pick up a change of clothes and left a note for Kay that I wouldn't be home that night.

I banished all thought of writing that night and sat by Audrey's bed, watching the miracle of her loving eyes. Milk and honey. Hot lemon juice. I wanted to reach into her and take out all sickness. I put my hand on her hair and thanked her from beyond the core of shyness within me for having let me come to help her, for accepting my love and my concern.

"It's I who should thank you," she protested.

I shook my head. "I have so much love in me," I said. "And no one has ever wanted or accepted it."

"Oh, I'll accept." She sat up quickly.

"Will you?" I asked. "Will you always let me love you?"

"You bet." She lay back down against her pillow. "The shrimp was delicious."

I gloated. Privately, though, I meandered through a trail of memories of trying to love, trying to give myself. I had nothing to give except myself, complete with melancholy, complete with my obsession for working and writing, complete with my desire for a human companion to share the road I traveled from one end of this life to the other. I had tried on so many roles of loving. Lover, wife, mistress, mother substitute, child. In all of them I had been inadequate. I either retired them or they retired me because of lack of passion or too much abundance of myself. I fit well into loving itself, into the giving and the yearning. But I did not fit into consistencies or into roles. As for Audrey, I wanted to love her forever as I loved her now. Audrey sat up again and put her arms around me, tightly.

"You can love me as much as you want. Always."

"You sure?" I asked with manufactured pathos, designed to disguise the fact that not only did I want her to say yes, but I also wanted it to be the truth.

"Positive!"

"But already I've failed you grievously." I was fishing now.

"How so?" she asked. "I don't remember."

I remembered perfectly. Her teasing reproach when, three days earlier, preoccupied with my own thoughts and our scintillating conversation, I forgot for the first time in the month since I had started seeing her, to light her cigarette as I was lighting mine in the car. 'Oh, soon you'll be taking me for granted,' she'd teased me, of which unbearable accusation I reminded her now.

She laughed. "You'll just have to remember all the little rituals," she said, which prompted me to get up from the side of her bed and bring her another concoction of hot milk and honey. This soon soothed her to sleep. I turned off all the lights but one and remained sitting beside her, watching her face. Finally I turned off the last light also and stretched out at her side. She pressed against me and cradled her head on my shoulder.

Her illness lasted several days. She bravely taught her students and saw a few clients and came home absolutely spent. I juggled my waking hours between my job, getting to the apartment occasionally to pick up more clothes, and Audrey's house. During one of my short stints at the apartment, Kay complained that I wasn't ever there. But the next day she cooked a chicken soup which I was to take along with my respects to the ailing Audrey.

Audrey told me on the phone that I shouldn't bother to come all the way by metro with chicken soup in my pocket. She could eat the tuna in her closet, and I should stay home and write instead. I opted for delivering soup after all, and the combination bus and metro ride, steaming soup container in hand, gave my emotions a much needed lift of amusement.

I was determined not to get sick myself while loving Audrey back to health. I didn't. I only got restless. At night I found it difficult to sleep, though body and mind were exhausted. My writing was moving farther and farther away from me. I couldn't expect to produce overwhelming poetry in the fifteen minutes that remained from my lunch hour after shopping for groceries or maybe taking an aimless stroll around the business district so as to feel a blessed spell of solitude. One night, lying sleepless beside Audrey, I felt the fear that what little talent I had wasn't merely being postponed, but was falling away from me altogether, like an old coin that had fallen out of use.

I slipped out of bed and went to the living room to sit in Audrey's rocking chair, thinking, listening to her breath from the other room. I remembered the day she had taken me for a twenty mile ride to show me the first peonies in a suburban garden she had discovered by chance on an errand the day before. I thought of the art exhibit she had taken me to, only to have us find it closed. "Oh, good," she rejoiced. "Then we can always go home." She'd rolled down the window of the car as she drove and shouted happily: "Hey, world!" Now I listened to her breath as she slept, and words formed in my mind: "Your breath is my breath."

"Andrea," she called out sleepily. "Andrea, where are you?"

Guilt surged at having been caught dreaming. I went to the bedroom, knelt by her side of the bed, explained where I had been, asked if she needed anything, told her that I was right there if she did, told her that I loved her, that I wanted her to go to sleep again.

"Come back to bed," she mumbled.

"In a little while," I said.

She fell asleep again. I tiptoed back to the rocking chair and felt, if anything, even more fragmented than before. Yes, I wanted to lie down beside her and sleep. And yes, I also needed this moment by myself. And yes, I loved her. And yes, I was afraid of having that love usurp all other things in me. And yes, even that wouldn't be such a terrible fate.

But I was sad. I felt cornered. I felt my personal space shrink to an endless frantic rush, an endless desire for having more time—enough to lead the three different lives that I would have liked to be leading simultaneously. Writer, lover, and earning a living. I kept listening to her breath, her being, her sleep, and loved her through all the ache inside me.

I was afraid she might wake up again and miss me again. Also, I wanted to sleep as she did. Finally, with a lurch of resignation and anger against myself, I tiptoed to the hallway between kitchen and studio where she kept her unframed paintings and her liquor stash. "No" seemed to come at me from more nerves than I was aware of owning. But resignation won. I poured a large glass of vodka, rinsed out the glass in the predictable drowsiness that came on quickly, brushed my teeth carefully, and sank down on the bed. Audrey turned and put her arm on top of me. I felt condemned and forgiven, both, by her gentle touch.

In the morning, waking to Audrey beside me, I felt restored by her love. The sun streamed through the white window lace. I felt enormous energy. It was the day before Easter. The orange cat stepped over my head like an old indignant gentleman. Not only did I occupy his space in bed, making him seek out smaller and less comfortable places, but, what was more, breakfast wasn't served yet.

I got up and tiptoed downstairs to the basement, preceded by the senile tomcat, and followed by the three more mannered ladies, the two dogs and the other cat. Pied Piper fashion I hummed to them all the way downstairs, laid out their food in their respective dishes, then raced upstairs and treacherously closed the basement door on them.

"Alone at last," I rejoiced, folding myself again into Audrey's arms. Not having performed Pied Piper tricks in the basement, she never quite woke up and mumbled that she loved me.

We woke next to the melodic ring of her golden alarm clock with the only alarm noise she could tolerate. She said she had searched for it for nearly all of her fifty-two years. I reached across her to turn it off and she caught me in her arms so that we woke up properly, letting our eyes rest on the morning of each other's faces.

§

Audrey had two clients scheduled that morning. On her way to the office which she sublet from her psychologist friend for weekend and occasional evening hours, she dropped me off near my apartment. I walked the rest of the way through the chilly morning, bought a croissant at a café I passed, then eggs and onions at the grocery store around the corner.

Kay was out of town to visit her parents so I had the apartment to myself, complete with choice of music—the Supremes singing Impossible Dream, with me as backup voice. I decided to try my hand at Easter eggs. I took pressed flowers and leaves and wrapped them around the eggs with yarn, then dropped them into the boiling onion skin water already turning red. I soon discovered that the patterns were not going to take well—the flower petals were too delicate, the yarn not tight enough. By the sixth egg I had figured out how to perfect my method, cut out the letters of Audrey's name from duct tape, and dipped that egg into the color broth with far more vibrant result.

I daydreamed myself into a state of consciousness that had lurked in my head all during April, a seed idea now blossoming into sudden images. Cutting tape and handling the round smoothness of my eggs, I saw it more clearly than before: a vision of men and women bowing to each other, waving to each other with serenity, then separating, withdrawing from their enmeshment with one another, from the struggle and the toil, the sometimes enchanted and sometimes violent love for one another. I knew they were going home, back to spheres that were more intimately and more naturally their own. One by one they stood up and withdrew from the uneasy meeting grounds of fireplaces, linden trees, and cocktail bars.

I saw a wide expanse of grassy plains. A last couple stepped out of their embrace to separate and follow the brothers and sisters who were beckoning. It looked like a choreography of peace that sent them into a dance of rest from one another, a choreography of pride, of gentle gratefulness, and much relief. A world came to completion as I saw the women lead each other away hand in hand, and the men, with their arms around each other's shoulders, moving in the other direction. They were going to a place where each could find, among their brothers and sisters, a fresher consciousness, a remembrance of the essence of their being, unmixed with the shame and confusion that had grown around them during centuries of strife and struggle for power, and the resulting imbalance that had made the world grow old and worn with viciousness and mutilated joy because they didn't know their own essence anymore. It was the end of a very old and tired world, its phase of dying from confusion. It was not, however, the end of all possibility of world.

I don't know where the vision came from. I thought of Joel briefly—how I would say goodbye to him precisely in this fashion, gently and with relief, as though he were a mythical creature for me, an angel, the most beautiful man I had ever met. As I had met him, so I would separate from him, a coda to the life of confusion I had led so far. I longed for Audrey. I longed for everything else to be over and done with. But I would not get to see Joel again to consummate this final farewell until more than a month from now.

When Audrey came from work I proudly demonstrated to her my coloring project. She dutifully praised even the misbegotten flower and leaf designs. She was, however, overjoyed with the egg that bore her name.

§

At Audrey's house that afternoon, she showed me for the first time the room whose door had been closed every other time I had been there.

"When I bought the house, I planned to see clients here. But zoning wouldn't permit. Though every once in a while I did it anyway." She shrugged and laughed.

It was a small room with bookshelves and a desk. I thought it would be a perfect work space for me. A print of a unicorn hung over a sofa by the window and a large drawing of a guitarist with a cruel mouth hung over the desk. I did not like him. A romance novel, with a swarthy, longhaired hero looming over a blond white-skinned lady on the cover, lay open on the sofa.

"You're reading that?" I asked.

"Yes," she said. "It's very good for sleepless nights. The best part is, there's always lots of trouble, but in the end truth and goodness always win."

She must have seen the glimmer of scheming in my eyes, but we did not yet speak of my using the room. I was too shy to ask, and she too proud to offer without being asked.

§

In the kitchen that day I listened to stories of her childhood, things that swam out from way back in her memory. There had been poverty and hardship, much neglect, and some craziness. Audrey showed me photographs of an amazing array of identities. A little girl with pudgy cheeks and somewhat dull eyes with her family in front of a wagon. A young woman with brightly painted lips and sleek wavy hair. A woman with long dark hair reaching down to her knees, severe and proud, almost matronly. Pictures of houses she had lived in, places she had visited. Fragments of a life-time spent. Fascinating, and alien to me, images from a wooden box, unsorted and coming at me helter-skelter in prints whose edges were cut straight or jagged, according to the fashion of the photography industry of their time.

I felt lost in the presence of so many fragments of life that took Audrey to endless memories I couldn't share. Her eyes glittered with memory and I was left out. The only photograph that didn't make me feel outright lonely was the one she kept on the desk with its many shelves and organizing slots in her studio. Her graduation as Doctor of Philosophy, her eyes bright, her face in profile, looking up from the small frame of her shoulders bearing the heavy gown. Her hair was straight then, otherwise she was completely familiar to me in every feature of the photograph—the energy, the enthusiasm, the look I knew so well, her eyes half searching, half knowing.

"How did you come to live here in the East?" I asked.

"Other than to wait for you here?"

"Yes."

"I guess I just came," she said. "One of my brothers lived out East at the time. I moved to Baltimore at first. I lived in the harbor area. Do you know Baltimore at all?"

I knew very little. Once I had stayed with a man near Johns Hopkins in student housing by an alley way that had "No parking" and "No standing" signs and was infested with rats. In the first floor apartment the windows were barred with heavy iron rods, but that did not prevent the occasional scary lewd comment from a passing drunk.

Audrey had lived in the harbor area.

"Most of the houses were occupied by retired sea captains. Old men who spent most of their time sitting on their front porches, smoked pipes in silence and watched the world go past. These were my protectors. I felt safe walking the streets because of their presence and they never let me down. If a stranger came up to me on the street and so much as started to talk to me, three or four of them would leave their chairs or benches and start down the steps of their porches toward us. This was enough to make anyone unwanted leave me alone.

"I was very beautiful then. I had long light hair which I wore like a train floating down my back. But I was mute. I never even talked to a single one of my protective captains. Our bond was one of silence. Sometimes, when I was by myself, I would practice talking. I started writing then, too, as part of my attempt to get my speech back. I was convinced I had lost it. I called myself Melanie then."

Audrey had mentioned her Melanie phase before. I was puzzled about the light hair. In her photo as a stern young adult her hair was dark. I didn't get around to asking. Melanie had come from the West, having lost against the world and wanting a new one. She had erased her past together with her name. She wanted a future without memory. Melanie Anderson. She wanted to be as Scandinavian as she thought she looked with her floating light hair. She wanted a self-made identity that she could live in. Anderson.

"I probably picked that name to have it sound close to yours," she said.

I knew she had been "Melanie" for a few months, possibly even years, in her early twenties. But so far she'd only mentioned Melanie in passing. I wanted to know what in her world could have wounded her so much that she became mute and then boldly gave birth to herself again in a totally different identity. I fantasized about such things at times—to appear in some unknown city or town, pretending amnesia, starting all over as a mystery woman. The closest I had ever come was a three week stint cleaning floors in a Norwegian dormitory for medical students, dreaming of taking singing lessons and making music my art.

"Well, for one thing I was near crazy," Audrey said. "The aching sort of crazy, you know, when you do what you do without understanding. I just wanted to move into a new world. The change of name seemed drastic." Suddenly she laughed. "To think that there are still people walking the face of the earth today who knew a mysterious mute young woman called Melanie Anderson!"

This wasn't enough answer for me. "But then why did you become so crazy?"

"Come on, Andrea!" She laughed again, this time at me. "To live in this world and not go crazy?"

Later in the kitchen, fixing supper, debating whether we should have any of my masterpiece Easter eggs already and deciding to be patient until Easter morning after all, she painted for me at least one of her sufferings. It came up in a round-about way. She couldn't remember the name of either title or author of a book she wanted to recommend to me. I merrily tried to help out by asking about themes, descriptions, which only resulted in Audrey growing more and more irritated.

"I can't ever remember anything!" She twisted her hands. "Ever since I had those shock treatments, there are times when my mind blanks out completely. It's scary. I used to have a perfect mind, just like everybody else. Now I have to work so hard at remembering anything at all."

I no longer minced garlic. "You had shock treatments?" Moisture crawled down my back.

Audrey shrugged her shoulders. "Yeah."

"What on earth for?" I asked as cautiously as I could, trying to disguise my feeling of shame at my unease. "I mean, what can have been so bad that you needed shock treatments?" The more I tried to pull myself out of my embarrassment, the further I slid into it. It was my turn now to be confused and then ashamed of my own confusion and mistrust.

"It wasn't bad at all before I had the shock treatments," Audrey said, looking at me through eyes contracted into slits. "And there certainly wasn't any valid need for them."

We stood silent for a moment. I was reminded of a friend who had told me a horror story of callous and dismissive hospital personnel who had administered more shock treatment than his doctor had ordered.

"Audrey, please tell me what happened," I asked, hoping and fearing, both, that it was a mistake in her case, too.

"Oh, I was in this state institution. That was the place where you got put when there wasn't anybody else willing to take care of you. My mother was running around with a new husband somewhere. The family was split up, and this was the place I had to go to. I wasn't of age yet, you see. Kids who're not of age have to be put somewhere. So there was this one nurse at the institution, the head nurse, who had the hots for me. She wanted me, and I didn't submit."

Listening to her lilting voice, I felt hypnotized.

"She was used to having her way," Audrey continued. "She made that clear to me. But I still didn't submit. So she sent me in for shock. To make me submit. Periodically she'd come by to ask me, 'Are you ready now?' And I still wouldn't submit, and so she sent me back in for shock. I remember the times before the shock treatment. I'd try to memorize my name. I'd say it to myself over and over and over, so I wouldn't forget. After the shock, of course, I didn't even want to remember. Eventually that's all that my life seemed to consist of, her asking, 'Are you ready?' and the shocks." Audrey shrugged her shoulders and went back to tending vegetables in the frying pan. "Is the garlic ready?"

Hastily I bent over the cutting board to mince my garlic some more.

"That'll do." Audrey took the cutting board away from me and added the garlic to the vegetables. I leaned back against the refrigerator.

How can you love woman, I wanted to ask, if a women has done that to you? Instead I asked, "How did you get out?"

"Of the institution?"

I nodded, wishing I still had garlic to mince. It was hard to figure out what to do with my hands.

"I don't remember exactly. I'd written to my mother to come and get me out, but she didn't. I think eventually my sister came and signed me out. But I wouldn't have had to stay much longer anyway. I was almost eighteen, and at eighteen you can sign yourself out. Before that I needed someone else, someone over eighteen, to sign for me, and so I had my sister come and sign me out."

"Did you ever . . . ?" I began asking with all the violence of compassion and concern I had in me, then stopped short of completing the sentence. Audrey came to the refrigerator where I still stood motionless. Her wooden spoon in one hand, she placed her other hand on my shoulder and looked deep into my eyes.

"I don't mind talking about it now, Andrea. You don't have to be so concerned." She smiled. "It's all very, very long ago. If you were going to ask if I ever submitted to her, the answer is no. I didn't."

"Jesus, Audrey. She could have destroyed your mind completely." What a saint Audrey seemed to me, talking so calmly, no matter how long ago everything had happened.

"Yes. She could have. She tried. But she didn't. I got away. You know, to this day I don't even know what she saw in me that she had to have me at all cost. She could have had a lot of other girls more easily." Audrey made a rumbling sound way back in her throat.

"But it's so obvious," I said. "It was a massive game of power. The one who resisted naturally became the most important one. To break a proud spirit must be the ultimate victory and power. Oh, Audrey, please make me shut up. Please let me hold you for a while."

"For sure."

She put down her wooden spoon. The vegetables burned and we proudly ate them burned later on.

§

We spent that night with our arms wrapped around each other, waking from time to time to make sure that we were still there, then falling into sheltered sleep again.

On Easter morning, first the animals woke me. The orange cat now had a strategy. Stepping on my head at dawn was the surest way to trigger breakfast. The second time I woke, it was from the awareness of morning and sunlight through white curtains. It was Easter. Audrey was no longer by my side. Instead I woke to the smell of turpentine.

I tiptoed to the door between bedroom and studio, which she always kept open. She stood at her easel, applying paint, stepping back, picking up paint with her brush, the tension in her body like a spring of energy. It was like a delicate, powerful dance. In the mirror behind her I could make out that she was working on the city rising from the water across which her golden dragon flew. I remained motionless until she noticed me. When she did see me, her body changed currents. A flow of tension rippled through it. A flow of softness replaced it. She laughed.

"Here I wanted to serve you coffee in bed, and then I forgot to notice when you woke up."

"Unforgivable," I teased her, then told her I didn't want to disturb her painting and was sorry that I had already distracted her.

"Oh that?" she said, snapping her body into a second's imitation of her previous tension of concentration, then loosening it again with a shake of her head that sent her brown curls flying. "It'll come again," she reassured me.

"Come on," she said and led me to the kitchen.

"Where are our Easter eggs?" I asked.

She produced the basket from the top of the refrigerator. I reached in and pulled out the egg with her name on it.

"You eat that," I said.

She took it and turned it around in her hands." I don't know if I want to eat this one at all," she said. "I may want to keep it forever. You made it for me!"

"There is no forever," I reminded her.

"Oh?"

The truth was, I wanted to keep the egg forever as much as she did. It was nothing but self-effacing bravado that made me encourage her to eat the egg and made me watch her break the shell.

"Now what do we do?" she asked when I had eaten one of the less successfully decorated eggs.

"You should paint again," I said.

"And you?"

"I'll sit down somewhere and write."

She considered me with her diamond eyes.

"If you'll let me, I'll go to your unused room and write there," I said.

"Would you like that?" she asked.

"Yes."

She came along to install me. I trailed my bag with notebooks with me, looked around the room, bowed to the unicorn which would hang indifferently behind me as I wrote.

"You really don't mind if I work here?" I asked her excitedly.

"No, why should I?"

I didn't tell her what was on my mind, but I hoped to work here often. To have her close by, doing her own work. To be close to her and yet not be an intrusion. To work separately and yet together. To be with her.

She brought me a fresh cup of coffee and left me for her golden dragon. I began feeling the power of being, just possibly, at home, and I began to write.

The hours flew. There were a few times when we both stopped working, came to each other, hugged each other silently, with smiles in our eyes, and with love, but without words. I did the outline of a vision that I planned to work on diligently every day, filling it out from its different angles. It was a vision of a woman's sorrow and despair, and her determination to drag herself through it by the stories that she told herself. Sheherazade and the king in one.

Nagging hollows in my stomach finally transported me back to a more mundane level of existence. My hands trembled, my stomach gurgled things I was embarrassed to hear. Did my body have no respect for art? One egg and many cups of coffee simply didn't last into the early afternoon. I peered in the studio door. Audrey didn't notice me. I tiptoed to the kitchen, opened the refrigerator and found not even bread. Nothing even vaguely appetizing in comparison with the vision of something warm, greasy, and satisfying that my brain dictated. I looked at a prism hanging in the window. No, not even the beauty of broken sunlight had the power to satisfy me now. Why was it my bad luck to suffer from a human body with its trivial demands? I knew, from unhappy experience, that if I didn't eat something soon, I'd get crabby. All right, then, I would have to face Audrey with the shocking fact of my mortal needs. I turned around and saw her standing in the kitchen door.

"Whatever are you doing?" She laughed.

"I was getting advice from the fragmented sun in one of your prisms," I said. "It says, if you're hungry, you must eat. But your refrigerator is uncooperative, and so I have to come up with an alternate plan of action soon."

"Can I help?" she asked.

"Oh, please."

"There's Mario's up the road. He's got so much food, he has to sell it!"

"Salvation," I cried. "Let me see your hands."

Audrey stretched them out openly, looked at them in puzzlement.

"They're not trembling," I remarked, stretching out my own for comparison. "Don't you ever have to eat?"

"Oh, sometimes," she said. "In fact, I'm starving. Being older, I simply don't starve as publicly as you do."

"You call this starving?" I stroked my hands over my hips.

Audrey shrugged, put on a wise smile and said. "Let's go and get something to eat regardless."

Throwing our usual vegetarian preference to the wind, we indulged in enormous steak and cheese subs, with everything except onions, but including double servings of hot peppers that made smoke come from our mouths.

§

In spite of our age difference, I couldn't see myself as anything but an equal. A man twenty years my senior would in all likelihood lord it over me. Not Audrey, though I didn't pretend to myself that she was younger than she was or that I was older than I was. It wasn't necessary.

I hoped that the equality between us would never become unbalanced, for I was also awed by her almost overpowering strength and the seductive temptation in me to lean against another, stronger, human being. Please stay my cinnamon and dragon woman, I prayed silently, or do anything else, but don't fall into the temptation of becoming my mother, Audrey. I am your lover. Don't allow me to become your daughter.

No, not you, she seemed to respond to me, putting her arms around me gently, smelling of patchouli and leaning her head against my shoulder.

Dusk set in and I didn't want to turn on the lights yet. I wanted to sit still and think for a while. Audrey. So much goddess, and so much of earth. When it got dark, I fell asleep on her sofa and didn't wake up until it was time to go and meet for our Easter gathering.

§

With a few potential celebrants dropping out, there were only five of us who finally set out for Dumbarton Oaks to celebrate Easter with a box of crackers, a candle, a bottle of wine, and our spirits rising. Audrey, Kay, Kay's friends Maurice and Brendan, and myself.

We entered Glover Park at the gardens, next to a house that Kay and I had once picked out as one we would gladly accept if it were donated to us. We walked past the botanical buildings where I had once acted the part of a goddess in a friend's movie. We walked in silence until we lost the city lights behind us and the mists rose before us and we reached the murmur of a brook and night song whispers of the woods. Dogwood trees gleamed in bloom and a mild wind carried sparkling scent to us. We found an open hillside in the blue-white silence that hushed us, too, to whispering. There we lay our belongings down in the grass, then separated to go our different ways to do our private ceremonies. Soon I was alone with the misty hillside. Steps lost themselves away from me into the distance in the shape of a star. The moon looked full and hung huge between blown clouds, sometimes covered, then milky again in white glory. Milk over gold.

I didn't go far. I walked toward the shimmer of a dogwood tree straight ahead, one of its branches bowing low as though reaching out to me. I was wild with joy. My fingers, clammy with the April air, touched the silky petals, stroking, caressing.

"Speak to me, tree," I whispered. A smile spread through me, telling me I wouldn't hear what the tree had to say to me if I didn't with all my heart believe that I could in fact hear. And then I heard within myself my echo of what I could not yet hear in the tree's own language: "I want to be like you." And the answering echo: "And all I have to do is be like you."

I raised my arms and stretched to imitate the branches of the tree. I looked at the moon. I wasn't precisely ashamed of being human, only a little skeptical and apologetic that being was, for me, still such an effort, such a pose mixed with dance and wanting to please and longing for the confirmation from some unspecified source that I was doing it exactly right.

I stood like that, unfolded in a dancer's pose, for a long time, swinging back and forth between my smiles and my sadness, then letting the sadness slip away. A light rain began to fall. The petals of the dogwood responded with a whisper, catching, then releasing the water as it fell to them. When all of my sadness was washed down by the droplets of rain that touched me, I felt ready to return to our human meeting place.

Just as I let go of the tree, I heard Maurice's voice coming up the hill toward me in the first notes of a song. I stepped back into the shelter of the tree to let him pass me. He stepped out of the mist, walking steadily, his head bent back a little, singing his lei-ei-ei to a dark melody. Then I heard another voice respond, Brendan's, from the direction of our meeting place. I stayed hidden for a few more moments, then left my tree and walked toward their voices.

A candle Brendan had lit flickered at eye level. Three shapes moved near the flame, and just as I stepped into their range of vision, I saw Audrey from the corner of my eye as she came up the hill toward the lit candle. Audrey and I reached those waiting and singing at the same instant. We greeted one another and them with shy smiles.

Brendan had moved our belongings underneath the shelter of a tree. Kay stood beside him, her lovely face shining, crowned with clear joy. Maurice knelt and poured wine into the wooden bowl we had brought. With a smile he accepted a dogwood flower Audrey picked up from the ground and offered to him. He dropped the flower in the wine, to swim, light and white, over the dark liquid, sanctifying. We sat down in a circle, Audrey beside me, and offered each other the bowl.

"Don't swallow the flower," Audrey whispered to shoo away the probably too sanctimonious look on my face.

I swallowed the wine as well as the laughter without spilling either. "I didn't."

We took our last draughts, emptying the bowl, and blew out the candle. Its heat had cracked the glass of the copper-framed Mason jar in which we had kept it burning. Somebody apologized. The jar had been mine. I laughed at the loss.

Audrey and I walked side by side. Kay came between us suddenly, taking both of us by the arm.

"I wonder how often we've done this before," she said. Recently she had begun to study past lives.

"A few thousand times, no doubt," Audrey replied with the characteristic wise smile on her face.

"I have never been here before," I said with envious conviction.

"Maybe you simply don't remember," Audrey said.

"Perhaps," I said, but still didn't believe that I had ever set foot on this earth before. True, perhaps I believed the way I did because it was easier, for now, to learn than to recognize. My heart and soul felt young, a child's heart, a child's soul, eager to discover rather than remember.

Audrey looked mystical and mischievous. Many dark curls bounced and touched her shoulder, placing her somewhere between angel and elf. She carried the wooden bowl, with most of our things inside it, on her left shoulder, her arm a graceful circle around it. Mist thickened between us the further she pranced away from me. At times it looked as though she were stepping straight into the edge of the world.

My heart knew with a tender beat that I wanted to follow her wherever she went, even if she were to step over that edge. I trusted her. Wherever she chose to go, I would find ground for my feet as well. Wherever she chose to go, I would follow, with or without fear.

§

One does not, apparently, step out of the world like that on a misty Easter night under a still nearly full moon. We passed around the jug of wine, its remnants more ample than what we had modestly consumed under the protection of the dogwood tree. Soon we got silly. Brendan saw in Audrey some resemblance to a Russian princess, now conveniently named "Audreyvitch." All five of us huddled in Maurice's car to take Brendan home, because he had missed his last bus.

I was tired from the wine and the night and even the love I felt in me and could barely contain. Audrey sat next to me in the rear of the car. She performed silly gestures with a finger puppet she had discovered on the seat between us.

Before falling asleep in the apartment later that night, I called out to Audrey who had already returned to her house on the other side of the river, alone. I called to her spirit, giddy with memories and sleepiness, first "Audreyvich," then "Audrey witch." Most beautiful woman.

I called her to me.

§

After Easter came a month of confusion, difficult to bear in some of its splendor and destructiveness.

"We should welcome confusion," I explained to Audrey once. "Originally, the word means 'melting together.' Will we please confuse one another?"

On the human level of our lives, commingling with one thing is a separation from something else. So much of my life began to mingle with Audrey that I sometimes stood bewildered and tried to save something from my former self that she hadn't touched yet, to hide it in privacy, clinging to it, not able to give it up yet.

Mixed with my love for her was suddenly fear. She was so powerful. We called each other equals. Our respective friends called us equals. I wanted to be consumed, commingled with Audrey. And yet I was afraid to be consumed.

The more I gave her my time, the more parts of me were busy carrying themselves off into the distance. This was not new to me. Whenever people had come close to me, I had a whole parade of existential ants inside me, carrying off bits and pieces into safety. What was new to me, however, was that I didn't really want anything carried off into safety this time. Only the habit was still there, the habit of scurrying and whisking things away.

In this intricately woven background of ways out, I was suddenly face to face with Audrey. Now I wanted a way in. The old network carpet of ways out still lay intact on the ground of my being. Human voices in me clamored, warning: This is too new. You shouldn't commit yourself so quickly. Divine voices whispered more calmly: This is. Accept it.

§

She gave me a ring.

"Part earth and part sea," she said when she slipped it on my finger.

A frame of gold clasped a red coral as though with golden hands. I was not yet very good at accepting gifts and stuttered bashful gratitude.

"I hope you don't mind that I give you gifts," she said with a wistful apology. "It's natural for me to want to adorn my beloved. And I want you to know, I've worn this ring for a few days, so it would have my energy in it."

My own apologies: "I want to love you so much, Audrey. No one has ever let me love the way I need to, the way I am able to. I want to love you that way."

"I accept," she said.

§

Each time she came to the apartment, Audrey still burst in with her original exuberance. "Where is she?"

Soon I learned to recognize her step, light and precise, past my window, and I would run to the alley to celebrate her coming. We would stop for a moment, then stretch our arms toward each other.

Where is she? Where is she now?

§

I often worked in Audrey's study now. I came up with a new concept of writing prose that would compensate for the limited time

I had to practice my craft every day. I called it mosaic writing to make the concept sufficiently appealing to myself. Tiny pieces of color, one of which could be written each day, like tiny pieces of different glass, to be joined in one figure, with the bold coherence of a rough outline of connective bronze, or, say, the suggestion of a plot. And the theme, like a light behind a stained glass window, created coherence. I immediately set to work on an apprentice piece in this manner, which I meant to have finished by the time I was to take my vacation at the end of May. One small mosaic piece each day.

SUMMER

The end of May approached. My journey. To see Joel to say goodbye. Many times I caught my breath and held it, intending to take the leap, intending to tell Audrey, and maybe even have her dissuade me of the need to go.

By now Joel had arrived back home at his river. He responded to my original letters written with the exuberant affection of first separation. He wrote with great joy, with zest, with gratitude and growing wonder at the thought that I would actually come out to see him.

He wasn't the only one wondering. I didn't want to go anymore. Why should I? To fulfill what undestined thing? We had already parted. I had journeyed worlds of consciousness since then, and I was ready to remain parted.

Yet, the plans were made and the plans were good. I had been stuck in the city for months. Two brief excursions to New York the previous fall, and no vacation at all since August when I had started my job. My plane tickets were already paid for. The trip promised an exciting chance of a lifetime to safely navigate the wilderness with an experienced guide. I loved rivers, just as I loved the anticipation of adventure.

I tried to tell Audrey about all this. The more I tried, the more difficult it got. I slowed myself down with images and dreams. Pity held me back, pity at her innocence and at such false reassurances as she gave me. One day at a party, she pointed out a young male artist she had picked out for me as a lover in case I couldn't find it in me to love her, being a woman. He was gorgeous, arrogant, and totally unappealing to me. But Audrey said she would have tried to make a match between us, if necessary, just to ensure that I would stay in her periphery in case it didn't work out between her and me. I loved the promised freedom in this gesture.

I made many aborted attempts at saying things to Audrey, to all of which she merely responded, while my courage faded, with the sorrow at my going away for ten whole days in a row. Early on I had written to Joel about my growing love for Audrey. He responded with gentle greetings to her and regrets that he had not met her.

What I told neither one of them, couldn't possibly tell one or the other, or, for that matter anyone at all, was that the only way I could let myself go in Audrey's love-making was to imagine Joel hovering over me and then entering me as she caressed me. It frightened me and made me feel wrong, and yet the physical release it gave me pleased Audrey.

I told her once, on a ride from the hospital where I had been visiting a friend, "Joel wrote from Oregon. He sends you greetings."

"Oh?" she said.

She did not seem to want to hear more. At the time it wounded me. I did not want her to be indifferent, and deep within myself I felt unshed tears. I stared out of the side window of the car at spring greenery, at sunshine, trying to keep my tears to myself, managing, but thinking, Audrey, this too is part of my life, and you shrug it off with a small 'oh.' And so I will be silent, but such silence is dangerous. It will bring loneliness to both of us.

One night we went to see a movie together, a new rendition of Arthurian tales. When my personal hero, Perceval, came on screen, tall thin, his young face looking faintly crazed, Audrey handed me the bowl of popcorn we had smuggled into the theater.

"He reminds me of . . . ," I started.

"Me!" she said, probably remembering the pictures in my ancient book I had shown to her one night in April.

"He also reminds me of my friend Joel in Oregon," I whispered back, feeling almost evil at bringing up the forbidden subject again.

"That's an illusion," Audrey insisted. "It's me."

That night, lying in her arms, I dreamt I had wrapped my arms around her and leaned my head against her shoulder. She stroked my hair to comfort me. "You really don't like men very much?" I asked her in my dream. "No, not much," she replied. "But you must realize that I still do," I told her. "If you do," she said, turning her head away, "I don't want to hear about it."

I woke from this dream feeling a fresh layer of loneliness, deeper than anything I had known before. It was as though my world was splitting into two halves for me, one of which I could share with the woman I loved, and the other one I had to live out by myself, dangerously walking the edge of my sanity.

Audrey kept asking what was wrong, but I couldn't tell her. I already felt condemned to silence and fear and unease, even when magical things happened in her presence.

We did have many angel moments between us, and they eased much restlessness in me. Sometimes they were just seconds of simplicity between us. Small breaths of wind for our flames, like the first time she growled at me as we cherished each other's bodies. The surprised way I learned to growl back, the roughness in my throat suddenly finding its own melody. Playing at predator and prey, and liking it.

It was difficult for me to come back from that world to find myself sitting at the typewriter at the office with its regimen of due dates, numbers and small tragedies of errors taking place around me without mercy. My boss buzzing me to his desk with twice-rung impatience. Messengers with urgent faces searching for files that weren't where they ought to be. The clatter of typewriters. Red entries in calendars demanding respect and immediate attention. In this unnerving onslaught of tasks designed according to some Kafkaesque scheme, the smiles from our separate world layered the frantic clutter with a sheen of unreality.

We invented methods for communication. She had the privilege of being able to call me between clients and classes in privacy, whereas at my desk there was no privacy. So when Audrey would greet me with her sparkling "I love you," I would survey the paper shuffle around me, the people performing its choreography, and then I usually decided to beg her, "Say it for me too, please."

So she would whisper, "You love me?"

"Yes. Exactly," I would reply. "Except, please say it louder, as though I really mean it."

"You love me!" she would shout.

§

It was comforting to sleep in one another's arms on nights I spent with her without fear of the future. Once, just before falling asleep I remembered a vision she had told me the day before.

"I could suddenly see you when you were already older," she said, touching my face.

"What did I look like?" I asked.

"Oh, much the same," she said. "Your hair was shorter and you didn't have bangs. You were very sad."

Well, weren't you with me? I wanted to ask, unable to imagine myself as sad as the pity on her face suggested, not as long as she was by my side. I didn't ask out loud, afraid of an answer I didn't want to hear.

Now in the middle of the night, not sleeping alone as in a beautiful Sappho poem, I drew my arms more tightly around her to change whatever future sadness her vision foreshadowed by not believing in it.

§

She picked me up to go to the zoo where she planned to study large wings so she could paint her dragon Auriel. I heard her steps at the window and rushed to the door to greet her. She stood in the door, flooded with sunlight. Later, at the bird exhibit, she pulled out her sketch book, stepped on the lawn that kept others off through habit, though there were no prohibitive signs, sat down and began sketching. I watched for a while. She paid no more attention to me.

We agreed to meet at the exhibit of the river otters when she was ready to stop drawing. I walked away from her slowly, turned back a few times to look at her. She was absorbed in her task, lovely, small, and vibrant with attention to the birds flying up in front of her inside the wire mesh of the enormous cage.

Just as I passed the eagle cage, one of the eagles swooped with widespread wings from its perch at the roof of the cage. I wanted to run back and call her, but of course it would have been too late. The moment of magic was already over.

It was the first time in days that I had leisure moments entirely to myself, to think, to try to answer my own questions, and to deal with secrets that were tied up in me and almost strangled me. Joel had told me once that river otters were his soul's animals, to whom he was attached by some inexplicable affinity. His words at my ears: "Whenever we come across otters at the river where I work, I stop and put everything aside and simply stand still to watch them for a while. Everyone is used to this, so they let me be when it happens."

Joel. To whom I, too, was bound by some measure of mysterious affinity. He also had things to show me about freedom. Alternatives. The freedom of joy that did not want to own or even claim another's being for itself. Joel who had held me and absorbed me completely and had gone away before there was a chance for him to no longer feel honored and enchanted by my presence.

In April, when he had stood on the sidewalk waving goodbye, I had painted in my mind a future of seeing him again from time to time to let us refresh in one another that part of us which makes human existence not mere searching, but also endless joy. Then I had thought, perhaps we could just meet once a year or so, to tide over the knowledge of joy, year after year, until we would become quite old, having touched each other's lives again and again in an affirmation of being.

Now, sitting on the stone block wall looking down on the river otters below me as they swam their endless joyous circles, I knew that instead I would only see him again on one more single mission of farewell. It would be a farewell not only to Joel and the magic we had experienced between us, but on the grander scheme of my limitless fantasy, it would also be a quiet and calm farewell to years and years of having sought, in vain, a permanence of love with a man. The image I had dreamt in my waking dream the day before Easter had kept recurring. It rose again now. Men and women drawing apart from one another into opposite directions. This image became mixed now with my sentimental yearning to say goodbye to Joel, not, as I could well do, in the careless fashion of simply gliding out of one another's awareness at a safe distance, but in a conscious goodbye of choice.

"He has given me so much joy," I whispered more to myself than to the busy river otters. "He has not caused me any suffering. That's why I will be able to leave him, and the others beyond him, without bitterness or regret while I follow Audrey to her side of the world."

I saw myself as one of the gentle ones, one of the lucky ones, one who would not be condemned to turn toward the woman who was meant to be my destiny from the ruins of shame and disgust, or from the desert of anger and hatred, or from the jungle of despair, but on the clear road of choice, recognizing the call of my own kind, and following it without ill will and with a song on my lips. Joel had given me joy when I had already begun to walk the road I was now walking. He had stood at the crossroad smiling. I wanted to see him one more time, to thank him for letting me pass, to thank him for being there to witness my passing, to tell him where I was walking, now that I recognized the road, and to tell him how beautiful it was walking there.

It was good to sit in the cool sun of early May dreaming all this.

Why could I not simply enjoy the dream and leave the living of it unlived, when its meaning was already clear before me? Or—listening to the other side—why should I? I had the confidence that I could live it without harming anyone. I didn't want my farewell from the realm of man-love to be a daydream or a memory of some blind act of the past taking place unmarked. I wanted it to be a conscious act, a sexual act, something that I could witness with open eyes. I wanted the act of separation to be clear, noble, and heroic, so that I could return to Audrey, washed from my past and ready to give myself to her in a clean commitment. Unless I said goodbye to him in my fashion, I was afraid Joel would remain unfinished business for me.

My mind justified its own laws like a talented gymnast. I did not feel frivolous in following my thoughts to my own logic's conclusions. I felt, in fact, especially pure and innocent just then. I felt that, though my heart had already chosen, my mind and my body were spinning me an intricate plot to give me a perfect vehicle for my choice. In the boldness of that image I felt no fear, nor the least inkling of shame or betrayal of either Audrey or Joel. I felt strong and proud of myself, and gentle and affectionate toward both of them, Audrey, the woman whom I chose for life, and Joel, the man whom I would unchoose.

When I chose Audrey for my life's companion, I did not want any possibility of longing for the unknown or the unfinished, to exist in me. I wanted to finish what was unfinished without loose ends dangling from the hem of my life. The things one trips on. I wanted to convert the old shapes of attachment into new shapes of friendship. I wanted to undo the acquired desire for a man as my lover, the only choice I had been taught from the day I was born, by going through the act of love with a man consciously, but with little remaining desire, then none. I wanted to triumph over my past. I wanted to extricate myself from the mesh of things I had been taught: whom I should love by law or convention, and whom not, and how I should conduct myself accordingly. I wanted to unravel the thread and then weave my own new tapestry with it.

I wanted to be free.

I felt a great power of innocence in me, a power strong enough to bend the world. I saw myself as a young woman walking back to the crossroad in order to choose the road Audrey had already taken, not following it merely on impulse, absentmindedly pursuing the patterns of pebbles on it, or grass along its margins, just because of being dazzled by their haphazard beauty. This time I wanted to elect the road by looking as far as I could see, considering its hills and its trees, its narrowing and widening, where I would have to duck my head or shield it with my arm, and where I would be able to walk upright. So that I would not have to return to the crossroad ever again to sit down and wonder whether I had made the right choice. I believed in my innocence and I felt wonderful.

There were other mind-dreams I followed partway. I regretted the child I never had, the daughter I had often dreamt of. Curiously, I had fantasized about having one single daughter since the time I was a teenager. Lilith-fashion. No father in sight. Depending on what phase of life the fantasy engaged me, the father had left me, or more frequently, the father was simply unknown, untraceable. Never yet, in my fantasies, had the "I" of my fantasies taken the responsibility of leaving the father myself.

I remember early banter in my teens with first admirers: "I never want to get married. But I want a child." "Oh, I can help you out with that." Or fantasies later of bearing a certain man's child, but then cancelling the fantasy itself because of the knowledge that he would eventually claim the child as his. Now fantasies of having my child began spinning around Joel also. I had no commitment to him. I would be free to take my child, my hoped for daughter. Audrey and I could raise her.

It was a lovely image in my mind, but short-lived. I knew one didn't live life quite as mythically as all that. In my fantasies, Audrey would be happy and gentle with me and my child. But in external reality, the timing was not right. If I were to get pregnant now, it might be possible for her to care for us. But I couldn't be sure. In the reality in which Audrey and I lived, I didn't know whether her love would be strong enough.

Audrey. Andrea. Joel. A daughter. If I had a child, it would involve more than my own body and more than my own mind and desires. And so I understood that I would retain my sanity, stay on the pill, and remain human and childless.

"But Audrey," I whispered to myself and to the river otters below, "if I were a goddess, I would have my child, and we would raise her in the spirit of freedom."

Daydreams and a wild kaleidoscope of feelings. I felt as though I had the world at my feet. But when I looked again, it was only the river otters swimming their rounds in merry silence, flipping backward and forward, and the image of Audrey as I had left her behind, sitting in the grass, drawing birds' wings. Or sitting at the table in her house, telling me: "I love your mind, Andrea. It can take everything and slowly turn it around and around, looking at it from all angles." I conjured up the image of Audrey turning her own small hands, as though around an invisible ball.

Yes, it can, Audrey, I answered to that flash of memory with a sigh inside myself. Not only does it describe a circle, but it loops over into infinity. It reaches through a larger world than this, now touching the earth, now touching things that are not of the earth. And sometimes it sees almost too much.

Post somnium femina triste est.

I lowered my eyes to cut off the dream, opened my bag, and took out my pen and a letter I had promised to translate into French for one of Audrey's friends. I was still working on this, turning my head slightly to look for verbal inspiration in the distance, when I saw Audrey stand beside me, a few feet away, looking down at me with her diamond eyes, her mouth slightly open.

I jumped down from the stone wall. How beautiful she was. As always, my first awareness of her presence went through me like a frothing waterfall of joy.

"So here you are with the river otters," she said.

"Yes, look at them." I put my pen away and motioned for her to lean over the wall with me. "They swim and swim and swim, and they never seem to grow tired."

Sometimes they followed each other around the little pond. Sometimes they swam separately, but never for long. One of the pair would choose to follow the other, slim brown bodies gliding through the water, then emerging, walking a long tree stump soundlessly. The only sound either of them made was the splash when it entered the water again, with carefree movements of slow play, yet with all the intensity of seriousness.

Audrey and I stood close to one another now, elbows touching in a deliberately open secret with which we could outwit the disapproving public into not noticing that we stood there, two women loving each other. Against their rules. Without their knowledge.

"I want to steal you," she said.

"Steal me?" I giggled with surprise.

"Yes, steal you. You and your joy. Surely you haven't created all this joy all by yourself."

Joel, I thought.

"I want to steal you from your parents, your siblings, your friends," she continued.

"And animals," I added. "Especially river otters. Not sure I can be stolen, though. I'd much prefer to give myself freely."

She smiled at that.

After a while we came up with possible methods of trying to distinguish which of the two otters was which. A young girl came and let herself into the exhibit to feed them, throwing small fish to their long, sleek, arching bodies, wet hair sticking in tiny triangles to their sides. When the feeding was over, most of the other onlookers left again, children with their enthusiastic questions, and adults with their occasionally wrong but always authoritative answers that made Audrey and me exchange private grins, and later, out of earshot, mischievous imitations. People crowded around us in clusters, then created gaps of solitude. I leaned deeper into the sandstone rock and put my hand on Audrey's arm.

"Look," I said.

I wanted to show her. This is how you can look at my life without seeing. This is how you can know without knowing. These are his animals, and this is what I will have to finish before I can be with you completely. So that there will be no way of turning back.

§

The nights we spent together were enchanting, though sometimes difficult. Over and over she would call me "my woman." Sometimes I heard a quiet crying in my heart and wondered if she could hear it too. I didn't subscribe to a view of the world where people could belong to one another. For her, I decided, I would make an exception. But I couldn't be hers yet. In silence I promised I would be hers as soon as I could. I would come to her not as a refugee, but as one who was whole again and totally her own. Then I would give myself to her.

There was no betrayal in my heart. Betrayal wasn't even part of my personal vocabulary. Audrey had to practically teach me the concept. She considered so many things in her past betrayals. For my part, there was only the wish to give myself, once I became whole again after reclaiming myself.

The discomfort that I did begin to feel more closely, again and again, was tiredness and fragmentation. Audrey began to feed me vitamins on those mornings when I woke up in her house, five different ones, selected according to a scheme which I didn't bother to investigate. The important thing was the beautiful care of being fed something in aid of my flagging energy. My mind was nourished simultaneously with the lovely mix of images of medicine and love. My favorite was a shiny pink ball of royal jelly.

"The stuff that queen bees get fed on," Audrey told me with an enigmatic smile.

Audrey herself, by some other scheme, took twelve vitamins to my five each morning. "Of course I need more vitamins than you," she said. "After all, I am older."

I liked to sit on the sofa by her small coffee table with its delicate-looking bronze top. Sometimes she came to sit with me, but usually she went to sit in her rocking chair next to the fireplace. On occasion I sat down on the carpet at her feet, placing my cup right next to hers on the floor to create a ritual image of togetherness.

"The trouble is," I regretted once, "I only get feasted on vitamins and yogurt when I am here. Won't my body rebel, getting feasted one day, and the next day the meager deal of merely one multiple and one Vitamin C? Provided that I remember to take them at all?"

"Well, then you must simply come and live here permanently," Audrey said as though it were a matter of utter simplicity and no great importance, while she lightly stroked her poodle's long curls.

§

Audrey and I agreed that it wasn't a burden at all being partly divine. It was the strictly human parts that made for hardships.

Imagine a goddess, joining her lover at night, then rising from her bed at dawn, putting on eternally unruffled robes of splendor, taking up her silver bow and gracefully stepping into the day.

Then picture instead the hasty selection of garments from the closet when a mortal decides to spend the night with her beloved. Can't wear the same thing to the office two days in a row. Do I have everything now? What all did I need to do tomorrow? Toothbrush.

"But you can always use mine."

Is it Tuesday? Then I must take my checkbook along. And a pen. And would you really lend me a clean blouse? 'Cause I haven't had a chance to do my laundry in ages. At least, thank heavens, we're the same size. And isn't it a good thing that I always wear clogs? They go with everything. I'll have to have one of the heels fixed soon, though. Comb. No, I better take my brush.

"But I've got a brush at home."

"Yes, but they say people shouldn't share brushes."

"Oh, come on. All lovers share brushes."

Then the defiant stance of stepping out into the street, dressed in jeans, a wide elegant skirt slung over the shoulder. Yes, anyone who cares to notice: This isn't a trip to the dry-cleaners. I'm going to spend the night with my beloved!

"Oh damn, I meant to take a book along to read on the Metro."

"Forget it, darling, I'll lend you one of mine."

"But I'm not in the middle of one of your books just now!"

Then imagine the goddess again, striding, that's true, but never entitled to see the lover's helpless yawn in the kitchen, the rubbing of pink fists over morning eyes, the blinking, being persuaded, after having discovered that the stockings one took along in haste had a run in them, to wear a pair of the beloved's purple ones. The nervous protest.

"Oh, come on, how would I look like in the office in purple stockings?"

"Ravishing, dear."

"But positively everyone would notice!"

"So?"

"What do you mean, 'so'?"

Mentally already embracing the moment of showing up in the office with purple stockings after spending months solidifying an image of understatement. Preparing for imaginary comments of those who dared to comment with imaginary pride: Yes, don't they look nice?

And the way of leaving the house, Audrey in the door, waving her hand, still dressed in her summer-sky-blue terrycloth robe.

§

Goddesses do have the advantage of not growing tired. Women, in spite of vitamins, do. Nerves fray, small tasks remain forever unaccomplished. This was the flip side of sitting with Audrey at her table, talking, looking, feeling the peace of connection, growing gently superior, even to ourselves.

"You know, they say people have to engage in creative arguments, creative conflict, whatever they call it."

We didn't. We had never yet raised our voices, never yet spoken to each other in anger. We were growing proud because we began to believe that we were capable of living without that ingredient of human experience. Only the tiredness I had in me kept undermining me. True, I did not raise my voice. Instead I created a silence of frustration when I could not be alone long enough to refresh myself. So many impressions, so much longing. Sometimes I drew a magic shield of hostility around me, believing that it could not be seen or felt, avoiding the mirror of Audrey's eyes, which held at first concern, later mockery, then pity, gentleness, and helplessness. And when I did look into that mirror, I failed to acknowledge what I saw.

One day she came to see me at the apartment and I was so tired, I couldn't think straight. I was torn. I wanted to be with her. I also wanted to work. I was too much on edge for enjoying either. Rest and solitude seemed such a waste. I was cantankerous.

Her bright: "What shall we do?"

My moody, shoulder-shrugging: "Well, I don't know."

Quick shame. My wanting to make her a gift as amends. She was looking for curved stairwells to use as model for those that were leading up into space in the painting of her golden dragon. I knew some beautiful stairwells in the former Georgetown University library and suggested I would show them to her. Her grateful, energetic "yes" unfortunately served only to remind me that I did not have such bottomless energy as she did. My moodiness, my envy on our way there, took much of the gift away again. I heard my own voice make unfriendly remarks, or else my own shrill silence.

Audrey was strong. She enjoyed the stairwells anyway. And then I started to enjoy them as well, through her eyes, as I enjoyed her loveliness, stepping up and down between the tiers of the great hall, looking down on the wide open space in the center where a few art students were at work on their own creations. I even enjoyed looking with her, and through her, out of one of the high windows.

But I did not enjoy myself. Loving her so dearly in the few moments of bright energy, I mostly felt my own frayed essence. Why could I not be as lovely as she was, and so filled to the brim with life, and spilling over?

"You need sleep," she said sanely when she delivered me back to my apartment.

I both pitied and hated myself for the ungraciousness in me, the "now-she-will-not-love-me-anymore," the clinging for a wonderful goodbye that didn't materialize. She only pities me now, I told myself. Maybe she is angry, too, and I too tired to apologize?

After she left, I drowned my tiredness in mocking wine until I slept. I woke a few hours later, my throat metallic, my pillow reeking of wine. Heavy with despair at myself, I got up to fill my glass again, not wanting to be awake at all. I encountered the ugly scuttle of an enormous cockroach in the closet. I sat on my bed, trembling, the closet doors pulled shut again. The brim full ashtray on the nightstand had ashes spread around it, gray on the scratched black wooden top. I touched candle stains on the carpet from old feasts. Not caring anymore, except for wanting to escape my ugliness, I opened the closet again, pulled the wine jug from the cardboard box in the corner, filled my glass with the blub-blub-blub-blub of red wine, felt a devilish grin spread inside me, downed one full glass, then filled another, feeling better already. Drowsy. A third glass would finish me off. Checked the alarm clock five times. Had to get to work in the morning. Three more hours of sleep. The third glass tasted like poison and instant cure all in one. I'd done this before. Being ugly. A burp. Another grin of self-disgust. Then sleep again.

Morning. Hurried motions. Scrubbing my body, the smell of

wine still in my nose. I opened the windows, praised the stale smell of cigarette butts that would camouflage the rest. Grabbed the necessities, stepped out into the gray morning, onto the bus, into the office. Smiled. Quiet and intense, controlled nerve ends trying to untangle from the clutch of toxins.

A little shy, perhaps, keeps to herself a lot, quite lovely. The traces of debauchery can be washed away. How stupid you all are, but I can't blame you, for I'm so very clever, so discreet. And so ugly to myself. But even that will fade. As long as you all keep believing the appearances.

It was a miracle to find respect and balance for myself again as quickly as I did. Or else an amazing habit, a bright facade.

Love me, if you can, though I am ugly. Just love me, and you will, somewhere along the lines, love my ugliness as well. I am not arrogant enough to burden you with that. The shamefaced, shame-bodied brightness of distortion. Lo, how innocent I am. I am shining and golden. You have said so yourself. You must not know that I fall asleep to the perfume of cheap wine. No wonder I cling to the feeling of being loved while never quite trusting it. Who in their right mind would love me, were it not for my clever charades? And all along I wanted so desperately to show that I was worthy of being loved. For the world was my mirror, and if it could love me, even in disguise, then maybe, just maybe, I was worthy.

It did take considerable acrobatics of the mind, the body, and the emotions to reestablish a sense of well-being. For two days I didn't see Audrey, though I mastered brief telephone conversations with aplomb and charm. Regretted that I couldn't see her. Had things to do. The laundry, for instance.

I was still tired, though getting better. I swelled into the shaky bud of confidence of feeling worthy of her love again. Though she didn't know my images of shame, at least they did not attach to me like visible, audible, reeking scabs of ugliness.

§

Two nights after I had saturated myself with self-loathing, Audrey came to have dinner at the apartment. She and Kay scintillated over the frying onions, while I was still largely "a little shy, keeping to herself a lot." We ate in harmony, they with their sparkling conversation, I with my quiet smile, sipping the wine with a delicacy that would never give away my recent nocturnal extravagance. I felt lonely, a little bored, a little set apart from their innocent world in which I only participated via fraud. We were stacking plates in the kitchen when the telephone rang. Since it usually rang for Kay, she picked it up.

"Oh, hi. Hold on," I heard her say, then, covering the mouthpiece, to me: "It's Joel."

"Which Joe?" I asked grandly, knowing two in town who were respectfully interested in me, myself not thinking much of either.

"No, Joel. From Oregon," Kay said and handed me the receiver.

"Joel!"

I gasped. I reached for the telephone as though in a dream where too many impressions overlap.

"Hi," he said joyfully at his end of the line.

"You were supposed to call collect," I said, still keeping up a pretense of grand manners. "I thought we had agreed on that." I wanted to say nothing personal whatsoever in front of Audrey.

He explained it was cheaper calling this way. Later, I could always pay him back half of whatever telephone calls we would make. I agreed, though I knew he would never collect his half. I heard Kay mumble something to Audrey. From the corner of my eye I saw them leave the dining room where the phone stood next to the kitchen doorway. Audrey's eyes briefly met mine. Her mouth was slightly open, her eyes veiled over.

"Well, how are you?" I asked slowly, myself almost as incredulous as the look in Audrey's eyes. I went as far into the kitchen as the phone cord allowed.

Joel was exuberant. He made me laugh. He thanked me for my inspiring letters. He was so glad that I would be out in Oregon to see him in just a few weeks.

I thanked him for his letters and the flowers.

He told me he could barely hear me, that I needed to speak louder. I responded in an unaltered voice. He repeated that I had to speak up.

"I can't speak louder," I said. "I'm already screaming as much as I can. Can you hear me now?" I wasn't screaming at all, of course. I was trying to hide this call. Not only from Audrey's ears in the other room, but also, perversely, from myself. Sweat trickled down my neck. I felt like a thief. We didn't say much at all. I told him that Audrey was visiting. We had just had dinner.

Well, he had merely wanted to hear my voice and was glad that he did—even if he could only just barely hear it. And if I had a guest as precious as Audrey, he didn't want to keep me on the phone. We said goodbye and I slowly replaced the receiver.

I still felt as though in a drugged dream's slow motion when I walked into Kay's room where Audrey and Kay sat on the floor. Kay looked up with an odd smile. I was vaguely aware that I had started to mistrust her.

Audrey did not raise her head.

"Joel sends greetings to both of you," I said. "He's such a joy."

I sat down with them. But their conversation, whatever it had been, had broken off when I entered the room and for a while all three of us said nothing. Gradually, awkwardly, we stumbled upon some subject. After a while Audrey excused herself to go to the bathroom.

"Thanks for taking Audrey to your room, Kay," I said when we were alone. "It would have been even more difficult to talk otherwise."

"I didn't do it for you," Kay said, hostility radiating from her. "I did it for Audrey. She's incredibly sad, you know."

"Yes, I suppose I'll have to talk to her about this," I replied, still confident that things merely ought to be brought out into the open fully and then Audrey would understand me and love me all the better for it. Besides, with her psychic abilities, wouldn't she know everything about me already anyway? But I felt harassed by the hostility in Kay's voice. I felt shame and guilt at leading what must look like a double-life, suddenly exposed. Kay herself, of course, had two lovers, but they were meticulously informed of one another's existence.

Overriding previous plans, I went home with Audrey that night, to be with her, to prevent her from surrendering to a sadness she didn't deserve, to convince her that I loved her and that there was nothing to fear. But of course the fact that I thought and saw that it was necessary to go and to reassure meant that I was very much aware of dangerous currents between us. We were distant, not ready to speak. For now it was easier to be together in cautious silence. We avoided all allusion to Joel's call or to my trip later in the month, no matter that it was probably on both our minds. Certainly it was on mine.

We didn't speak of it until the following weekend in Audrey's kitchen. Suddenly and simultaneously we couldn't bear the tension any longer. During the delicate days of silence, our minds had separated and gone their different ways, interpreting, trying to put together, and, most probably, misinterpreting what we observed in silence.

"You never told me you were going there to meet him," she accused." You said you were going to visit a friend."

I was dumb-founded. For I had told her. I had conveyed to her greetings from Joel. I had, with my own mind's private meandering, assumed that she'd known all along.

"I didn't make the connection," she now told me. "I didn't know it was the Joel you once described to me as your 'perfect young man.'"

"Then you'll also remember that I called him 'perfect' because he was leaving."

"And now you're about to head straight after him?"

I was wounded by the implication of man-craze in her voice. "I'm not heading after him. I'm going on a vacation out there. I haven't had a vacation in months."

"And you're going to spend it with the man you're in love with," she said bitterly.

"I'm going to see a friend," I defended myself. "I'm not in love with him." It was true, I thought. I had been in love with him, but I wasn't now. I loved Audrey. Couldn't she see that?

"But you were lovers when he was here."

"Yes. Or, more crassly, we slept together."

"And you're going out there, and you'll be lovers again."

My mind tap-danced through definitions. I didn't want to admit to things that she would misinterpret. Yes, I was going to sleep with Joel. And no, I did not think I was going to be his lover.

"I love you, Audrey," I said helplessly. Love was a feeling, a heart commitment, not an act of the body.

"Yet you're going out there to see him."

"I'm going out there to say goodbye to him," I said.

"Write him a letter."

"It is something I have to do in person. I saw it in a vision." That ought to clinch it for her, I thought. But no such luck. "And on a more mundane level, I'm going out there on a goddamn vacation that I planned for weeks before I even got to know you."

"Why not go somewhere else?"

"Because I have paid-for tickets in my desk. Special fare. I can't cancel them and get my money back."

"Throw them away?" she suggested lightly.

Throw them away? Did she, could she, have any idea of what money meant to me? Was she asking me, for the love of her that was so new, to cancel all that I had ever done and planned independently? Already? It seemed too early. I was disturbed. She couldn't want to own me like that. Not so soon. Not without me freely consenting to being owned. Which consent, if it were possible to give at all, I was not ready to give now, not until properly conducting my self-imposed ritual of saying farewell to my past, which had not been one of woman love. She could not demand this. I could not afford to give in to threats of jealousy. It would mean that I let myself be subsumed in her will—which was strong—without unfolding mine. I could not.

Suddenly she frightened me. I felt as though I had misunderstood something, misinterpreted something I had taken for love. Was I only worthy of her love if I acted in accordance with her wishes?

Yet, suddenly my own ideas of freedom of thought, action and ritual, seemed nauseating to me as well. I began to see that they made no sense to her, that she wouldn't be able to see them for what they were, but would see them only through the distorting lens of jealousy. She would not see me as preparing myself to make a commitment to her, but as betraying her. And once the specter of betrayal was raised between us, it would soon become a two-faced demon. It would escalate a power battle between us. I did not want to be involved in a battle. Especially not with her. I wanted to set myself free to love her.

Suddenly, against my will, I was drawn into a warrior stance. I was afraid of jealousy. I was afraid of being owned, or not so much of being owned even, but of feeling owned. It would send me spinning to find avenues of escape, when all I was hoping for was a way in, not a way out. Her jealousy would have the power to make everything seem other than it was. It would not listen to explanations. It would not comprehend that the only way of holding me would be the sure paradox of letting me go. I was suddenly afraid that I would have to learn to fight for myself.

Nothing and no one had ever before mattered enough for me to be willing to fight like that. I'd always been so ready to leave, quickly or slowly, quietly or with a lot of clamor. I didn't want to leave Audrey. Ever. I understood that I wanted to stay with her for the rest of my life. Which meant that I would have to stand up to her, for both of us.

I wasn't standing. In my mind I stumbled while my body squatted on the kitchen floor, my head pressed against the refrigerator door. We'd both argued ourselves into heat. Our minds had long sloughed off clarity. I cried. I couldn't comprehend this. I was battered by the impressions that washed over me. Audrey's words, her questions, her assertions of her own self—all made sense to me, word by word, and image by image. I could see her position. But it wasn't mine.

We were no longer attuned to each other. Otherwise we might have understood what our issues were. From my perspective, there was a lot of snarling in her, and a lot of whimpering in me. We were both defending ourselves in this battle, each of us believing the other to be launching wild attacks. Had I been more attuned to her, I might have seen the horror in her face. But I was trapped in my own circle of fear and cringing. Audrey, too, was not attuned to anything except her own suffering. I believed she too couldn't see the horror in me, the fear of being sacrificed, nailed on the cross of her judgment and jealousy and my love.

We resolved nothing. We simply tired into an uneasy truce. We began to concede things to one another, infiltrating each other's territory again with some measure of love and giving.

"I've never felt jealous before in all my life," Audrey said with wonder, almost pride. "I've never cared enough."

I, too, had unprecedented feelings to concede.

"I've never done anything except comply with others' wishes. I've always assumed that eventually I would have to, and would want to, move on. I never had the will to stay. So there was never any reason to fight for anything which later, moving on, I would have anyway."

Now, however, she cared, and I wanted to stay.

§

I carried images of her with me, memories of voice and touch. I wandered around the office, carrying messages, coffee cups, or files, and suddenly, talking to someone, I would find my free arm moving in a graceful Audrey gesture. I'd quickly raise my eyes to the ceiling and hold them there, another of her gestures, while my nerves would tingle with delight at carrying this mute "Hi, Audrey!" to my brain. When people told me that they felt good in my presence, I answered them by giving my head the quick backward motion that, I was sure, made them see Audrey's dark curls fly for a moment, instead of my own straight blond hair.

I told Audrey how I now met her everywhere, even within myself, and she confessed that she too would sometimes sit with a student or client and suddenly discover herself doing or saying something I would have said or done. We couldn't get over this: that we were able to meet each other in ourselves.

§

Her house in Maryland was nearly renovated now. Audrey had

given up the idea of moving there herself.

"Too far away from everything."

It hadn't been when she had bought it, of course, but it was very far now, given the fact that I didn't drive and that the idea of living together was growing in both of us. Often it seemed as though that was what we were doing already, if it weren't for my ritual of stopping by the apartment periodically to pick up a change of clothes, or to spend a token night "at home," intending to work, but more often ending up having long discussions with Kay.

Instead of fighting, Kay and I dramatized our estrangement and resentment. There was the time, for example, when Kay saved a pot of moldy noodles I had inadvertently left out of the refrigerator through two days of absence. When I returned, she confronted me with the carefully preserved nauseating smell of oversweet pink and green mold, and the task of getting rid of it, which I managed to do while, without Kay's knowledge, crying bitterly about the visual and olfactory messages that came through clearer than anything Kay might have said with words.

I knew Kay loved Audrey in her fashion, and I knew Kay loved me in her fashion, but there was a natural selfishness of new lovers about Audrey and me that tended to make us want to exclude all else and all others. Only Audrey's actual presence in our apartment made me feel safe from Kay's outbursts of hostility, for Audrey never failed to inspire Kay and tame her with continued wonder, and with the wish to be included somehow.

So, when Audrey mentioned that her house was nearly finished and only odds and ends remained to be accomplished, Kay enthusiastically suggested a final chore party with lots of willing friends chipping in and making the cleanup into a festival.

"I can make it the last weekend in May," Kay suggested.

"Yeah," Audrey said coldly. "That would be the weekend Andrea won't be here." For this was how Audrey now measured time.

"That'll be perfect." Kay was still advocating her idea. "We'll surround you with activity. You won't even notice."

Audrey pursed her lips in a disdainful smile. Of course she would notice. She already noticed it now. It was on her mind all the time.

"That you should choose to be with another," she hissed at me when Kay wasn't paying attention. The rift between us widened.

§

Audrey woke me with a kiss. "I dreamt last night," she said. "I sat on a hillside combing my hair with your yellow comb. Far below me was a river. On the shore you and Joel were playing. You were both happy, laughing, and busy being alive. But I was up on the hill, combing my hair with your yellow comb."

Her dream haunted me. I felt diminished by it. Audrey seemed like a wise woman watching the frolicking insouciance of children from the distance, combing herself in patient beauty with my comb. The dream felt like a slap in my childish face.

§

Then I proceeded to hurt myself. I was staying at Audrey's house so much that it had become almost my home. It was natural now to go to the study and work for a while when she had other things to do.

I remembered the first time I had used it and how she had stood in the open door, telling me how delighted she was to see me sitting at her desk, in her house. She had spread her arms: "Everything in this house is yours, Andrea. Everything I have is yours to use." A moment later she warned, with sternly raised eyebrows, but a smile playing around her lips: "Except, of course, my journal!"

She had a ritual. Every morning she sat in her rocking chair by the fireplace to meditate. Sometimes she wrote in her journal. I'd seen it often, lying on top of the magazines and books in the rattan basket by the window behind the chair. It was a gray simple journal, the kind I had used years ago when I first began journaling myself. I used that kind long enough to follow its price increase from eighty-five cents to a dollar and thirty-five cents. Nowadays I used larger notebooks.

In the past I hadn't been above intruding on other people's privacy by stealing, on occasion, a glance at personal writings. With Audrey's journal I'd never even felt the temptation. It was sacred to me, especially after she had impressed its sacredness upon me with her words. Often I passed it with a gentle silent greeting: "You who contain Audrey's innermost thoughts and are sacred." I wanted to share everything she was willing to share with me. Never in my life, however, would I spy on anything she meant to keep from me. It was respect and it was love. It was trust and the knowledge that I would never forgive myself for violating her privacy in any way.

Forbidding me her journal as the only exception eventually became the perfect Bluebeard setup. You may open all doors, except the one. Now that I was hurting from her dream, I fell prey to the lure of the forbidden thing. I didn't even feel it coming.

It happened on a Saturday morning when she had gotten up early to meet two clients. It was the one day in the week when we had the chance to reverse roles. Instead of getting dressed along with Audrey and have her drop me at my apartment where I would wait for her with lunch when she was done with her clients, I accepted her offer to let me stay and get up leisurely and settle down to work until she came home. I watched her slink away to take a shower, rubbing her eyes, then reemerge, dancing with wet hair, while I was again languishing in bed after having fixed coffee for us and hidden nuts in the red day-pack she always took with her, since she normally gave me a parcel of nuts when she sent me off to work from her house. She wouldn't find the nuts until she opened her bag in the office, and then she would smile. I watched her get dressed, flirting with me while putting on her red bra, in response to which I coyly pulled the sheets half-way over my eyes.

"I love it when you lie in bed while I have to get dressed and go out into the cold and cruel world!" She sat down next to me to sip her coffee. "Mostly I love the idea that I can later come back!"

This day I, for a change, stood at the door in an orange robe she had assigned to me from her wardrobe the first night I had stayed with her. This time I waved to her from the door as she walked out briskly, not looking back. Then, at the car, she turned around with her radiant smile, waved to me with a graceful turn of her hand before getting into the car. Suddenly she opened her car door again, jumped out, stood still for a moment, holding the door of her car.

"I love it when you wave goodbye to me from home," she said.

She jumped back into the car, and I watched her drive away until the car turned the corner.

"I love you when I wave goodbye to you from home," I whispered after her.

I went back to the bedroom and stretched out on the bed, cherishing the feeling of being so in love. Cherishing the images I had of her. Audrey of morning. Audrey of rubbing sleep from her eyes. Audrey of carrying dance in her body. Audrey of walking away.

Soon I felt her absence. The house felt lonely without her. I sighed, finished my coffee, and slowly got dressed.

I tiptoed to the study with my shoulder bag that had my notebooks in them, smiling when I realized that I was tiptoeing in an empty house. I plugged in the typewriter, got myself a fresh cup of coffee and continued with the story I was working on, a story of despair and loneliness that almost made me feel guilty in the writing.

But being sheltered and in love now didn't mean I had entirely forgotten what the other side of living felt like. The words wanted out.

Pretty soon I got stuck on a phrase, and there was no more coffee in my cup, and the ashtray had to be emptied, too. So I took my usual writer's trip to the kitchen to wait for water to boil, hoping that back at the typewriter the phrases would meanwhile resolve themselves and wait for me to return to gather them onto a fresh piece of paper. I brought the empty ashtray back, just to see what the phrases were doing. Nothing apparently. In the kitchen the water was still not boiling. So I sat down in Audrey's rocking chair, invoking her spirit to be with me while waiting for at least the completion of coffee.

One day, I thought, I'd learn the patience to meditate as she did. In so many ways my mind was fragmented. Did one close one's eyes? I closed mine, bending my head to my left shoulder. But of course one didn't meditate while waiting for coffee. For what if one should get lost in one's meditation, and the next thing one knew, one had managed to ruin Audrey's only coffee pot? When I opened my eyes again, they fell on Audrey's journal.

I loved her, and those were her thoughts. I found myself curious and fled to the kitchen to be at least physically out of the way of temptation. I poured my coffee, walked back to the study via the bedroom rather than the living room to avoid the vicinity of temptation, and closed the door.

Only I could no longer concentrate at all. I longed for reassurances that Audrey loved me, seeing that I loved her so much. Her journal would tell me. But she had told me herself. On the other hand, she had also told me a dream in which I acted like a little child. And every time the subject of my vacation came up, she grew more miserable and couldn't understand that I would go there to make an end of my past so that I could come back to her without leaving unkept promises and unfinished business trailing behind me.

I wanted to know that she loved me exactly how I was, either known or unknown to her. And part of me was afraid that she, in fact, did not.

On my way to the next cup of coffee, I didn't even look in the direction of the rocking chair or journal, but passed them as though wearing blinders. On the way back, I put a shot of brandy in my coffee to fortify myself against both the growing misery in me and the temptation.

It was too late. Next thing I knew I was kneeling by the magazine rack, studying the exact position of the journal. Then I had my hands on the journal, almost crying, listening to all the noises on the street.

"I don't have to do this," I told myself. "She loves me more than I will ever know. Why search for confirmation?" My other voices were not slow to answer. "Don't you want to know her completely? Shouldn't you? To love her you must know everything. Aren't you perfectly sure of your own love, which could bear anything?"

Of course I was afraid of her journal, given our current condition of not speaking, or alternatively haggling in evasive ways, about my upcoming vacation. Less than two weeks away now. I should have been content with my fear, which was bad enough. But I wasn't content. The last written page was yesterday's entry. Today she had left too quickly to go through her morning ritual. Also, my presence probably kept her from it. The words I read from yesterday crept at me with a cold wave of hatred. Black on white. Or was it blue on white? Two paragraphs of despising me while trying to keep her judgment contained.

Why should Andrea be different from any others? She's young, and she's lovely, or so she thinks. Reared in our wonderful inventions of free love, free sexuality. Why should she be different? And why, or how, could I expect her to be different?

I don't want her to have another lover. But there it is. She wants to have one. What am I to do or say against it? If she needs to be just like all the rest, and if she wants her other lover, then all I can do is let her. And bear it. In whatever way I can. I've seen it all, I've heard it all. I can't stand it. But there it is. She's young, and she wants another lover. And there is nothing I can do except let her go. Why should she want another lover? Why shouldn't she? Why shouldn't she have any number of them? It's the fashion of our times. All I can feel is frustration and shame. So let her have her lover. Who, after all, am I?

Darkness rushed across my brain. But now, having committed my sin of spying, and being paid for it with precise justice, I couldn't even afford to faint. I had to banish the black from my vision, for I had to get up and close the journal and put it back into its proper position. As though I had never touched it.

So this was what I looked like to Audrey. An uncouth horny kid who wanted 'another lover.'

The phrase reeled like a curse in my head. I felt sick to my stomach.

Of course it was what I looked like to Audrey. Since I was in fact going to meet 'another lover.' But where, in her blunt analysis of truth, were my dreams of freedom, of gentle farewell to all men, my good dreams, my holy dreams of doing precisely what I needed to do in order to be with Audrey without having the fear of old desires dragging lamely behind me? Or leaving old possibilities open in order to revert to them in maudlin future fantasies when Audrey's arms, for whatever reason, should not be enough for a time? Where was all that beautiful dreaming of crossroads and passing through them by choice, so that the choice should be final, and mine?

I wanted to live my own myth. And it looked ugly now because I had dared to look at it in a mirror of thoughts other than my own. Hold the myth up to the mirror, and it isn't the mirror that gets tarnished, but the myth instead. In my myth I saw myself as one walking a road of freedom, gathering the gift of myself, and coming home with it in order to give myself fully. In the mirror, I saw a reflection of filth, lust, running after a man, after sex, and my face was one of selfishness.

All over the place I saw the accusation "child." This was what I looked like to Audrey. I felt slimy under the splinters of shame that she couldn't see me in another light.

I closed her journal and put it back with care, then leaned against the open doorway dividing living room and dining room, crying. And when I couldn't bear the opposition of the two worlds anymore, my world of myth, and Audrey's world of cheesy judgment, I went back to the brandy bottle and poured more into my cup. This time I left out the coffee. The drink felt like a bitter promise of forgetfulness warming up my veins. I went back to the journal and opened Audrey's ugly mirror again. There, I could bear it better now. This. How I looked to her. Now I was only sad. So what else? I thought. I turned back a page, another. I came upon my name again. I read.

"Tonight in the car the words she said. And my sadness in knowing that she may want children, and that I don't want to be the cause of her denying herself that experience. And yet I love her, and I want her to be with me. And yet, I cannot give her children."

Here, then, was Audrey with a mirror shining at least with compassion. I even remembered by the date the words I had said which made Audrey think of this. We had been driving to her place. We were happy. In my exuberance, and carelessness, I said lightly: "To think that one day I'll sit, old and gray, among my grandchildren. And this is what I will tell them: Grandchildren: you will, of course, not believe this. But I knew this beautiful woman in person. And I loved her beyond anything. And she loved me a little, too." And now I wished that there were a way in which, short of admitting that I had read her journal, I could officially know of her fear, and tell her a thousand times that I didn't want children. That I wasn't meant to bear children, that I wanted to be with her. What would I do with children if I didn't have Audrey?

Then I felt bitterness again. That the mirror could know so little about me, that I was so alone in my love of her. I went back to the cold pages, read once again how young I seemed to her, how irresponsible. How insufficient. "She's young, and she wants another lover."

I wanted her love back, even the love of this morning, her spirited goodbye, the way love had looked to me before I knew her private thoughts.

I went farther back in her journal and found early words of love from a time when she had first felt me like a sunrise inside her. I could see her sit in her chair writing them. I could see the happiness rising in her, the small words. "Andrea. I love her." "Andrea, I love you!"

But somehow, these words of love came too late now after all that tarnished mirror stuff. Or, chronologically, they came too early, were already outlived, already outdone by the contempt she felt for me of late.

I replaced the journal a final time, lining it up at the twenty degree angle over the top magazine, exactly the way I had found it. I fled into another drink, fled into the lesser pain of tiredness, my arms and legs feeling weak now, almost deliciously so. I managed to fall asleep on the sofa in the study. Until the telephone rang to wake me up with Audrey's voice telling me her client sessions were done and asking me, how was my morning coming along?

"Not so well," I told her. "I'm tired, I'm restless, and I can't concentrate.

"Well, I'll be back soon now," she said, her voice full of exuberance.

I walked through the house, checking if everything was in its place, mostly of course to satisfy myself against the hidden and irrational fears of some god-sent spectacle of punishment that would have wafted the journal away, so that Audrey would eventually ask me about it and I wouldn't be able to hide my guilt. I decided to read a book while waiting for her and pulled one in the bedroom from its shelf, *Lesbian Images.* That would be safe to be found reading, I thought. But when I heard her car in front of the house I changed my mind and considered it not safe after all. I put it back and guiltily rushed to the study, so as to be able to emerge from it just in time for her to open the front door.

"You don't look well," she said. "Are you ready for some lunch? 'Cause I'm starving."

I was not ready for lunch and my stomach was queasy. I comprehended little of what went on during the remainder of the weekend. At first I was too preoccupied with appearing normal after having drunk too much. I was in the shadow land of knowing that things were wrong with my body and my mind, both, and constantly afraid it would show on the outside as well, hence acting with total self-consciousness. Then gradually I became poisoned with the mistrust and cold anger I had read in Audrey's journal, though she showed me none of those in person.

§

We had an absurd argument one day when she came to the apartment after work and Kay was playing grating music much too loud for Audrey's frail nerves after hours of intensive work with clients. She asked me if we could go to her house instead, and I both wanted to and didn't want to. Finally I found myself standing on the street, watching her green car drive off, and in it Audrey with a shrug of indifferent shoulders. I watched a moment too long, for just when I began to run after her, the traffic signal changed from red to green and she turned the corner. I reached that corner, still running, only to watch her turn the next corner and be gone.

Kay, none too enthusiastic, said, "I thought you were going to spend the night with Audrey."

"No," I said moodily, watching Kay hem the skirt of Sharon's wedding dress.

"Sharon's coming over later to try this on," Kay said with a sigh. "I wish I hadn't agreed to do this, but now I have to finish it."

Well, I thought bitterly, Andrea is now going to her room to cry. Which I did, until Sharon arrived and visited me in my room. I greeted her with sulky complaints: "Well, the music is too loud, and I can't stand it."

"So ask her to turn it down," Sharon said.

"I can't," I said, barely managing not to stomp my feet. "It's her apartment too, and she can do whatever she wants."

"You're being silly," Sharon said.

"Yes," I agreed without glee.

So Sharon left me to my fate too. Too unmanageable for all of you, I thought with the self-righteous satisfaction of the badly wounded. Not a minute later the music stopped. It made me laugh. I made my way to the kitchen, hoping to run into Sharon, which I did.

"Thanks," I told her with a sheepish grin.

Sharon smiled with bridal grace. "It was simple. I merely said I'd turn down the music a little. Kay said, 'Sure, turn it off if you want.' And so I turned it off."

"Remarkable," I said.

I took Sharon out for a drink, an abbreviated version of a bachelor party. We sat down in the garden of a restaurant. She talked with the calm happiness that had become hers. She spoke of a peace she felt within herself. Her eyes were bright with belonging, and her mouth was soft and wide with loveliness.

I turned my wine glass around and around in my hands and

finally said meekly:

"Sharon, I am very much in love."

"Ah," she said with her bridal smile, as though all being in love was nowadays a gift from her. "And who's the lucky man? Joel? Or should I ask, who are the lucky men?"

I laughed. "It's even more complicated than that. I'm in love with a woman."

I watched Sharon's eyes. They simply looked back at me. "Yes?"

"Her name's Audrey. I met her through Kay. At one of our parties to which you didn't come. I don't know if you've ever met her."

"I think I may have," Sharon said. "She's an older woman? Teaches art and does spiritual work?"

"That's her." I blushed.

"I met her sometime last year," Sharon said." I don't remember her terribly well. We talked a little, not much."

"It's awkward for me right now, because, well, obviously it's the first time I've fallen in love with a woman. I don't know much about it. Except that I love her very much. She's beautiful. And it's strange now, of course, dealing with the world around me—same world from which I have just barely emerged myself, you know, and where it's simply not terribly usual for a woman to love another woman as I love Audrey."

"Well, if you both understand each other, it should be easy to keep a low profile. You don't have to go around with a sign on your back saying I love a woman, do you?"

"No," I said. "I don't have to, but that's just it: Sometimes I kind of want to. Except you're right, it isn't necessary. I don't even know exactly why I'm telling you."

"Perhaps because I once told you that I've been with a woman once?"

No, that wasn't it. I didn't even remember her ever telling me that. It was more that I wanted reassurance once again that loving Audrey was all right. Better yet, that it was perfect.

Sharon laughed. "Poor Joel, I suppose. He's quite in love with you, you know."

"No, not 'poor Joel,'" I protested. "I feel a lot for him. Only, being in love with Audrey changes everything of course."

"You're still going to see him in Oregon, aren't you?"

"Oh yes," I said quickly. "Sometimes of course I have the urge to cancel everything and just stay here with Audrey. It would make everything simpler. But then I get afraid. She has a lot of power over me, and I'm scared. There's this strong urge to give up everything that doesn't have to do with Audrey, in order to assure myself of God knows what."

Sharon looked at me steadily through all my helpless stammering and crooked smiling. "You don't have to make a choice right now," she said calmly.

I sighed relief and helplessness. "No, I don't have to make a choice now."

At that moment I envied Audrey her past experience. At least she had already loved women. I only hoped that I wouldn't fall off the cliff we were climbing. Yet it seemed there was always some foothold still.

I love you, Audrey, I prayed quietly.

"I love Audrey very much," I told Sharon.

"I'm glad," she said. "You look happy saying it."

"I am," I said.

§

The day of Sharon's wedding, I gave a poetry reading at noon. Everybody else was busy with the wedding and only Audrey came. She wore a long red and black dress in honor of the occasion and looked so enthralling that I regretted it wasn't she who was reading, but merely I instead in my shy violet skirt with a coy white blouse.

Later she stood in the street, her dress fluttering around her legs, her unused all-occasion jeans folded over one arm, waving with her free hand as Kay and another woman and I drove off to the wedding. I longed for a time in the future when we would be invited to events together, recognized as belonging with one another. The longing surprised me with delight. Whenever I had been labeled as being part of a couple in the past, I had chafed against it, at first mildly, later more vehemently. Now I wanted it.

I also noticed another phenomenon as I looked down on my pale violet skirt. For years now, I had been understated in front of other people, especially men, who would claim my companionship. Never would I dress up for a man, for example. In my mind's own judgment, that would look as though I were out to get him. For Audrey now I wanted to be beautiful. I wanted to shine.

As I looked at Sharon in her light wedding dress with its now perfect hem, and her face calm and soft with radiance, I acknowledged that there were separate ways of going this life's path not alone.

§

For now I returned to Audrey's dreams. They came in throngs.

"I'm afraid you won't come back," she told me. I didn't know at the time that one is only always most afraid of one's own specters. Her fears embarrassed me, woven into such beautiful dreams. Often, waking, I could feel her glance linger on me, and I would pretend not to notice.

"I am afraid for you. It's such a dangerous journey on that river. Something might happen, and . . . ." Invariably she would break off.

"I had this dream three times now—there is a special place in the river—it's dangerous. The water is brown and fast, there's an eddy that could pull you in."

I did not want to hear the threats of her dreams. I did not want to be spooked. But dark eddies, not of water, but of my mind, washed over me all the same. Her earlier dream. Her journal. The fear that I would be washed away by my love for her into denying all else that was part of me. I knew it would be possible, and I knew I couldn't live like that for long. As a vegetable, yes, perhaps, but not as a full human being.

I cried a lot. I knew it was possible for me to give myself up to another's love, especially to one as powerful as Audrey's. But there was a heaviness around her now that was difficult for me to deal with. An eddy of fear threatened to engulf me, an eddy of love tainted by jealousy.

"I'm afraid you'll drown," she told me.

I was drowning already. I felt as though I were reaching up high for breathing space, but there was none, and I was drowning for lack of it.

"I've dreamt this three times," she repeated, probably in response to the signs of dismay in my face.

I said nothing. What do you want me to do? I asked in a silence of anger and discomfort. You're afraid I'm going to sleep with Joel, and I am. But you will not say this. You will threaten me with dreams. You will threaten me with the power of magical predictions, and with the power of fear. So that I won't be able to come or go in my own time, at my own speed.

"There are strong rapids. I can see the place, but I can't describe it. The water is dark," she said.

And you are sitting on top of the mountain, my Lorelei, and perhaps you are singing, and, yes, perhaps we will indeed drown. Can you not love me? Can you not trust me?

"I'll come back in ten days," I said. That was all that mattered.

And then I will be yours. Exclusively. Forever, I added in my thoughts.

She sighed. I didn't understand that she, too, lived her own myth now, the myth of the seer, the myth of the lover losing the one she couldn't warn. To death. Or to a man. Or simply to loss. I didn't know then that she was living the myth of losing me in her own fashion, as I was living, in my fashion, the myth of freeing myself for her.

§

The night before I left, Audrey prepared a special dinner. Shrimp. Which I had prepared for her when she was sick. Shortly before dinner I found her packing vitamins for me in the bedroom. She had them all spread out on the bed and filled individual plastic bags with them, her head bent, her hands mechanically reaching for the various pills by color, stuffing the bags. I stood by the door, watching, wanting to do something. She looked touching, forlorn in her determination to sadness. She rolled up her down jacket, which she was loaning me for the trip so that I would not get cold. She stuffed the vitamins in the hood and fastened the hood over the rolled up jacket to make a compact parcel.

"There," she said with gruff satisfaction. "Your body's taken care of."

We went to eat our shrimp. We said little. From time to time one of us attempted a joke that didn't come off. Finally, after swallowing my last gallows' shrimp, I blurted out, "Audrey, I don't want us to be so glum!"

"What do you want me to do?" She laughed angrily and shot me a slit-eyed glance of contempt. "Dance? All right, I'll dance for you."

She jumped up from her chair, turned her back to me and stomped an impish, ugly dance for me through the living room, her curls flying, her arms held up stiffly in the mock grace of her anger.

Her dance felt like a fist to my stomach. It hurt me beyond belief. Nevertheless I stood up and caught up with her and took her in my arms, and she felt small and helpless as she collapsed against me and let herself be held. Finally our distance ebbed away and we felt one again. We made love to each other for a long time, her beautiful skin against mine with the tingling sense of belonging she could make me feel. As she touched me, an image formed in my mind. Water lily. I whispered the word over and over, as though it were her name. Water lily. My beloved. Water lily.

I already drifted inside the peace of sleep when she recalled me with these words: "It'll be so difficult not making love to Joel." I felt drawn back into the torn world of our misunderstanding. I turned my head away with a sigh. She turned out the light and laid her head on my shoulder.

"I love you, Audrey," I said.

§

On the way to the airport we didn't say much. We progressed like a sad medieval parade. I couldn't understand why she insisted on driving me to the airport when my going was so painful to her. She probably couldn't understand it either. I had planned to get an airport limousine downtown. She was adamant about rearranging her schedule to have a few hours free in the middle of the day. She didn't want me to go, but as I was going, she wanted to take me.

I looked at her from time to time. Her face was poker-cold, concentrating on the traffic.

She looked as though she couldn't believe what she was doing. Cold anger mixed with disbelief, an intent line pinched her beautiful mouth. I remembered a Native American saying remarking how white people have thin lips and how thin lips are a sign of not being generous.

Audrey, who had some Native American ancestry, had very thin lips. Now. Not always. Something inside me cried for both of us.

When she came to the apartment to pick me up together with my green backpack, which she insisted on carrying, lugging rather, to the car, I probably gave her the greatest pain yet, the image of being full of joy and anticipation about my impending trip. I couldn't contain my joy, it was in all my motions. I hadn't traveled for so long, and I was going far away to an adventure I never had before. Journey adrenaline was humming through me.

After a while she couldn't bear me looking at her. She made me look away by giving me a heavy-lidded sideways glance of contempt, her eyes drawn to a half-closed command. It was the kind of look that matched her journal's opinions about my childish cruelty. Yes, I was cruel for permitting her to chauffeur me to the airport. Perhaps cruel for going at all. For the last time, I told myself.

Through the image of her mirror knowledge, I felt distorted again. I knew that I had to get away from her. I could not be with her and feel so trapped and suffocated by her possessiveness, and so I chose the ultimate means of untrapping myself and in the process I ran straight into the maw of fire, blowing further jealousy into the flame. The child in me cried, wanting to be loved just for being who she was. The child in me also painted me grandiose visions of the golden-haired lucky one—myself—able to get away with everything, able to live her life freely.

Three times I met Audrey's eyes full of accusation and hostility. Then I turned to the window and began to sing, Dona nobis pacem. Give us peace. Let this cup pass by me. And I knew it would pass. I would sit on the airplane and would be able to forget the tensions between us.

The child in me kept wanting to cry tears that I didn't want to cry in front of her. There was also rebellion inside me. You cannot keep me against my will. As it is, you're pushing me away from you. Why must I feel so suffocated in your presence that I actually look forward to the moment when I will no longer have your accusing look on me?

I kept looking out of the window, singing my Latin words to no God that I knew of. Singing for the sake of singing. How can one love and be rendered so loveless at one at the same time? Dona nobis pacem. Give us peace. I love you, Audrey. Why must we be so distant? Why must I feel this idiotic need to assert myself against you? I love you more than words can say. Why must I fight against the accusation in your eyes by stubbornly insisting, yes, I am exactly as you think. A child, risking everything, and capable of getting away with anything. Why must I feel so compelled to show my own power? Why must you feel so compelled to have power over me? All I want to do is sink into your arms and forget that I ever wanted to go away. But you have my going in your eyes, strangely, bitterly, and I cannot stay. Finnegan's Wake, the daughter river singing little waves: "it seems silly to be flowing, but I canna stay." Forgive me, my Audrey, I don't know what I am doing, and yet I do know. I am driving myself to do it. And more literally, you are also driving me. This unreality. Dona nobis pacem. Give us peace. I want to stay, I want to go, and there is a heaviness, and a sliding, and a clinging, a collapse of myself that you cannot understand. Will not. In this I will always be alone. Give us peace.

We arrived at the airport and sat for half an hour in the parking lot, Audrey's head on my lap. My hand on her soft hair. Her red and gold ring on my finger over her brown strands of permed hair. Images to live by, to come home to.

Slowly I started clinging to myself again from this moment of melting into the sense of no world other than Audrey. Myself. What I was. What I was doing. How I was doing nothing wrong. I was simply being. Myself. Dona nobis pacem. Give us peace.

"Don't let your friends poison you against me," I begged. "I don't know what they will say when I am gone." I didn't have the wisdom yet to ask for the much more important thing: Don't poison yourself with bitterness against me.

Audrey gave me a suffering look, then sighed. "Well, I better be getting back to my life," she said.

She walked me to the sliding glass door of the terminal, but she wouldn't come in. At the door she gave me my backpack, which she had carried this far.

"See you in ten days," she said.

I wanted to reach out to hug her and kiss her goodbye. She shook her head lightly. Don't. We are two women. There are those who wouldn't like this.

"Oh, Andrea," she said softly.

"Bye," I said.

She shrugged her shoulders and I turned to go inside. I had to turn around to look at her just one more time.

"And don't forget, the dragon is flying with you," she hissed. "She'll be there watching every moment. There's nothing you can do without her seeing you."

"And will she also protect me?"

"That too," Audrey said. She pursed her lips and I wrinkled my nose.

Then I stood in the airport, the sun creating reflections in glass and clear plastic. Faceless voices announced distances and their mechanical connections. I was exhausted, leaning against a stucco pillar, staring at the red ropes of division between departing, arriving, flying. Perfumes and raincoats wafted by. Audrey, I thought, what will become of us?

§

I checked in my backpack, then sat in the airport lounge to

catch up with neglected business, collected in my spacious shoulder bag. Three days ago I got the ten first preview copies of my new book of poems, my largest collection so far. Suddenly it seemed so unimportant. The small hallelujah of being in print. Almost unnoticed, even by myself. I asked for a manila envelope at the airport post office window and addressed it to my parents. Time out for two minutes of pride to sneak another glance at my photograph on the back cover. Turning around, I looked with challenge disguised as modesty at the people rushing around me. May I present you with the unrecognized company of a published poet in your midst?

That was about it for my grand moment of pride. I went to have my thin package weighed and mailed.

To draw attention to myself, I asked, "Can it still go printed matter if I've written a personal dedication into the book?"

"Sure, that's all right," the clerk informed me, obviously not getting the momentous situation at all.

I strolled around, then returned to the post office window a second time to buy a postcard which I addressed to Audrey. "Water lily," I wrote, then spent fifteen minutes thinking of the next thing to write but only came up with this:

I'll be back in ten days.

Love,

Andrea

I boarded the plane. It took off, whereupon I ordered a Bloody Mary because Audrey had told me that was what she always drank to make it through a flight. I daydreamed out of the window into Washington disappearing below me. I'll be back in ten days, my Audrey, I whispered into the crystals condensing on the window pane. When the "No Smoking" sign went off, I fumbled for a cigarette. Sat up straight again. Reached for my notebook. Wrote about Audrey's hair, my pale hand in her hair, her ring on my finger, coral and gold, the gold fixture around the coral oval like tiny hands holding it up. Audrey's hair.

Quite suddenly the pressure of her powerful and demanding presence fell away from me. I knew I loved her forever. I began to respect not only her love, but also her jealousy. After this I would give her no cause for jealousy ever again. We would grow to know each other, and through each other ourselves, and we would be together, growing in trust, season after season.

I wrote her a letter, wrote about learning to respect her jealousy, wrote about the photograph of her she had recently given me as a present, explaining that I had not taken it along only because I would be out on the river and was afraid that it would get damaged. I wrote that I loved her in all the ways that fit on six or seven pages, and into the long stretches of unwritten daydreams in between the lines. I wrote her a poem about her hair and my hands.

In Denver I had to change planes. There was a two hour wait. I strolled around the terminal and found no post office, but only a gift shop with idiotic greeting cards, one of which I bought and discarded so as to have an envelope for my letter. I finally found overpriced stamps in another gift shop and mailed my letter. Then I sat down and watched a clock until I could safely assume it was late enough for her to be at home. I wanted to call her.

The pay phone was near impossible to figure out. I tried another, also with unsatisfactory results. But I was determined. The third phone, by some miracle, accepted my call and my coins. Audrey answered.

"Hello?"

"Audrey! I'm in Denver."

"Congratulations, I suppose," she said.

"I wish I were there with you."

"Me too."

"Audrey, I'll be back soon."

"Yes."

"I miss you."

"I miss you too, darling."

"I wrote you a letter."

"Did you?"

"I wish I could come back right now."

"Do you? What's keeping you?"

"Schedules. Old plans. I want to come back properly."

"I'll be here."

"Have a good trip yourself this weekend to New Mexico."

"I'll try."

"How are the animals?"

"Fine. They came to the door and were disappointed that you weren't coming home with me."

"I love you, Audrey."

"I love you too, darling."

In this manner we talked until the operator interrupted us to demand in a chirpy voice that I insert another dollar worth of coins. I complied. Pretty soon her bird voice came on again. At the third interruption I told Audrey that I didn't have any more coins. This was it.

"Do you want my credit card number?" she asked.

"No," I said miserably, having nothing noteworthy to say to her, yet not wanting to have the connection broken. The operator's voice piped in again, politely insistent. Audrey laughed out loud and repeated her offer to pay for the continuance of the call. I didn't think it was all that funny and repeated my pathetic no.

"Oh, well, take care of yourself then," Audrey said.

"I love you very much, Audrey."

"I love you too, Andrea."

One of us had to take the initiative and hang up first. Finally I heard Audrey do so. I went to board my next flight, ordered my next Bloody Mary, and took a nap.

§

Then it was Oregon. The landing. Scrambling for carry-on luggage and my coat. The ramp to the terminal.

And there stood Joel. My heart raced. He was staring at the arriving passengers and stared straight through me without seeing me, which gave me a chance to sneak around him unobserved.

"Waiting for someone?" I asked him from behind.

He turned around and caught his breath. "I was looking for you," he said. "I must have missed you."

"Must have."

He bent down to embrace me. I laughed because he pretty much had to kneel in order to sink to my level.

"This is so wonderful," he said. "You being here. You've shown me the city where I lived for years in an entirely new way. Now I can show you this place, the river, my home. It's hard to believe you're actually here."

I studied his face. Tan skin over fine bones. Deep long creases radiating out from his black eyes when he smiled, long and prominent front teeth. His dark glossy hair fell in thick waves into his forehead.

"I must be a sight," he apologized. "After work I barely gave myself enough time to shower and put on a clean shirt so I'd be here in time." I found out it was a five hour drive from where he lived to the airport in Portland.

"I've been traveling all day, too, you know." I matched his apology. "So we're both tired and grubby."

"Yes, you must be tired." He snapped out of slow motion welcome. "Let's get your luggage and get out of here."

The luggage from my flight already traveled on the round conveyor belt. I pointed to the green backpack with the blue sleeping bag cover strapped to it, from which much of the bright orange sleeping bag itself spilled forth.

"I only had a string to tie it with," I said. "I guess it didn't hold up very well."

Joel nodded. "We'll have to find a better bag, or else a proper string for the river," he said in a tone of voice intimating that he hated to tell me this, nevertheless, this sort of sloppiness wouldn't do.

"Where are we staying tonight?" I asked. "Or do we have to drive all the way to your place in Maupin?"

"No, we'll stay here in town," he said. "A friend left me keys to his house. He's gone for the weekend."

Joel took charge of my backpack despite my protestations that I would gladly assume responsibility for this haphazardly packed thing that decidedly had the looks of being put together by city hands. It wouldn't damage his reputation in the least to carry it, he insisted.

We arrived at his friend's house and it turned out that Joel did not actually have the keys, but that his friend was supposed to have left them for him under the rug in the front of the unlocked parked pickup truck. Unfortunately, the keys were not where advertised, no matter how often and how carefully we looked. Finally Joel, armed with screw driver and flashlight, decided on alternative means of getting into the house. Since the door was latched from the inside, he decided to unscrew the latch screws, after first knocking on all the windows to make sure that no one was by chance inside after all.

And if I had to spend my week's vacation in jail for risking a break-in the very first night, that was all right with me too, I assured myself. After three quarters of an hour, however, we were safely in the house without being arrested or otherwise interrupted in our shady work. We lay down on the living room rug and covered ourselves with our sleeping bags after Joel had fastened the screws to the door again and then discovered that his friend was at home after all, fast asleep in the bedroom, though, and interlaced with a girl who was also fast asleep, despite all the noise we had generated. Probably drunk, thought I, who knew such things.

"Good night then," I said.

Joel tried to apologize for the complications. I protested that, if I hadn't come, Joel himself would be many miles from here, sweetly asleep in his own bed, so no worries.

"Good night," he said into the dark around us. There was hesitation in his voice. Then: "It's difficult to decide what to do. We have a long drive tomorrow, and we have to get up early, and it's very late now. At the same time, I want to make love to you and hold you all night long."

I had forgotten the delightful almost monotonous matter of fact way in which he was capable of speaking of such things, his voice always with a quality of utter seriousness and respectfulness to it. It was refreshing to hear him deliberate between respectfulness and common sense and desire again. I enumerated back to him the many things that we needed all our strength for the following day, and I felt in me a gentleness toward him that compensated for the superiority I felt within me, since I was quite capable of waiting. I only wanted to make love to him one more time in order to satisfy my mind's mythologies, and we had ten days and therefore I had time to be patient.

But these were days of farewell for me, of which farewell I knew more than Joel did. And I felt the need in me to honor him for making it possible for me to take a gentle farewell from him and his kind. I felt the need not to take without also giving. So when Joel reached out and touched my face, then my neck, then my breasts, speaking now with his body, no longer with words, I pushed away Audrey's folded up jacket which I was using as a pillow, and opened my arms to his desire. This was for him and had nothing to do with me. It seemed only fair.

I tried to hold him to me as gently as I could with my body. My mind was far away. Flying through the past, through all the times I had held men in my arms. Through all the times my mind had raced away from them. Like this. Only with this difference: In the past my mind had merely been racing away. Uneasily. Finding me refuge from where I didn't think I belonged. Now instead, my mind raced both away from and toward. Away from this sexual act with its implications of belonging to a man. Toward Audrey, toward a belonging which my heart felt, which, for the first time in my life, my body felt, and for which my heart grew ever more impatient, the closer I felt myself drawing toward it. Never before I had known Audrey had I been allowed to go through a sexual act without having my mind rent apart from my body: The mind always tore itself away in self-consciousness and sorrow at its own flight; the body tapped into the pity of the mind and begged forgiveness for flying away through tenderness and touch.

Joel, I thought, perhaps it's a curse between us men and women, to have to bear this distance, this obligation to deny it with our bodies, and this soft silence to cover up all our doubts. Perhaps you too are thinking now how best you could please me and apologize to me for your essential distance. Perhaps, aside from procreation, we have all lain in the sexual embrace with the delusion, or the hope, that the other would be pleased, in spite of our own distance and because of our tenderness. What a world of distance I had lived in for so many years. And you. And your brothers. And my sisters. Our constant attempt to convince each other that we're not distant. This gentleness in our hearts we then call love, when sometimes all it is is a sigh of pity and a silence of mutual protectiveness.

And you, dragon Serena, who are watching this, as she told me you would, know that I needed to make this conscious once again, this distance I have lived for all these years. And this pity of lacking what we have called, in human language, union. Tell her that I must live through this, that I must know this once again, completely, before I can return to her, where there has been less distance every time we touched, and where my mind forgets to fly and race away, and brings me images of flowers from the depth when we touch. Water lily.

I managed to return to Joel just as he moved away from me, leaving the wetness of his semen on my thighs. We lay still for a while. Then I got up in search of the bathroom to wash myself. Carrying with me the once overheard remark that men do not like it when women wash themselves promptly of their emissions. Did men not know about the overnight smell of their semen, or the stickiness between one's legs, bearing their smell?

"Thank you," Joel said when I lay down again. I replied with a thank you of my own, meaning that I would always honor what and whom I was leaving in this shady way.

Then I pushed his arms away and laid my head on my own arms, holding the pillow of Audrey's coat, and clutching with my free hand at the peaceful scarab hanging as a charm around my neck, falling asleep to images of Audrey coming closer, cradling me into belonging.

§

We got up early the next morning, accepted a cup of coffee from Joel's friend and his lover, to whom we sheepishly explained our break-in.

We drove into the morning, stopped at a cabin restaurant to eat breakfast by a window overlooking a lake. It was chilly, but there was a fire burning. The mountains were still laced with snow. The wonder of it. Vegetation just about began to stir with spring, except on a long stretch of hillside where fire had some time ago stripped all possibility of bloom into black scars of lifeless sticks for years to come. Merely a layer of grass already insisted on its presence again on the ground.

The sky was overcast and I was surprised when Joel suggested that we stop at one of the hot springs to take a bath.

"Isn't it too cold?"

"No, you'll see," he said.

I was willing to have him take the lead. These were my last days with a man, and it seemed right that I should let him take the lead, especially as I had already gone against my own preferences by letting him make love to me the first night. The sense of being in control of my own destiny was already compromised. One more time I would play by the rules I had been taught from childhood, but for the first time without chafing against these rules. I would surrender, by choice, for ten days. I would witness the choices he would make as I would never again have to witness them directly, and as I would perhaps for the first time witness them consciously, because I was not distracted now by the preoccupation with gaining a space of my own in this preponderance of laws and rules.

We came to a weather-beaten wooden fence with a shed serving as bathhouse next to a small square of green water that smelled of rotten eggs and steamed into the chill of the air.

"Smells strange," I said.

"Sulfur," Joel explained.

"That's what hell smells like?" I asked.

"So I hear," Joel said. "I haven't been, so I can't say for sure."

I watched him undress. He smiled at me. I smiled back and undressed likewise, self-consciously projecting the requisite image of lovely lady baring her body without shame. Of course there was shame. There had always been shame at being naked in the presence of a man. Unease, vague fear, the amazing sense of vulnerability. A dark sense of willpower against the ancient rules of fear asserted itself in the willed pretense of simplicity, of fearlessness, of being secure within myself, and without shame. Underneath lay all the suffering that comes from seeming centered, solid, without being so.

This is what we have come to, I thought silently, a state where the woman feels endless shame and an endless desire to flee. The last flight, when every other flight is barred, is into covering herself into a coyness woven, prettily, from the rough fibers of dark discomfort. Conditioned by centuries of domination, all the essence of woman in me was trapped into this game in the presence of a man. The dark demand: Flee. Don't resist. But flee. And if you choose not to take flight, flee anyway. You will always find ways of doing so, preferably without appearing to do so. Conditioned to this: wherever a man is, the woman is only partially there.

I stood there, shivering in my naked thoughts, when Joel called me.

"Come into the water." He laughed. "It's warm in here."

Oh yes.

"Just a moment." I undid the necklace that held my scarab charm. I stripped off my ring.

"Oh, good," he said. "I forgot to tell you to take those off. Your necklace would have turned black in this broth."

"Well, I remembered," I said.

"It's a beautiful necklace," he said. "I noticed it last night. You didn't use to wear it, or the ring."

"No," I said. "Audrey gave them to me."

I stood still in one spot in the warm pool and felt the water bubble up pleasantly along my legs. I bantered with Joel. But my essence was not lighthearted. It drooped under a heavy sense of unease, discomfort, almost hostility, and the insistent messages from some part of me: Be gentle. He is good and beautiful. His mind doesn't know of the shame and the distance and the darkness which surrounds you like a shield. Honor him by being gentle.

I was in two worlds at once. The world of water, bantering,

towels, and playing at being. And then the world of knowing that all living was rent apart, precisely because of this, the play and the performance of being. The world was rent into men and women playing at being friends and being in union, but finding such friendship only in complicated enactments of longings that were not entirely there, except by virtue of many years of training and demands that they ought to be there. And always, in the wake of such knowledge, came the painful and confused moments of retraction, taught with precision from mother to daughter: Don't for anything let him share this knowledge that all this attentiveness to him is just a logical decision to honor him, not a full response of your being. There was the eternal see-saw between gentleness and caring, and the endless reminders in myself that part of my gentleness was based on falsehood and on the hope that the gentleness would nonetheless appear genuine, thus complicating falsehood several times over. Then came the sudden and jubilant feeling of triumph, feeling like a miracle in all its undeservedness, that I knew a union that was at once more simple and much deeper, and that I had the promise that this union would forever be mine. With Audrey. With a woman who was not forbidden to me by my own need for being. This feeling reconciled me with the world.

I reached for Joel's hand. "Let's go," I said with the exuberance of one who has suddenly received a great gift.

We drove the last stretch of distance to the small town where he lived in a trailer. Impression after impression anchored the feeling of triumph and wonder in me.

§

In the afternoon we spent a few hours packing—in my case, repacking—our belongings, including my intractable sleeping bag, into river-suited packages. Food, clothes, tent, the raft.

"That little parcel of plastic is supposed to carry us for five days?" I asked.

"Well, pick it up and feel how much it weighs," he said. "Does that convince you?"

"Seems sturdy enough."

We arrived at a small craft airport to meet our chartered flight into the mountains. We watched a rattlesnake in its cage, while doubts about our ability to fly that afternoon were radioed in by the pilot who was just coming back in from a previous trip. The weather—he reported clouds, wind, and poor vision—looked worse by the minute. But when he landed and found us still determined to go, he said we could give it a try. We loaded our gear into the plane and took off.

I sat up front with the pilot. If we were to crash, the least I wanted to do was to watch up close.

We didn't crash. The flight was magical. The pilot even flew a few unnecessary loops for my delighted benefit.

Late in the evening, daylight already almost gone after we had eaten in a ranch house and had pitched our tent and blown up the raft and anchored it in the river, Joel and I sat on the bank. I smoked my final cigarette, and listened to the quick rush of water.

"To think that we'll be on that tomorrow," I said.

"Nervous?" Joel asked.

"You bet," I said, then drifted into poetry. "But you know, here I sit thinking. What if I had a choice? To die on the river in the loveliest surroundings, with the mountains on both sides, and the water rushing all around us, and the crickets singing, and the water going on forever with its quiet melody. Or to die at home in my bed from old age."

Joel put his arm around me.

"And you know what?" I said. "I'll be happy to die in bed of old age."

Our four days on the river were the most serene I'd spent in years. I had no responsibilities other than cracking eggs for breakfast, or frying bacon, or throwing together a salad, or tending a fire for one of the meals that Joel had carefully planned and provided for. Our icebox seemed to contain infinite amounts of gourmet food that beckoned to be prepared and eaten.

Since I had never been on a raft trip before, Joel had planned this journey to be as leisurely as possible. We never spent more than a few hours on the river at one stretch. We went for walks. We spent hours cooking, cleaning pots, setting up the tent and taking it back down.

Time seemed to become whole again from the hectic fragmentation it undergoes in city life. Thoughts flowed and didn't constantly demand to be written down. There were too many of them to begin with, and oftentimes it was difficult to call them thoughts at all. They were pictures rising to the brink of awareness, then hanging there, too large or too little for the mind to know how to process.

I looked for Audrey in everything around us. The river, the swirling white water, the rocks, the flowers we renamed, the hills, the bends in the river. The clouds. Often I leaned back from my position on the raft and simply looked up into the clouds that seemed to drift more slowly than the swirling water beneath us.

What pushed up into my awareness was the thought that, unless I was with Audrey, I would forever be stuck on the fringes of my being. Not a terrible place. The feeling I had was one of being a translator between myself and the reality outside of me. The translations were good. But I longed to do more than translations. I longed to communicate directly, to be in touch directly. And this required love and sacredness, which one feels most directly with the one human being whose eyes one chooses to recognize, whose lips, in a moment of recognition, say: "You are one of us."

The world away from Audrey seemed impure, despite its beauty, and showed me how much I needed her in order to be one with the world, in order not to succumb to the slow drip of the human poisons of conditioning and psychological constraints around our beautiful, but slow and only just evolving natures.

I knew for Audrey and me there would be moments when we would cross the boundary of all constraints and feel pure being. I grew impatient to be with her again and to fulfill the belief that, with her, existence was a place where the world promised to cease being merely a colorful and breathtaking carnival in which I was free to jump in and out of rides. Not a terrible place at all, this carnival, but one which, in all its colorful unfolding, cried out for the bond of belonging, for being still somewhere.

The river was swollen with the waters of spring, beautiful, as all water is beautiful. Joel was worried about certain rapids and difficult rocks. He knew every potential spot of danger and every rock that required attention. Well ahead of time he would slow down or stop rowing and announce, in a precise and careful tone of voice, when I would have to start bailing. He spoke as though speaking to a child. And I was more than happy to obey.

Most of the time I had little to do. I felt more or less useless. Only when we went head first into a wild stretch of high water—sometimes a single wave filled the entire bottom of the raft—was I called upon to help out.

Joel and I shared the single tent he had brought. At first I was irritated with his tacit assumption that we would sleep together. However, I did not question or fight the arrangement. I wrapped my arms around Audrey's coat, bundled up night after night as my pillow. Joel and I did not share the same sleep, and we did not share our bodies.

With the same mixture of self-righteousness and curious detachment with which I didn't question our sleeping arrangements,

I was determined not to withhold myself if Joel were to make sexual advances. One morning, with the yellow walls of the tent announcing sunlight long before it came, he turned to me and began caressing my body. I silently said yes, take me then if you must. But even my silence must have carried so many mixed feelings that Joel, more perceptive than I had suspected, stopped touching me. I respected his quiet pride of not just letting himself be tolerated. Difficult as it was to talk about sex, we talked about it calmly, with lies and with truths, absolved one another, and got up in peace to start breakfast and to fetch water from the river for coffee and for pancake dough.

I felt hope growing in me that somehow Joel would be the one man who could understand me, who could remain my friend. Because of his perceptiveness, because of his pride, and because of his lack of need to send me spinning into guilt trips for having undone his manhood by neither feeling, nor faking, enthusiasm for it in that cold stiff moment of my gentle will to tolerate.

I wanted to tell him about Audrey. I had already made several false starts, beginning in my letters. It wasn't easy. His ears, though perceptive, were also selective. He spun conversations around, or turned them into wide-eyed questions about my fascinating friend Audrey. I would want to say, no, not just friend. Call her my lover instead. My one true love. At which point he would change the subject, or else I would perceive it so. One doesn't speak only in word language. He was courteous, he was undemanding and perceptive. Hope flooded me. I found him remarkable. For a man.

I have to write this down, this superior-sounding 'for a man.' I had not been brought up to respect men. My disrespect was not even something I knew consciously until much later, but I had it in my bones. I had been taught, in so many subtle ways by the important women of my childhood, that it was my fate as a woman to tolerate men, and preferably *the* man, to be sweet and long-suffering in my tolerance, to over-praise every man with immoderate flattery, and in every other way to do exactly as I pleased. Flee, fake the power of the king, and crown and mantle him with words, and privately turn into a comet of my own light. I had been taught tolerance, but not respect, not that essential ingredient for love. Now I was learning a glimmer of hope, a glimmer of respect for one who chose not to be tolerated. I felt hope for being able to leave with the friendly embrace of my Easter vision. Men and women parting from each other into their separate worlds. I hoped I might be one of those who parted with a smile and not with bitterness.

We came to the roughest stretch of our journey the day after the sex-conscious, sexless morning. Joel rowed with passion. As usual I sat across from him on the tarpaulin that covered our tightly packed belongings. As usual I clutched my coral ring and scarab necklace in my pocket. I checked for them endlessly, and found, ever again with relief, that no shock of waves and wild water had washed them away.

The water became rougher. My mind turned maudlin. Fine with me if all my possessions got washed away. Not so good if my life should happen to get washed away as well. On the topic of life, though, fate, do you hear me? If you want my life, feel free to drown me, but let my ring and my necklace drown with me. They are my dearest possessions.

Joel announced he was nervous about upcoming rapids. He decided to anchor the raft and walk ahead on the side of the hill to take a look at them before we attempted to run them. He stood studying the rapids for a long time. I smoked several cigarettes, collecting the butts in a plastic bag. I didn't want to offend nature more than necessary by smoking, and I didn't want to offend Joel by leaving cigarette butts, since his job was, part of the year, to collect the trash of ill-mannered tourists.

"We'll make it," Joel said. His voice was reverent and his face was pale. "You know all about bailing, and if I yell, 'forward,' throw yourself forward. I hope you don't mind my sounding like giving commands. I just figure it's best that . . . ."

"Command away," I told him eagerly.

"I don't want to scare you either," he said. "We'll make it just fine." Pause. Smile. "Or else this is famous last words."

As we approached the bend with the raft, Joel stood up, looked ahead, then sat down again to have better control of the oars. Then his yell. "Forward." We were surrounded by water from all sides. The raft hurled headlong into waves, stood almost upright, despite our forward weight. Then we were flat on the water again, rocking through turbulence. We were drenched with ice-cold water. But the sun was warm and there was hardly any wind to chill us.

I leaned back and shook water from my hair, my poncho. I watched Joel. He was still concentrating. His arms pressed into the oars. His eyes were filled with reverence and love for the water, full of attention. Black and glittering. Strongly at one with the elements.

I was spellbound. He was so beautiful. The magnificence of his eyes. I couldn't stop staring. Suddenly his eyes shifted and he looked straight at me. His face relaxed, his eyes turned into a smile of pure love. I returned the smile. I was completely in awe of him at that moment. I respected deeply. I felt as though our souls touched directly in greeting. And if it were possible for me to love a man, I would have loved him. But I no longer believed I could.

We stopped for a rest after the rapids. I went for a walk to find a river stone I had promised to bring home for Kay. I also wanted to find a nature gift for Audrey, whom I had promised nothing, and to whom I longed to carry everything. At the foot of a tall boulder on the side of the hill I found the stone I felt was hers—dark gray with pink stripes in a pattern that reminded me of snakes. No matter which way I turned the stone in my hands, the pattern didn't break but continued in a laced fashion like a mysterious band of containment. I found a pretty pebble for Kay also. We resumed our journey in less turbulent water.

Respect for Joel, awe, and at the same time not loving him and his powerful beauty enough, were impossible to keep in balance for long. I had an eerie feeling that I should behave properly as long as we were on this river under his command, proper being defined as somewhere very close to calculated flattery and submissiveness. It felt like an archetypical command to be gentle to him and to welcome his tenderness as a gift. There was a yearning to call the constant reminders to be gentle and well-behaved simply love. And all the while I felt shame—this confusion was what I had complied with and had been enslaved by all my life. I also felt triumph. This was what I would be able to have, without lies and confusion, in only a few more days. Forever. All I had to do was be patient. With myself. With circumstances.

I tried to detach as much as I could, in order to anaesthetize the pain while picking at the old wound of confusion again, trying to cauterize it while hoping for the cessation of its throbbing.

Yes. I learned. To see the sacrifice I had embodied for years. And the sacrifices I had made out of others in turn. Myself sacrificed to my own confusion, and others sacrificed to its consequences. But I made a valiant attempt at defending myself. I had not created this confusion. I was born into it. And so I learned also to forgive. And to ask for forgiveness that, in order to learn, I had to make for myself an example of myself and of another human being, a man. I was spooked by that, and I hoped, childishly, that my need for drama wouldn't be punished by humorless powers who would judge my need for self-knowledge a wild transgression of all propriety.

True, I once nearly did fall out of the raft, a surprise dunking as we were already coasting quite safely toward our journey's end. Joel held on to me until I regained balance. I felt as though I were churning myself, and Joel in my wake, through all the drama of the war between men and women. But there is no taking without giving.

I hoped I gave him some knowledge as I took mine. I hoped his soul would forgive me for using his willingness to be with me as fuel for my drama.

§

I forgot to think of the forgiveness from Audrey that I should also have prayed for. In spite of the strained quality of our parting, I somehow assumed that she knew what I was going through, and, even more importantly, that she knew why and that she supported me.

When we returned from the river to human habitation, my first wish was to call her, to tell her I was safe. It was difficult. Joel's trailer had no phone. There was a pay phone in the middle of town. A rough-looking man spoke endlessly, showing no signs of stopping. Joel had dropped me off, and returned for me after twenty minutes. I hadn't been anywhere near the phone yet. I didn't want to make a nuisance of myself and followed Joel back to the trailer, trying to be meek and accepting, but gritting my teeth and boiling inside.

This only resulted in my becoming a nuisance in spite of myself. I stomped out of the trailer finally, while Joel was offering me ice-cream as a consolation for the call I hadn't been able to make. Ice-cream! When I was nearly hysterical. Wanting to let Audrey know that I was safe. Hoping that she would care. Wanting, most of all, to hear her voice.

I found a motel. With no public phone. But in my determination I fought myself through to an office phone which I used, calling collect, exposed to odd looks from management, which for once didn't bother me.

I was stunned by Audrey's voice. Her lilting. Hello. My rejoicing.

"Audrey! We're back from the river. Safe. I wanted to let you know. I miss you. I'll be back in a few days. Do you love me? Say that you love me."

She loved me. Her own trip had been nice. The animals were well. But moody.

"I suppose they miss you too, Andrea. And on second thought, maybe they're just pissed that I left them alone the entire weekend. They spurn me. Kora won't even bark at me, much less come near me, ever since I'm back."

"I'll fix that. Put them on the phone and I'll talk some sense to them," I said. Meaning, oh, Audrey, let me play with you. I miss you so. Give me any way at all into playfulness.

"Kora, come here! Neige. You too. Andrea's on the phone."

I admonished the two dogs to heed and love their mistress. I heard Audrey's laughter. How I loved her laughter.

"Wish I could come back right now, Audrey."

"So do I."

"See you Saturday. I love you. Please love me." Begging.

"I do, darling. Come home soon."

§

Joel had to go back to work during the day. I rode on time. Thinking of Audrey. Thinking of Joel. Doing laundry. Wandering around town aimlessly. Dwelling on my future, yearning for it, virtually slurping it into the present. At night I slipped into Joel's arms. His roommate had obligingly cleared out for the occasion.

I didn't want to have sex with him anymore, but I felt compelled to by my own sense of fairness. It was the world I had been raised in, as a stranger to myself and to what I really wanted. Treating others, and especially men, as guests whose preferences had to be accommodated at all cost.

Sometimes I'd fall asleep in the trailer listening to music that pulled me out of my ache and guilt into forlorn lyrics. Songs of loss, and homelessness, and of despair.

I wanted to be back home. I whispered the word to myself. Home. As though I'd never had a home before. I also wanted to be normal, or at least appear so. I didn't want to appear ungrateful for Joel's welcome and for Joel's hospitality. I felt trapped. I felt my beautiful dream turn into rubble. I was vulnerable to everything in me that commanded, "Go on, degrade yourself."

The days faded away. I felt my energy sucked out of me and felt a puzzling kinship with Joel because he was young and as lost as I was in the world. He sensed my vulnerability. He tried to heal it by making love to me.

I couldn't sleep at night. One entire night I listened to a woman's voice at the other end of the trailer make man-appreciating cries for what seemed hours. I listened to my own discomfort in her bird-like voice. I saw her the next day, thin, shy. She had a small girl with her whom I managed to befriend. Did the little girl also lie awake and listen to her mommy's cries at night?

I liked Joel. Immensely. Waves of the intensity of my feelings on the river returned, when I had watched him with absolute awe. But I exhausted myself with confusion, with shame and with guilt, with impatience and yearning for Audrey, and also with the fear that she might not be there for me when I returned. Now that I knew.

Knew what? That I loved her? I had known that before. I was ashamed that it had not been possible for me to know without playing to myself this pompous drama of farewell to all men, while risking Joel's feelings, my own, and hers. I called her twice more. She said she longed for me. But her voice sounded tired. Distant.

I had one beautiful evening, two nights before my departure. Joel was invited to go kayaking with two friends. He wanted to go. Was that all right with me?

"Sure."

"We'll spend tomorrow and Saturday together," he pleaded, with himself more than with me.

"Only make sure you get me to the airport in time on Saturday," I said.

Suddenly it turned out he hadn't thought of my leaving as early as Saturday. Somewhere he had lost a day. Now it was out of the question for him to go with his friends, he said. He'd stay with me instead.

"Why?" I asked. There was nothing special for us to do. Most of all, I wanted him to choose the river over me.

"Because you're leaving so soon," he said. "And the river stays."

"And so do you," I said.

Joel went with his friends. They drove into the mountains where they would be able to follow a particularly beautiful stretch of the river downstream in their kayak. I went along part of the way, impatient for the luxury of being alone. I sat down on the side of the hill under a bridge by a crossroad, midway between where they would first put their kayak into the water and where they expected to end their trip.

I dreamt myself into a trance of Audrey. It was wonderful to be alone.

A future spread before my eyes like the shimmering ribbon of river before me. Now that I could come to her, cleansed of all the male-identification I had acquired early in life, there would be twenty, maybe thirty years for us to be together. Ten thousand days. If possible more. I wanted to live every single day of them close to her. I was breathless with anticipation.

All this was interlaced with my presence in a world to which I felt I didn't belong anymore. If I ever had belonged there. Now, not only didn't I belong, but I also had the joy of knowing I was leaving, even though I still had to pay attention to this world, to see its presence glide by like the river, to listen to its words.

Joel, at some point:

"I'm afraid if I come to your city again, you'll be too busy for me with your friends. You'll have found someone you love and who loves you as you should be loved. And you'll be too busy to see me."

"I hope I'll never be too busy to see you. I always want us to be friends. But, yes, I will be with someone I love. I will be. . . ."

"Don't tell me," he said quickly. "Not now."

Our last night. The final embrace, the final sexual contact in my life with a man. My body compliant. My mind filled with joy. My heart said farewell with gratitude for gentleness. My entry into this heterosexual duty of being had been brutal, and the continuance of it had many sharp edges of brutality. But Joel was gentle, and I wanted to thank him for that in silence. I did not have to run into Audrey's arms with wounds or for refuge.

I held on to his arms after making love that last time.

On the way to the airport Joel surprised me with the gift of having listened far more closely than I had thought. Out of the blue he began telling me of two lesbians who had lived with him as roommates once. No reference to me or Audrey. Just the memory and the unspoken connections.

"I lived in a house in Arkansas. They wrote and asked if they could live there with me for a while. I was gone much of the time anyway. They were beautiful, and there was so much love between them. They didn't need men for anything, least of all me. But I lived on the fringes of their love which flowed over into everything they did. I was happy, and honored to be so close to their love. Some of my friends thought it was strange that I would let them live there with me. Some of the people I knew even looked down on them, and, as a consequence, on me. But I admired and respected them. The few months we shared that house was one of the most magical times I can remember living."

I felt his words like a blessing. He had, after all, listened and heard my being. We could have spoken of so many things on the long ride to the airport, and he chose to speak of this particular memory.

There were dried flowers clipped with a clothespin to the glove compartment of the car.

"What are those flowers?" I asked, still feeling warm with blessing.

Joel looked at them and smiled. "I picked them for you when I traveled through Texas in April. Unfortunately they didn't keep, so I wasn't going to offer them to you."

They looked miserable and touching. Dried flowers as farewell. "I will take good care of them," I said by way of accepting what hadn't even been offered.

We sat in a pizza parlor, eating and drinking beer.

"I'm sorry you're going. But only partly so. I know you'll be happy," Joel said. "Once, when I was on the river, there was a blue bird . . . ." Joel smiled, with a shadow of the magic I had seen on the river in his glittering eyes. He'd already told me that story once. He had been in his kayak out by himself. He heard a knocking behind him, convinced it was an illusion. When he heard it the third time he turned. A blue bird sat perched on the fiberglass, looking at him, spreading its feathers to dry. It rode with him for a short stretch, hopping this way and that to avoid the droplets the paddle splashed up. Then it flew away.

"I'm so happy you came," Joel said. "And that you let me show you my small world here."

My wanting to reply: "I'm so glad you showed me your joyous world. And that it was you with me under this particular gate to freedom. Thank you."

§

I sat in the airplane wanting to sing. Of tenderness. Of freedom. Of having been let go, like this. I felt lucky and blessed.

My heartbeat was all future. Audrey. Are you there? Are you also counting the hours, beloved? Now I have nothing left that stands between us.

I was in a fever of anticipation. We would have thirty years stretched out before us. Maybe. As long again as I had lived so far. And I was flying home.

Into all of this came the announcement of the pilot. There was a bad storm over Washington. We might be circling for a while. There was no way of landing now. Suddenly we were rocked roughly, then rose again above the storm, though not before we had seen lightning flash. Somebody screamed.

I worried about Audrey. I checked my watch. She would be on the road by now, or shortly. There was no way to get in touch with her except by believing that our minds could touch. Don't drive, Audrey, I prayed. Wait, dearest, till the storm blows over. And if you're on the road already, pull over. It isn't important that you meet me on time. It is only important that you be safe. I love you. Please be safe.

My seat neighbor nudged me. "Are you sick?"

I smiled and opened my eyes. "No. Do I look sick? I was simply trying to relax." Not specifying whom or how.

I turned my face to the window before beginning my amateur attempts at ESP again.

Lighting tore the sky. The passengers were restless. The captain announced that the plane was running short of fuel. We would fly on to Baltimore, either to refuel or to disembark, the final decision to be made once we got there. On schedule we would have landed by now. Instead we took off for Baltimore. I called the flight attendant as he passed my row.

"Are they keeping people at the Washington airport informed of our safety?"

"I don't know," he said with breathtaking sincerity. I wished he would have lied.

We landed in Baltimore but weren't allowed to leave the plane. After forty-five minutes we took off to return to Washington.

"That was lightning again," someone shouted.

"We should have stayed in Baltimore, for God's sake," another yelled. "At least we were on the ground."

The atmosphere among the passengers was electric too, now. Stormy. Pessimism like percussion in the background.

Three hours late we landed.

I acted thinner than ever as I squeezed past whomever I could. We rode to the terminal in a bus. Then the terminal.

Audrey. Her hair was shorter, freshly permed. Her face was intent, serious, then, seeing me, she smiled an exhausted smile. I wanted to cry. From exhaustion, from relief, from the depth of my love.

"Hi," I said softly.

"Hello, Andrea," she said. We stood still and looked at each other.

"Okay, so let's go and get your backpack," she finally said.

"I was afraid you'd be on the road in the storm," I said.

"I was. I guess we were all pretty frightened." She laughed. "The terminal bristled. Now everybody's tension is going to fall away. Way below normal. People are going to be irritated with each other left and right, without knowing why. They'll think it's because she didn't bring the kids, for example, or because he came in jeans and without even having combed his hair. But it's simply the aftereffect of all this fear."

We passed an unattended cage with a huge dog whining. Audrey knelt by the cage, murmured to the dog, then went off in search of the owner, came back, went off again. We didn't leave until she knew the animal was taken care of. Then we had to hurry. Her own two dogs were in the car waiting, greeting us excitedly when we got in.

§

I was exhausted. At every traffic light, not daring to distract her at other times, I touched Audrey to make sure she was there, was real. I complimented her on her hair.

"You like it?" she said. "It was about time to have it trimmed and put into some semblance of order."

She seemed new, different. Lovely, but as though ages had gone by. I wanted to hear what she had been doing. On the telephone it had barely been possible to speak of anything real.

"One thing I did," she said, "I went to see a psychic I haven't met before. It was fascinating." Suddenly Audrey was lively with memory. "Daphne said one of my closest guides is the spirit of a bear. She said in one of my former lives I was an animal trainer, and one of the animals was this bear. I trained the bear with love, not force, so that its spirit came back as my guide and to protect me. Which, Daphne said, is why I have such affinity for animals. Daphne said I have a complete balance of feminine and masculine traits. She was excited about that. So was I, of course. She said she'd never seen anyone so completely balanced. She said this about my creativity: that I would one day do my best work with words. Writing of some sort. She also gave me a word of warning, or caution. Apparently my muse is capricious and difficult. Sometimes she will go away for long periods of time, and then there's nothing I can do except wait until she comes back. But she always does come back, and then my creative powers are very strong."

It felt magical being with Audrey again. Having her drive me to her house. Hearing her words. Listening to her images. Being carried along on her belief that there are connections between us and the world of spirits and powers, whose world we are able to tap, and whose wisdom we are able to ask if we trust enough and if we make the effort to believe. I could picture her with the bear she spoke of, coaxing a mistrustful, wild, and fettered being into trust and obedience.

"I asked Daphne about you, too," she said. "I simply said your name. Andrea. She described you very well. She said this about you: that you're very independent, and that you need a lot of freedom in order to do your life's work. She also said that I was the one person in the world who had the strength to give you the freedom you need."

On an impulse I opened the car window, in imitation of how she had once shouted her joy into the world: "World, listen to me," I shouted. "I'm all Audrey's now. Forever!"

"What?"

"I'm yours, Audrey. Forever. I just wanted the world to hear."

"But do roll up the window again. The rain, you know. Not good for the upholstery."

I rolled up the window with a sigh. So much for appreciation of my exuberance. I wanted to hear more about what the psychic had said about the two of us, but Audrey didn't tell me more. I would have loved to hear our relationship confirmed, outlined, irrevocably promised and sanctioned by higher powers. But I was content to take the promise of Audrey's strength to give me freedom. I was happy. Tired. It was so good to be back.

"What are those flowers?" Audrey asked. I had clipped them to my shoulder bag so they wouldn't get crushed in their brittleness.

"Joel gave them to me. He picked them for me in Texas."

It rose like a shattering scream out of Audrey, a deep howl: "Can't you ever stop?"

I felt as though torn in two by the vibrations of her rage. I grabbed one of the dogs and put her on my lap and stroked her frizzy fur with trembling hands in order to be in touch with something whole, something trusting, something soothing.

"I'm taking you to your apartment," Audrey growled, her voice trembling and rough. I tried to speak but couldn't find a sound. I simply continued stroking the dog on my lap.

After a while I reached for Audrey's arm and said her name in a whisper.

"Don't touch me!" she bellowed.

The car swerved. I withdrew as far as possible to my side of the car and clutched the dog against me for comfort.

Suddenly Audrey began speaking in a deep, jarring, monotonous voice, cold like needles of hatred scraping down my skin.

"I'll tell you something. Years ago I was in this hospital. I had to share the room with another woman. She was crazy. She was full of evil. She wanted to kill me. She said so over and over. She was tied to her bed. She tried to get up to get at me. Every moment I had to watch her try and reach for me. Her hands inches away from me. And when I couldn't see her, I could hear her. Threatening to kill me. Or screaming at me in her mad voice. Trying to throw things at me. There wasn't anything to throw. But it was hell. Her voice. Her hands reaching. I called for help and no one heard me. Or if they did, they pretended not to. Nobody came. I had to stay there for two days. It was pure hell."

I was frightened. Feverishly my mind reached for connections, finding none. My hands curled underneath the dog, lifted her up to press her against my face.

"And that," Audrey said, "that was the only other time in my life I have felt hell as terribly as I've felt it this last week. I couldn't sleep. I couldn't do anything. Couldn't concentrate on clients or students. Nothing. All I could do was endure. Listen. Feel the madness come on me. Like that woman flinging shit at me. And that's what you're doing to me. Threatening me. Trying to kill me."

I shook my head. Audrey stared straight ahead at the wet highway. Her jaw clenched. Her eyes fixed with an expression of fear and hatred.

"And I do not want to die," she hissed. "I do not want to die. Do you understand that? Can you?"

I couldn't grasp what was happening. I was lost in the torrent of her words. It was as though all this happened in a world in which everything I knew was irrelevant, in which it was not possible to reach out with a human gesture to beg her to come back. She spoke of death, accusing me of bringing death to her. I was helpless. I had no words of defense against her accusations. Her anger cursed me to a place where only righteousness would have found the sounds that would have cried back peace. I didn't have such righteousness. I only had trembling.

I tried small noises. "I love you, Audrey. Please . . . ."

She flung their ludicrousness back at me, her high voice piping back an affected version of, "I love you, Audrey, please." Then her low voice shattered even the ludicrous in that. "Don't 'Audrey, please' me!"

A dozen times I began with a new phrase, a new way of putting into words my incomprehension, my plea for mercy. A dozen times she cut me short with some far more powerful phrase of fury and contempt. Peaceful city lights glittered around us, meaningless, irrelevant, nothing to hold on to. We crossed a bridge that meant we were already on the way to my apartment, not to her house. I did not want her to drop me off like this, rage unleashed and cutting into me, threatening abandonment. I was afraid that I too would turn crazy shortly, was crazy already, against my will and without any defense.

"Don't take me to the apartment," I pleaded. "Let's talk . . . ." I wanted to say, let's talk like human beings. But I stopped short of completing the sentence, not daring to imply that her fury struck me as anything other than human.

"I am taking you to the apartment."

I wanted to be out of this situation. To be where I would not have to believe any of what was happening. There were moments when I gave up, felt nothing but the dog's fur against my cheek, soft shelter from reality. Then I came back briefly with a fresh effort.

It was useless. I felt as though I were someone else, miles away, watching my body and my emotions go through this. And from that distance of ten thousand miles away, I merely looked on in helpless sorrow.

But body and emotions themselves were not allowed the luxury of distance from sorrow. They were steeped into this lava of agitation, trying to swim out of its burning, molasses-like mass.

Audrey stopped the car in front of the apartment building.

"Get out," she screamed.

I had to remind myself to move. I didn't want to.

"Get out," she bellowed again.

My dazed motions were too slow for her taste. She shrugged her shoulders, got out of the car, walked around, opened the trunk, took out the backpack, slammed it on the sidewalk, then opened my door. Her mouth stretched into a vicious smile. Her eyes were full of hatred. She grabbed my arm and tugged. "Get out."

Parts of me moved, obedient to her voice, until I stood on the street. I felt as though all blood drained out of me, down into the pavement, anchoring me in this moment with roots of blood.

I watched her jump back into the car. Watched the car. Drive. Away. Myself standing. Simply still. With sorrow. Exhaustion.

Audrey. Who could not hear me. Could not see me. Anymore. Pavement. Gray. The backpack. Green. The wish to draw, from somewhere, laughter. None anywhere. Light a cigarette? No. First get inside. Pick up the backpack. Yes, that's it. There. Pick it up. Go inside. Foot before foot. Key is somewhere. That's right. Fumble. All you need. Lights are off. Good. Kay not in. Better alone. Pull the string. Light on. Yes. Table. Three letters. From? Pull backpack into your room. There. Make coffee. Or tea. Something. Milk in the fridge. Good. No wine. Never any. Kay can't afford. Okay. Sit down. Your bed. Nice. Yes. Time to sit. Tear open envelopes. No. Don't want to read letters. Cigarette. Yes. Match. In the bag. Red matchbook. Audrey. No. She went. Away. The car. Yes. In the car. Bathroom. Oh. Mirror. Face. Tears. Wash it. Pretty face. Cool. Water. Audrey. Window. No. She doesn't come back. Sit down. Ashtray. Yes. Sit. Calm. Perhaps. No. Later.

Despair doesn't come a cappella. It comes with every instrument of emotion in the book. The violins of self-pity wailed thinly: "My God, my God. My Audrey." Solid percussion ego droned prominently: "Shit, this can't be happening to me." Self-righteousness piped in tremolo: "I love you, Audrey. I do not deserve your hatred. I have a good heart. See me as I am. See me. I am innocent. I love you. Can you not see me?" Shrill cymbals of fear rang on. Underneath, and above all, sang the rich flute of sorrow, knowledge, and true caring. She loves me. I love her. So? Percussion ego. She'll come back. She'll call you next week. But the flute still cared. Yes, but if so, how? With strangeness and apologies for this scene? Acting as though nothing happened? Ego. Let her. Let her carry her burden. Whoever screams loudest is wrong. Let her come and court you with apologies. Then offer yours. Soft understanding. Harp of harmony. Flute. But she loves me. Ego. And? Is that your responsibility? It only goes to prove my point. She can't do without you. Yet. Wait, therefore. Flute: No, she can't do without me. But I, too, love. She is wounded. She screams. It is I who must humble myself. Percussion. Give her that much power? As though she doesn't already have too much of it? You with your fits of pity and human kindness.

No, mostly not pity or anything of the sort. Mostly deep caring.

Wanting to reach out. And touch. And heal. I did not mean her harm. Therefore what she suffered from was not real. But she didn't know this. She felt the wounds were real. Therefore they were. And if it cost my pride—and it would cost my pride—I would reach out once more. I loved her more than anything in the world. Certainly more than my pride.

I touched the telephone. My hand withdrew in fear. I touched again. Dialed her number. The ringing. The sudden hope she was not there, I would not have to do this.

But she was there. She answered.

"Audrey."

"Andrea?" Cold, exhausted, yet somehow hoping for something. Or so I believed, whichever was then dominant. Ego or caring.

"Please let's talk about this."

"What's there to say?"

I didn't know. Just let our voices glide. Talk to each other. Let our voices meet. Audrey's voice, dazed, far away. My own voice answered. Didn't matter what. Her voice grew calmer. My heart beat hope. Her puzzled question:

"But you come home to me, and you carry a keepsake from Joel, a bundle of flowers. Don't you see? Don't you see what that means?"

"But it means nothing, Audrey. It means that Joel wants to remain my friend. No matter what. . . ."

I didn't feel the wrongness of this until her voice came across, shrill with contempt. "Well, good for you. Then keep him. Keep your precious friendship."

Bang. Connection cut.

Frantically I dialed her number again. We had been talking. That was good. She had been on the point of understanding. I had to get through her fury.

"Audrey, listen!"

"I don't want to." Bang.

I dialed again.

"Audrey!"

"Leave me alone!"

The next time I dialed, the phone was busy. I called a taxi. Out in the street again. Sometime around midnight. Gave my directions. Distraught.

"Just let me get out right here."

In the middle of the night. In the middle of Wilson Boulevard. Near Audrey's house. I'd find it better on foot than helping the driver figure out this maze of one-way streets. I knocked on her door. She came to open. Looked at me with anger. Narrow eyes.

"At the risk of being a burden," I began with my much rehearsed phrase. "I've got to talk to you."

"I'm on the phone," she said.

"I'll wait."

She left the door open for me so that I could come in and returned to her phone call. I stayed outside on the steps to the house with fever licking my bones. She didn't make me wait long, although time at that point was hardly a reliable concept.

"Come in," she commanded.

I went inside and stood by the fireplace, flicking my cigarette ashes in it. For once she had no ashtray on the table. The dogs jumped around me wildly at first, then lost interest in my pathetic non-response to their joy.

"Sit down," Audrey said. But I couldn't yet sit down. I wasn't yet sure whether it wasn't better to leave again. Just go away. Consider my mission failed. I stood still, taking a drag from my cigarette from time to time.

"So what have you got to say to me?" she hissed.

"Not much," I said. "I simply wanted to tell you that I love you."

I began to see that coming here had been a mistake. Desperate grasp of a desperate heart. She was so cold I could get neither through that ice nor through her anger. "Now that I've told you, I guess I'll leave again."

I turned to walk to the door. She lunged for me and pressed her arms around me, not in a loving way. She squeezed me so hard that I couldn't move.

"Oh you! You stay now. And talk."

Slowly I shook my head. "I thought I could get through your coldness and your bitterness. And your indifference to me. But I can't. I must go."

"I'm not cold. I'm not bitter," she shouted, yanking at me. "I am furious. Do you understand? Furious! At you. Indifference? I can never be indifferent to you. I can hate you. Love can turn to that. But not indifference. Not you."

"I don't think I can bear your hatred," I said quietly.

"You will have to!"

I tried to push against her arms to free myself. They cinched strong and hard around me. I turned my head to the side and began to cry. It was as though I were watching, from far away, something in me beginning to die. The fragment of an illusion, as well as its inexorable death, pushing, straining toward its shattering. An illusion called innocence. An illusion called gentleness. An illusion called harmlessness.

I did not want it to die. It had been so pretty. It had been my mask to others and my mask to myself, my theme for nearly thirty years. I saw it slip away. I wanted to hold on to it, but there was nothing left to put my hands around. No little girl was there to hold up a torch of peace with a charming face and golden-haired enchantment.

Audrey loomed before me, her anger reminding me, her pain

reminding me, and those parts of her that had compassion also reminding me. The love I brought to her was spoiled for her and both of us could not bear this.

We went to sit by the fireplace, the dark cold hole of winter's fire, and talked to each other until the early hours of the morning, battled each other, wounded each other and healed each other. Then we went to sleep. Dawn was already reaching out.

§

The publication reading for my book was scheduled later that day. I dreaded it, for I could neither laugh nor cry anymore. So how was I to read to any audience? But I did remember to ask Audrey to set the alarm clock. Something in me was amused at such attention to detail despite all despair. We stretched out next to each other and reached for each other's bodies to sleep in closeness.

"Look," Audrey suddenly said in a voice where bewilderment of fear and pain were mingled. She raised her left arm and made me touch a hard lump in her armpit, twice as thick as the finger with which I touched it. I drew in breath with the sudden fear that caught me.

"When did this happen?" I asked.

"It grew last week," Audrey said, her voice gritty. "It simply started growing, and I just sort of watched. And it kept on growing."

"Have you seen a doctor?" I asked.

"Not yet."

"Will you? Next week? As soon as you can?"

Audrey nodded. "I guess so. I don't want to. I keep hoping it will go away."

I made her promise. Somehow, knowing full well that I was giving her the right advice and that I would have to insist on her taking it, I still couldn't shake off a strong feeling of shame within myself at not having the powers of healing at my fingertips as readily available as I had the powers of wounding. My Audrey, I thought silently, sadly, and helplessly, as I moved close to her side and laid my arm around her to hold her in my sleep.

The alarm clock was merciless with its reminder of reality. I wished I could simply fall back into my pillows and dedicate this day to Audrey and myself without venturing out into the world. Waking up around noon, with the thickness of exhaustion in my bones, the staleness of unbrushed teeth in my mouth, and the terror of the night before dancing in front of my eyes like a magic lantern of a malevolent kind, was hardly the proper state for poetic dedication. Difficult to immerse myself in the requisite intimations of immortality when my gray face stared back from the mirror, with bags under the eyes and the eyes themselves red from all that crying. I looked at Audrey's face, adorable in its matching pathos. Her body stumbled for balance in this new day while her eyes laughed beneath wild sternness. Her mouth whispered an endearment, then recommended the ludicrously simple measure of taking a bath.

"Though I loved the way you smelled last night. All sweaty and dirty from travel."

I was too exhausted to get caught up in any of the ordinary nervousness otherwise part and parcel of a poetry reading. I was unable to gauge what quality reading I delivered that day. I remember mentioning far too often that I was distraught on account of just having returned from a trip. The landing, I told my audience, had been frightening, in the middle of a heavy storm. Audrey and I exchanged knowing glances. I had to take care not to look at her too often, so as not to burst out laughing while I painted colorful renditions of my dreadful landing.

When the reading was over, we stepped out of the building into a fair ground with a fair in full bloom, the festivities dominated by a carrousel with old-fashioned animals, horses, lions, even an ostrich.

The first horses we picked to ride, on account of their color, weren't the ones which, in addition to going round and round to jingling music, also bobbed up and down in place. There was only one solution, to get back in the ticket line and ride again, this time on painted horses that also bobbed.

Audrey and I looked into each other's eyes. I watched her lean back, her arms extended like a dancer's, the polka dots on her sleeves fluttering.

§

Before the week was out we decided that I would move into Audrey's house. On Tuesday we carried the typewriter.

"That means morally I've already moved in," I said.

Thursday we talked to each other a dozen times on the phone, trying to decide which of us would tell Kay. Audrey finally volunteered.

Kay came to meet me for lunch. I first saw her on the other side of a downtown intersection, in a blue dress, smiling. When the traffic light changed and we met in the middle of the intersection, I saw she had tears in her eyes.

"Andrea!" She was happy for me. Sad, she said, for herself. "Who will warble soprano solos in the shower?"

I grimaced.

"I was at Audrey's house one night last week when you were gone," Kay told me. "I turned and looked around me, and I had this burst of thought: Soon Andrea will be living here. I just didn't know how soon."

None of us had known. It was barely three or four weeks since Audrey and I had first cautiously mentioned the possibility of living together and seeds of desire had been sown.

Speculation from the more somber side of reality: Did we both think we were doing the other a favor? Speculation continued: Did we both think we were doing something entirely for the sake of the beloved other, ready or not? I wanted to be with Audrey. Audrey wanted to be with me. I was at her house more than I was at the apartment. It would feel good to put an end to my vagrant life. Do I have all I need for the next two days? Notebooks. Damn, there's the letter in the top drawer of my desk that needs to be answered, but what the hell, I'll be at the apartment again the day after tomorrow.

And so, on Saturday afternoon Audrey came with her van. I packed my belongings in less than two hours. A few boxes. The wonder at how few things I owned. And even so, there were already too many things. I scurried past Audrey with a collection of empty wine bottles in a box. Shamefaced. Too shamefaced to escape notice.

"Look, I don't want you to know what I'm carrying out, Audrey."

Suspicion on her face.

"Okay, Audrey. They're empty bottles, from the days when I was a closet drinker in the truest sense of the word, you know. Would you like to see the bottles now?" In spite of the aggressive tone of voice, the shame deepened.

Audrey shrugged her shoulders. "So? Who hasn't gone through that?" Understanding. Blind, or from experience? Anyway, I was at last rid of the bottles.

Another private moment of carting things to the garbage room. This time I was able to conceal them from Audrey. They were small enough. Joel's flowers. Dry, miserable, and accusing. Audrey's voice cutting into me a week ago: "And then you come back carrying his keepsakes!" Joel's voice in the car: "I meant to give them to you, but obviously they haven't kept very well." My flattered pronouncement: "I'll take good care of them." And now my fearful laughter at myself. I used to be someone who prided herself on keeping promises.

Well, some things must change, I told myself. Such rules were all very well when I had only myself to consider. Now I chose to consider one I loved also, and no matter which of the ancient rules got violated, I would not carry detested flowers into her sacred house. Let this then be the first symbol of the many changes I was ready for. Green, rusty rim of dumpster yawning open for the flowers. So. End of strict adherence to old rules of my own making. How did it feel? I silently apologized to Joel. All right. I hated the deed. I loved Audrey. There, that was done.

We carted box after box into Audrey's van. Enough to work up a sweat, but not much in terms of a dowry.

"When I bought the van, I thought I needed it for a different reason. But this will do, this will do," sang Audrey. "Oh yes, this will do very well. Carrying you and your belongings home."

A passing fantasy of hers had been to drive around the country as an itinerant portrait painter. "And I very nearly did. I had already decided not to renew subletting the office. Made all kinds of plans for saying goodbye to students and clients."

"Audrey!" My own cry of relief, mixed with untasted potential of despair, metallic threat to my heart. "It would have been lovely for you, of course. But I wouldn't have met you!"

"Well, I stayed, darling. I stayed. Look at me. I am here. I am yours."

Audrey ran up the steps to her house and turned around spreading her arms: "Welcome home," she called down to me.

There had never been a place for me that felt so much home as did this house already. What had I ever called home? Three continents that I had lived in, together with their assorted rooms, their designated, borrowed corners. A little girl walking around with schoolbooks strapped to her back, blinking up into the sun: I don't really belong here. I suppose I must stay a while. They seem to think I belong. Later, weaving dreams through city streets, knowing perfectly well I had fallen from some star to be of comfort to someone on earth. After that mission was accomplished, then I would be able to return to my star. Teenage years, passing groups of young people hanging out in the park, strumming guitars, but myself merely passing, envious and yet too proud to ask to join. In recent years the occasional moment of having my eyes caught by the soft light from some window, my heart touched, but my body passing by. Now: Home. My heart beat in recognition. If Audrey was nothing other than the great enchantress who made me feel this illusion of home, then all I could think was: Thank you. I had longed for this feeling all of my life.

I stopped in front of the painting of Serena. How I had tried to tempt Audrey on that first night we had seen each other to leave me the painting. Lend it to me for a while. Her brief hesitation, followed by her decision that she had to take her dragon home after all for varnishing.

"She wouldn't leave you with me," I whispered to the dragon. "So I simply had to come live with you."

We had used Serena to communicate, especially in the beginning. "I'm in love with your dragon, Audrey. Will you tell her that?" "How wonderful. She'll be delighted." "It's easier falling in love with a painting than with people. People are the pits." "Isn't that the truth?"

One time in Oregon, when I had walked by myself, I saw in every cloud the shape of a dragon, the shape of the love that protected me. Serena.

Suddenly Audrey stood behind me. I turned around and looked at her beautiful eyes. Did I have to tell her about my private communications with her dragon? I didn't think so. She held out a glass of champagne.

We put the boxes in my room. I practiced the sound, "My room."

We mingled my skirts and blouses with hers in the closet. "Now they're all here," Audrey laughed. "Your dresses and mine. But we'll need a dresser for you."

For the time being she cleared out part of hers in the bedroom. For the time being we mingled everything from socks to underwear and T-shirts.

"I wouldn't have believed that I would ever let anyone put her underwear next to mine," she rejoiced.

We drank more champagne in the kitchen. "This is your house now!" she exclaimed. "Say it. Say, 'my house'."

I shook my head. "Our house," I finally said with some effort.

One doesn't come home and instantly lose all habit of traveling and having nothing to call one's own except the body and a few choice rags to cover it, as well as the mind and pieces of paper to spill it on from time to time.

"I wanted to have the whole house cleaned up before you came." Audrey pointed with her foot at a ball of dog hair lying on the carpet in the living room. "I wanted everything to be so perfect. But there wasn't time."

"What do we need perfection for?" I teased her.

"I like perfection," she said sulkily. "Still, the important thing is that you're here. At home."

Even as few possessions as I prided myself on owning, moving them always revealed how many more of them there were than I really cared to be responsible for. All that baggage of past. We were tired that evening, and lost and happy.

Audrey laid her head on my shoulder before falling asleep. "In four or five weeks, darling, you'll be settled. Then you can begin writing," she mumbled contentedly.

Her mumbled words coursed through my tiredness like electricity. Four or five weeks? I'd wanted to start immediately. How could I possibly bear to be away from my writing that long without growing restless beyond tolerance? How could I survive being away from my journals that long, from my stories, my poems?

"What's the matter?" Audrey must have felt my arm stiffen.

"Nothing," I said, then amended, "Yes, this." I explained the core of my impatience.

We laughed about it, and underneath the laughter, our eyes held pity and compassion for my dilemma.

§

Living with Audrey turned everything that had been trouble or effort before into a sort of magic. Chores became mixed with delight. Doing the dishes at night with tired bones, remembering Audrey's touch while handling the ceramic. Disgust with dishes from the night before still in the sink, and scrubbing them with love so that she wouldn't have to. Tiredness mixed with dreams. Daily tasks were wrapped in blankets of bliss.

She never asked me to do anything, much less our dishes, unless the spirit moved me. But move me it did. How could I bear having her get up in the morning to face more imperfection than was absolutely necessary?

Going shopping was an adventure. Taking the garbage out on Tuesday nights was an adventure. Putting books on the shelf she had cleared in my room was an adventure. Not writing was an adventure. Getting dressed in the morning, slowly reassembling myself for the day, while listening to her hum melodies was an adventure. I made sporadic entries into my notebook, with a wish to stretch the day, just half an hour longer, and a wish to be able to concentrate.

Hardly anybody intruded on us during the first days of living together. I treasured being alone with Audrey. Our neighbor on the south side, our first visitor, stopped by once to borrow something and called half an hour later to say that she had never seen Audrey so beautiful before. Ah yes, we knew we had the golden energy of belonging, the promise of growing strong enough together to let the power spill over on others, for inspiration, challenge, and comfort.

Soon the things in Audrey's house began to mesh with the things we spoke of, weaving into my consciousness a whole web of being, feeling, seeing. We would sit under the blue and yellow geometry over the headboard of the bed, blue shapes lining a wide road beginning at the bottom frame of the picture, and from there narrowing off into a mysterious distance.

"One day we'll go up there together," Audrey said.

§

"You never speak of your family, Audrey," I said because being with her reminded me very much of family things, seed images of home, waking up in the morning, watching my father and my older brother at the breakfast table, my mother rushing around, myself just sitting in the corner, watching, savoring the smell of hot chocolate that my mouth forgot to drink with all the fascination of home and purpose going on around me.

Whenever I received letters from my parents these days, I received them with a gentle, grateful feeling, and the wish to feel free to tell them how I was beginning to build a home like theirs now too.

Audrey, however, didn't seem to have much contact with her family. Sometimes I looked at the small family photograph. An old-fashioned truck, the father tall, virile, the mother with an intent expression on her face, something between defiance and scorn, looking straight into the camera, but her eyes dull, as though a heavy weight pressed down on her lids. Two brothers. A sister. Audrey herself, small, pudgy, the youngest. I wanted to be in that picture somehow. Maybe as a blade of grass.

"Yes, my mother is still alive," Audrey said. She told me her mother was in an institution and not doing well. Audrey had gone to see her a while back, and found her paralyzed, listless, a vegetable compared with the vibrant woman she had once been.

"She doesn't say anything." Audrey blinked. "I've offered to help her. Financially, for instance. She won't accept. I don't even know whether it's pride or simply apathy."

I was convinced that we would both go to visit Audrey's mother some day and manage to bring her joy. Then there was Audrey's sister. I had always longed for a sister.

"Were you very close?" I asked starry-eyed.

Audrey laughed. "Only when we banded together to stand up against my mother. Sometimes she'd completely forget about us. She'd leave us at some street corner in Los Angeles. 'Wait for me here,' she'd say, and we'd wait and wait and wait. Meanwhile it would be the middle of the night, and we'd begin wondering whether she had in fact forgotten about us once again. So of course we had to rely on each other. We wouldn't have any money or anything, so we'd just walk back, miles and miles and miles, the two of us. It took us six hours one night to walk home."

§

Under the blue and gold geometry of the bedroom ceiling we exchanged our vows one day.

Audrey: "Tell me that you'll never go away again."

"I will never go away again."

"Promise?"

"I promise."

"Forever?"

"Forever."

"Not for a single day?"

"Not for a single day."

"Except . . . ," I said sheepishly two minutes later. Audrey fell back onto the bed laughing.

"Except what?" she exclaimed. "In your mind you're already leaving me again."

"It's not that I want to," I protested. "Back in January I promised my boss that I'd housesit for him in September, and that I'd take care of his dogs. How was I to know I would fall in love with you and therefore be unavailable?"

We decided that this was a promise which, in the new hierarchy of things, I wasn't bound to keep. As difficult as it might prove to be for me to assert myself against authority, I would give notice that I couldn't housesit after all. If he couldn't find anyone else, then Audrey and I would take it upon ourselves to find a replacement.

§

We made elaborate plans, all generated by Audrey. I privately planned quietly to withdraw to my room and write world literature. The public plans were these: We would paint the ceiling of the bedroom dark as night and decorate it with bright stars, and, perhaps, a moon. The important thing would be the stars. How would we get them to glitter with our mortal resources? And then, how would we get ourselves to glitter to match their presence?

Soon I discovered, in snatches, that there was this possibility: to live our own legends in imagination. I'd stare at Audrey's paints in the studio, Audrey herself concentrating, for the time being, on her golden dragon. In my mind, however, she presently became the itinerant portrait painter which, a while back, she had wanted to become. I saw her travel in her van which, in my imagination, became a little more old-fashioned than the one standing outside in the driveway with all its modern contraptions. She would set up her magic tools, a combination of dramatic things as well as the dramatic energy in her nerves, her arms moving in the magical fashion that would endow canvas and color with a dimension beyond mere matter. I could imagine a portrait of someone taking shape. I was still in love, for instance, with the magnificent face of the old woman hanging over the fireplace. Veins drawn so refined that a light seemed to be shining through her features. I could imagine the model, exposed to Audrey's eyes for the duration of the sitting. He or she would not merely walk away with a fresh portrait under one arm, but also with a piece of enchantment. A process of pure magic captured there. As for myself, I thought I would make a perfect backdrop for Audrey in all that magical activity, the mysteriously silent blond creature in the background, lovingly regarding the scene with huge, soulful, melancholy eyes.

"Hey, Audrey, next time you dream of going off somewhere as a portrait painter, let me come along. I'll be your apprentice, fetch things and so on, and together we'll become a legend. You the magician. I some kind of silent background muse."

Again and again I would imagine us like that, on the road, resting in one another's presence, and for the outside world conjuring up a ritual of magic. Until then I could always watch her paint in the more ordinary privacy of our present surroundings, for example the three gladiolas I had bought her recently so she had something to practice with when she said she was at an impasse with her golden dragon. When she painted, I was theoretically free to retreat to my own room to write, but often I stood in the bedroom door instead and watched her. I hoped some day she would ask to paint me.

In my mind the images merged, and pretty soon there was one predominant picture in my mind, made up of Audrey, the painter in the studio, Audrey the gypsy painter on the road, and Audrey the bear trainer whom her fellow psychic had seen. Gypsy, artist, and animal trainer. There was yet another merging, the male vision of

Audrey, suggested by the psychic's verdict: she's the most perfectly balanced male and female person. I saw her spread her arms, her face taut with concentration, as dragons sprung from her canvases and bears rose on hind legs with complete trust. I wanted to be part of this picture that was filled with so much tamed wildness.

Sometimes, when I was at home alone, I stood in front of the mirror, fancying myself a gypsy girl. I would put on two skirts, one on top of the other, and admire in myself the perfect counterpart for my beloved's energy, dressed in colorful skirts, seeing the shadow of her love behind me, proud, powerful, and yet tamed into tenderness for me.

I asked her questions. "Audrey, do you remember the time when you were an animal trainer? Can you see it?"

"Oh yes," she said with an enigmatic smile.

"Was I there?"

"Oh yes. You lived in a stone house. I came to see you."

She told me in that segment of reality we loved each other powerfully, but not yet perfectly. That's why we lost each other somehow. Meanwhile I had no further problems believing that I had truly lived before, even though I still could not come up with even the tiniest vision or memory or awareness of such a time. The images Audrey gave me from her own visions became part of mine. I imagined myself in the window of a house, blond, radiant, consumed with love for her, yet aloof somehow, and thus failing her love, as she in her darker gypsy pride in turn failed in her love for me.

We promised each other this time we would not fail. This time we would master our love, and thus become free from the destiny that returns all lovers to earth again and again, until they complete their understanding of each other and their love. It seemed like a commendable task to complete what we had, according to Audrey, tried and failed at many times before. Now, holding on to each other's arms, how could we not be filled with confidence that, this time we would succeed?

"What were we like when we knew each other then?" I asked, riding on the beam of my imagination.

"As lovely as ever," she teased.

"I mean, was I a woman then? A man?"

"You were a woman." Audrey looked at me with far-away eyes, as though remembering. It made sense. Standing in the window, waiting for my lover—waiting, a woman, always waiting in a stone house of forbidding conventionality. Waiting for my lover to come. Surrounded by the pressure the stone walls exerted all around me.

"And you?" I asked." Were you a man or a woman?"

"I was also a woman," she said. That surprised and delighted me. I could no longer imagine her as anything other than a woman. A courageous and unconventional woman, training animals when I was still waiting in a stone house, weakened by the stone culture which had refined me.

I was confident that in this life I had the necessary courage. In this life I would have the strength to stand by her, and to stand by my love for her.

§

Yet in this life I also found myself short of courage in lots of ways. Our new life together was not a continuous and uninterrupted stream of bliss. Rifts slashed between us. Doubts. There were thoughts we carried when we were apart, and there were fears we could not share even when together. I don't know what dark areas of her mind Audrey had to navigate on her own. I had glimpses of them, but the darkness I learned to battle with was strictly my own.

She would come home from work, exhausted, sat across from me at the table, poked at her food with chopsticks. Stared at the red place mats. Then suddenly she shook her head, put on a shy smile, a sparklingly arrogant air of laughter, trying to make light of it all.

"I can't believe it. Jealousy. I hear nothing but jealousy all day long. Everywhere I go. Left and right. As though there is no other theme left in the whole world. Jealousy."

I poked at my own food by now, could barely swallow. I was afraid to talk, with Audrey of all people, about jealousy. I remembered, with constricted throat, sitting on the airplane, heading toward Oregon and Joel, with the pompous generosity of feeling: I am learning to accept and to respect her jealousy. After this, there will never be cause for her to feel jealous again.

"And I can't stand it anymore either," Audrey said in sing-song voice. "Everybody does the same. Remember the gay couple I told you about the other day? Well, one of them came to me last week, complained about his sudden inability to get it up. So we fixed that. I found him a metaphor. Think of an umbrella opening when you want to get an erection. Andrea, it worked. The metaphor works for him. He can get his erection again. He can have his sexual intercourse. And you know what he did, Andrea?" Audrey's voice escalated into a crescendo of indignation. I didn't dare look at her when she continued. "He went out and had himself an affair with another man. Went out and cuckolded his lover, just because, oh, joy, he suddenly could again."

"He turned promiscuous!" Audrey screamed at me while I still stared at my dinner plate, then at hers. On both of them the food turned cold and gelatinous. The judgment between her spoken words was that I was henceforth personally responsible for all jealousy in this world, and for all cuckolding and all betraying of unsuspecting, righteous love. If I had incited her mind to be preoccupied with nothing but jealousy through my actions, then the responsibility for that fever in her brain was indeed mine. Whether I wanted it or not. I did not want it.

I wanted to give Audrey my innocence. I did not have any innocence to give. I tried to manufacture innocence. I couldn't pull innocence out of my sleeve or hat. I couldn't fashion it craftily out of thin air.

I loved her, and I wanted innocence and purity for myself, so as to be able to give them to her, only to realize that I didn't have either.

I woke up from a dream of Joel one night. It was a dream of farewell and it made me very sad. I called out his name with longing in my dream, and as I woke up, dream images were still so vivid that, for a moment, I didn't know whether I had called his name out loud or only in my dream. Cautiously I turned around to look at Audrey. She slept, though fitfully. Suddenly I remembered her enthusiastic face a few days ago, as she told me, "Oftentimes people who have a special connection will dream each other's dreams, even when they are miles apart. Maybe someday soon I'll dream your dreams."

Not this one I hoped. Carefully I took her sleeping body in my arms and placed my cheek against her cheek. She mumbled something in her sleep, returned the pressure of my skin against her skin for a moment, then drifted away from me slightly, although she stayed in my arms.

§

My body decided to play along in my education. I missed my next period.

I had gone off the pill as soon as I had finished a cycle after coming back from Oregon. What a relief from an enslavement to hormones that would keep me from bearing the children of men with whom I was not prepared to raise children, or whose children I wasn't prepared to raise by myself.

Now a missed period. It wasn't that it had never happened before and that each time the matter had been happily resolved a few weeks later with the familiar blood between my thighs. Now, however, it happened in conjunction with Audrey's jealousy. I couldn't talk to her about it. I couldn't talk to anyone. I was alone with this worry. Every time Audrey pronounced the word jealousy, I felt the knife point of exactly how alone I was.

The pain of feeling guilty, asking nonetheless, with ardent prayer to a deity I normally didn't address, that life produce the proof of innocence.

Two weeks after I missed my period, the true creeping began. I didn't know about home pregnancy tests, so I went through the phone directory on the sly. Who could give me a cheap and effortless pregnancy test? I couldn't go to my regular doctor because my medical plan was part of a clinic which, as one of its unpleasant side effects, had lengthy waiting periods even for scheduled appointments. One might be scheduled for ten o'clock and be lucky to finally manage to see the doctor at a quarter to one. What if Audrey should call me at the office while I was at the clinic? What if she should ask me later on: Why were you gone? Where were you all that time?

I remembered a clinic run by women two blocks away from my office. Years ago I had accompanied a friend there when she needed an abortion and someone to sit with her for comfort.

I called and got instructions. Next morning I slunk to my study from the bathroom, hiding my first morning urine sample, secured in a drug store bottle and wrapped in several plastic bags. Then I sat with Audrey through breakfast. I nearly choked on my vitamins. She had me petrified with fear. Nevertheless I managed to smile and go on my crooked way.

"Call after two o'clock for the results," a woman at the clinic told me.

I spent the morning in agony. Of course I wasn't pregnant. But what if I was?

Damn columns of numbers. How was I supposed to concentrate on typing? Twice I talked to Audrey on the telephone. The wonder that she couldn't sense my fear across the miles. The suspicion that, perhaps, she could. And then what was it that kept her from dashing me further down into this despair in which I was already, but perhaps not as deep down as I was capable of going? Yet. No way could I be pregnant. But what if?

Two o'clock came. Slowly I reached for the telephone. Was anyone in my office listening? How could I ask? How should I phrase this? Would they manage to be discreet on the other end? If the answer were yes, then what would I do?

I dialed. The quick respite of a busy signal at the other end of the line. A trip to the lady's room to smoke a cigarette. Returning, dialing again. Busy. Typing a letter for my boss. Trying again. How again was I going to phrase this?

"I had a lab test done this morning and I am calling for the results."

"Just a minute."

My nerves congealed and became solid pain, solid trembling in the process, as I gave name and date of birth.

"Got it. Your test was negative. But it says on your chart here that the date of your last period was seven weeks ago. If you don't get your next period within two weeks, you should have the test repeated."

"Thank you."

Relief. With just a small drawback. This was not the end. This was really nothing more than a respite. Two weeks. Then all of this might begin all over again. But for the time being, preliminary joy, gratitude, relief.

On the way home from work I exuberantly bought a bunch of flowers for Audrey. Chrysanthemums. At least for a while now I could show her my enthusiasm without feeling the absolute weight of duplicity on my shoulders. I wanted to dance with her that night, dance my relief under the guise of untroubled joy. I wanted to play and sing and dance with her for the next two weeks straight. Then, if doom was necessary, I would face it. For now I had two weeks.

The joy was short-lived. Fear has its own life, like a monster corrupting joy in its path. Everything I touched seemed tainted with a guilt which I myself found hard to understand, and harder yet to live with. What had I done? I had not willingly harmed Audrey and never would. Before we had ever really gotten to know each other, I had fallen in love with a young man, and I had promised him to go and see him at such and such a time. Then I had stuck to my promise. It had seemed all right to go and say goodbye, it had seemed ingenious to make an extravagant statement to myself concerning the end of my life of deferential relationships with men. But the specter of Audrey's anger and the guilt it whipped up in me was stronger than any reasoning.

§

Right in the middle of all this, Toby called one day. Surprise. Haven't heard from you in ages. Ought to have dinner some day. Well, sure, why not? Perhaps this was my time to venture out into the world again from my seclusion with Audrey.

When I told Audrey of my date with Toby, she wasn't pleased, so I quickly offered to call up Toby and ask if she could meet with us for dinner, too. Toby, for his part, didn't like that idea. He wanted to talk to me alone and mentioned he was a little overawed by Audrey from the two times he had met her. Audrey in turn said she wasn't surprised at all that Toby wanted to see me alone.

"I don't even particularly want to go," I told her. "But if I don't, I'm putting you in charge of my life."

"And? Would that be wrong?"

"Yes, because I don't know where it would end."

"Go then," she hissed. "I know, by the way, where it would end. In bliss. In paradise. But you don't want that. You want freedom to be with men."

She was wrong. Her idea of paradise would have ended with me becoming a doll, and her losing interest, and we would both have failed.

The night before I was to meet Toby, we went to friends of Audrey for dinner. We sat outside in the garden. Laughter fell on my ears like a distant thing that belonged to others. My mind was heavy with Audrey's mistrust.

Suddenly Audrey shrieked. All of our heads, in the darkness lit by candle flames in jars, turned simultaneously. Audrey had already jumped the fifteen feet to the vegetable patch where the house cat was in the process of attacking a baby bird that had fallen out of its nest. Audrey must have seen some movement to pinpoint the scene of trouble so quickly, so exactly. Now she stood there, baby bird in hand. I could hear its faint chirping. For a while she just stood like that. The men were making jokes about the situation. I wanted to somehow hold Audrey in my own hands, protect her and shield her from the pain of the warm wingless bird body in her hand, as well as the pain of the careless laughter assaulting her.

I grew sad with the knowledge that shielding her was impossible. Later, at home, I watched her try to feed the bird with a mash of egg and grain we cooked up, and she held it out to the bird's eager beak on a toothpick. Time and again the tiny beak would open with longing, exposing the wide pink lining of the mouth. Time and again the toothpick with egg mash would be offered. Time and again the bird rejected the manufactured food.

"It's too frightened," we said. "We'll try again later. We'll try again tomorrow morning."

Audrey took the bird to work with her. Even that didn't seem to be enough.

"I don't know if I should take it at all," she said sadly. "It'll only be a further shock to its system, riding in the car. But I can't leave it here by itself. It's so small, Andrea. I want to save it. It's so small."

During the day she called me several times. No, the bird was still not accepting food. She would go back to her friends' house in the evening and try and see if its parents would accept it back. It might be possible. She would simply try. She would hang up the basket and wait and see if the parents would go near it. And of course she would continue to try and feed it with pap at home. Put vitamins into the food. Simply keep trying.

Meanwhile Toby called. He couldn't make it to dinner as early as we had planned. Could we do it an hour later? I said fine. When I spoke to Audrey again, I told her I would be at home around nine o'clock.

"What?" She was furious. "You said you'd be home at eight."

"Yes, I did," I said. "But Toby couldn't make it as early as he thought, and so everything got pushed up an hour."

"I don't like this," she said. "First you say one thing, then another. I can't rely on what you say at all."

"I'm sorry, Audrey," I said. "It's merely a change of plans."

"Change of plans, change of plans!" She hissed.

I was just about to suggest that I cancel all plans with Toby, when Audrey said coldly that she would see me a nine o'clock, or else thereabouts, stressing the word 'thereabouts' to emphasize her mistrust and contempt, and then hung up. We did not speak to each other again that afternoon, and I duly, and a little listlessly, made my way to the bookstore café where I had promised to meet Toby.

I waited outside and watched him swagger up the street. When he too saw me, he spread his arms with Prince Charming flair and held them out for the entire block he still had to walk toward me, which he walked slowly and with total consciousness of effect.

"Well, how are you?" he asked loud enough to be overheard by anyone who had even the faintest interest in observing this charming tableau of two old friends meeting.

"Fine," I said. "You? You look good."

"So do you," he said with rare generosity.

We threaded our way through the bookstore and sat down at one of the tables outside.

"Well, what have you been up to?" His smile, designed to be endearing, looked disturbingly vacant. This was all wrong, I thought. Why was I here at all when I would be better off with Audrey? But I stayed.

"I fell in love since I last saw you," I mentioned, studying the menu. "I believe I've met my soul mate."

"I'm so happy for you," he said. "Who's the lucky fellow? Do I know him?"

"It's not a fellow," I said. "I'm in love with a woman."

Toby dropped his wooden cappuccino stirrer, then picked it up again.

"Hm," he said in a small voice balanced between confusion and suppressed laughter. Finally he regained control and looked straight at me, his eyes warm and smiling. "Well, I'm certainly not prejudiced," he said forthrightly.

"Didn't think you were," I reassured him with a broad smile of my own.

Finally, when there was no more question of suppressing uneasy laughter, Toby asked, "Was I that bad?"

Well-phrased under the circumstances, for all I could on the spur of the moment answer to such a question was a plain, "No."

When what I really wanted to say was, hey, Toby, this has nothing to do with you. Despite the fact that you're pretty enough to pose for cigarette commercials, you don't come into the picture at all.

"Is it Audrey?" he asked.

"Yes," I said.

"I'm not prejudiced in the least," Toby repeated. I remembered the dropped stirrer. "That's something I had to deal with in my last relationship too. Rosalie. You know, I already knew her last fall when you and I were together. She's almost twice my age. Black."

He proceeded to tell me at great length how very special she had been. Brilliant, had authored a book on politics. It sounded painfully familiar. I too had been special at some point.

Rosalie. Turned out the poor thing had been a washout for Toby, too, and they had broken up. His choice of course.

"You know, when I last saw her, she swore that she would always be after me. 'Hon,' she said to me, 'if I'm ever around you anywhere, you can bet your sweet life that I'm going to seduce your sweet ass!' She was really stuck on me."

I saw helpless gloating on Toby's face as he repeated Rosalie's words. He was almost touching in his boyish pride, but shame trumped compassion. For all he knew I was still stuck on him too. I felt embarrassed that I had let this situation, even this dinner, happen in the face of incurring Audrey's anger, in the face of risking her already shaky trust in me, in the face of her sorrow about her dying baby bird. And all that merely for the sake of my own ego insisting I needed to have and see friends. Friendship? With this asshole?

"Well," I said, checking my watch. "Nice seeing you again, Toby. I better get home now, though."

He said goodbye to me with a smirk, suggesting that he understood I had to jump whenever my lady said so.

On the way home I was depressed. I walked up the steps to the house. Neither Audrey nor her car was there, though the porch light was on. The basket in which she had carried the bird around with her all day hung from the porch roof, empty.

I was filled with premonitions. I call her friends' house and asked for her. Yes, she was there. She came to the phone and spoke to me in a small, aching voice. Well, had I finally made it home? Yes, the bird had died. She had just buried it. She'd stayed on, not wanting to be alone at home.

The accusation of my having gone out was never spoken, but I heard it all the same. She said she'd stay another half hour. No need for me to come over to meet her. I didn't particularly want to. I wouldn't be a great comfort. Well, see you later.

By myself after the phone call, I played back her coldness, the distance and the tiredness in her voice.

I wanted to cry out. It wasn't my fault that the bird had died. Nothing was my fault. But no one was there to hear my self-defense. I was tired also, exasperated. And envious of Audrey's purity. Here I was in the throes of a human depression, woven together from all kinds of factors, not the least of which was Audrey herself with her unsettling jealousy and possessiveness. I wanted comfort. Instead I was faced with no comfort at all, but only her far more reputable sorrow, which made my little depression pale by comparison. She, my loved one, had a death to grieve over. The death of a bird which her fragile imagination sanctified. Whereas I had only the misery of human life and its sordidness.

I went to pour myself a drink. Why must she be so pure, and I so sordid with my ugly little human woes?

By the time she came home my mind was bearably fuzzy. We hardly spoke. She asked me how my evening had been, sounding as though she really didn't give a damn. I told her "depressing." She shrugged, clinging in silence to her purer sorrow. Clinging, perhaps, also to a few shreds of contempt for me.

I found a piece of paper on the living room table the following day. Was I supposed to read it? It described Audrey's struggle for the bird's life, her sorrow that she was so powerless to help it, and that it was so small, so fragile. That it had addressed a nerve of responsiveness in her, of power and of hope, and then it had undone everything by dying. That it had not been able to trust her enough to accept nourishment from her. That the will to life in her had no power over the fate of death around her.

I cried for Audrey, her sorrow, her helplessness, and her defeat, and also for her loveliness.

Then I cried for myself. Other peoples' sorrows were a dangerously vulnerable place for me. They typically counted more than my own. I didn't know how this had started, or where, and if it would ever end, this guilt in me for crying over my life when there was always someone with a more valid pain. The laughter of, "Well, what if you have no God? There are those who don't even have bread." Or, "So what if someone was unkind? There are those who have to bear far greater misfortune with grace." Or, "What if people mock you for being female? There are those who don't have the luxury of being merely mocked."

Gradually, over the weekend, Audrey closed the distance between us. We had sparkling moments, and every time her heart seemed light, I forgot the difficulties that existed between us, as though every day were a fresh day to live without memory of what went before, as though every smile of hers were the original smile, and as though she too were capable of accepting every gesture of love from me as a new thing, a sunrise that didn't contain the failures of the day before. Her mouth formed words: "This cannot be said in words, my dearest one, my beautiful one. It simply is." My mouth agreed with a kiss.

Audrey had once said that the two of us were part of that portion of humanity that didn't run away from pain but rather ran toward joy. A minute distinction in the movement, but very important for those who were doing the moving. Sometimes I wondered, though, if we weren't lying bravely to ourselves about the direction we were running. I certainly felt imprisoned in concepts of sorrow, in a life lived according to semantics of stern suffering. How could we affirm joy, describe it, live in its language? And ever again the same conclusion: the language of sorrow had the larger vocabulary by far, and the heart of sorrow had the greater wealth of detail.

Sorrow in so many colorful nuances. With the insecurity of my would-be joyous heart, I was constantly prey to the fear of losing love. My fear muddied the love I had only just found.

§

Kay called me at the office. "Hey, chief! I want to see you. And there's a package for you from Joel."

A leap of joy in me. I met Kay at her office and started unwrapping incense sticks. I remembered the night Joel and I visited the house of one of his friends whose house smelled of the most beautiful incense. I had asked her its name, already thinking of it as a gift for Audrey for the house. What a beautiful gift. Only, in my insecurity, I now didn't feel entitled to bring his gift of joy home openly. Suddenly, in the middle of downtown Washington, in the middle of Kay's office in which, fortunately, at the moment no one else was present, I broke down crying.

"My God," Kay said, wrapping her arms around me, surprised at the sudden flood of tears. "Andrea. What's the matter?"

I pulled myself together and began to tell her of the terror of Audrey's jealousy, of my insecurity in the face of it, of the wheels it set spinning into some direction of destruction. And I could see no way of stopping it, except by love and by strength, praying that those would be enough. How it undermined me. If I couldn't believe that I was innocent, as I had once believed, concerning Joel as much as concerning everything else, then how could I have the strength to cope with what was attacking my essence? So strong was the undermining power that, even as I talked to Kay, my friend, I grew suspicious of myself, wanted to check myself. What business, after all, did I have to talk in any negative way about Audrey whom I claimed to love? It was no one else's business if she was jealous or if there was anything between us that wasn't entirely bliss. Was it my own ego, or Audrey's, that I wished to protect? And what difference did it make?

Kay suggested I ought to consider moving out and not living with Audrey for a while. I was stunned. Didn't Kay understand that I loved Audrey, everything included? Had I spoken so unlovingly that Kay instantly thought I would be better off away from Audrey? Couldn't even Kay support me and understand me without questioning the value of my love?

Suspicious of myself, I soon grew suspicious of everything around me. I carried suspicion home with me as well, in the guise of a loving smile that fell flat after working its momentary magic. I smuggled the incense into the house surreptitiously rather than with the pride of joy with which I would have preferred to bring it, and only casually brought it out later on to give to Audrey, "Oh, by the way, look, a friend sent me this for us."

Audrey and I ended up in an argument. She grabbed the bronze top of her coffee table in anger, aiming it at me, then reconsidering. She lost her grip. The bronze fell on her foot. With a scream of humiliation she fled to her studio and locked the door. Half an hour of pleading later, she finally let me in, having withdrawn to a chair in the corner again, where she sat investigating her big toe which was already turning purple.

"I love you," I shouted at her helplessly.

"I love you too," she mumbled.

We put ice wraps on her toe. I fixed something to eat, which Audrey consumed in bed. Then she read quietly and I lay down beside her, pretending to read likewise. I couldn't take in a word, though. I watched her from the corner of my eye, and if I didn't watch her, I held her in my mind. The miracle of being with her. The miracle of being close to another human being and to go through this upheaval of emotions, and yet loving so strongly that I was not tempted to run away.

Suddenly she put her book away and said, "I hope one of us will always have the sense to say a word of love, and to wait out whatever else happens. Storms. Anger."

I hoped so too. We were close that night, nursing each other's love, each other's guilt, each other's wounds. According to her words, all I would have to do was to remain steadfast in my love for her. All would be well if I could only always be sure to find the words of love.

Before it ever approached healing, Audrey's toe became blacker. Sometimes she laughed about it, called it a casualty of love.

§

Toe notwithstanding, we went to the beach for the weekend as planned. She picked me up after she was done with her one Saturday morning client that week and we started off in her van. I was already familiar with its precarious fan belt which had broken the weekend before and threatened to give us trouble again. I was already familiar with its use as transporter of my limited belongings from one place to another in one single trip. Every once in a while I looked back at its roof that looked, for the time being, like any old van's roof.

"You sure we can sleep up there?" I was skeptical.

"You'll see," she sang.

I began singing a song I had recently composed for us. The words weren't my own, only the melody. Ancient words of women's love for each other, variously preempted later for men's purposes. "Whither thou goest I shall go. Your people shall be mine, and your

God my God." I remembered sitting in an Irish house years ago, reading the only novels that were available, and finding this phrase spoken by a women to her man. Words of loyalty. I heard the strange echo and immediately felt a sense of theft. Futile to argue with a book, though. The important thing was that I had reclaimed the words. I sang them over and over. "Whither thou goest I shall go. Your people shall be mine, and your God my God."

A few days ago I had written them, together with my melody, into Audrey's music book that she had just bought. She had started singing lessons. She hadn't found my writing yet because I had put it toward the back of the book, wanting her to find it someday by chance during one of her lessons. Now I regretted that it was quite so far back in her book. It would take a long time for the remaining pages to fill up with musical notations before she would finally come upon it.

Crossing the first bay bridge was thrilling. I hadn't seen the ocean for so long.

The first campground turned us away. No space left. It was beginning to get dusky. We were hungry, too. At the next campground we got a space and canceled all feelings of deprivation. The place where we had to register served simultaneously as the counter for the general store. The clerk was finishing a sale.

"Peanuts and three lemonades. Will that be all? That'll come to a dollar and eighty-five. And you, do you need an electric hook-up for your van?"

"No," Audrey said, then turned to me. "Or do you have your typewriter along? She's a writer," she explained to the clerk. I burst into laughter and shook my head. "No electricity then," Audrey declared.

A little while later she got to demonstrate to me the as yet hidden mysteries of the van. With the crank of a handle, she raised the roof. This, miraculously, turned the remainder into a bed. All the mosquito nets and white lace curtains for comfort and privacy were in place. I climbed up and down half a dozen times to investigate the magic and then got ready to take up our sheets and blankets, at which point Audrey finally stopped my enthusiasm.

"Don't you want to go and get something to eat?"

"Yes, of course," I said naively. "But then when we get back, we don't have to bother with all this anymore."

Audrey laughed out loud, at which point I managed to synchronize realities again enough to realize that our temporary house was also our only mode of transportation, and we couldn't very well drive all over the place with the roof of the van raised like this. Not only was it possibly unsafe, but probably also against the law. I climbed down and after a few moments we had an ordinary van again.

Audrey wanted to take me to a restaurant she knew from previous trips. "Once I came here," Audrey told me with glittering eyes, "and I ordered a whole quart of their crab soup and took it away to my motel room in a plastic container. Then I sat there all night, eating the soup straight out of the container and reading a book."

"Do you miss that?" I asked.

"Miss what?"

"Being alone like that. Doing the luxurious things one does when one is alone? Spooning soup and reading books all night and feeling on top of the world?"

Audrey smiled a dream of memory. She shook her head. "No," she said. "It was beautiful. But I don't miss it."

I looked at her with guarded admiration, masked in spirited conversation about art and our future life together. She had been alone much of her life, though also apparently oftentimes not. She had lived for fifty-two years learning this life. How much she touched me with her courage.

I was inspired by her vivacious presence. I was happy to be at the ocean, to eat with her, to scribble poetry on place mats, just to be with her. Fleetingly I thought of other people's energies. I typically got entangled in their commanding energies. I politely halted mine and then invariably found my own energies dwindling. I listened to others until I could no longer listen to myself.

This was different. Audrey's presence simply heightened awareness. The rims of the mussel shells that lay empty before us on our table became tangible, white, brown, and black with smooth sharp edges, just because I was with Audrey. Her essence broke open ancient knowledge in me, dressed it in vivid colors, or else washed old colors free of all protective coating of gray. There was nothing to protect from Audrey. She had no intention of taking anything away from me in order to distort it.

I jotted an old poem on the napkin, one of the first I had written. A sunrise at the ocean. Many years ago in an Italian village, at four o'clock in the morning, I went to the edge of the ocean with my father. Dawn was about to break. We looked for shells. "Suddenly a secret trembling. . . ." I tried to remember the rest. Other lines of other people's ocean poems came into my mind. "The sea is calm tonight, the moon lies fair upon the strand. . . ."

"Let's go and take a walk along the beach," she said.

The path to the water led through boardwalk jingles. Ice-cream parlors were still open, filled to capacity with teenagers sporting sleek longing and blaring radios. Their hearts beat with the sounds of promised love and romance, no doubt. Sharp edges of energy among them. Pizza places, youngsters sitting on the steps, girls with long tresses of luscious hair. The loud smell of beer. Gift shop windows. A couple walked past. A child trailed along on his father's hand, raptly listening to the father's sonorous words about sailboats, while the mother's eyes turned to the windows. She obviously wanted to stop, but realized she might as well give it up. Daddy and son weren't interested in such things. Her lips tightened with acceptance.

Then the beach. Desolate. A few shreds of plastic fluttered on the sand. Debris of a day of sunlight. The sand just lay there as though longing for the return of people, taking on a life of its own. Not ugly. Merely neglected. The wind blew through the darkness. The sounds of the boardwalk behind us came through as a whisper.

Water patiently licked at the sand, spilling its endless white foam. Again. Again. Again. Gathering. Crowned. Then sweeping down like a gesture of homage.

The gift of the ocean at night was solitude. We were alone. No one could see me holding Audrey's hand. We were invisible. Standing together. Cool wind stroked our hair, just like it stroked the waves. But we could still look up and see other human figures through a spray mist of distance. I let go of Audrey's hand and started a game of stepping as close as possible to a receding wave, daring the ocean. Spill out your water again. See if you can catch me with your tongue of water. In this game, inevitably, there was always gleeful defeat, wet shoes, socks, and feet. I took Audrey's arm. Come, race with me. Then I let go again. I headed up the slippery wood of a small pier, straight into the extension of the shore, where water swirled beneath the solid footing of planks. A playful wave broke over the wet wood.

"Audrey." I turned and ran toward her, giggling.

Her answer breeze of mist. "I can't walk very fast tonight. Much less will I run, Andrea. My foot, you know."

I caught my breath. "Oh my God, Audrey, did we walk too far already?" I had forgotten about her foot.

"It's all right to walk a little," she said. "Come on."

We went farther. Wounds of our human condition. Audrey's black toe. The table in the dark house crashing on her toe because she didn't throw it in my face. I wanted to kneel to her. Not, however, in the wet sand. I didn't have a great desire to find more sand than necessary later on in the washing machine.

I loved Audrey. This time. This breath. This moment.

Then I stood still. My eyes wandered over the sky, the water, the beach. Human figures. The lonely erections of life guard towers. So much wind. So much fluttering. I turned my gaze to the ground. Look. A crab. Skittering toward the water. Washed away. I looked down at the water. The endless gathering and breaking of waves. The moon overhead, playing with the water. Creating a celebration of light for us. Audrey. Look. Oh, look. How the crowns of the water catch the light over there. Like a fine line of lightning, of fire. How the ocean spills them out for us like garlands. Let me put my arms around you. Like this. Yes, we can stand close together like this, even we, two women loving each other. While the firebrands sear the water in silence.

Her hair was damp with mist. Her eyes were clear and steady against the rolling and swirling flutter of being. Could she see me too with her steady eyes that witnessed everything in motion? And could she love?

Could she really love me?

Two on the beach. For a long breath of wonder there was unity. But such unity fades with the return of ordinary consciousness. Was she cold perhaps? Were we walking too far? Could she bear my silence? And could I bear hers?

One of us said: "Oh, let's sleep standing up here at the beach. Please!"

The other one, regretting not having taken the opportunity to speak first, now having to take the sensible part: "After we've already paid for a lot in the campground?"

"You're right. After all, why collect a sizeable parking ticket for abandoning the van in the middle of the town square and sleep without shelter when we've already paid for shelter?"

We wandered back the way we had come. From time to time we

turned to stand still, to look back at the light on the water. Soon we lost the angle where the light of the moon and the light of the lamps hit the water for the exact magic of shimmering garlands. We walked up the modest incline to the street where we found the van.

Audrey rummaged in the icebox and found us two bottles of beer. "Not as cold as the term icebox would suggest," she said.

No. I both wanted and did not want to have a drink just then. It would help me sleep and I needed sleep. There had been so many impressions. They would keep me awake for hours, and there was the next day which we wanted to spend in the rare luxury of doing nothing at the beach. But I knew having a drink would make me feel heavy. It would make me feel as though dragging the habit of city ways out here into this shelter of magic. I sighed and started drinking.

With a familiar fuzziness in my head, I helped Audrey change the van into a bedroom again, raising the roof, folding out the mats, tucking in the sheets. Laughter of mildly intoxicated satisfaction. What do we ever need a house for again? And could we not soon go on that fantasy portrait painting and poetry spinning journey through the country?

We climbed into each other's arms. I loved Audrey's touch. Her tenderness, the lightness of her fingers against my body, my excitable skin.

But just as the heaviness in my head took on the strongest effect from that misbegotten bottle of beer, Audrey's gentleness changed to wildness. She held me strongly with one arm, and with the other hand she began to imitate a man's love, pushing her fingers up and down inside me, strongly, wildly. I wanted to beg her to stop. Don't make love to me like a man. Please don't do that. Images of being fucked by men mocked my brain. The relentless ramming, withdrawing, making rough sensations without pleasure, now imitated by Audrey's hand, her eager fingers, eager for something, to give me pleasure. Not knowing that, like this, she couldn't. Suspecting, probably, and hoping, that, like this, she could.

I was thrown back to the old trap of silence, of not wanting to stop the illusion of one who wanted to give me pleasure and was convinced, or at any rate hopeful, that pleasure was what I felt. I did not want to speak, and yet I wanted her to stop. Don't touch me like a man, my Audrey. Don't. Oh, please don't.

I pulled away from her, but her arm held me strongly. My pulling away together with the moaning of not physical but other pain, the pain of memory, the pain of being abused, seemed to serve only to give her the false clue that I was growing excited and wild under her pseudo-masculine touch. I was trapped in my mind's baffled silence of despair. Moaning. Moving. Not speaking. Praying for her woman touch, but praying in the dumb bewildered silence that has not yet learned how words can be used for necessary prayer. Incredible, perhaps. But real. For the words of freedom were not yet born in me. Audrey. Please stop. Please love me like a woman. Stop trying to imitate a man. Instead, the shame of such reflections as, 'what if she truly likes to do this? Then I must love even that.'

So I stayed silent, sick in my mind. I bit into her shoulder. Hard. My teeth clenched around her flesh as though spreading and sharing the pain, as though helping my mind to wait this out. And all the time my heart was begging her to love me like a woman. My body was tired. And finally, lulled by its unshed tears, my body fell away into dull sleep.

By morning—bright, dewy, and full of bird twitter around our heads right underneath the branches of trees—the pain was all slept away. Privately I made a vow, rather habitual in its nature as I sardonically reminded myself on the way to the bathrooms, to stop drinking, and amended that vow quickly into the easier version of at least never again drinking beer, seeing that it only served to render me heavy and unhappy. Back at the van, I furtively inspected

Audrey's shoulder. My bite mark there seemed mercifully mild. With feelings of regret we dismantled our mobile bedroom. I felt sentimental about putting the sheets and mats away and pulling down the roof over our bed in which I had slept as close to the sky as I ever would.

It was a hot day, suitable for letting one's brain fry lazily, as every self-respecting woman deserves to do at least once in a great while. We went to play in the water. We lay under the umbrella we had brought. We went for a walk. We rubbed each other's skin with suntan lotion, celebrating with furtive delight this permitted public touch.

Audrey wore a violet bikini which made me give up on the book I had brought along to read. Instead I lay on my stomach with pleasantly sun-heat-diffused awareness and looked at her for hours. How beautiful she was. Her gorgeous woman body. So small, and bearing so much energy in every fiber. At times I closed my eyes and dozed in the sun. Once, when I opened my eyes again, Audrey knelt beside me in the sand.

"I'd love to kiss you now," she murmured.

"Well, do it," I said and watched her face pinch into a bitter sadness.

"There are people who wouldn't like that at all," she said harshly, as though accusing me together with the rest of the world.

A wave of disappointment flooded over me, because of her fear and my compliance with her fear. I remembered lying awake one night after a similar comment. The dogs had barked wildly. We had both gotten up to take a look and, if necessary, to protect each other. Checked a thousand times that the door was locked, that everything was in order. The almost guilty fear that, first of all, we were only two women. If that wasn't enough to challenge mankind to attack our vulnerability, we were throwing even greater provocation into mankind's face by being, on top of the fault of being women, so audacious as to be in love with one another. Guilty of being female, guilty beyond that, of loving that state of grace in one another. Guilty of squandering our energies on the sustenance of one another, rather than donating it, as society had established was our duty, to the greater glory of malekind. Lying awake that night and listening, close to three o'clock in the morning, to a helicopter cruising above our fear, feeling personally addressed, lying awake through the nightmare of fear: what we are doing is not what they like. The loud droning made the corners of the house vibrate, reinforcing all fear: they might be coming for us even now. We were sinners in the eyes of men. Though we had not slapped their faces, nevertheless, we took our valuable woman-energy (for men admit that some of our energy is valuable) away from them in order to devote it to each other. This was not what they liked. Beware. They still had all the power. Beware.

And now to see the shadow of that fear in Audrey's pinched face, to hear it in her voice. To feel it in myself.

Quick. Change the subject. Avoid remembering having seen this in each other's eyes. Avoid. Be happy. Withdraw into the solitude of secrecy. Yes, laughing with each other on the way home from the beach after a long walk, stopping in a public shower building. Neither curtains nor doors at the shower stalls. Looking at each other's bodies, naked. Soap in our hair, in our eyes, and on our lips as we kissed each other, as we danced in and out of each other's shower stall. A few places where fear couldn't touch us, because we were alone and protected. In woman territory.

We stopped at a road stand with fruit and vegetables and their specialty, double-yolk eggs.

"Well, yes," Audrey said. "Two yolks, you know?"

Suddenly the van began making noises unfortunately already familiar to us from the recent breakdown. It had to be the fan belt again. It was already dark. Would we make it all the way to Washington? Was the engine overheating? Let's pull off the road. Close to a gas station. See what we could fix. For though I couldn't drive, I had at least some familiarity with this particular fan belt problem already.

We were a good team. Audrey? Yeah. Start the engine now, let me see what happens. What do you mean?

Suddenly a large man lumbered down from a truck stopped behind us. Came close, leaned over the opened back of the van with creepy familiarity.

"Need any help, ladies?"

Those were his words, but his body distinctly said "broads." His eyes were not on the van at all, but alternatingly on my breasts and on Audrey's. Behind him another man, same size, same attitude, shuffled toward us.

"Maybe we could tow you."

Was there a double entendre in tow?

"No. We're fine. Just a small problem. We're fixing it."

Audrey, for God's sake, please get the van started. Let's get out of here. This is not woman territory.

One of the men grabbed Audrey's arm. "Let me give this a try."

Audrey slipped his hand off politely. "It's fine, sir. We've got it under control. Come on, Andrea. Let's get going. It'll work now."

Pray that it does. Pray that it does.

It did. Only after putting distance between us and the men did Audrey allow herself to turn pale. My hands were shaking. No words between us, only the pain of persecution meeting in each other's eyes.

Then Audrey's voice, half sobbing. "Jesus, I love you, Andrea. I never want you in that kind of danger."

An echo of sobbing in me responded with the knowledge of other dangers that we had already both lived through. The violence of the masculine world at its most forceful, at its most contemptuous. How could our suppressed sobs rise from so deep down within us if we had not already known the danger, faced it, run away from it, at times not fast enough to escape its mutilating energy entirely?

§

Back in the city. Back at work. Kay called me during the day, which needed a spice of some kind to get me through my nostalgic mood. I longed to be back at the beach.

Kay puzzled me with a question. "Is everything all right with you?" Then, after an affirmative answer, "Did you call me on Saturday?"

"No. I was at the beach with Audrey. It was wonderful. I haven't been at the ocean for so long."

"Hm." Kay tried to change the subject.

I steered her back. "Why did you ask?"

"The phone rang," she said. "When I answered, there was someone on the line sobbing, saying nothing, merely sobbing. I was afraid it was you. Which is why I listened to it for quite some time. I tried to get the other person to say something. Nothing. Merely the sobbing. And then a hang up."

"Oh, my God, Kay," I said. "Have you had other strange phone calls lately?"

"Not really," she said. "Every once in a while someone calls and then hangs up." Which wasn't that unusual.

We ended the spice of that strange conversation embedded in an otherwise dull day with lightheartedness. "Well, we'll either find out who phoned in those tears. Or else we won't."

§

Later the sweet cinnamon of Audrey's call. Laughter.

"Darling, I've got to tell you this."

It sounded important enough to abandon conscientiousness and business correspondence for a few moments. Besides, homesick for the ocean, I needed any and all cheer that came my way.

"Listen, I am wearing my light blue blouse," she said between splutters of laughter, her voice laden with significance. The blouse she referred to was a pretty, pleated, light-blue affair with a wide and fairly low neckline and short sleeves falling in a soft triangle over Audrey's lovely narrow shoulders. I called it her angel blouse and it now apparently revealed a love bite near the neck.

I tried to apologize.

"Apologies not accepted," she said. It turned out it came in handy in a session with a tragedy-filled client whose day went uphill starting the moment she saw Audrey's neck.

From then on, the rest of my day went uphill as well. I walked home from the metro stop finally, with the mild evening sun caressing my bare arms, coming around the corner of our street, seeing the van parked in the driveway. My heart seemed to skip a beat at the sight, then made up for it with a series of extra-fast beats. The knowledge that I belonged. The sweet certitude that I had a home, that I had a love. That in less than three hours Audrey too would be home from work. We could discuss her shoulder once more, and I could tell her about the feeling I had when turning the corner to our house.

The phase of feeling I belonged lasted until Thursday. Thursday was the night Benny and Sharon were to come over for dinner at our house, our first guests from my past.

What if the subject of Joel came up? He was still Benny's best friend.

We had already gone over Audrey's pain so many times since that first night after I came back. I was afraid I could not bear her fury once again. I made myself ill with fear. Added to that was that I was to have my follow up pregnancy test the next day. I was so alone in all this.

I wanted Audrey. I wanted her with all the freshness and all the innocence of my heart. Yet, wherever I looked, there was neither freshness nor innocence anywhere.

By the time I got home from the office on Thursday, I had worked myself into a frenzy. I dropped my bag on the floor in my room and made straight for the liquor shelf. Anything to soothe my nerves, to dope away my fears.

I stumbled over Neige's pink plastic ball in the kitchen and remembered to let in the animals and to go to the basement to feed them. Hi here, animals. I moved slowly, trying to slow down my fear as well.

Listlessly I arranged food and utensils with which I intended to prepare our meal on the counter. I was about to slice into the first eggplant, when I lost my nerve and sat down on the kitchen floor weeping. I looked at the red telephone on the wall until I had the strength again to get up and dial Benny and Sharon's number.

"Hi," I said.

"Hi," Sharon answered in her rich, warm voice.

It was an ordeal of politeness, mixed with my wild need to be let off the hook. I explained to Sharon vaguely why it was that I was disinviting them for dinner. No problem, she said, they had food at home which she could easily fix. She understood, she was not offended—didn't we have a long tradition of breaking dinner dates for any old reason in the book without breaking our friendship? And neither would Benny be offended. Only sad at not being able to see me. It had been a while. Did I want to talk to him? Not particularly. Anyway, hope you're all right, and I'll see you soon sometime.

Then I called Audrey. Hi. I just wanted to let you know. I asked Benny and Sharon not to come to dinner. I can't handle it tonight. I just can't. But that's all right, Andrea. Just as long as you're all right.

Hey, I'll be home soon, Andrea. I want to be alone with you anyway. Questions. Answers. And solicitude. Back and forth. Just wanted to let you know. It's all right. I'll see you soon. Take care. I love you. Do you? Oh, say it again. No matter what, I love you. I love you. Do you hear? I love you.

The wash of relief. The pilgrimage to another drink to celebrate relief. Until tomorrow's pregnancy test. And if that came out negative as well, then I could truly celebrate. Then I would gradually rebuild my armor of innocence which I had lost without noticing. But lost it was, for here was I, dragging myself finally to my room, sinking down on the sofa, then getting up again to rinse the glass. Ought to replace Audrey's vodka supply someday soon. Glass rinsed. Brush teeth. Again. Better. Drink coffee now, eat some cheese to hide the liquor breath. Sleep. Until Audrey is back. I'll be all right then. Fear. Can't handle. It'll be all right. She loves. Me. Does she? Oh yes.

When Audrey came home I woke up, but was exhausted, befuddled, sad, just barely awake enough to know that she was holding me, that she was humoring me, forgiving me, the whole nine yards. She was understanding, she was sweet. And yet she would not be able to go with me through the hell I was scheduled to go through the following day.

Was I pregnant? Of course not. I would never have a child. Would I be with Audrey for the rest of my life? Would we conquer the fear, its danger, her anger? And my anger? For there was that, too. Who was she to force me into this state of fear? My anger grew into nightmare visions. Babies flushed down the toilet, left in garbage cans. Knitting needles stuck up against the womb. For not much more than this. Desperate women clinging in this fashion to their chosen love, or to the myth of purity that was expected of them. What kind of a world was this that we lived in? Where even my Audrey could not live without being compelled by God knows whose myths to rake me over the coals of her possessiveness? Audrey who loved me. What, then—and where—was love in this world?

§

In this frame of mind I went through my second pregnancy test, the result of which put my practical fears to rest once and for all. But the procedure cracked me with its humiliating secrecy and loneliness, with the wedge it put between Audrey and me.

Once more I crept with my furtive bottle of urine from the bathroom to my room, to hide it in my shoulder bag beneath one of the notebooks.

"See you tonight, then, darling."

On the telephone, later: "Hi, darling. Well, no, nothing new since I saw you this morning."

§

All weekend long I wore smiles and excitement and danced around Audrey. Mind over matter? Peace over fear? We went to a bookstore in Alexandria. Enormous shelves full of forgotten enchantments. It had been months since I had finished reading an entire book. I was overwhelmed by the mere prospect.

"Will we sit together tonight and read whatever we get here?"

"Sure, if you want."

"I want."

The promise of a refuge I was so used to. Reading. Getting lost in other worlds, or alternatively finding myself in them. What should I choose to read to break such a spell of fasting from the written word? Suddenly I was faced with too many choices all at once, and with a nervousness in me that I thought I had long outgrown. Would she judge what I chose? Quick silent incantation. Mind over matter, peace over fear. Of course she wouldn't. She loved me.

I could never limp long in her presence. I looked up to see her stand by a shelf, hip braced solidly against the wood, a book in her hand, radiant. She was complete in herself, unshattered by anything I could do. So long as we were able to hold on to our respective completeness, we could be sane, and happy, and blissfully in love.

After a while she turned to meet my glance and whispered a bright "hi."

Hi, Audrey! Hi, carnival of butterflies in my stomach.

The book I chose, because it was on sale and I had looked at it once or twice in a distant past, and also because it was so deliciously large, a thousand pages or so, was Norman Mailer's Executioner's Song. Odd choice, of course. What would a macho-man's crowning achievement be doing in a lesbian household? There was my old joy-anger at Mailer to begin with. Ever since I first read him, I had hated everything he wrote, and loved the way in which it was written. If there was a God, how could He allow someone like that to write so well? Merely to inspire someone like me to write better? Small comfort. Nevertheless, I wanted to learn from the man's superior craft.

So there I sat later that night, fat volume of Mailer on the table, my hands holding the needles and green yarn with which I had begun knitting a sweater for Audrey. I was good at reading and knitting at the same time.

Within the predictable thirty or forty pages, the book began making me sick. Gary's attitude. Out of prison. Looking for a fuck, finding it. Meanwhile Mailer pontificating between the lines about the God-given man-approved bliss of just such a commodity. Nicole, the perfect Eve of a heroine. Cock-worn, yet cock-worshipping bitch. And all of this coated with the amazing sugar of the best writing, the best craft I had encountered in a long while. Precise, clear, beautiful writing. And then the vague discomfort closing in on me again. There was no method known to me by which I could read a book—or for that matter live a life—not personally.

The gorgeous writing drew me like a magnet. The contents unsettled me. If I had gills, they would have turned green. Furtive glances at Audrey who sat in her rocking chair, absorbed in a book on psychic healing. Hm. What if she were to look at the book I was reading and came to the conclusion that my reading of this book reflected an unvoiced desire on my part to be once again "in the company of men?"

Back to square one. The rage about Joel. And you, she might say. You constantly complain you don't have time to read, time to write, time to do anything at all. The first book you pick up is written by some goddamn male chauvinist and full of the glory of his hero's prick. Why don't you go back to your men? Why don't you go back to Joel? Whom you were so eager to visit in May?

Suddenly Audrey looked up from her book and laughed at me. I laughed back at her. Yes, we would master our respective fears. I saw the love in her eyes. And no book written by some male chauvinist idiot—always bearing in mind that he wrote like an angel—had the power to disturb our peace. We belonged together.

"Look, I have almost half the back of your sweater done," I said. "It's going to be beautiful."

The light in her eyes loved me. How little we knew each other, and yet how very closely we knew so very much.

§

Monday became a day of glory. I had gathered, from off-the-cuff comments, that Audrey was currently in financial straits. Amazing to someone like me who neither knew much about money, nor cared much, except to acknowledge how useful it was, and to be glad that I could always earn enough in one legitimate fashion or another. Audrey gave me hilarious lectures on the difficulties going hand in hand with making the so-called "decent" salary.

"The moment one makes over twenty thousand dollars a year, one begins looking for tax shelters, and even so, one gets into a great mess."

One year she had in fact jumped from making under twenty thousand to suddenly an impressive over forty thousand.

"When the time came to pay my taxes, I paid them, of course. And then I had to borrow money in order to be able to buy food. Now I'm doing much better. Now I employ an accountant."

Nevertheless, right now, tax time was on the horizon, together with an unexpected sudden demand for a loan repayment. Due to my usual frugality, I had something over three thousand dollars in my savings account. True, two thousand of them did not belong to me, but were in the nature of a long-term loose personal loan ("if you spend them, so be it; if you can repay me, so much the better"). Honor within me demanded repayment. But at the very earliest these two thousand would be needed in a year or so. It was pleasant to have them on hand already. Still, they were sleeping in my savings account. And Audrey needed money from somewhere. Why not make it easy and give her these to keep until next year? A two thousand dollar loan. And a one thousand dollar gift.

I got to the bank six and a half minutes before closing. The luxury of writing out a savings withdrawal slip for three thousand dollars and a deposit slip for the same amount into the checking account. Rich for one moment in life. I reached the teller three minutes before closing and endured the heavenward rolled eyes.

"You have to get his approved by a manager," the teller said in a reluctant voice.

Be glad to. But then it isn't my fault, is it, if I have to transact a few minutes past your closing time.

Transaction completed, I raced home. Wrote out a check to Audrey and placed it on the center of the table where she would eventually see it. Then I went about my business, humming, pretending hard not to think about it anymore.

When Audrey did come home, the check proved to be too invisible in its tiny blue shape on the center of the table. I had to manipulate her attention to it.

"Andrea," she shouted. "This is beautiful! This has never happened to me. That my young, virtually indigent lover should present me with the means of escaping debtor's prison."

"But I would have visited you," I said. "As it is, maybe next year we'll go together, and if we're lucky, they'll give us communicating cells."

I was being waltzed through the living room, the dining room, the bedroom, and halfway through the kitchen. There was a mixture of surprise and love in Audrey's eyes. Pride also, and happiness. It meant we belonged together. For wasn't it the most telling commitment to mingle finances?

§

I was looking forward to the long weekend of the Fourth of July. As always, I wanted to do everything all at once, read, write, be with Audrey, spend ten days worth of energy in the space of three days of luxury.

I still indulged in the perversity of perusing Mailer's book with the duplicity of admiring and despising it simultaneously. I was already two hundred pages into it. Thursday night I allowed myself the absolute of indulgence, staying up late in my room, reading, reading, reading, while knitting the sweater for Audrey. Audrey went to bed at ten.

"Wake me up, darling, when you come to bed."

"I want to stay up very late, though."

"Doesn't matter."

Midnight. I heard Audrey go to the bathroom. Then she stood sleepily in the door of my room.

"Andrea, are you still reading?"

"Yeah, does the light bother you? Maybe I should close the door?"

"Oh, no, don't close the door. I want to see your light if I wake up. I want to know that you are there."

"Do you want me to come to bed?"

"Um. No. Not until you're ready."

Three o'clock. I felt luxurious with the silent hours of the night in solitude. I resolved to do this more often for the benefit of my soul. It felt good. It was rare for a working person. Only on long weekends like this. It was refreshing, hours of pleasing myself, as though I actually were a woman of leisure, no matter that it was the middle of the night.

Quietly I extinguished all the lights, including the lamp at Audrey's bed, which she had left burning. Her curly hair on her pillow, her small face crushed with sleep. I tiptoed to my side of the bed and slipped in, maneuvering animals out of the way in the dark where they had nestled against Audrey and where, instead, I wanted to nestle now. She woke up briefly in the ensuing commotion. Dog bodies plopped from bed to floor. Cats climbed over her indignantly. When we were all settled again, she rearranged her sleep-warm head on my shoulder.

"It's late," she mumbled.

"Yeah," I whispered. "Go back to sleep. I love you."

"Much?"

"Very much." With her head on my shoulder I finally fell asleep, body and soul filled with love for her and the need for her closeness, her skin touching mine.

I woke up late and right into the calm before the storm. Audrey had been up early, burning for action, faced instead with a sleepy lover finally scrambling out of bed close to noon. What should we do to celebrate having the day off?

I opted for drinking coffee first.

"You were up really late."

Reproach?

"I'm sorry. But look, I finished the whole back of your sweater."

"I wish you would have been in bed with me all night." Sulking, mixed with desire and accusation.

"I'll be in bed earlier tonight." I wouldn't be able to sleep, since I just freshly ruined my schedule, but that didn't matter. If she wanted me in bed early, that's where I'd be. Early. I loved her.

But by evening the storm had broken loose.

"You don't want to be with me at all. Take last night. You were up forever. My God, how long you can stand it without wanting to be with me? You always want to do things separately. You don't care for my company at all."

Limp, unavailing defense. Followed by an appeal to sympathy. "It's just that sometimes I want to be alone. Don't you?"

Absolutely the wrong thing to say under the circumstances. The flames flared higher.

I withdrew to my room. Audrey followed me three minutes later with a bundle of my collected skirts and blouses gathered from the bedroom closet over her arm.

"Get out!" she screamed. "You want to be alone? So I don't want you to live here. You don't want to be with me. Take these and get out."

Wry mocking flared up over the fear inside me. "In the middle of the night?"

"I don't care. Just get out."

"Well, I can't. I don't have a place to go. I have to stay here. I'll close the door and you won't even know the difference. If you want me to, I'll look for a place tomorrow."

The doors shut between us. I cried behind mine. I opened it once, to see that the bedroom door was closed also. I shouldn't have looked. It tore something apart inside me. I shut my door again and cried some more. My clothes lay in a heap on the floor.

I waited until I heard her go to the bathroom. Took the opportunity to tiptoe over to the liquor shelf next to the kitchen, took a whole bottle of vodka with me in case I wouldn't have another opportunity for foraging. There. Alone. Abandoned. Angry. Desperate. I didn't have a place to go. No place to call my own. Not this, which was hers, regardless of the fact that I gave her half my monthly salary for rent. No place to call my own. I drank myself to sleep. How easy. For the time being.

Saturday morning we met with gray faces in the kitchen. Mutual apologies. I'm sorry. I love you.

It didn't last. Somewhere I said a wrong word, and the whole thing started all over again.

Audrey stood in the door frame to my room, screaming. "This is our famous Fourth of July weekend. How quaint. How lovely. The first night you spend by yourself, reading. The second day you sleep. The second night you drink yourself into a stupor."

My collected skirts were still lying in a pathetic heap on the floor the way she had dumped them there the night before, untouched. The liquor bottle was hidden out of sight behind the sofa.

"Audrey, I love you," I whispered.

"Audrey, I love you," she mocked in a shrill voice. "And I love everything else in the world as well. Everyone else. Joel. Anyone. Especially male. This is your splendid creation. Rejoice. Audrey and Joel together are your fantastic choice in life."

I felt the blood rush to my head. A long time ago, when she was new to me, when everything was new to me, when I didn't know yet that I was meant to love a woman, I had in fact exuberantly thought I loved them both. A man and a woman. Her psychic abilities, no doubt, intruded on my privacy. But then why did she have to hate me with such knowledge now when everything had changed? When I, who had never wanted to belong to anyone, was determined to belong to her?

I cried in despair. Her name. My love for her. My feverish fear that I did in fact not have a place to go if she were serious about all this. At least not yet. How would I manage? And why should the burden of leaving fall on me? Move again, after I had barely moved in? Why should I leave when I loved her so? I was in utter disbelief.

Audrey's sudden scream hammered the ultimate nail into my crucifix of confusion. "You whore!"

She reached out and slapped me and drew blood on the bridge of my nose. I didn't even notice the blood, only the pain inside me. She backed away from me with a look of terror and a whimper of despair.

"Oh, my God, now I've done this. I'll never forgive myself for this. I've hurt you. I'll never forgive myself for this."

"It doesn't matter," I said miserably.

I was so tired, it truly didn't matter to me. It wasn't the slap which caused the pain anyway. It was the intention to hurt me.

We were invited to a party that afternoon. I told Audrey to go. There wasn't much use in our being together, though the blood on my nose had shaken her free from the immediacy of her hatred.

She left, I stayed behind. Sipped vodka. Lay on the sofa, brooding. Somehow I couldn't believe, didn't want to believe, that such violence was possible between women. I was bewildered.

There was a knock at the door. First reaction: Knock away. Nobody at home. Another knock, insistent. I peered out of the curtain. There stood Kay, dressed in a pinstriped white and violet summer dress, holding a bicycle. Face intent and serious. I sighed and went to open the door. Her radiant smile.

"Hi, Andrea."

"Hi, Kay." Amused question in my eyes. What brings you here?

"I couldn't spend a whole afternoon in the neighborhood without visiting you. So I borrowed a bicycle and came. The party was dull anyway."

"Well, come on in, then," I said. Should I hedge politely or opt for being blunt. "Can I get you something? Wine? Juice? Did Audrey send you?"

"Um. Not really"

Conclusion: Audrey had sent her. Kay in shining armor. To rescue maiden in distress.

We talked for two hours. Kay was concerned for me. For Audrey, too. She loved us both. I, finally inspired to put an end to outside scrutiny of my personal life, got up to call Audrey at the party.

"I'm sure she'd like that," Kay prompted. I wasn't so sure, but I called anyway.

Audrey sounded tired, not overly enthusiastic. "Frankly, I would rather be at home with you."

"Then don't stay too much longer."

"No, just a little while."

We spent Sunday in mutual admiration for weathering our latest argument.

I saw Audrey caught in the snares of the grandeur of suffering. And here was I, with too few tools yet to be a winning advocate in the defense of perfect joy. We're all brainwashed into believing in the nobility of pain. Our whole language abounds with subtle shades of pain. I couldn't subscribe to that. Whereas my lady did. She had been fed the myth of noble darkness for many more years than I, and it appears she had swallowed every morsel of the gruel. And I had no persuasive language yet to change her mind.

So far only the language of pain was indeed precise and eloquent.

§

I went to work on Monday and faced the sympathetic questions as to the marks of passion on my nose. Gave rise to speculations.

"What happened to you, poor thing?"

"Hm. Of course you won't believe me, but I ran into a dragon."

"Likely story."

"You see, I live with a painter. And the lady has a golden dragon on her easel. So suddenly the studio is dark, and I am in a hurry as well as absent-minded. I ran straight into the corner of the canvas. Wham."

Only the company's Korean chauffeur questioned my tale. "Looks to me like you ran into some man's fist," he said, poker-faced.

I grinned because I was able to reply quite truthfully, "No, Sir, I did not run into a man's fist."

I dragged myself home from work. No energy for writing. Read a few pages. Little energy for that. Lay down on the sofa, thought of Audrey. Took her call.

"I'll be home soon now."

I danced through the living room. Tortured the piano for a while. Started dinner. Fried some vegetables. Tofu. Smuggled in an unorthodox egg. As I heard Audrey come to the door, I turned down the flame.

I shouted: "Audrey! Thank God you're home. I missed you so."

I fell into her tired arms. Not too tired for my weight. "Can I get you a drink? Juice? Dinner will be ready in a minute."

"Darling, I love you."

Her eyes twinkled, her tired body melted into the rocking chair.

I lit a cigarette for her. Her eyes. Oh, her magnetic eyes. Gray tonight. I knelt by the rocking chair. Stared at her with rapture. Caught, from the corner of my eye, a weird light flickering. Transcendence? Already?

"Shit, no!" I yelled and leapt for the kitchen where the neglected frying pan had caught on fire.

Audrey, one leap behind me, poured salt while I held potholders, the straw kitchen witch, and other flammables out of the way. We made a splendid team.

We sat down on the kitchen floor, now that the fire of passion was extinguished, to laugh the laughter of relief. Then up again to open the windows and get the animals out of the smoke. The Lhasa, out of fright, shat on the studio floor. So, what shall we have for dinner? Perhaps we ought to go out, what do you think? And remember you keep telling me that we'll never be bored with each other?

§

We never did bore one another. There was the weekend of the cucumber. Friday night Audrey returned with treats she had bought.

"Can you believe it?" she asked. "Before you, my refrigerator was stocked with crackers and yogurt. Now suddenly the adventure of real food. Blueberries. Cheese. Couldn't think of what kind of cheese you would like, so I got us three kinds." And the cucumbers. She pulled them out of the shopping bag like rabbits out of a hat. Little babies. Pale green. Gnarled shapes. "Aren't they cute?"

"Yeah. Cute enough to go to bed with."

Oops. I hadn't meant it that way. There was a flicker between laughter and hatred in Audrey's eyes. Intense stiffness took over her face, the decision to ignore the idiotic remark altogether.

I must have turned bright red, reading in her eyes what she had heard in my words. Phallic shape.

For half an hour we tried to salvage the situation. Then one of us must have become tired of trying and we argued. After two hours of that, we were back at arguing about my having gone to Oregon to visit Joel.

Cold, self-righteous challenge in my voice: "Audrey, is every conversation we have with one another going to end up in an argument about Joel?"

Audrey's reply: "Honey, we were lost on that subject the moment you opened your mouth after I pulled out the cucumbers."

"Sometimes we don't speak of cucumbers at all, and yet we end up arguing about Joel."

"If you hadn't gone, we wouldn't be stuck with it now."

"But I did go."

Hatred in her eyes: "Yes. You did go."

"And we will never be finished with the subject?"

"No. We would have to go back to the time before the end of May for that."

"We can't do that," I said.

"No," she said.

I didn't believe her. I had tiredness in me, but also buoyancy, stemming from stray remnants of my old belief in my essential innocence. And from my trust in Audrey's love when her eyes weren't clouded with the madness of hatred. But when her eyes went dark with things I couldn't change, I slunk away to my room, to my books, those that I read and those that I hoped to write.

§

My writing became more sporadic rather than less so. How I longed for it. My chief enemy was tiredness. We talked about my writing instead of me doing it. I told Audrey of the many things I wanted to write. Of things that no one else would ever be able to write because they were woven specifically from the texture of my life.

"You will write them, darling," she would say.

I hoped so very much. For the longest time all I had now were helpless sketches in my notebook, moments of inspiration captured in a few words that carried me back to vivid recollection, then, upon rereading, gradually grew pale and insubstantial. Instead, I followed Audrey around the house, never growing tired of watching her, enjoying her.

"Audrey, sometimes I am afraid," I told her once. "Of what happens between two people. Afraid that one will always be likely to put aside her ambitions. To become subsumed in the life work of the other. I don't want that to happen to us."

"Yes," Audrey said solemnly, caressing me with dreamy eyes. "Sometimes I fear that, too. Your writing. It's so important to me. You're right. I am afraid I could get drawn into it, subsumed by it, as you call it. Forget my own goals. Just concentrate on you."

What? It was me I was talking about. Not her. Didn't she see that?

She didn't. I could see it in her eyes. Two strong wills meeting on the crossroad of divergent understanding. Would we go her path, or mine? Or would we achieve the miracle of cutting out a new path for both?

§

At night I couldn't concentrate, not even on reading. Never mind writing. Visions of Audrey in my mind, her face when she was angry. Her face when she was tired, irritated. But when I chose to, I could remove myself from that and think of her face all smiles, all beauty, all the cosmic perfection that she corresponded to in my own longings. I could get paralyzed with fear. What if it was true that the most deeply touching love was that from a safe distance? In proximity we always seemed to botch the crystal-clear perfection we could keep intact with distant longing. I had already spent the greater portion of my life enjoying precisely such safe longing.

I still recalled echoes of words she had said in the past. "I was prepared to love you from a distance. Simply to look at you from time to time." So she wasn't exempt from this danger any more than I was.

Was it only possible to love distantly? The tendencies were there. And were they universal? Fear now reached my stomach. Paralysis. Can't love. Neither of us could. None of us in this whole world could love, except what we didn't have. Part of the curse of being alive.

Paralysis? Hell, no. I would get up, shake off loneliness like a dog shakes off water. Sneak to wherever Audrey was. Play "Honey, I need you" with my eyes. She never let me down. Not when there was play in my eyes. At such times I wanted to come down to earth. I didn't give a damn if our souls were linked forever, just our bodies, now, sufficed.

"I love your shoulders. They're so small. So little and so round. Mine are so square and solid, and far too large."

"But I love your shoulders. Anyone can have small shoulders. Now, strong and square ones like yours . . . ." Her hands brushed over the flattered skin of my substantial shoulders.

"No," I insisted. "Small shoulders are nicer. More delicate."

We'd end up in front of the mirror, comparing shoulders. Unshakable in our respective convictions.

"Small shoulders are nicer."

"No, large ones."

"Well, they're yours."

Weren't we lucky that it turned out we got what we liked best of all. The red and flawless taste of her made me think of flowers, sunlight, fields of wheat, then nothing.

She came home with an armload of new clothes one day. A flounced jeans skirt for herself. A dark blue skirt, the color of cornflowers, for me. A cornflower blue T-shirt for me. A purple dress with gold trim for herself.

"Next weekend, let's go and get some new shoes for you."

We did that too.

The best part about buying shoes was the long debate over a pair of suede slippers, looking like a pair of dancing shoes with suede lace to tie around the ankles. Audrey stood for a long time admiring them on the shelf. Size six. Everything about her was small. Her shoulders. Her feet. Her face. As opposed to my solid Nordic dimensions. The only thing not Viking about me was the fact that I was not very tall.

"Audrey, get these shoes," I pleaded with her. "They'd look so pretty on you."

With growing passion I argued the case of her being worthy of extravagant things to adorn herself with. I loved being in the persuasive role of celebrating her.

§

The road we traveled crossed all borders that I had been raised with, borders of the sacred and mundane, the serious and frivolous. Until there were no more borders. Life was a part of everything, and everything was of great importance.

Sometimes we solved the problems of the world in the course of a single conversation as we spun visions of our future like a tree sprouts branches. At other times we might transform a sultry waitress in a deli into someone only too delighted to bring us a glass for the bunch of daisies Audrey had just bought for me. We had magic. Whatever we touched became infected with it because we had the grandeur of happy moments, whether they were brought on by philosophical insights or by a bunch of flowers. We connected things and they, in turn, connected with us. The trademark for all this was Audrey's laughing face.

By herself she had magic too. Beautiful tricks with her eyes and her mouth. She played my nerves like an instrument, especially the nerves that were the keepers of my desire. I wanted to learn, to teach, to see, to show, to hold.

One warm night we sat on the stone rim of a fountain, toes dangling in the water, splashing gently. Over at the street corner, a blond woman pushed a baby stroller, the woman dressed in pink, her face puffy and childlike under layers of motherhood, loving and tired and petulant. The color of her dress made my mouth taste raspberry. Air brushed my skin. Thousands of colors claimed my attention, the city dust blue of the sky, the green assertion of grass in the cracks of the fountain's stone walls, the white of the water swirling in the creamy center of the fountain.

"Audrey," I whispered, "when I'm with you I can see."

She blinked her diamond eyes at me.

"When I was with other people, I couldn't see like this. My mind was always ahead or behind, and never where I was. Two states of similar gray. I was never really there. Always in some sort of focus that another's presence would impose on me. I could never see. Like this. With you."

The skin around her eyes crinkled. I realized it wasn't necessary that she understood me precisely.

The occasional force of such ordinary moments shook loose something in me that had always cried, or else felt called upon to cry, for the unusual, the mythical, the heroic. I didn't need to be special anymore. I only needed to be with Audrey.

Suddenly my whole life was special indeed. All gray was gone.

The clashes were gone. There is no language yet for the vibration of joy in my nerves that I felt. Words reduce now, as they did then, the scope of the flight of my soul to specifics, and specifics, out of context of the feelings that surround and cloth them with love, appear ridiculously small. I lived them fully. I can recreate in naked and impoverished words their memory, but just barely.

§

Saturday mornings when Audrey saw clients, I would trek through the basement to pick up dog shit, old dry turds, medium soft turds, occasionally some fresh. My heart laughed because now Audrey wouldn't have to do this, and somebody had to eventually.

More heroic yet were the maggots I found one day in the bottom of the garbage can in the basement where we deposited the empty dog and cat food cans. That time Audrey was home. I slunk up the stairs and stood in the doorway of her studio, ready to go away again since she seemed busy.

Audrey sounded prepared for the worst when she saw me stand there, dilemma personified: "Yes, darling?"

My voice was tiny: "There are maggots in the garbage can."

"Oh, damn," she said. "We probably left it there too long and didn't cover it."

"So what am I to do with them?"

"Well," she replied, experienced, "You take out all the garbage, with the maggots, and put it into the sun. They'll die there, 'cause they need moisture to live. And the ones you can't get out easily you drown with a lot of Ajax in water."

"Oh, okay," I said, pale, dreading the work to be done, and slunk away again.

"Do you want me to do it?" Audrey called after my receding shadow. Oh yes, if you would, please.

"No," I said, feeling proud that she didn't have to. It was bad enough that I would have to deal with the wiggling creatures. The mere idea that my unearthly beloved should have to do this? Far better I took care of it.

The feat accomplished, I returned from the basement, hands shaking still, my mind full of memories of wiggling white worms, for the hero's embrace. I never had to slay any dragons for my beloved—especially not dragons, seeing that Serena hung in the living room guarding our souls. But maggots, yes.

§

It was a blessed time for me. I never doubted that it was the same for Audrey. Her eyes were so happy when she looked at me. Miracles were commonplace now. At first, after my return from Oregon, we had cried together over the lump in her arm, I with my tears, and Audrey with her tearless eyes—she tried to explain to me once why she could not cry wet tears like everybody else, but I couldn't comprehend it entirely, too many unfamiliar medical terms surrounding the membranes of her eyes. Later we had nursed her arm according to her doctor's "wait-and-see" instructions. I brought her hot wash cloths at night and insisted on renewing them several times. She smiled at me indulgently as though it were child's play. Can you undo the damage you did? Three Ave Marias, though you're not even Catholic? Gradually we gave up. She didn't, for unspoken reasons, want me to fuss over her any more. Perhaps my fervor had been slipping. Secretly I would sometimes feel her arm, and sometimes openly when she invited me to. And when she asked, "Do you think it is growing smaller?" I would say, "Yes." though I could not tell the difference. I felt the yes in my wishes, in my needs, and that was enough.

Eventually she made an appointment, after all, to have the

growth surgically removed. It seemed sensible. We were both scared. Five days before her surgery, the growth really did begin to shrink. Three days before the operation it was hardly there. Then it was gone. The operation became unnecessary. And I was, more than ever, ready to believe in anything, even in my own magic in constellation with Audrey's and with the love I felt between us.

§

We experimented with different lifestyles every other week. At first I cooked most dinners. Audrey declared that, indeed, she knew how to cook, but wasn't inspired to do so. For the time being, I, on the other hand, was inspired. At the same time, however, I was also inspired to spend my time writing, or being with Audrey. As usual I was frazzled. Overextended. Fragmented. So we decided on this scenario: cold dinner, cottage cheese or yogurt. After all, when we had been on our own, that had been our respective staple fare, barring a few mayonnaise sandwiches at my end. But then I longed for the evenings when we would sit at the table together, sharing a leisurely meal. Luckily it turned out that Audrey missed that lovely, though danger-fraught, dinner hour also. Danger-fraught, because we might, by chance, end up speaking to each other. For example on the subject of jealousy, or of my wanting to sit in my room engaged in endless hours of reading or writing, or similar landmines. Still, at least I'd have her face in front of me while eating whatever haphazardly prepared vegetable or other concoction would be our lot, frequently in a scorched condition due to my exuberantly dejected fragmentation.

Try cooking with an earth-shaking poem on your mind just once. The food rebels. The muse throws a tantrum. And I slyly wondered what ever happened to Einstein's firstborn child whose cradle he allegedly rocked with his foot while concocting his theory of relativity.

There were lovely days of mercy when we determined we deserved to go out to dinner. After Audrey enchanted the waiters, we'd sink into each other's gaze. Such dinners were exploration times. The choice of walking the nine steps to my room was ruled out. And our frugality stood in the way of any argument, no matter how tired we were. Argue over a meal we have to pay for so dearly? While there's cottage cheese in the refrigerator? During one such dinner we reminisced about our childhoods and fantasized what it would have, could have been like, had we met each other as children.

Audrey: "You wouldn't have liked me. I was dirty and unkempt. Sometimes I had to walk back from school because my mother forgot to comb my hair. Some days the teacher made a point of it, and some days not. The walk was an hour each way."

Andrea: "You wouldn't have liked me. I was sickly, though clean. My mother was conscious of appearances. She made me wear two pairs of stockings one winter after some boys walking behind us made fun of my thin legs. I was a bookworm, too. I loved learning. I was damn smart, too, with the saving grace that I was also rather fresh. Not your ordinary teacher's pet."

Audrey: "I loved learning too. But no, I was no teacher's pet, either. I wanted to please the teacher as all hell. I wanted to be smart and bright. But I was always so dirty. Barefoot. I simply sat there and said nothing, so that they wouldn't notice me too much with my uncombed hair. I didn't want to risk any more walks back home than absolutely necessary."

Somewhere, though, our pictures overlapped. True, Audrey had spent her days running barefoot on the stubbles of wheat fields, just because she could and nobody else could, not even the boys. But she also went to the store of her Japanese girlfriend's father where everything was magical and delicate. She never bought candy with her trifling windfalls of allowances or gifts. When she had money, she went to the Japanese store to buy paper flowers. Not the expensive kind that came in little seashells, but the cheap ones that were simply wrapped around a tiny pebble. She'd drop them in a glass of water and sit and watch them unfold. She'd keep on watching, transported for hours into a world of pastel paper swaying in water. She loved everything delicate and fragile.

Audrey was running, curly-headed, wild across the wheat fields, while I was sitting in the castle gardens a ten minute walk away from home, dreaming of adventures of all kinds. I was a prince in wait of dragons. I was a gypsy orphan, waiting for the sun to set or rise. I dreamed or read of things that Audrey actually did when she picked up rattlesnakes by their tails, twirling them around her head. Or else she sat still with the grass and the flowers under a redwood tree. I merely took my pet hamster to the park in a basket. I never lived in a tent, never walked for miles to go to school. Life was fragile, but I always had more shelter than Audrey, more stability. Ultimately we agreed that she was the earth-bound gypsy child, dirt on her hands, whom I admired endlessly, and I was the frail city-daughter, thinned out between the high walls of civilization, whom she wanted to protect against any and all.

"We would have, too, liked each other," we concluded.

I pictured her again, standing alone with her sister for hours at some Los Angeles street corner, waiting for the mother who had left and forgotten them there. It was the middle of the night. They had no money and darkness loomed around the two shivering girls. Even now I wanted to cry for the tiny, fragile, helpless gypsy Audrey. But then she gave me this image, filling out old songs that used to move me, her hands gesturing at eye level as though painting her miracle into the air.

"One morning I remember best of all. We'd been traveling early, way before sunrise. I was still tired from loading our father's wagon. I'm huddling by my mother in the pre-dawn chill. On the road again.

The wagon climbed uphill. My sleepy head leaning against something, the side of the wagon probably. Unwilling for this to be day already. And then suddenly the top of the hill: The sun rose before us and the valley was filled with orange poppies. As far as you could see. The color of the earth with its bright poppies repeated in the sky. We stopped the wagon. All I could do was look. In silence. Orange, poppies, and sun."

Audrey's eyes held them all for me. Orange. Poppies. And sun. The earth had given itself to her, and now to me in her words, in her eyes.

§

"I want to show you something," I said one morning when I was ready to go to work. "Come with me to the Metro station."

Obediently she put on her jeans and a T-shirt and walked with me. It was a sunny morning. Warmth streamed around us like a blessing. I walked with excitement in my blood.

"There," I said.

A fence at a garden, two blocks away from home, with poppies wound around gray wooden fence posts. Waving their flower heads in the morning breeze. Civilized poppies, also climbing up to the light, but with delicate colors. White, pink, and misty violet, faint shadows in their centers.

These colors were also life. These colors were mine, faint and yet bold in the surprise of the city. Cultured, made pale and delicate, but persisting in their presence, whether or not anybody cared to look. Audrey's eyes were bright with her diamond smile. Perhaps she understood. I had been tamed in the wilderness of the city, like these flowers. And I was ready to show her my life, wound around a fence post like a flower.

I could hardly bear to leave Audrey that morning. Finally I

stepped onto the escalator down to the subway. I looked up and saw her stand at the light end of the tunnel, smiling, waving her hand.

§

She called me at work barely an hour and a half later. Her voice was filled with love, but also with strangeness. Could she come downtown to have lunch with me? Wonderful idea. She'd never done that before. Had wanted to for a long time, had been too shy to ask when we first knew each other. Later too busy on the one day in the week she had completely to herself. But her voice had a strangeness to it—sweetness and awe, but mixed with awkward breathlessness.

"Is something wrong, Audrey?"

"Oh no." I heard light laughter in her voice, soft, unconvincing reassurance. "I'll talk to you at lunchtime. When shall I come?"

She came at one thirty. She'd never seen the office I worked in, so I gave her the grand tour. I introduced her to a few of my office co-inmates. I was bubbly and excited.

For a treat I took her to have pizza and tacos—we couldn't make up our minds as to which we wanted more—in the Connecticut Connection underground Metro arcade, where the likes of me, secretaries, clerks, shop girls, and on occasion their bosses, took lunch to the smell of fresh bread on one side and that of fresh chocolate chip cookies on the other. The pizza was under a dollar a slice and the plastic atmosphere always amused me with its pretensions of being a self-contained small hub of glitter chic and inexpensive elegance.

She was worried about a young friend, Sonja, a fragile spirit as well as an heiress to a considerable fortune, and her family seemed oddly reluctant to allow Audrey to see her on an impending visit to Washington.

"And then, this morning . . . ," Audrey began, then didn't finish her sentence.

"This morning?" I prompted her gently.

"This morning I went into your room," she said in a very low voice, not looking at me. "And there was an emptiness in your room that I felt like a presence. As though you were gone. Forever, Andrea! The room felt cold. And the cold and your absence from it came over me like a wave of terror. I can't explain it. You were gone, and I could feel this terrifying emptiness in your room."

It took me a moment to process. The despair in her eyes was real. She had felt something ominous, and she was helpless, even smiling now, at the impossibility of describing it right, and at the absurdity of her fright. Through all the stammering and brave smiling, I could feel a seriousness in her, and it touched me.

"I won't leave you, Audrey," I promised. "Whatever it means, this thing you felt this morning, I'll be there for you. I'll be with you."

Audrey looked at me with a grateful smile. My words must have sounded preposterous in the midst of plastic all around us, the white spray-painted café chairs we sat in, the downtown lunchtime voices humming with discussions of bosses' unfairnesses, office managers' laughable idiosyncrasies, and companies' deals, and now and then a woman's voice floating across it all with a description of what some "he" had said to her, and later on done, on the occasion of a certain dinner date followed by a movie.

"I wish I could tell you what to do about Sonja," I said to avoid addressing the scarier issue of the empty room.

"I already did one thing." Confidence came back into Audrey's eyes. "I called Larry. He's a psychic I've already referred a few clients to. He's been on my mind for a couple of days now. So this morning, after that experience in your room, I was in such a state that I finally looked up his number and called."

I nodded.

"He answered the phone, and before I said anything at all, he asked, 'Audrey? Is this Audrey?' He's been expecting my call since yesterday. He even knew my name! And you know what? I have an appointment with him this afternoon. Usually he has a waiting period for private appointments, but while he talked to me, he went through his appointment schedule and found a free hour at four this afternoon. Isn't it amazing? He told me he thought he was fully booked for another week or so. He said he thought he had already made an appointment for four o'clock today."

I was in fact amazed. Also the tiniest bit uneasy. This was something I knew so little about. But it made me happy to see her eyes light up.

She escorted me back to my office building when my lunch hour was up, but declined the dubious honor of coming back up the elevator with Muzak misting its victims with pleasantness. I stretched out my arms to her as the elevator began to close and she did the same in graceful exaggeration of yearning, to the amusement of the black man who had entered the elevator with me. Audrey wore her light blue angel blouse. My bite marks on her shoulder had in the meantime faded.

As the afternoon wore on, I felt apprehensive. I couldn't get in touch with her at all, this of all days, because she had errands to run before going to her appointment with Larry and wouldn't have time to call. I had to wait patiently until I got home before I would find out anything. I tried to calm down. Hadn't I only just seen her, which normally I didn't have the good fortune to do during a work day? And it would only be a mere four or five hours until I saw her, held her in my arms again. Then three hours. Two. One. I wanted to fling myself out of the office, the elevator, the building, jay-walk, and race past all other pedestrians, as well as squeeze myself as the first one out of the metro tunnel at my home stop. Instead I took step after step with great deliberation, as though praying—undecided agnostic or, on occasion, pantheist that I was—for protection for me, and for Audrey as well. I wanted to take her by the hand and go with her to my room to show her that the emptiness she had experienced, my icy absence, was possibly a warning of some sort, but not a reality that we had to contend with. I walked as though on clouds, feeling in me a great sweetness of care.

She was there, tired but happy. Everything was bound to work out well regarding Sonja. At first, when she had mentioned Sonja's name to Larry, he had seen her as a child, a small girl, overwhelmed with questions about the universe. Sonja apparently also had psychic gifts that were troublesome in the context of her ordinary life. But she would pull through beautifully, and none the worse for the struggle. Audrey's own task, for the time being, was to send Sonja loving thoughts of energy, and to hold herself aloof otherwise. To let things take their own course as they must.

"I asked Larry about us, too," Audrey finally said.

"What did he say?"

She gave me a long, quizzical look. "He says that you are innocent." She lingered on the word a while, as though trying to find out what it could possibly mean. Parts of me sighed—noiselessly, of course—with self-righteous relief.

"When I said your name," Audrey continued, "he said he saw the image of a white horse running, a large white mane flying in the wind. He also saw a purple flame, which was the light of both of us joining in the flame, rising upward. Purple is a very spiritual color. It's the light of our souls."

I wanted to hear more. There wasn't any more. Just these fragments. Innocence. A white horse. A purple flame rising.

"What about the room?" I asked.

"I don't know," Audrey said.

"But the purple flame. Does that mean our souls are safe? That they will grow together, be together, join, whatever may come?"

"Yes," Audrey said simply.

I hugged her and waltzed her through the living room despite her tiredness.

I spent the weekend pondering her experience, both the apprehension and the relief that filtered through Larry's words. I had repeat moments of delicious self-righteousness at the verdict of innocence. It made me happy. Whatever metaphors Larry's message was masked in, it seemed to contain a promise of happy solutions, both with respect to Sonja and to myself.

§

The next week flew by with exhausting speed.

I anticipated the weekend with dread. Friday night I was supposed to meet with Kay with whom I hadn't been alone for a very long time. Audrey would leave us a few hours to ourselves, then join us. Then, either Saturday or Sunday, we would see Sonja. I had promised Audrey I would be with her for that.

The question was, as ever, when was I going to have any time to do my work? Never mind relaxing. With mounting self-pity I survived the week nights with more drinks than I had taken of late. Exhaustion gathered around me, the need to sleep, the fear I wouldn't be able to, frazzled as I was, without shutting off my mind with a sleeping draught. Audrey would be in bed, studying or reading, and I'd quickly take a drink or two in my room, then fix a publicly weak one to take to bed with me, and then, before I'd know it, I'd be asleep.

"You know," Audrey said once, "I admire your ability to fall asleep so quickly. You hit the pillow and next thing you're gone. I'm often awake for a long time, merely trying to fall asleep."

I didn't particularly admire that ability in myself, because I knew its not altogether natural causes.

By Friday afternoon, though, I actually looked forward to meeting Kay after work. To brag of my happiness with Audrey. To tell someone about my wondrous life.

Then Audrey called. Could she come and join us sooner than we had arranged? She didn't want to be alone at the house. Sad things were happening. I was disappointed about missing out on alone time with Kay. But Audrey's feelings were more important, no matter what. She did sound sad. She didn't want to discuss it on the phone, but said it had to do with Sonja.

"Tell you what," I said. "I'll come home first. Then we'll go to Kay's place together. Would you like that?"

"Yes," Audrey said. "Thank you, Andrea."

She met me at the metro station, her face tender with grief. The mutual friends, with whom Sonja and her family were staying, had called. They said it would be better if Audrey didn't come to the picnic on Sunday afternoon, or to the luncheon on Saturday. Audrey's presence would only cause confusions and resentments and other feelings that nobody wanted to deal with. It would be best if Audrey considered herself uninvited.

I simply held Audrey close. There wasn't much I could say. But I could show her that I felt with her the grief of being accused of being a potentially harmful intrusion in a loved one's life.

At Kay's apartment, Audrey perked up. I admired her. I felt happy for her. I heard her banter with Kay. I simply watched.

Then suddenly I slithered into an ugly wave of jealousy. I was ashamed of it from the beginning, but shame didn't do much except heighten the discomfort of the onslaught of petty jealousy. Here I had sacrificed my time alone with Kay, and now Audrey usurped it completely. Kay was fascinated with Audrey. Who wasn't? I might just as well not have been there. I couldn't believe, or control, what I felt happening to me.

Something raged inside. In moments of near sanity I berated myself. What was it I wanted? That Audrey should thank me for having drawn her out of despair? But she had thanked me. What more did I want? I couldn't stop the rage from gnawing inside me. I filled cup after cup of red wine and drank it, growing more sullen in the process of watching this happen to me as from a great distance in which I grew scornful of the ease with which other people, specifically Audrey, pulled in and out of despair without leaving even traces of it.

I was angry. Also very tired. I wanted to go home. But couldn't. Because I couldn't drive, and it was Audrey's car anyway. Meanwhile Audrey and Kay were exceedingly joyful, and I really and with genuine generosity did not want to disturb their world of enchantment.

They were talking about psychic phenomena. Audrey described how her dragon painting had come by its name. She'd been alone in the house, and sounds had formed in her chest, her throat, her mouth, as though by themselves, slowly, Sss . . sssr . . chr . . Serena. How she had repeated the name. Serena.

How lovely she was telling her story. I felt unbelievably left out. By the time they noticed anything odd about me—for after all, I had a reputation for being the quiet one—it was too late. I'd sunk too deep out of their jolly companionship and felt like a trapped intruder. Audrey tried to pull me back into the conversation. She suggested a three-way poem. Each of us would add line after line to unseen preceding words. I knew perfectly well that this was for my benefit. I felt like a sulking child, being indulged by its sane and wiser companions. So I furiously behaved like a child, penning my few lines with scorn, trying to behave, and yet trying to get it across also that this was in fact what I was doing: behaving, for their benefit. Enjoying myself I was most certainly not. And I wanted them to know that.

Whenever I was sure Kay wasn't looking, I darted fiery glances at Audrey and mouthed the words: "Why do you hate me so?" At first she tried to read the words from my lips, then shook her head, then shrugged her shoulders. I never knew whether she comprehended the words or not. What I was sure of was that I was sinking deeper and deeper into the boiling inside me. I don't even remember how we finally got home. No doubt I said a few apologetic times that I was tired. No doubt Audrey loved me through these moments of despair, though I made it as difficult for her as I conceivably could. Behold, Audrey: your lover, the baby.

§

Audrey didn't seem to bear a grudge. After two Saturday morning clients, she came home, tired and with a terrible headache. I still felt guilty about the night before. She didn't even allude to it.

"You should sleep," I told her.

"I wish I could," she said, "but I don't think I'd be able to. My head is pounding."

"Then lie down for a while at least," I said.

"It's not going to do any good," she said, but then asked, "Would you lie down with me and hold me for a while?"

"I will."

I was still trying to work off last night's karma, but already also weaving on today's love and tenderness. I took her in my arms and asked her to describe her headache to me. Was it like darts? Like needles?

"How do you know?" she asked.

"Well, I've had a headache or two in my day." I said. She laughed, but laughter seemed to hurt.

"Close your eyes," I said. "Can you see the arrows?"

"Yes," she said weakly. "They're gray and silver and very fast."

"Can you make them turn blue?" I asked.

"How?" she asked back.

"I don't know," I said. "It was just a thought."

"But I can!" she suddenly exclaimed. "I can make them turn blue!"

"Then how about some deep green among the blue?" I simply went on inventing. She could visualize the green also, to both of our surprise. We both knew I didn't have the faintest idea what I was doing, and yet it seemed to work.

"Now change their motion," I said. "Make them swirl, make them swish around very gently. Can you do that?"

Before I knew it, Audrey was asleep in my arms, breathing deeply, relaxed. Perhaps it was simply the warmth of my body against hers that lulled her to sleep. I lay awake, guarding her sleep with tenderness. It felt good being able to make her come to rest when she needed it.

She woke up an hour later. Her headache was gone. She was in an adventurous mood. Brave adventurousness, as we both knew, since this was the day when we should have been at the luncheon with Sonja. Neither of us mentioned Sonja's name. But I knew she was on both of our minds.

"So what shall we do with the rest of the day?" Audrey asked brightly. "Do you want to go out to dinner? For a walk?"

"Yes. And yes. In a while."

Though Audrey was full of energy to do something right away, an irrational hope made me want to wait.

"I want to get out of here soon!" she insisted.

"Yes," I said.

I tried all delaying tactics I could come up with, languishing about. I was filled with a wish more than hope that Sonja might get in touch. When the phone rang, we were both in the bedroom and I darted for it, expecting to hear Sonja on the other end. Instead it was a wrong number. I realized that my hopes were silly, stemming from overconfidence in some kind of knowledge beyond myself that I didn't have after all. Brought on no doubt by having sent Audrey to sleep through a fluke of gentleness. I, too, now gave up on Sonja.

"Okay, let's go," I said.

Audrey went to the bathroom to wash up and get changed. The phone rang again. I picked it up at the kitchen extension with the impatience of, 'what is it now?'

"Audrey?" a joyful woman's voice asked.

"No, this is Andrea. Hold on, let me get Audrey."

"She's there, then?" the woman asked excitedly.

"Yes, yes," I said, amused at the urgency in her voice. "I just have to go get her."

"This is Sonja," the woman said.

I nearly dropped the phone. "Hi, Sonja." Blood pounded in my ears. "Yes, hold on, I'll get her right away."

I covered the mouthpiece of the phone and shouted, "Audrey, Audrey! Phone's for you!"

For some reason Audrey didn't hear me. Later she told me she hadn't even heard the phone ring.

"Hold on a moment, Sonja," I said into the telephone. "I still have to get her."

"But she is there?" Sonja asked again.

"Yes." I raced through the bedroom and nearly bumped into Audrey coming in through the other door. "Didn't you hear the phone?" I said. "Get it! It's Sonja!"

Audrey snapped up breath, looked at me, as though for help, then flew to the kitchen to pick up the phone. I danced like a goblin until Audrey called me.

"Is it all right," she asked me, voice calm, eyes full of liquid fire, "to have dinner with Sonja and Peter tonight?"

I threw up my arms. "Of course," I said. What else had we been waiting for?

Audrey lingered over arrangements, consulting with me at every new suggestion, giving me a lovely sense of importance in her life. "That would be an idea. Let me just ask Andrea if that's all right with her."

I felt proud, as though both the vanishing headache and the connection with Sonja were personal accomplishments for me.

§

We met Sonja at a restaurant run by one of Audrey's clients. I liked her tremendously and was surprised at how strong and competent she seemed in view of Audrey's description of her frailty. I liked her husband as well.

"I think he trusts you," Audrey whispered to me. "Which is wonderful. Because that means some of the suspicion of me is gone as well."

At some point a gentleman Audrey's age, with white hair and gold tooth, asked Audrey to dance. She declined but referred him to me, and I accepted.

"I love to watch you dance," she told me later. "You're so graceful. And the best was: there you were dancing with a man, and I didn't feel any jealousy at all. Perhaps I'm over all that. Finally. Of course I wish you would have danced with me. But beyond that, I knew that no dance, no gesture, and especially no man could come between us."

"That's because, when I dance, I dance only for you," I said. "And when I do anything else, I also do that only for you."

We talked about dancing, about Sonja, and about our happiness in being together way into that night. We were happy. We made love. Afterwards we lay awake in silence, holding each other, feeling the blessing of being close.

§

All of that Sunday, we played. Audrey brought up a trunk from the basement. She pulled out garment after garment, among them a long, silky light blue gown. She made me put it on.

"You look like royalty," she said.

I looked in the mirror and was pleased. To tease her, I put on the curly wig that stood on the dresser. Brown short curls, much like her own, replacing my long blond hair.

She shrieked.

"It made you look ten years tougher," she said with relief when I took the wig off again and brushed out my hair. "But the blue gown? I wish you'd wear that always. You look like a queen. And that's what you are. My queen."

I looked at my regal outfit with misgivings.

"You should at least wear it all day today," she conceded. "So that I can see you like this."

"Even when I go to the airport to meet my friend Lisa?" I laughed and pictured myself traveling on the metro with long-flowing robes, and long-following eyes all around me.

"Yes!" Audrey exclaimed.

In the end I didn't dare. I wore the normal faded jeans and T-shirt.

§

I had a glass of wine with Lisa at the airport. When she left for her gate I called Audrey to come pick me up. Waiting for Audrey I felt sad, as though something was over, finished, gone. I stood waiting in the blazing, dusty heat of July. I would miss Lisa, with her splendid long black hair, her gentle face, and the secret aching in her to attract some dashing lover, while none would ever be worthy of the sweet solemnity of her life.

Audrey came and was gentle with my fragile mood. The sun was beginning to set, briefly painting the roofs and monuments golden. I wanted to be alone with Audrey. At home. Quiet.

We stopped at a fish market and moved from stand to stand, comparing prices, watching men display their masculinity. There is a certain tough carelessness of holding a fish up into the air just so that seems to go with stained undershirts, muscled arms, and a challenging glint in the eyes under greased forelocks. Almost as if taken from God's picture book of what a fishing crew member should look like, though God must have taken some inspiration from existing people, such as Marlon Brando or James Dean.

We picked out our fish and took it to a shed where fish was custom-cleaned for twenty-five cents a piece. Audrey and I stood in line. It was hot and the smell of fish was strong. I craned to watch the cleaning procedure. A huge black man in a wide brown plastic apron took fish after fish, held their scaly plump bodies about a foot away from his chest, then scraped off the scales with quick strokes of his axe-shaped scaling knife. The fish bodies seemed to quiver with dance-like resiliency even under his tight grip. It took only seconds. Then, with another knife, he gutted each fish with a few quick cuts. It looked graceful, the swiftness of the fish cleaner's motion culminating in an elegant toss of the cleaned, gutted, headless fillets on the table between himself and his customers.

I was stunned. How could something so inherently brutal look at the same time so graceful? I felt repulsed, then drawn again to the grace of the violence. Something in me wanted to scream. Instead I only stared. I looked at Audrey. She gave me a mysterious, indefinable grin. My heart contracted. Was this my Audrey who couldn't bear baby birds dying? A shadow came over her eyes, then in an instant it was replaced again by laughter.

I wanted to leave and go outside. Who cared whether we had fish for supper or not? Thoughts attacked me: Girl, if you can bear to eat fish, you ought to be able to bear to see how they acquire their pan and oven ready condition. So I had to stay, didn't I? Finally though I could not bear it any longer. The smell had become sickening in the heat. If you can bear one thing and not another, then that's the way it is. I'd leave. Any minute.

I told Audrey that I wanted to wait outside, if that was all right with her, because my stomach felt queasy from the heat and the smell. She looked at me with compassion, then some more laughter, and said she'd be fine waiting her turn in line by herself.

I sat on a wooden ledge right in front of the shed, close enough to the door so that none of the men in the vicinity would consider me lurking and in need of attention. It was getting dark outside. Noise surrounded me, but it stayed at a distance, as though something had drawn an invisible circle around me and everything outside of it was far removed. I felt tears rise to my eyes and tried to fight them. When Audrey came outside with her innocuous package of fish, she spoke to me softly and pulled me out of the fragility of aimless despair.

By the time we sat at the dinner table, three candles lit between us, bittersweet Japanese music on the stereo player, and the fish in aesthetic white, flaky portions on our plates, I felt I was back home in the light of our being. After a few mouthfuls of food, I told Audrey about my feelings at the fish market. I dutifully laughed about it, although I didn't much feel like laughing. I ended the tragic-comic report of myself by raising a forkful of the tender fish to my mouth in demonstration, saying, "So, anyway, for the benefit of stomach and taste buds, I can in the end easily suppress all fine sentiments concerning the fate of other living creatures." Simultaneously, as though by arrangement, we bent down to hand a few scraps of fish to the cats who caressed our legs with longing, so as not to be found solely guilty in the food chain.

We sat together in silence. It felt as though there was nothing left to say. Our hands lay close together on the table without touching. It seemed as though even touch was now superfluous. I felt our closeness, our being, wash over me like an endless stream of peace pulsing back and forth between us. Even love seemed too simple and too limited a word for this. I thought of Audrey's words she liked to use for occasions like this: "It has no name. It simply is." I smiled. Even that still seemed less than there was. But the smile itself, as though in waves, spread all over me. To be allowed to feel this. A joy that had no name, no framework for comprehension.

When we drifted out of the connection, I felt sad to comprehend things with names again. Audrey's face. The shape of her eyes. The color of her hair. Wherever we had just been, we couldn't stay there.

Audrey put it into words: "I wish we could keep this moment forever. Just like this. Without any change."

Life seemed impossibly short. Twenty or thirty years in her company seemed too short suddenly. Even forty years would only give us fourteen thousand six hundred and ten days together which seemed barely enough. She promised to do her best to live another fifty years, in case I stuck to my old plans of reaching at least eighty.

"Try for at least seventeen thousand more days," I begged. That too seemed too little. But perhaps by then our souls would be so linked that any other mode of existence would not dare to take us in separately.

"If I should die before you," she said, "would you sit with me and tell me I belong to you?"

§

Daily life, the usual culprit, tested us beyond bearing, fragmenting the interweaving of our beings, shattering what could be shattered. On Tuesday we planned to meet with Sonja and Peter once more. But Audrey called me early that morning. Their plans had changed. The meeting was off.

"I feel sad," Audrey said. "As though something is lost. I hardly even know how to talk to you. It's as though words are invading my mind and I can't say to you what I want to say. I want to say over and over and over again: I think of you a river. I want to say to you I want the pleasure of your company. But that isn't what I want to say at all. Yet over and over the words. I think of you a river. The pleasure of your company. I don't speak like that. These words aren't mine. I don't know what's going on."

"Can you meet me for lunch at least, even if Sonja and Peter can't make it?"

"I could, yes," she said after a moment. "But perhaps it's better if I don't. I have a lot of things to do and we'd have to eat very early. At eleven or so, and I know you prefer to go much later."

"I don't mind going early, Audrey," I said. "I'd like to see you very much."

She decided she'd rather get her chores done. Then we'd have more time for each other in the evening. We were going to a meditation group led by the psychic Larry with whom she was very much taken since her appointment a week and a half ago. We'd also have to eat, and the house needed to be cleaned, and she needed to sit down to pay bills and straighten out all kinds of things.

"Do call me again later," I begged her.

"Yes, I'll call you," she said.

She called me right on the dot at eleven o'clock. Her voice was uncanny.

"Andrea, something strange happened. Maybe it isn't strange to you. A man just called and asked for you. He wouldn't leave his name or number, but he asked for you by name. I gave him your work phone number and then I immediately thought that perhaps I shouldn't have done that. I don't know. It was so weird. That he wouldn't leave his name under any circumstances, and that he wouldn't give me a number to call him back. I don't know what to think. I don't know what to do. At any rate, I wanted to warn you in case he calls you. Do you have any idea who it is? And why he would call you? Like that? Leaving no name?"

I didn't know. All I knew was that Audrey was unbearably disturbed. Her voice came in soft dry sobs. I racked my brain and couldn't come up with a solution to the puzzle. I'd only moved so recently. Old friends would have my work number, but not my home number. I grew frightened, both of the mysterious caller and of Audrey's jealousy. I tried to get her to describe his voice, tried to recognize it in any way at all. No luck.

I was inundated with crazy thoughts. I felt something evil heading my way and I couldn't stop it.

My mind searched in all directions for a simple explanation that would shed light on this darkening muddle of premonitions. Who was it that had called me, knowing my name? And what was Audrey thinking in her fragile state of mind that made her voice crack with sobs? I waited for the call at my work number, so that I could ask, "Oh, so-and-so, was it you who just called my number at home?" But no call came.

Later in the day I talked to Audrey, and she asked the same question. Had the mysterious caller ever called me at work? No. I had no clue as to who he was.

I was sensitive to everything—especially my fears—and when I went to the ladies' room, I discovered that my period had started. Confirming, thank God for little things, my non-pregnancy. Some relief at least. Though it didn't take away the overwhelming fear into which I had worked myself since Audrey's phone calls.

§

We both came home from work drawn and exhausted. I fed the animals. Audrey sat down for a few minutes of rest. Then we headed out again for the meditation group. We didn't speak much in the car. I tried to break through the tension between us.

"Something very mundane happened to me today," I said.

"Oh?"

"Yep. I got my period."

Audrey looked at me briefly before concentrating on her car maneuvers again. "So you did?" she said strangely.

"Yep," I repeated. "You might as well be forewarned, should I fall into any unusual moods."

"Thanks for the warning," Audrey said and laughed, not kindly.

She parked the car. Her vibes were daggers. Her silence was painful. We were early. I touched her arm.

"Audrey," I said. "You're very strange tonight, and I'm very sensitive. Perhaps I shouldn't come along. Perhaps you'd rather go to the meditation by yourself. I can't tell. I don't much want to go if you don't want me there."

"As it happens, you're already here," Audrey snapped, looking at me coldly. "Think I'm going to drive you all the way back home?"

"I could wait for you." I was sad, but also angry. Did she have to snap at me? Didn't I already have enough problems? "I wouldn't mind at all."

"Well, it's up to you, isn't it?" she said unhelpfully.

I looked around to see some landmark where we could meet in a few hours' time. But I was so tired, I couldn't think constructively. I ended up tagging along with her through long corridors inside a tall building. We got to the eighth floor where Larry lived and did his work. A small group of people was gathered already.

"You're new here?" someone asked kindly.

Audrey began talking to people she knew. I hid from people by studying, for appearance's sake, the bulletin board, and then the bookshelf where a number of spiritual books were for sale. One title disturbed me. "How to use your power. For money. Relationships. Success." Was that all anybody was ever interested in? If I wanted money, why use spiritual powers? Why not simply go and study law or medicine? After a while I sat down in one of the chairs set in a large circle.

Audrey came to sit beside me. She seemed happier now and smiled at me.

"How do you like it so far?" she asked.

"Don't know yet." I smiled back.

"Larry won't be here tonight," she said. "I'm kind of disappointed. I wish he would have been here."

A pregnant woman with sultry eyes and a harsh voice began to deliver the evening's teaching. I missed the relevance of a joke made about "man loving man" until Audrey bent to whisper into my ear, "Larry's gay."

The woman explained the position and function of the seven chakras, as well as their colors. I tried to memorize everything.

The guided meditation that followed gave me a wonderful sense of well-being. I felt at peace, even amused, because as we were visualizing ourselves climbing up the length of our spines in seven steps, I followed directions too eagerly and found myself having arrived at the back of my neck when the voice of the meditation guide informed me that I should still be somewhere down along mid-spine. Oops, I thought giddily, and sent my visualization back down to where it was supposed to be.

"You arrive at a precious place where you get to be totally alone with yourself, utterly loving, and utterly forgiving and at peace with yourself," the guide spoke slowly into my nerves. "You have a key with you. Open the gate and look around. This is the part of yourself that nobody else can ever touch, where no cares of daily life can intrude. If you want to, wander around, or, if you prefer, sit down and rest."

Suddenly I did have a golden key in my hand, an ornate, old-fashioned key with a loop at its end, solid, but not overly large. I opened a door in front of me and came into a spacious cave-like place filled with a mild golden shimmer. A patch of sky appeared overhead and I left the cave into an open field of gold. I sat down in a sun flower, spreading myself along its petals into the sunlight overhead.

I rocked for a while. Then I jumped down from my sunflower and began walking again. I was at the seashore by an old castle, walking up in spirals on a paved road. The castle stood on a steep cliff that fell to the ocean. I looked out at the world, feeling like a peaceful shell around a seed of sadness. But it was also a seed of promise. Slowly I walked back to the cave, passing the sunflower, the golden field, a chrysanthemum I hadn't seen before. Then I stood back at the gate.

I was happy when we ended the meditation. In an adjoining room coffee and cookies were served. I could barely speak yet, even when Audrey sat down next to me, though there was much I wanted to tell her. For now, all I could do was smile.

The teacher with the harsh voice wanted to practice psychic sensitivity with us. She had written the names of various fruits on index cards and placed them into envelopes she now handed out.

"Imagine yourself in the supermarket, going through the fruit and vegetable section, picking up your fruit. Smell it. Touch it. What does it feel like? Look at it and notice everything about it. Taste it. When you feel you have recognized your fruit completely, open your eyes." Here she laughed. "So I can know when you're done, or at least most of you. And don't be disappointed if you can't identify a fruit. It doesn't always come at once."

I picked up a sense of orange at first. The texture of its skin attracted me. Something wasn't right about it, though. I couldn't smell much. Suddenly I had the taste of strawberries in my mouth. I doubted them for a respectful moment, and then decided that the taste was so delicious that I was going to stop taking everything so seriously, and that I would simply open my eyes and keep tasting this delightful strawberry flavor. It was cool and fresh and sweet. The moment came when the teacher invited us to open our envelopes. Was my sweet strawberry going to be vindicated? Should I have stuck with the orange? Suddenly I wanted very much to be right.

When I opened the card, it had "STRAWBERRY" penciled on it in capital letters. I was delighted. Just then I noticed Audrey's inquisitively smiling eyes on me. Well? her eyes seemed to ask. Well? I asked back with mine. It was obvious that both of us had 'guessed' correctly. A coincidence amused us afterwards. She had briefly doubted her orange for a strawberry, just as I had doubted my strawberry for an orange.

§

When we left for the night, the day's troubles and fears and nervousness seemed to have dissipated. The premonitions seemed wiped away. I was chatty and wide awake and felt up to all sorts of antics. Both Audrey and I wanted to talk to each other all at once, and I felt she was as bubbly and hyper as I was. We stopped at a hamburger place and treated ourselves to enormous salads, feeling entirely too pious to eat a quarter pounder.

I was reluctant to give up the evening by going to bed. But it had to be done. I wanted the effervescence to go on and on, and I wanted to linger on the memories of meditation. Audrey eventually persuaded me to reason. I was in the process of undressing and flinging my clothes around the bedroom, singing to the cats and the dogs, barely refraining from doing somersaults across the bed, which would have landed me straight in a pile of books and carefully balanced ashtrays and a glass of juice on Audrey's night stand. She stood at the closet with her back to me.

Suddenly she turned her head and asked with a grin: "Do you love me?"

"Yes, yes, yes," I shouted, dancing toward her. She held me at arm's length.

"Do you love me only? Of all the people in the world?" she asked in a light sing-song voice.

I hesitated, touched strangely, the question, coming straight into my euphoric feeling of being in love with the whole world tonight. Why ask like this? Something put me off. Couldn't she see, feel, sense how much I loved her? My Audrey. My world.

"I love you," I said. But I felt challenged by her attitude. "I love other people too. I love my friends. But, Audrey, I love no one as I love you. I love you best of all. Not only. But best."

An unpleasant shadow came over her face. She dropped the arms that had held me. She stepped back. A frown burrowed in between her eyes. The eyes themselves drew into a slit of contempt. My God, she's thinking of Joel, I thought, shocked and wounded. He hadn't crossed my mind until the frown had appeared on her face. I'd been thinking of Kay, Sharon, Lisa. I felt as though she were deliberately causing me pain.

Because of hurt and pride I didn't say what was on my mind. Not Joel. I wasn't thinking of Joel. I just wanted her to leave me alone with her jealousy. I couldn't bear being nailed down like this for affirmations of love. And, of all moments, now when I had just felt so happy and strong. I made no disclaimers, merely said "I love you" once more, this time in a weak and miserable mixture of accusation, wounded pride and defiance. Audrey, I love you. My heart ached with the emptiness of the words and the surrounding silence. I love you, but I want you to know it without stupid and inadequate words. I want you to know it from the core of yourself.

"Oh, God, I'm so damn needy," she said.

"You're not. You're not. I love you so." I rushed to hug her.

"But not exclusively, no?" she said. I stared at her wide-eyed. She sighed, shrugged her shoulders, began undressing, lay down beside me and slipped her head on my shoulder. I felt incredibly close to her.

"I love you," I murmured over and over again before I fell asleep.

I woke up in the middle of the night to go to the bathroom. She wasn't beside me in bed.

"Audrey?" I asked, puzzled. Not a sound.

One of the cats was in bed with me, and as I got up I heard the dogs stir in the living room, shuffling toward me. I came back from the bathroom, blinked my eyes, frowned, and tried to comprehend. Where was she? No lights were on in the house, merely the faint glow of the porch light which we always left on during the night. I tiptoed to the living room.

She lay huddled on the sofa wearing a T-shirt, a blanket wrapped around her. I walked to her side and touched her shoulder lightly. She was fast asleep. I wanted to wake her but something inside me said, no, leave her alone. She needs the sleep. And so do you. I felt heavy as I tiptoed back to bed. Bewildered. And so drowsy at the same time that I fell asleep again at once.

The alarm clock woke me up at seven. I reached across Audrey to turn it off before I realized that there was no Audrey to reach across. She wasn't beside me. I remembered. The living room. The sofa.

It frightened me. I got up quietly and walked over to see her. Yes, there she was. Asleep. Looking small and fragile, her skin gray with sleep. I felt like crying. I stared at her. Then I went to the kitchen to make coffee. I made a cup for her. As always. Or rather, not as always. I put it on the brass coffee table beside her, hoping it would wake her up with inviting morning smell. It didn't.

I washed, got dressed. Sat in the rocking chair between her and the fireplace, rocking and looking at her. Wishing she would wake up. Checking my watch. Smoking one cigarette after another. I didn't know what to do. I wanted to speak to her. About last night. My failure to convince her how much I loved her. I considered calling in sick. Didn't dare do that either. I simply didn't know what to do.

I took the animals to the basement and fed them. They came back up through the door I left open for them. They were as quiet as I was, none of us waking Audrey.

It was time for me to go. I went to the sofa. Bent over Audrey. Touched her shoulder, touched her awake. She moaned and turned over, opened her eyes a slit, closed them again. Her face looked drawn.

"I have to go to work, Audrey," I said.

"Oh yes," she said.

"Are you all right?"

"Hmm?"

"Are you sick?"

"Mm, no," she said.

"Do you want me to stay home and not go to work?"

She shook her head tiredly.

"Are you sure?" I dreaded having to call in to say I wouldn't come in. But I dreaded even more leaving Audrey like this.

"I made coffee," I said when she didn't reply. "Do you want me to bring you some?"

"No," she said.

"Do you want me to turn off the burner, or leave it on low to keep the coffee warm for you?"

"I don't know," she said. "Turn it off."

"Audrey, I wish I didn't have to go."

She shrugged her shoulders.

"I love you so very much," I said.

There was the shadow of a smile on her face. Not nearly enough to wipe out the gray of sleep and, possibly, pain.

"Are you sure you'll be all right?" I asked again.

Her body told me to leave her alone. I put my arms around her shoulders, so thin in the washed-out T-shirt. I kissed her mouth. It was dry from sleep. She didn't resist, but she didn't kiss back. I pressed her shoulders, not wanting to let go. Knowing that if I was going at all, I had to go now. I stood up.

"I'll call you," I said. "If you want to, sleep until I call you. I'll call you early enough so that you can get up in time for your class."

"Okay," she said.

I felt empty and sad. I went to the kitchen and turned off the burner. I walked past her to the front door. She had rolled over again, facing the back of the sofa, perhaps asleep again already. I felt tender and protective toward her.

"Bye, Audrey," I whispered at the door, loud enough for her to hear me if she was awake, quietly enough so as not to wake her if she was asleep again. She didn't respond. I closed the door behind me soundlessly.

FALL

I called the house at nine thirty, reluctantly, feeling all the tenderness well up in me again. She answered on the third ring.

"Hi. This is your wake-up service," I said in an attempt to sound cheerful.

"Thank you," she said.

"Did I wake you up just now?" I asked.

"No. I've been up for a while."

I felt as though there were a circle around her that I couldn't penetrate.

"Will you call me later?" I asked.

"No doubt I will," she said.

She called at four thirty in the afternoon.

"Hi," I said, happy and expectant when I recognized her voice.

"Listen," she said, "I merely called to let you know that I won't be home tonight."

"What do you mean?"

"I just won't come home tonight. I thought I'd let you know ahead of time."

"I don't understand," I said. "What happened?"

"Nothing," she said.

"Audrey, what . . . what is it?" I asked. "You know I can't talk very freely at this phone." Furtively I looked around me to see who might be in spying distance of my conversation.

"I know you can't talk," Audrey said.

I cleared my throat, stalled for time. "I wish you'd tell me why. I'm worried."

"Don't worry," she said in a cold, even voice. "There's nothing to this."

"Then why?"

"Simply because." She hung up.

In a daze I finished my day's correspondence. When my boss called me into his office impatiently to have me correct this and that and to type a label for something or other, rather than the envelope I had provided, I simply kept performing in sleepwalk mode. Then I went home and lay down on the couch in my room, then on the living room sofa, in the same position in which I had found Audrey in the morning, trying to feel close to her.

When it was time for her to be finished with her last client, I dialed her office number. My hands trembled. I was surprised that she answered at all. That she answered right away.

It was after eight o'clock.

"Audrey!" I said with relief at hearing her voice. "Tell me it isn't true."

"Tell you what isn't true?" she asked.

"What you said this afternoon," I said. I really didn't want to repeat and pronounce it. "That you won't come home."

"But it is true. I will not come home."

"Why, Audrey?"

"Because I can't bear it."

"What? What can't you bear?"

"You," she said. "You and your, what shall I call them, affairs of the heart? Your men."

"What are you talking about? I don't have any affairs of the heart. I don't have any men in my life."

"Strange men calling you in the morning? And Joel's love letter?"

I had received a letter from Joel recently. He had been sick, had written to me in the gentle mood of coming out of a sickness, of remembering neglected friends. Yes, he had signed the letter "love, Joel." But it wasn't a love letter. It was a friend's letter. Not a love letter. It wasn't because I didn't allow it to be such. I told Audrey so.

"I can see his words," she said. "He writes to you of love."

"Have you read the letter?" I asked.

"No," she said. "But I can see the words even so. I could feel them as he wrote them, and I can see them in front of my eyes. Now." She almost howled. "I don't need to see the letter in order to know that!"

I didn't believe her. Despite her psychic abilities, I felt if she could see anything, it was because she had gone through my mail. Which wasn't pleasant. And yet, if she had done so, she must know that it was only an innocent letter full of affection.

"What does he mean," Audrey suddenly asked, "when he writes of plums? Of a poem?"

"I sent him a bottle of plum wine for his birthday," I said. "And I sent him a poem I had written."

"You wrote to him secretly? While living with me in my house?"

So many possible defenses, and at the same time none that mattered. I hadn't written to him particularly secretly. As a matter of fact I had written to him rather openly. About being with Audrey. About never again wishing for anything else. About hoping that our fluke of an affair could turn into a friendship under the circumstances, rather than ending with the cheapness of having merely been a double-header affair. As it happened, I hadn't written to him from the house either, but during one of my lunch hours.

During which I had also mailed that fated birthday package in the middle of June, which now was belatedly acknowledged. "Thank you for the plums."

"Is that your secret symbol?" Audrey asked in a menacing voice. "Plums? How quaint. How romantic."

"It isn't, Audrey," I defended myself. "I wanted to keep his friendship."

"With secret favors? Plums?"

"I don't see what's so terrible about that," I said. "I merely sent him a bottle of wine."

I tried to keep my innocence in focus. I certainly couldn't hear it in Audrey's voice.

"Anyway, there's no use discussing it," she said.

"Don't hang up," I begged.

"What do you still want to say?"

"Please come home."

"No."

"Please, Audrey. Please don't do this. Please come home."

"No."

"Where will you stay?" I pleaded.

"I'll stay in the office tonight." The woman from whom she sublet office space only worked nine to five daytime hours at the office.

"Please come home," I begged, straining for plausible reasons. "It'll be so uncomfortable."

"As it happens, it won't." She laughed. "The office is very comfortable." She was right, of course.

"But I want you here," I cried.

"But you can't have me."

"Audrey, I want to hold you. I want to talk with you. I want to know where you are."

"No," she said. "You can't. And after tonight, you will never know where I am anymore. Never!"

"Audrey, don't say that," I gasped.

"You'll never know where I am anymore," she shouted. Then she hung up, and when I dialed her number again, I got a busy signal.

I darted for the liquor stash. I had to forget this. I simply had to. But instead of pouring myself a drink, I changed my mind and darted right back to the telephone. More than anything else, I needed to talk to someone. I called Kay. She spoke to me for a long time, maddeningly philosophical and calm. I told her I didn't know what to do. I was hysterical. Should I go to Audrey's office? Should I move out of the house so that she could come back home? I loved her so. I didn't want to be in her way if she wanted me out of it. And I didn't want to be out of her way, if she wanted me in it. Kay, you knew her way before I even met her. What would she want? What should I do?

"Well, what do you want to do?" Kay asked.

That wasn't the point. Or rather, it was. I wanted to do what Audrey wanted me to do. Didn't anybody understand that I loved her? Didn't Kay understand? That I would do anything? To have her back, or not to have her back, according to what was right for Audrey, the most beautiful, precious person in the whole world to me. No, perhaps Kay didn't understand. Hadn't we sat together on quiet evenings, no more than three or four months ago, talking ourselves into a streak of ecstasy at the idea that poets and artists and our kind should always be free, should never be enslaved to another human being, shouldn't ever have to heed difficult lovers? If I'd heard myself talk like this then, I wouldn't have believed it. I would have laughed, joked about plenty of fish in the sea, with a few perhaps more viable than any fish currently at hand, or rather slipping out of hand.

Kay heard me talk, but for all I knew she didn't hear me. She heard the past. She heard what she expected to hear. She heard her own present. But she didn't hear me.

"Maybe you're right," she said. "Maybe it would be better for you if you moved out of Audrey's house."

But I hadn't asked what would be right for me. Only what would be right for Audrey. And I didn't want to leave. At all. How could I trust Kay if she was capable of suggesting such a thing with total calm?

"Perhaps you aren't meant to be together now," she said.

How could she say that? She had seen us. She had witnessed the magic.

"Perhaps you're simply not ready," Kay said. "Obviously you're suffering from Audrey's jealousy. Obviously you're trapped. And so is she. She must suffer a lot, not to want to come home."

I didn't want to leave the house, my life, or Audrey. I felt so defeated that the thing I wanted least seemed the punishment I thought I needed to agree to. But where would I go? Kay had already found a new roommate.

"You'll find a place," Kay assured me.

I didn't want a place. I didn't want to share an apartment again with a roommate. I didn't think I was able to afford one on my own. Above all, I wanted to be here, in peace, and in love with Audrey.

"You could stay with me for a few days. I'm sure Mel won't mind," Kay said. Mel was her new roommate.

After an hour of talking I felt more wound up than before. Finally I said goodnight. And then I finally did take recourse to the liquor shelf. Downing a few hours' worth of sleep.

§

When I woke up, my head spinning, I called Audrey.

"How are you?"

I wanted to hear that she loved me, that she had missed me, had been lonely for me.

"Fine," she said icily.

"Audrey, I can't bear this," I said. "Will I see you tonight?"

"No," she said.

"What are you going to do?"

"I don't know yet. But I will not come home. I can't bear it, and I can't bear you."

"But what do you want to do?" I asked in a sob.

Least of all she wanted to talk to me. Reluctantly I replaced the telephone receiver. I didn't want to end the conversation, but there was nothing I could do with her coldness.

Next I called the office and lied to the manager.

"Terry? It's Andrea. I won't be in this morning. My friend Audrey didn't come home last night and I'm worried. I want to find out what happened."

"Sure," she said.

"I'm going to call her office and try to find out anything at all. Then I'll call you back," I promised with great pretense of responsibility.

"Don't worry about us. I'm sure the office will function for a few hours without you. But do call back and let me know what happens, please."

"There are a few letters on my desk that need to be typed."

"I'll go and see what has to be done. Just get your mind at ease about your friend."

"Thanks, Terry," I said.

I waited half an hour, then I called the office again, lying my crafty way through further excuses. My boss told me to take off all the time I needed, and that they cared for me at the office and to remember that they were there for me. I thanked him.

That was that. With a relieved and somewhat evil feeling of

triumph I hung up. Something in me laughed when I dialed Audrey's number, which was of course answered by the office building's receptionist. "Dr. Bergen's office." At which point, having done my duty, I hung up again. I had called her office, hadn't I? For a moment I seriously considered getting dressed and taking a taxi to Audrey's office, just for formality's sake. To lie as little as possible. But I felt much too weak and sorry for myself for that much effort.

I went into the basement, made sure that the animals' water bowls were filled and that they had plenty of food. Back upstairs I carefully locked all the doors from the inside. Then I poured myself glass after glass of brandy, vodka, peach liqueur, anything at all we had in the house. Soon I found myself rocking on the floor, just sitting there, rocking, waiting to pass out.

Oh, God, to simply pass out and sleep again, and hope that by the time I woke up again, things would have taken care of themselves. Somehow. Of course they always. Did. Would. I always woke. Up. I always. Went on. Doing whatever. It was. I was doing. Didn't want anyone. To find me. Here. Like this. Got up. To check. The doors. Again. Yes. Locked. When was I. Going to. Pass out? Another glass. Would do. If I dragged. Myself. Across. To the shelf. And then. Took the glass. To the bedroom. Lay down. In soft. Pillow. Glass? Where? Are you? There. At the. Oops. Side. Bitter. Yet sleep. No, sweet. No, I was. Right. Bitter sleep.

Kay drifted into my mind.

"Kay?" I said, puzzled. Hadn't I locked the doors? Her face thin and gray with—what? Pity? Worry?

"Yeah, it's me. Don't you recognize me?"

Foolish question. But Kay wasn't supposed to be there. What was going on?

"I bolted the doors," I stammered.

"Yeah," she said, unsmiling. "I climbed in the back door."

"How?" I asked.

"The animal way," she said and, with some difficulty, smiled. "Didn't think I was going to fit. But I did."

"Why?" I asked lamely.

"Audrey called me. She tried to get in, but the doors were bolted from the inside. So she called me. She tried to call you too, but you didn't answer the phone. So I tried to find a way to get into the house, and I finally hit on the animal route. Christ, Andrea, we were worried about you."

This upset me. Shit, Audrey didn't come home, said I'd never see her again. And then I didn't even have the right to get drunk in peace without people worrying about me? What business of theirs was it what I did to myself? What if I wanted to get drunk? Had I bothered Audrey at the office last night after she had hung up on me and I was wild with worry and with fear? Had I sent the imperial army after her? The anger sobered me up. I looked at my watch. It was three thirty. It was daylight outside.

"This is still Thursday, isn't it?" I asked.

"Yes," Kay said, suppressing a smile.

"Afternoon?" I asked.

"Yes."

"How come Audrey knew the doors were locked?" Or less politely in my private thoughts, what business does she have snooping after me? When she's supposed to be at her school? I furtively checked out the alarm clock on the bed stand and found it duly set for a generous hour before she was due to be done with her last class.

"She came home to pick up some things. But she couldn't get in."

A moment of compassion. Poor thing!

"Where is she now?" I asked, concerned. Poor wanderer, out in the streets. Or rather, probably back at school teaching, without whatever it was she had wanted to get.

"She's here," Kay said. "In the living room."

Now she was telling me. What was I doing talking to Kay when Audrey was here?

"I want to see her, for God's sake," I said. "I want to talk to her!"

"Are you sure?" Kay asked.

"Yes, for crying out loud. Audrey!" I did cry out loud.

"I'll go get her," Kay said when there was no response to my call.

Kay slunk away, looked back at me once. All right, so I wasn't a pretty sight, okay? Disheveled, probably gray in the face and with bags under my eyes, and my eyes glassy. So what? Audrey was here, and I could actually see her.

She came in, dressed in her jeans skirt and the blue angel blouse. Tears came to my eyes. She was so pretty. I loved her so. She stood by the bed and looked at me as though from an enormous distance. Her eyes were clouded.

"Audrey," I whispered and sat up to touch her.

She stepped away, shaking her head. All of her movements looked as though she were floating. I knew I had my brain full of liquor and fuzziness. But I also knew that I couldn't have looked nearly as ghostly and as far away as she did.

"Audrey," I said again. "I love you."

She looked at the floor. "I don't know what to say."

"Aren't you back to stay?" I asked.

Audrey said nothing beyond an occasional repetition of the fact that she didn't know what to say. After a while Kay's head appeared in the doorway, smiling apprehensively.

"You talk to her," Audrey said in a low voice. Then, without looking at me again, she turned away, head first, as though her body would have to follow her then, and walked out of the room. She still looked as though she were floating.

"You ought to come and stay with me tonight," Kay said.

"But there isn't room at the apartment for me any longer," I protested.

§

I didn't want to go. I didn't want to be treated as though I were mad. Audrey's eyes fearful, distant. I was a perfectly normal human being who had elected to get drunk. For no one to see, for no one to know. Sorry about Audrey's bolted doors and all, but it was she who'd failed to come home last night. If she hadn't, I would now be at the office, not drunk; and she'd now be at school teaching, not here.

"I think you better come with me now," Kay said. "Audrey packed a few things for you. They'll tide you over for a few days. We can worry about everything else later."

So. It was already all arranged. Andrea ousted by decree of Audrey, and with the help of always glad-to-be-meddling-in-other-folk's-tragedies Kay. I was disappointed, a feeling gnawing at my nerves like a starved animal. I was also terrified. To be thought crazy if I were to resist, with a hangover mixed with this unbelievable sense of disillusionment. And no fight in me.

So be it. I got up, got dressed. Kay steered me to the door. I could barely believe it, but I followed her. A taxi was already waiting outside. I couldn't believe that either. How crafty. There was no point in turning back to fight this last humiliation. I sat down in the taxi. Crying. Before leaving the house I had looked back into the living room area. To see Audrey. To catch a glimpse of her. No matter what, I loved her.

"She's out in back. In the garden," Kay said.

Not even a goodbye?

"I want to say goodbye to her." I forced myself to be assertive.

Kay shook her head. "Not a good idea. She's very upset."

And what about me? I was relegated to sit in the back of the taxi, Kay patting my hand and giving directions to the driver. To her apartment.

I didn't want to eat. I didn't want to, couldn't sleep. I didn't want to go to work the following day. That part was easily arranged. I called in sick, and this time without lies.

"I could call in sick for the rest of my life," I told Kay. "I'll simply tell them I've a heart condition. Which happens to be perfectly true."

At work they weren't surprised. They asked about Audrey. I told them she was fine but needed to be alone. I was, in the meanwhile, temporarily staying at my former address. Well, get some rest, they sympathized.

I tried. Mostly I wanted to hide. Which I did, as much as I could, in Kay's sleeping corner with the curtains drawn. I watched her sleep during the night, watched her be indifferent to how what she had helped arrange would affect me. She slept the sleep of the self-righteous.

I knew it would be hard for me to like Kay after this. She was a drama aficionada. She loved to direct and play supporting roles in other people's lives. I had watched her do the same to other friends. Now she was acting on behalf of Audrey, with whom she was fascinated, with whom we were all fascinated. Within a relatively short period of time, though, after doing her part in helping Audrey and me to part ways, Kay would forget Audrey in the unfolding drama of her own life. I would not. Kay had no idea what this meant to me.

§

Mel, Kay's roommate, was pleasantly accommodating about the

intrusion in his living quarters. Friday night, before going off to spend the night with his new girlfriend, he sat on the carpet and played his guitar for me. I sat on the sofa, feeling safe enough in his company to cry quietly. Between songs, Mel told me that this is how he had spent the last few months before becoming Kay's roommate: sleeping on a friend's sofa, or alternately crying on it, about a broken relationship with a woman. He felt it was a favor that, given the opportunity and need, had to be passed on. The revolving sofa of lost lovers. He had a new lover now, though his heart was back with the old one still. One of those things.

In the meantime, he simply sat here and played the guitar for me. When Kay came home, he stopped abruptly, said it was time for him to go. Kay confided to me, starry-eyed and with sympathetic joy, that she'd never seen him break through this self-consciousness to play music for anyone as audience in recent years. Which explained his rapid disappearance when she came. It touched me, being singled out for generous compassion.

While Kay bustled around in her corner of the apartment, I simply kept on sitting huddled against the corner of the sofa, pretending to write into my journal, but doing little else besides crying. After a while Kay went to answer the phone, and I understood from the protective turn of her back toward me that she was talking to Audrey without wanting me to know. I went to the bathroom and sat on the floor. There wasn't anywhere else to go for privacy, Kay's, or Audrey's, or mine.

"How is she?" I asked Kay when she was finally off the phone and I had emerged from my bathroom floor crouch.

"Who?" Kay asked with a guilt-stricken look on her face.

"Audrey," I said. "Didn't you just talk to her?"

"How do you know?" Kay asked, convinced no doubt that she had carefully not mentioned Audrey's name or said anything revelatory while I was still within hearing distance.

Should I lay claim to psychic gifts of my own? I might even fool her. Something within me laughed. Quietly and bitterly. It was so obvious.

"I know by the way you turned your back to me when you answered the phone," I said. I laughed out loud now at the sound of pathos in my voice.

"She's fine," Kay said with a companion smile to my laughter. "She told me to tell you at some point that you're welcome to use the house on Sunday for your guests. I might as well tell you now."

I had totally forgotten. I had promised to provide breakfast and a few hours' worth of babysitting for two baby cousins whose parents were attending a family gathering, to which I had been invited also, had even managed to get Audrey invited along, both of us knowing all along that it would be far too difficult to go in the end. Now I'd have to call them and cancel even the remnant of extended family spirit, the babysitting part. Audrey's generous offer to feel free to use the house notwithstanding, it would be too much for me right now.

"And where will she be?" I asked.

"She's at the beach right now. She'll stay there until Sunday night."

So there. For the time being, I did know vaguely where she was, despite her threat that I would never know again. Defiant triumph in the midst of despair. Later that evening I made, under Kay's congenial supervision, a considerable dent into Kay's vodka supply. We talked during the laborious process. I was raw with loss. Some of the things she said in her detached fervor burned like branding irons.

"You move too fast, Andrea," Kay said.

I didn't know where to hide my face in shame. Should I have pretended indifference and let Audrey chase me? Should I have been full of strategies, having met the one person I felt was my destiny? How does one move when in love? How other than with direct precision toward the lover? And how was I to know any different, not having felt and shared such magic before? Yet having wished for it all of my life?

I looked into Kay's young, dark, satisfied eyes, pleased that in her detachment she had already found the definition of my dilemma. The mirror there described to me an Andrea who jumped at the sound of love, and at the closeness of sex. Andrea, older than Kay, but moving through the margins of love and physicality with much less finesse than Kay herself. Andrea, the pushover. Not as adept at juggling two lovers at once, which was Kay's specialty of the moment, with spare candidates on the waiting list. Accusing me of moving too fast.

"It's fun watching you get drunk," she told me with perfect gentleness cutting straight into my pain.

"Is it?" I asked. At least I served some purpose here, entertaining Kay's lust for scandal.

Much of the night I spent awake again, watching Kay sleep. A few times I got up quietly to fill my blood, which was turning too sober, with the tingle of energy loss again, with a few moments of hope for sleep and fuzziness. Until sweat on my face tickled me awake with fear that it was in fact something other than mere sweat. After all, I was lying in cockroach territory here, on a thin mattress on the floor.

Toward morning I woke from a terrifying dream. Green snakes wound through my consciousness, not threatening, just winding their magnificent shapes. Then I dreamed steps at the window, Audrey's steps, memorized in my unconscious from the many times she had come for me past the window to the back door. Tap tap tap. I actually saw her on the steps, almost at the door, her hands stretched out as though to knock. Then, with a shriek, she flew up and away, far beyond the reach of my dream calls to her. Quickly I shook myself awake in self-defense and lay awake for hours, afraid of her shriek and her flying away each time I closed my eyes. I watched Kay again in her deep, untroubled sleep. I watched the gray dawn of a rainy day.

When morning light was solid, I crept away from Kay's sleep space and sat in the corner of the living room sofa. It smelled musty. I held my notebook in my lap like a security blanket, but its empty pages remained empty, my mind longing for action, not reflection. Being guest here now, I felt compelled to remain quiet until the hostess awakened. I thought of, but didn't write, a letter to Audrey that I knew would never be sent. Dulcinea. To dream the impossible dream. To go where the brave dare not go. To burst in where angels fear to tread. Marching to hell for a heavenly cause.

When Kay got up and Mel returned from his night's brave philandering, I felt mightily in the way again. Weary body sitting in their living room, with a mouth too full of sorrow to bid even good morning in a civilized manner that didn't immediately call attention to my pain. This time I couldn't even retreat to the bathroom for privacy, for sooner or later they would want to use it for their Saturday mid-morning rituals.

The dream image kept spooking me. Audrey's hand reaching out to knock on the door, her body flying away with that uncanny shriek. What if anything had happened to her? And I wasn't there to help? I tried to comfort myself and reassure myself about her well-being. But I couldn't. I didn't even know any of her friends whom I might call for reassurance. The only one I knew adequately by first and last name was currently in Italy with her lover at some unknown address. Everybody else I'd met or heard of on a first name basis only. How was it possible that I was so cut off from her that I couldn't even reach a common friend? Except Kay, who forbiddingly turned her back to me when Audrey called.

Mel left again and Kay made for the bathroom. I knew her elaborate habits of hygiene and took the opportunity of her time spent in the shower to make a few phone calls. I needed to do something. I needed to be in touch with someone who knew Audrey. I was concerned about her. But most of all I wanted to be in touch. I decided on a cloak-and-dagger course of action, which satisfied my need to not be passive. I knew the name of the psychologist from whom Audrey sublet office space. I found her in the phone book and dialed her number.

"Am I speaking to Karen Espontes?"

"Yes." A tidy, confident voice.

"The psychologist?"

"Yes."

I quickly stated my dilemma. "I don't know if you know about me."

"Yes, I know who you are from Audrey."

She failed to save me out of my dilemma by knowing only that there wasn't anything to do, that Audrey would come out her pain, and so, her friend hoped, would I.

"I guess I just needed to talk to someone who knew Audrey." I found myself apologizing, confronted for the first time in my life with the benign indifference of a therapist. That was alright, too, the comforting voice told me in all cool friendliness. Nothing gained, nothing lost. I had wanted to touch Audrey with some ingenious maneuver. I had failed. That was all.

I was off the phone and into the sofa corner once again where I could, however, not bear it for very long. Kay went through casual Saturday morning brunch preparations when I quietly put my things together and told her with a radiance of heart and mind that I knew now what I would have to do.

"What's that?" Kay asked.

"I'll have to go to Audrey's house and take care of a few things," I said evasively.

§

It seemed too risky to tell Kay that I planned to go and incinerate my past by way of burning all my notebooks and letters. Kay might have been horrified by the idea, as I would have been myself under ordinary circumstances. But these were not ordinary circumstances.

The idea gave me a great deal of pleasure. I can't change my past for you, Audrey, but I can show you and myself that my attachment to it amounts to nothing. Anticipation sang in me. I can't burn my past either, of course, but I can burn my careful records of it. I can burn these things that once were meaningful to me.

I told Kay I'd probably spend the night at Audrey's house, since Audrey wasn't planning to return. Kay's repeated invitation to come back and spend the night at her apartment didn't tempt me. But I promised her I'd call if dark thoughts should come knocking. Gently I closed the door of Kay's apartment behind me, slowly, to hide the force of elation inside me.

It was raining. I held up my face to the rain as though it were a blessing. Wash the tears away from me. Wash the sadness away. I hummed to myself. In sat in the back of the bus so that I could continue singing in a low voice. Later, as I took the long escalator down to the metro station, a tall black man quietly stepped up behind me and held his wide umbrella over both of us. When we were out of the rain, he walked on past me with a light smile but with no words exchanged between us. I took that as a good omen. Life promised to be kind, voluntarily and without obligations.

When I arrived at the house I took out the box of letters. They would be the first to go in my ritual of dedicating myself to the future, not the past. In the basement I found a black metal tub with a lid—what would one do with it in ordinary life? Roast turkeys? Soak hand-washables? In my extraordinary life it would serve me as a burning vessel. I took it up to my room and carefully placed it in the center after removing all flammables from the vicinity. There went the first letters, sizzling into black at the touch of my match. Whoosh—the past into ashes. It was a feeling of thrill.

I thought of Audrey's story of burning her novel manuscript once. "Oh, sure, it felt wonderful, page after page in the fireplace. Afterwards, of course, I felt sorry." Well, there was no chance of my feeling sorry afterwards. I wasn't burning a work of art with which I had become temporarily disillusioned. I was burning my way free to Audrey instead. Not like another lover of whom she had once complained to me. "And do you know, under the bed, the very bed we made love in, she had the letters of old lovers bundled in a collection?" Oh, Audrey, Audrey, now you will believe my love for you, I hummed to myself.

Pretty soon it became obvious, however, that burning the past in this fashion would take an unbelievable amount of time and patience, added to which was the fact that the ashes made themselves independent and began drifting up in flakes, and the smoke, though of moderate proportions, was stinging my eyes.

I decided to move the operation to the fireplace. What more obvious place to conduct my rite? I had a few doubts concerning things I ought to know about using a fireplace, about which I in fact knew nothing. But I was impatient. I did check for the smoke exit, and the smoke did in fact exit properly instead of returning into the room. Soon the letters were all gone, also some photographs and many memories of love and friendship. I regretted some of the latter, but it couldn't be helped now. I was in a radical mood.

Then came the notebooks. More difficult. As they were, paper stacked and bound, they refused to burn. I had to tear out sections and feed them separately into my passionate sacrifice.

What I should have known about the fireplace but didn't think of, sweating in my T-shirt by the hearth, was that concerned neighbors might well notice the smoke and wonder about it on this midsummer Saturday blazing with heat. Worse than that, though the smoke left the house, it got stuck in the sluggish air instead of rising.

Soon there was a knock at the door. The next door neighbors, both husband and wife.

"Is everything all right?"

"Sure," I said, wiping sweat off my face. "I'm merely burning some old papers."

"Aha," the woman said. "Well, good, so long as everything is all right. We just noticed the smoke. In fact it came straight into our kitchen. So we were afraid something in the house had caught on fire." Slight accusation in her voice, though phrased lightheartedly, didn't escape me.

"I'm so sorry," I said. "I had no idea the smoke would bother you. I'll stop right away."

"Nah, that's all right," the woman said. "We're about to leave the house anyway to visit friends. Which is another reason we came over. Audrey asked me to feed the cats, and I guess I'll do that now before we leave."

"Oh, I'll feed them, since I'm here anyway," I said.

"Are you sure?" she asked with a devious smile on her face which was either a commentary about my general predicament or a questioning of my sanity. I wondered how much Audrey had told her neighbor when leaving for the beach with the dogs.

"I'm sure," I answered, smiling back with as much certainty as I could muster.

Hardly had I closed the door behind them, I slumped down on the sofa, trembling with shame as well as amusement. Trust me to get caught with a lit fireplace in the middle of a hot, muggy summer afternoon. What wasn't burned yet would have to remain unburned for now. After all, at least all the letters were gone, and the most recent notebooks containing all traces of Joel.

I went to the basement to feed the cats. The orange tomcat treated me with disdain. Could he sense that I was in disfavor? But Missy was still on my side, or so I pretended to myself while stroking her black and white fur.

"Meow," she said.

"I love you, too," I replied.

§

Back upstairs I stared at my two incomplete ash heaps. I had had my fun. Now I'd have to figure out a way of getting rid of the evidence. I had just emptied the contents of the tub into the trash can when the telephone rang. I prayed it would be Audrey. Instead, a man's voice asked for me.

"This is she," I replied. Then everything fell into place, before he even identified himself. Tuesday morning's unsettling caller.

Two weeks ago, while Audrey was at the office seeing a Saturday morning client, he had called and asked for a friend whose calls Audrey had agreed to accept for the duration of the friend's stay in Italy. After all, some gallery might wish to make her famous. This gentleman calling was, however, merely looking for a modeling job.

I hadn't liked his voice the first time we spoke. High, nasal, and persistent in a whiny way. Besides which he had originally interrupted me in a bout of verbal composition, and I truly did not know of any artist in need of a model. He was very good, he assured me. How nice for him, but this didn't bring any artists in need of his services to mind either. Audrey was doing dragons, Kay was doing abstracts, and other than that I knew a few writers and a lot of office folk. There was no advice or help I could possibly give him.

He wouldn't give up. He simply stayed on the phone, repeating how good he was and how cheaply he was willing to work. Finally I offered him this in order to get rid of his endless repetitions: the other person living here was an artist, and though she wasn't working from models, perhaps she might know someone.

If he would leave his number and she could think of someone, I would have her call him. But no, he didn't want to do leave his number because he was staying with friends and didn't want to impose on them by giving out their number. Weird in retrospect, because he did feel free to impose on me to give him my name—something I was not in the habit of doing—and then calling back not Audrey, as I had suggested, but asking for me by name, no doubt to give the impression of familiarity, just as he had done by using Audrey's friend's name.

And then he failed to call me at the office after he had whined his way in similar fashion into Audrey giving him my office number. By not calling me at the office after doing all that, he had caused a lot of confusion and spook in our house. I was angry, understanding everything now. He had incredible persistence. Despite my anger, he kept me on the phone another ten minutes.

"Tell me, why didn't you call me at the office number the person gave you when you called here on Tuesday?" I asked.

"I meant to," he said. "But then I didn't get the chance."

"Oh," I said, trying desperately to find a way of reproving a person who had by such simple omission created havoc with my life. Finally he did get off the phone and I on the phone to Kay, relating to her the whole story. It sounded banal in the retelling. It was, in fact, banal.

Kay sympathized, but never quite understood that I was describing the straw breaking a camel's back without even being deliberately deposited there. I also told her about burning my past. Hearing that, she first of all moaned, but then calmed down. After all, she agreed, my notebook scribbling was so prolific, I was probably doing a favor to posterity by removing a portion of it. English students of the future were obliged to thank me for the act of kindness. We talked for about an hour. She invited me back to the apartment, but I preferred staying at Audrey's house.

When I got off the phone, I decided that cleaning up the fireplace could wait until morning. I let the cats back in and fell on the bed, trying to communicate my love to Audrey in supernatural ways, though not convinced that any messages that I might attempt to send via ESP had any likelihood of reaching anyone, much less their intended recipient. One measly success with penciled strawberries does not an able psychic make.

I fell asleep and woke when the phone rang. Nobody spoke at the other end of the line. After a while there was the click on the other end hanging up.

I looked at the clock. It was just about midnight. My mind went into gear. What if it were Audrey? What if she had come back from the beach and called to find out whether I was there or not, in other words whether she could come home or not? If it was Audrey, I reasoned, and she was back, there would be one place she could go to, her office. If I called her office phone, I'd get her answering machine and could leave a message. So I dialed. To my surprise, the receiver was lifted, but nobody spoke.

"Audrey?" I asked. "Audrey?"

I heard the click of hanging up.

So she was there. Now what should I do? A moment later I called again. Exactly the same routine was repeated. I said her name twice, then the connection was broken. That proved it. She was there, didn't want to speak to me, and was probably put out by my staying at the house, because, not wanting to speak to me, she definitely would not want to see me. I would call again and say as fast as I could, "I'mleavingthehouseyoucancomehome," before she could hang up again. I dialed. To my chagrin, the line was busy now. I dialed Kay's number, no matter that it was now half past twelve.

"Hello," she said sleepily.

I tried to explain to her what I thought and why.

She didn't seem to comprehend anything, so I cut myself short and simply said that I'd have to spend the night with her after all, and could she please leave the alley door unlatched so that I could get in. I would latch it again after I got there. It might take me an hour or longer to get there. Kay sleepily agreed to unlatch the door and I spared her further elaborations as to what all I would now have to do.

I ordered a cab. I gathered shoes, coat, and a skirt to wear on alternate days during the week. What Audrey had packed for me as I was dismissed on Thursday in Kay's company was minimal. I took the knitting I had started for Audrey from the closet. I would finish it during my exile. The last thing I took was her framed self-portrait. It was unwieldy, but I would not leave without it.

"And if you ever throw me out and I cannot take you with me, I will take your picture with me. Everywhere," I'd told her when she happily presented it to me.

At the time I had been telling her fairy tales. Once upon a time there was a woman so wise that the king himself came to ask for her hand. She consented to marry him gladly. One day he got angry with her and ordered her out of the kingdom. As he commanded her to go, he allowed her, in a fit of generosity, to take one thing with her besides her clothes and her shoes, and he allowed her to choose for herself what she liked best. The next morning he woke up inside a sack, and the sack in the middle of the wilderness, and as he sleepily tried to comprehend his surroundings, she clarified it all for him. "You told me to take with me what I liked best from the kingdom. So I took you."

Oh, to be in a fairy tale. Instead, I tried Audrey's office number again and the line was still busy. Whereas my taxi had arrived. I hesitated, standing in the center of the living room, the bag with my clothes in my right hand, the picture in my left. Through the front window gauze curtains I saw the taxi driver come up the steps. Time to go. The only consolation was that she could feel free to come home now. Her home. No longer mine.

I gave the driver Audrey's office address. At the front desk I inquired whether the desk attendant knew if Dr. Bergen was in. Not to his knowledge, but I was welcome to check for myself. So I went through the hallway to her door, unable to hear a sound behind it. I sat on the floor and composed a brief note, which I slipped under the door. I left a similar note in a discrete envelope at the front desk, telling her it was okay for her to go home, I was no longer there. My heart beat wildly. When I turned my back to the desk attendant, I cried.

Outside again in the muggy night, I started walking. After a while I reached a public phone and called a taxi. I waited a long time. No taxi came. All I had been able to give as address had been the street corner, and the name of the gas station, now closed, at which I made my phone call from the public phone on the outside wall. A police car passed the gas station and me for the third time now. They stopped the car and asked if I was all right. Yes, waiting for a taxi, I told them. I made another call.

This time the taxi dispatcher told me that taxis could only be ordered from a residential address or an open business. But, I argued, I was standing out here in the middle of the night in the middle of the street, trying to get to a residential address, and previously nobody had questioned that fact. However, the dispatcher informed me, this was most likely why no taxi had come to pick me up in the first place. She couldn't send me one? I pleaded fruitlessly. The answer was no.

It was then that I noticed a crack diagonally across the glass of Audrey's picture. Too much traveling for the two by three foot glass frame. Short of kissing the broken glass over her crayon face, I stroked it lightly with my hand, remembering the day when I had touched the unframed portrait and marked one of the curls of her hair with my fingers so that a streak of crayon was blurred. My shock at realizing what I had done. Audrey's laughter, so what if it's art? I love it when you mess my hair, even in my self-portrait.

I wanted to cry at my lonely gas station, with the police car still cruising. Concernedly, I hoped. I began walking again. If necessary I would walk to Kay's house. I was tired. It was hot and muggy. The street was practically deserted, well-lit, but lonely. After about a mile I began looking for apartment buildings that might have visibly occupied lobbies. At last I found one and asked a suspicious person whether I might order a cab from there and wait for it in the lobby. It took a great display of helplessness and weariness to get him to consent. The weariness wasn't an act. I felt as though I couldn't go a single block further. At long last I was rewarded by a taxi that landed me at Kay's doorstep at three o'clock in the morning, dusty, sweaty, and too tired for anything except to crawl on top of the cot she had pulled out for me. When I came in she didn't even wake up. I latched her door, took the unwieldy, broken glass picture into my arms and fell asleep.

§

I went back to work on Monday. The massive piles of letters to be typed waiting for me were a relief—familiar ground. In addition, I was surrounded by people who didn't give a rat's ass how my private life was going but were glad that I was back to alleviate my boss's panic, for he had come to trust me and my skills, but was vociferously suspicious of everybody else's. Papers had to be stapled correctly. Flat staple neatly lined up with either top or side of paper. Nothing else would do. And nobody could unscramble the messy drafts he typed as easily as I could figure out his anagrams.

He showed his relief at my return by singing cheerful tunes in my vicinity, one of which, unbeknownst to him, touched me especially, as its lyrics went, to a racy melody, "money's gone, girl's gone," and the lucky persona of the song feistily didn't give a hoot. Unlike myself.

By Monday night I was crazy with longing to put things right with Audrey. I composed a letter full of appeal and self-abasement. Forgive me. If you knew how I suffer, surely you'd come to my rescue. I decided to hand-deliver the writ to her house and once again went on the extended bus and metro journey. I meant to sneak around the side of the house, get over the gate and slip the letter in by way of the animal door where Kay had squeezed through the Thursday before. Audrey closed that exit at night before going to sleep, after coaxing the dogs out for one last time before morning. This way she would find my words that same night still.

I advanced unseen and unheard. Usually anyone approaching the house at all, even just passing on the sidewalk, was greeted by a ferocious concert of the two dogs barking. But I banked on the fact that my existence was old hat to them and would not give rise to any vocal outbursts of anxiety. They didn't disappoint me. Everything was quiet.

I was just about to pull the rod that held the gate in place to keep the dogs in the garden—and from there it was only two steps to the house—when the neighbors' car pulled up at the side of the house, with the headlights shining on me and my maneuver. The dogs reacted to the car with barks and I reacted to the lights with dread, and pretty soon there was a whole lot of commotion. Adrenaline fizzing, I ran back to the front of the house and threw my envelope on the doormat at exactly the same instant as Audrey pulled the curtains from the front door glass window. We stood looking at each other for a moment, her face serious, stern, and, in my assessment, disapproving.

I ran down the darkness of the street, back into the Metro and the bus and the temporary shelter of Kay's apartment. I kept seeing

Audrey's face at her door. She'd worn her orange guru dress. In the safety of my current distance I longed for her to smile at me again, to welcome me again. But I also still had shock in my bones. How she had frightened me, or rather how frightened I was capable of being when faced with her. Surely a more civilized and unafraid person would have said: "Good evening. I couldn't stay away. I brought you a letter. I love you."

The next day I hoped Audrey would call me. She didn't. And I didn't dare trouble her existence again on my own initiative. She called me on Wednesday morning at work, however.

"I love you," she said angrily. Oh, thank God. "I don't have anything else to say."

"Wait," I said. "Can I call you back from another phone, so I can say something real?" I pleaded.

"Okay," she said. "But I really don't have anything to say."

Oh, but I did. "Please let me call you. I'll just be a moment. Are you at home?"

I raced past the receptionist and informed her I would be absent from my desk for an unspecified amount of time; moreover, if she saw the phone light on in one of the two unoccupied offices, that was me, making a private phone call, and if anyone asked for me, I was unavailable. The receptionist smiled at my excitement and promised complicity.

"Audrey," I said when she answered the phone, "I want to talk to you."

"Well, you're talking to me," she observed.

"Ah, I also want to see you."

"I have to think about that."

"Oh, please say yes," I pleaded.

"I don't know," she said. "I don't know if it's a good idea. I don't know if I want to."

"Well, I want to," I said more calmly than I thought I was

capable of speaking. "Please think about it."

"All right," she said. "I'll think about it. I'll call you and let you know."

I spent three hours sitting on guard at my desk. I didn't dare go to lunch or even smoke a cigarette in the lady's room. When I absolutely had to leave my desk to get a file or make a photocopy, I made sure someone close to my desk knew precisely where I was going, lest I should miss what seemed to me the most important call of all my life.

"All right, I'll see you," Audrey called to tell me.

"Thank you," I said. "When?"

"I don't know."

"Tonight?" I begged. "Because tomorrow is Thursday and you'll be tired from your clients at the end of the day," I added to rationalize my impatience.

"All right, tonight then," Audrey conceded.

"Where shall we meet?" I asked, barely able to believe my good fortune. "And what time?"

"You get off at five thirty, right? I have a client until six. So let's say seven o'clock at my house."

This puzzled me. I expected her to suggest a more neutral location. But I wasn't going to question anything now.

"I'll be there," I promised.

I decided to go to her house straight from work, though I'd be early. I still had the keys and let myself in. I went to the basement and fed the animals. Then I sat down in one of the rocking chairs. I waited the whole delicious hour, sitting still and thinking of her coming.

It began with daydreams and I ended up in something much like a trance. I felt myself surrounded by soft golden light and I murmured to myself, addressing Audrey. "You are surrounding me with love." I was vaguely aware of the time and checked my wrist watch now and again, but the feeling with which I responded to the time of waiting was so sweet, I hardly wanted to interrupt it. I was certain I would hear her car when she pulled up to the house.

At seven o'clock she wasn't there yet, but I felt secure in my trancelike state. I waited a few more minutes, then decided I would get up and greet her at the door. I stood up and walked to the door slowly, determined to wait there standing, only to find that I was much too dizzy, much too weak. Some doubts started to pierce my golden feelings, and the minutes kept seeping away. I listened for cars.

I responded to the phone slowly, thinking at first it couldn't possibly be for me, then realizing that it might be Audrey to tell me she was running late.

"Andrea?" she asked into the phone.

"You are surrounding me with love," I whispered.

"I didn't know where you were." She sounded concerned and angry.

"But I told you I would be here," I whispered. Something sounded wrong.

"Well, I'll be there as soon as I can," she said.

"But where are you?" I asked.

"I'm at my office. But never mind that now. I'll be there in half an hour. Just don't go anywhere in the meantime."

Of course not. Where would I go? I didn't understand at all. Meanwhile she had hung up and I walked back to the rocking chair, puzzled, still slightly dazed, though slowly all my golden feelings drained. I grew sad and ashamed, already knowing exactly what was going to happen. Finally she was at the house and I did meet her at the door.

"Are you all right?" she asked, flinging her red backpack on the shelf next to the door.

"Yeah, I'm all right," I said, but tears started down my cheeks, and in an attempt to hide my face, I stumbled and had to hold on to the wall. Audrey took my hands and led me to the sofa. I couldn't stop crying.

"You'll be all right," she said. She wore a white skirt and a bright red blouse and she looked absolutely beautiful, though distant and stern.

"Have you been drinking anything?" she asked.

I shook my head. It occurred to me that she thought I was under the influence. I had to explain somehow.

"I'm ashamed," I cried between chattering teeth. "Because we obviously had our signals crossed."

"What signals?" she asked in a distant voice, which I didn't like, but which had a soothing effect on me all the same.

"You must have meant for me to meet you at your office, but I understood house instead of office." I nearly choked on the pacifying words. I knew she had said to meet her at the house. What was she trying to do? I didn't understand.

She nodded. "Do you know why you misunderstood?"

I knew I hadn't misunderstood. Nevertheless, I said obediently, "It's because I wanted to hear you say to meet you at your house." How could I continue this groveling? And yet, I did. To pacify.

Again she nodded.

I felt sick and vulnerable, like a child chided for telling the truth. I was horrified. Why would she do this? Did she truly believe what she pretended to believe? To pin some craziness on me? Or was it a strategic move? To force me to show how far I would go in appeasing her, how great her power was?

"You have to learn to distinguish between your inside and the outside," she said distantly.

Slowly I raised my face to look at her. "Can you do it?" I asked.

"No," she said with utter seriousness. "I couldn't possibly go through that with you. I couldn't bear it."

"That's not what I meant," I said, realizing that she had understood me to ask whether she would work with me as a client. For the first time since she had come in the door I was capable of smiling. "I meant, can you distinguish between your inside and the outside?"

"Yes, I can," she said without hesitation.

I wanted to love her, trust her. And I knew I'd have to lie about some things for the rest of my life with her. I was in much too vulnerable a position to declare that I didn't believe her. Even before tonight's blatant mix-up she had created, I had seen her suffer from wounds of her own creation projected onto the outside. Injustices done to her by others—so many others, come to think of it. I felt caught in a wave of sadness again, and compassion for her, even admiration for her self-confidence, no matter how misguided. I loved her, sitting there before me, so sure of her judgment, so sure of being right by just saying so.

My tears of shame had dried.

"I guess this meeting of ours has miscarried. I'd hoped so much from it," I said.

Audrey smiled. "I do love you, but there is so much you have to learn. How to deal with people."

"That's a pretty tall order," I said. "I've never been too keen on that. How do I start?"

"You practice," she said.

"How do I practice?"

"You practice with other people."

I stood up from the sofa. "All right," I said. "I will go forth and practice with other people."

"I do love you, Andrea," she said again.

I wish I could have honestly said, 'I know', but that felt too risky. "I hope so," I said.

"Are you hungry?" she suddenly asked. "Have you eaten

anything? Do you want anything to eat?"

"No. No. And no." How much I loved her. "I think I should go now."

She nodded and smiled. Suddenly admiration and love did seem to come back into her eyes as well.

"Do you have enough to wear?" she asked. "I know most of your stuff is still in my closet."

"I'll manage," I said. "Look, I even got a pair of new shoes."

Audrey frowned down at my sandals.

"Don't you like the ones I got you?" she asked.

"Yes, I like them." The shoes she had given me were the only ones I had taken along. "I thought I needed at least two pairs of shoes in the world. And I didn't know when I'd be able to come here and pick up any of my others. So I got a new pair."

"They're nice," she said with obvious displeasure. At my independent action? At the waste of money when I could have acted like a civilized human being and gathered my worldly possessions from her house?

We threw together another bundle of things. With mixed feelings I followed her to the bedroom to take some more of my skirts and tops out of the closet. Our sacred place. My mind so aware of the bed. My eyes constantly tempted into its direction. My mind constantly admonishing, don't look there, don't even turn your head. My body obedient, looking strictly at the closet.

I picked things to take. Audrey was a marvelous assistant. For every thing I selected, she added two more, with the authority of someone sending off a child to camp, the child being deemed incapable of making her own best choices, underestimating, for one, the situations it would encounter out there in the varied and sometimes cruel world.

I was quiet now. I was tired. I didn't want to participate in the finality of this packing process much longer. I worked as rapidly as possible. Anything she suggested for me to pack was fine with me. Suddenly she put her arms around me.

"My darling, my darling," she said. "I wish it weren't all so difficult."

"Difficult?" I asked.

It seemed like a simple parting of ways. And, just to keep fate busy, there would still be enough things left in her household to ensure my eventual return to collect more. The books. The desk. As I reached for the final garment of this night's departure, she took me in her arms.

"I wish I could kiss you," she said.

I lifted my face to her from the plastic bag.

"What's keeping you?" I asked, tiredly.

Parts of me felt triumphant, though. So you want to kiss me? See, here is my body, my mouth, all open to you, my life and my love. I am waiting for your kiss. I will not abuse it. I will not put any obligations on your kiss. I never have. I love you, and you know that. I am yours, and you know that.

She moved her mouth close to mine. Then stopped.

"I wish I could kiss you," she repeated, sweetness and desperation in her eyes.

Something broke inside me. "But you can't," I said, tears welling up in my eyes again.

"I can't," she said. "I want to so much."

"I'm holding still," I said, not as calmly as I wanted to. The pain of her reluctance burned like poison.

"Why?" I finally asked.

"You know," she said mysteriously.

I knew? It would be easier if she said what she meant.

"Why?" I repeated my question.

In answer she moved her face close again. I could feel her breath on my lips. Stopped again.

"It's you and Joel," she whispered in a heart-rending sound. "I see you and Joel in an embrace and I can't kiss you."

"Maybe someday you will," I said. "Please take me to Kay's apartment now."

"Do you have everything?" she asked as we piled sundry plastic bags and parcels at the front door.

"Yes," I said.

"We've never really had a courtship," Audrey said in the car. "We'll have one now. We'll have it very slowly. I'll get to call you up and make dates, and all that sort of thing. And," she added a little sadly, "I will slowly get rid of all the bad feelings."

She came in with me to say hello to Kay. We spent another half hour fantasizing about the courtship we would have, after which I would eventually be allowed to come home again. As far as I was concerned, the shorter the courtship was going to be, the better, as I couldn't stay with Kay forever and dreaded the thought of moving to an apartment, then back to Audrey's.

We set our first date for Friday evening. It sounded exciting and romantic. And absurd. Here we were, two people who had lived with each other, were planning to do so again in the future, and now we went through these strange steps of distancing in order to get back together again.

"I'll call you tomorrow night," Audrey promised, her eyes full of magic.

We hugged each other and I saw fear in her eyes as I moved my face in order to kiss her goodnight. No, a kiss still wouldn't do. I brushed her cheek with my finger instead. She danced out the door. I heard the motor of her car. I was sad and also happy. If she wanted her courtship, then that's what we were going to have. A courtship.

§

As promised, she called me the next evening. We talked for over an hour. We picked a venue for our first date the following night. This took us ages. I wanted what she wanted, she wanted what I wanted. Audrey finally ordered me to choose. She could pick me up at Kay's or I could come straight from work to her house. I didn't want to choose. The more she urged me to, the more it felt like a test in which I had a fifty percent chance of failing and thus losing her once again. She recommended that I visualize the two places and then tested which of them felt right. And so I did.

"I'll come to your house then," I said.

"All right, darling," she said warmly. "I love you. I can't wait until you come. Goodnight."

"Goodnight."

Suddenly I had a strange feeling in the pit of my stomach. Fear. I persuaded myself out of it and went to say goodnight to Kay. We talked for a bit, then the phone rang and Kay took the call.

"Bonsoir," Kay said happily. Beaming, she came back into the room. "Pour vous," she said.

"Who it is?" I asked.

"Who else would it be?"

I went to the phone.

"Audrey?" I said.

"I hate you," she screamed at me. I felt as though the world came crashing down on me.

"Audrey, why? What happened? We just talked. You said you loved me."

"I went to your room after we talked," she hissed at me. "I hate you. I never want to see you again. And you will never come to live here again. It is, after all, my house. Not yours. It never will be."

"What did you find in my room?" Tears almost made words impossible.

"That I hate you," she screamed. "I hate you."

"All the same I love you," I sobbed.

Somewhere in between the words the line went dead. I leaned against the wall, holding the receiver and feeling like a wounded animal. Kay came dancing toward me.

"What did she say?" she hummed happily.

"She says she hates me," I whispered.

"But she doesn't," Kay cried. "She loves you!"

Kay wanted to take me into her arms, but I shook my head and she backed off. Wounded animals don't want to be touched. I went to the sofa and cried until sleep took over with its comfort of unconsciousness.

In the morning I woke up early, washed my hair like an automaton, puzzled that I could do anything at all. Then I called Audrey who answered the phone with her cheerful public voice.

"Audrey, why?" I asked. "What did I do that made you change in the space of ten minutes last night? Was it choosing to meet you at your house again?"

"No," she said, weary now, "it wasn't that."

"Can you tell me?"

"I don't know," she said. "All right. After we spoke last night, I went to your room and pulled open one of the drawers of your desk. There was a letter from Joel on top. And I couldn't bear it."

"Oh," I said.

What else was there to say? So I had missed a letter, from Joel of all people, when I had passionately conducted the burning of my past. "I thought that I had burned all letters," I said numbly. "I'm sorry that I missed one. It wasn't my intention."

"This thing about Joel is driving me crazy," she said. "And you never even told me what happened with him."

I felt the heat rise to my chest. That was because I didn't want to tell her. Clever Andrea. Careful to hide what would hurt Audrey most, and yet never lying. Now she was about to ask me point blank.

Don't, I pleaded with her silently, please don't. What earthly good can it do? And I cannot lie to you.

"Andrea," Audrey begged. "I have to know."

I still tried to squirm out of the answer. "What do you have to know?"

"Did you sleep with Joel when you were in Oregon?"

I felt I was burning up with silence.

"I have to know," Audrey kept on pleading. Then she played her trump card. "It would help me."

"But you already know," I said.

"You need to say it for me to know. You need to say it for yourself and for me. It will help me," she promised. "Did you sleep with him?"

All I could think of was the lisp with which she pronounced the word 'sleep,' and how I was about to pronounce my own death sentence, for I didn't know how to lie to her. I wanted to be able to. It might have saved so much. But I couldn't. Deep down I knew that each time you lie about yourself, you diminish the world.

"Yes," I finally said.

"It's good that you told me. I did know of course. But now it's cleaner. I wish you had told me before."

"But I couldn't, Audrey. How could I? I don't want to hurt you. And I knew telling you would hurt you. I even dreamed about it, early on. I dreamed you were telling me that I shouldn't tell you about any man in my past, and specifically not about Joel. You acted tired of the subject, superior to it, what have you. And so I didn't tell you. I dreamt that I shouldn't tell you."

"That was your dream," Audrey said scornfully.

I felt duly rebuked. Otherwise I might have been able to smile at her sulking tone of voice. That she should question my dreams, she with all her psychic aspirations and beliefs. I felt in no position to argue.

"You called my psychologist friend while I was at the beach. Why didn't you tell me?" she asked out of the blue into my momentary silence. "You weren't going to tell me that either, were you?"

She sounded hurt and betrayed again.

"I haven't had a chance to tell you, Audrey. There wasn't time," I said. "With everything else going on."

We had seen each other exactly once and talked on the telephone for a few more times, and each time had been so charged with emotion for me that all else was unimportant. Couldn't she see?

"I see," she said, sounding, however, as though she could in fact not see at all.

"Audrey, it wasn't a betrayal, or a deliberate secret I kept," I insisted.

"I guess not," she said.

I sniffled into the phone when it was time for me to say goodbye.

Audrey informed me that she did not think it wise that the two of us should meet that night. As for myself, I was neither afraid anymore of her hatred, I thought, or of her distrust. If only I could be there and wrestle with her through it. But she decided that I could not be near her; almost, I thought, as though to be able to mistrust me the better for it. Later she might ask, accusingly, why did you leave me to struggle alone? If there would be a later.

§

What Audrey called "Joel" was something larger, something that did not perhaps properly concern me at all, much less Joel. It could be something that, for reasons of Audrey herself—not mine, not Joel's, not anyone else's—might never get mended. As soon as I noticed these thoughts in myself, I accused myself of falling into

Audrey's trap of gloom, visions of dark forces and betrayals. And now I had a new trick of despair as well. Now, in addition to all other pain, I could accuse myself in Audrey's voice: "But this is your gloom, not mine."

I moved through the day in a trance and spent the evening with Kay who supervised me once again as I drank copious quantities of her vodka and told me once again what fun it was to watch me get drunk. She told me that my way of deploring my fate, whenever I felt fit to deplore it, was to make gentle fun of it, heroically, mocking. I failed to recognize the heroic part of it.

I slept on Kay's sofa in the hot apartment one more time. I was relegated to the public sofa now, no longer in the privacy of Kay's sleeping corner. Sulkily I turned my head to the wall and tried to be sure that my body was at all times covered by sheets, despite the heat, in order to preserve some show of modesty in my unsheltered position. But mostly my lack of shelter came from within. I felt like a tramp, and if I could have, I would have disappeared into the woodwork. But I was too large.

§

Newspaper in hand, I set out apartment hunting. "Today I will find an apartment," I told myself, glancing at the sofa where I had slept lately in uncomfortable exile.

The places I felt able to afford were crowded with seekers. One apartment I really liked at first sight was snatched away from me by a woman with a second's greater determination on behalf of her tongue-tied friend who ended up with it. I felt crazy and incredulous at being turned down. Dejectedly I walked down the stair among several other rejects. A couple with a small baby. A few foreign students, one of them a cheerful young Syrian who started up a conversation with me. I wasn't interested. Especially not in cheer.

But I was polite.

"I have a place," he said. "A two bedroom apartment. My roommate left. That's why I'm looking for a smaller place. You could stay at my apartment, for now."

I shook my head. Perhaps in Syria it was possible for rejects to make makeshift arrangements among themselves. Certainly I wasn't going to be living with a man, much less one whose culture I didn't know anything about.

What if he'd misinterpret things? My honor was at stake as though already compromised by the mere idea. Suddenly, through my silent indignation, I comprehended that for the past few minutes he had been telling me that his mother and sister were staying with him for a few months, so that I could feel properly chaperoned. Had my thoughts been that transparent?

"They can stay in my room," he said. "They wouldn't be in your way at all. Why don't you come and look at the apartment, and then you can always decide whether you like it or not."

So I sat in his living room and met his mother, Elaine, and his sister, a shy young girl of seventeen, giggling about her name. Hassna. And giggling even more at the pet name version of it, Sasa. I communicated with Elaine, the mother, in broken French, with Gen, the son, in good but imperfect English, and with Sasa in the language of smiles.

After half an hour's worth of conversation and plenty of good will, Gen and I drew up a handwritten contract for the coming month. I had a home again. A room of my own. With a bed and a desk that its previous occupant had left and not yet claimed. The closets were filled with the two women's clothes, beautiful, bright dresses. Elaine gushed something in French, and Gen translated with his ever cheerful face that they would move their belongings out of the room shortly. When did I mean to move in?

"Today?" I asked, shyly acknowledging the preposterousness of such speed.

"But of course," he said. What time would I come? Late afternoon? Fine.

Jubilantly I ran down the street, new keys in my pocket. I had wanted to find a place, I had found one.

In the afternoon I moved in my belongings, laughing with Kay over the fact that they now consisted of two plastic shopping bags, both, however, with designer labels.

Gen invited me to use the family's dishes. Kay gave me sheets and a nightgown. Suddenly I no longer had anything to worry about. I could begin to build my life again. I spread out on my new bed with relief. Elaine and Sasa had already moved their clothes. I looked at the clean white walls and the empty closet and listened to the highway traffic outside my window which I would have to get used to.

I got up and unwrapped, first of all, my notebook. When I placed it on the desk by the window, I found a small box. "From Sasa" it said. I opened it. There were cinnamon hearts in it. I nearly cried as I picked up one and let it dissolve on my tongue. It felt like a blessing from Audrey.

And if I couldn't live with Audrey, then I would spend the rest of my life writing of her, or to her, I thought. I would wait for her forever, of course. Aloneness, and the immensity of the word forever, didn't impress me at all.

Underneath all of my sadness, I also felt a great relief. The barren walls around me were white and calm. After the intensity of struggle with Audrey and with myself, I would have peace again. I was pleased with myself. In a single morning I had found myself a place to live. There would always be a place for me in life. What I needed now was some rest. After placing my pen next to the notebook on the desk in readiness, I went back to the bed to lie down.

Sleep evaded me, but I let my mind wander into a reverie. Sweet images followed one another, flowers, colors, Audrey's face. Until I was suddenly in the grip of a waking nightmare. I saw a penis coming at me, very erect, very pink, very large. I couldn't stop it. It was as though it were pulsing straight through my head, and I was unable to move out of its way or stop it. I lay there in paralyzed terror. Finally, as the relentless image came toward me again, I managed to deflect it so that it had to shoot past me. And then it was gone and I could move again.

I jumped from the bed and paced the room moodily. Why me? Okay, so I was telling myself that my life was fucked up. So what? Who needed a subconscious anyhow? All it did was pursue me into even the most innocent attempts at daydreaming.

How my heart yearned for Audrey. Not for the mad one who lived in her world of suspicions, jealousies, betrayals, and strange powers, but for the one who had gently and sweetly told me that she would never go very far away from me.

§

My life with Gen's family began. These were strange weeks, filled with sadness and desperation while I darted around reassuring the world that I was just fine. It seemed somehow appropriate that I could barely communicate with those I lived with.

Audrey telephoned me once to tell me that no matter how mad she was at me, or how much she felt she hated me, this was not the truth at all, and anyway, some things had to be taken care of. For instance, I must go and find a therapist for myself. She had done some research and found me a number of potential ones that I should try to connect with. She overrode my hesitations that I was unable to afford one by promising to pay for my sessions. This made me feel uneasy, but I said I would try, and I promptly made an appointment with the one I had liked most over the telephone for the following weekend. What Audrey wanted was still my command.

I met the gentleman on a Saturday afternoon and was duly unsettled by his suggestion that I had deeply ingrained problems which would take years to sort out. Bullshit, I thought stubbornly. I wasn't the first, nor would I be the last, human being sentencing herself to therapy to placate someone who requested it. I didn't particularly want to change or be transformed or adjusted. All I was here for was to show Audrey that I was making an effort at what she thought I should do.

There were other things I had to take care of which seemed far more important to me. One was to see to it that the cracked glass over Audrey's self-portrait was replaced, so as to clear that imperfection from the slate of fate. No, they told me at the hardware store over lunch, they couldn't replace the glass for me. But gradually it occurred to one of the gentlemen that replacing the glass was really only a matter of cutting fresh glass, then unbending and later on again fastening the nails that held the backing in place.

The young black woman at the register asked, "That a picture of you?"

"Me? No," I said. "It's a picture of a friend."

"Looks like you," she said.

"I suppose that's why we are friends," I said, smiling triumphantly.

I stormed out of the store before bursting into tears. We were exactly not friends just now. I wandered through the streets, the newly framed picture under my arm, feeling lost and forlorn.

We should be friends, my heart cried out. We even look alike. People can see it. It's all so obvious. Why can't we be friends again? And lovers? I sat down on a bench to hold still for a while under the force of all this emotion.

It seemed as though the world around me was in sympathy with me. A gust of wind sent late summer's first yellow leaves whirling at my feet. It hurt me that summer was gone. This beautiful summer. I thought of spring. Audrey showing me peonies in first bloom at the fence of a neighbor's garden. Now fall. The first leaves spinning. Winter coming on.

§

I wrote cards to Audrey. Letters. Some I mailed, others I tore up. There was never a reply. I spoke to Kay who had spoken to Audrey. Kay's attitude was still that she was not to repeat any news about Audrey to me. Strange. I could never figure out why. Sometimes it made me feel like a slinking thief, trying to steal information about the one I loved, as though information was something that belonged to her, and I would violate her by having it.

I continued living and began writing again. I noticed how little I had written since falling in love with Audrey. In between my journal entries or first lines of poems, I kept penning messages to Audrey.

One day I sat at an outdoor café during lunch hour feeling good. The sun was a bright, rich autumn blessing. No leaves whirled that day. Those that had sent me into sadness before had been premature. It was still almost summer. Life was beautiful. True, I had lost my love, but I was happy to be alive, and grateful to her. I started writing a letter to her explaining this, and thanking her. For everything. My growing, my joy, my life. I felt the warmth of my love for her glow like a sun inside me. This was a letter I wouldn't mail but carry to her house instead, this evening when, I knew, she would be with a client. There was nothing wrong this time about going to her house. I was not sneaking. I didn't feel guilty. I knew somehow that it was the right thing to do.

I opened her mailbox and was just about to simply drop my envelope and turn and walk away. But something compelled me to look at what letters were there. Maybe mail for me?

And indeed there was. My joy was wiped out by the sudden searing of dread. There was a letter for me from Joel. I didn't want it to be there. Mostly I knew that I couldn't leave it there. As happy as I had been before, so did I feel crushed now.

So this was what had compelled me to come here, I thought to myself in my magical frame of mind. I took the letter and ran down the steps, ran all the way to the subway stop. How was I going to get rid of this? On the train I went through my bag and found an old unused envelope addressed to Audrey. I crossed out the address and readdressed it to Joel, and wrote on his unopened envelope to me that I was sorry, but I didn't want his letter. I couldn't even explain why I didn't want to be in touch again. My reasons were too absurd for his precious world of sanity and joy. Please forgive me, Joel, I whispered. Forgive me for any ache this might cause. Forgive me in your lost world of joy.

Gen, Elaine, and Sasa asked me to go to a festival with them, but, exhausted, I begged off. I watched them go out in their colorful party attire. I was beginning to regret not having gone with them when the telephone rang.

Audrey's voice poured over me like brilliant light.

"Andrea. Thank you. That's all I want to say. Thank you. I love you."

Exactly what I had wanted to hear, but now it felt tainted, because of my own shadow of guilt due to that letter from Joel. Yes, it did seem as though Audrey were speaking to me from the sunlight of her life while I stood in the shadow of mine. Her words rushed over me like beautiful spring rain. I couldn't get Joel's letter out of my mind. I wanted to deserve her love for me, but how could I? She didn't even know that my mind was full of Joel and the narrow escape I had had by removing his letter and replacing it with mine, one she apparently liked very much.

Finally I couldn't help but tell her what was on my mind. It didn't seem to affect her at all. She thought, as I had, that surely some higher being had made me do the journey to her house in order to spare her the grief of finding Joel's letter herself. Other than that, the event seemed to have nothing to do with her. She wanted to speak of other things. For instance, could we see each other soon? As far as I was concerned, immediately. How could she not know that I was dying to see her, and somehow also worn out with waiting and with no longer believing?

§

I agreed to go to her house straight from work the next day. This time it was her clearly declared initiative, and she promised that it wouldn't upset her that I would be coming to her house. She was a woman in love. Jimmy, a gay friend of hers, would be there and would go to dinner with us, but afterwards we might have some time to ourselves. I was glad at the prospect of a friend, a sort of lightning conductor to allow the initial tension between us to disperse. Audrey. A few words on the phone, and my world was all hope and love again.

I went to her house as arranged. We went to a Chinese restaurant with her friend and, together, entertained him by showing off how much of a team, how magical a couple we were. So, for instance, when the waiter came to take our order for drinks, I calmly closed the drink list and, unsmilingly, ordered a drink called "Suffering Bastard."

"And I will have the same, please," Audrey said, solemnly bowing in the waiter's direction.

The waiter, inspired by our mirth, addressed me with a huge smile. "You don't look as though you are suffering," he said.

"But then neither are we bastards," Audrey said.

I wanted to hold her in my arms. Instead we hugged each other with words. From time to time our eyes met. All the ancient enchantment was there, though for me there was anxiety as well. We would not always have Jimmy around. At some point we would once again be alone together. Then what?

Audrey offered to take me home, and on the way, Jimmy having been left off elsewhere already, we stopped at Audrey's house. Missy, my black and white champion cat since the day I was the first stranger she didn't shy away from, came to sit by my side. We sat in the living room talking. About Jimmy, for instance, who was gay, but who was currently contemplating leaving the ranks. He had met a woman, possibly a goddess, for whom he was prepared to give up his preference for men. We wished him well.

It is difficult to be in love and not wish that blissful state for everyone else on earth in equal measure. After a time Missy got up and walked over to the door of what had been, briefly, my room.

"Yes," Audrey smiled. "I can't keep that door shut. I've tried, but she goes over and opens it again. She's been doing it all the time."

Oh, faithful animal, I gloated silently. Someone in this house was on my side.

I told Audrey that there was one thing I wanted to do. I wanted to get rid of Joel's letter which had escaped my burnt offering of the past and which Audrey had found on her day of hatred. She was reluctant. I thought it would be good if we did this together. Then there would be nothing left of him in our lives.

"It's the room," Audrey explained her hesitation. "I haven't been in there since I found the letter that night."

"Yeah, so?"

"It's not very pretty."

"So, let's go and get it over with," I said. What could be so dreadful about the room I had once lived in?

"You're not going to like it," Audrey said, but then took my arm and we went in.

I was glad she held my arm when I saw the desk. It looked as though a wind had swept across, a fierce and evil wind, full of rage.

Pieces of paper were torn and scattered in a gust of destruction. I had never seen anything so desolate in all my life.

WINTER

I have loved Audrey for over thirty years now.

In her eyes what I did was shabby. In my eyes what I did was life. I couldn't convince her. She almost convinced me.

That magical late summer we spent another dream-drenched week of courtship, then Audrey went to California for two weeks to visit friends, and when she returned, she asked me to move back in with her. I did. Two weeks later we were back at her rage and my powerlessness. She stabbed the nearly finished canvas of her golden dragon with a kitchen knife many times. I stood beside her shivering with eerie knowledge. I held two realities in my mind at the same time. I would have given my life for her. But not like this, not in shame. Not in an ugly farce of both of us shrinking in stature to where we did not want to, were not meant to be. Belatedly I performed numerous rituals of small sacrifice. Perhaps the gods were kind in refusing her to me, because I might have been tempted to sacrifice myself in ways a woman is not meant to sacrifice herself.

I went on a drinking binge. She kicked me out again, and this time she didn't let me come back. She had a new live-in-lover by Halloween. It was the one and only time I stalked her house, carefully disguised with a seasonal wig, after our final separation in

September. I saw a middle-aged woman, not Audrey, sweep damp leaves off the front porch with a broom, looking very much at home. This took my tender ego's breath away. It injured something sacred in my heart. I had been willing to devote my life, and to her it had just been a game of sex and companionship. Perhaps I started healing then. Perhaps not.

For a long time after Audrey I was not beautiful. I was afraid she had wanted me only for the pleasure of spitting me out. The gold she had advertised seemed shabby, stingy, like dirt. I kept trying to save some of my own gold over into reality. It was not easy. I realized I had already inadvertently lived the favorite part of my life the moment I wrote into my journal that I loved, and was loved by, a younger man and an older woman. And I hadn't paid enough attention or celebrated enough when it happened.

All of the following year she told me she was too busy to see me. Once she refused white roses I sent her. On a Sunday in spring I went to visit her house openly rather than stalking by hidden underneath a wig, but she called the police who encouraged me to leave but didn't arrest me.

I saw her again once before I left Washington. We were guarded and distant.

I waited for her for five years.

The last time I saw her was twenty-eight years ago. I was just married, to a man, but not Joel. We walked together, she and a woman friend, me and my new husband, a dancer, in the sun-drenched streets of Santa Fe. She was beautiful.

I am older now than she was when we first met. I have often wondered how many times these intervening years, had she asked me to, I would have gone running—no flying—back to her. But she never did ask, so no one will ever know. I mellowed my pursuit. Once my white roses were refused and the police came to coax me from her house, I accepted the verdict that I was a nuisance.

For a while I wrote Christmas and birthday cards, but I stopped when there was no longer a reply. It wasn't that I was bothered by the idea of my Christmas card hanging strung up with a thousand others over her mantle piece. It was more like I wasn't in the mood to be a vexation as, sometimes, unwanted lovers are.

I knew I had tried to live the fairy tale of my life without communicating to the other players what their roles would be. The princess was uninformed. Even the prince was uninformed. That made me the dragon, I guess, and I was afraid if I had told them what I was up to, they wouldn't have agreed to play the part I meant for them to play. And they didn't.

People who have been close to me since then all have formed their judgments. These range from Audrey being a cold seducer to her being a lunatic, to her being someone who simply couldn't handle being loved. I have my own judgment, too. When I was with her, I simply didn't have enough power yet to be good to her and to myself at the same time.

I have never loved a man the way I loved Audrey. I don't know if it is possible for a woman to love a man like that. In my experience love for men has usually been mingled with elements of duty and benevolence, pornography and feeling hunted. With Audrey it was like ocean waves around my heart, lapping in play, or wild and huge, and always alive, my soul stirring my body, my body sweeping up my soul in a surge of desire. I haven't loved another woman like that, either, though. Maybe it was that once in a lifetime thing I've always loved to believe in, and I blew it for lack of power. I am grateful I had it for that little while. I still miss the magic. In my heart she is pure sun dust, glittering on water, in the branches of trees, in morning light breaking through the window in shafts of expectation, alive, in motion, full of beauty.

I wrote a blessing for myself the year we were first parted: May you never hunger, may you never thirst, and may you never touch without learning. I have been lucky. I have been granted all three.

ACKNOWLEDGEMENTS

Thank you to all who have directly or indirectly helped to make this book a reality.

Thank you to Mary Riser and Michael Schulte for reading drafts of the manuscript and for valuable input.

Thank you to Joani Reese for making connections.

Thank you to Ariana D. Den Bleyker for seeing the potential.

Thank you to the editors of *Loch Raven Review* for publishing an excerpt under the title "Plaisir d'Amour" (Fall 2012).

Thank you to Teresa Lewis for the author photo.

Thank you to Michael Schulte who, like the sun, illuminates my life and makes it possible.

ABOUT THE AUTHOR

Beate Sigriddaughter, www.sigriddaughter.com, lives and writes in Silver City, New Mexico, Land of Enchantment. Her poetry and fiction have received several awards, including four Pushcart Prize nominations, and are widely accessible online. She has also established the Glass Woman Prize to honor passionate women's voices.